The Editor

MADELYN DETLOFF is Professor of English and Professor of Global and Intercultural Studies at Miami University, Oxford, Ohio. She is the author of *The Persistence of Modernism: Loss and Mourning in the Twentieth Century* and *The Value of Virginia Woolf.* She is coeditor, with Brenda S. Helt, of *Queer Bloomsbury* and, with Diana Royer, of *Virginia Woolf: Art, Education, and Internationalism.* Her essays appear in a number of venues, including *Modernism/modernity, Hypatia, Feminist Modernist Studies, Women's Studies, JMMLA, Journal of Lesbian Studies, Literature Compass,* and *English Language Notes.*

NORTON CRITICAL EDITIONS
Modernist & Contemporary Eras

For a complete list of Norton Critical Editions, visit
wwnorton.com/nortoncriticals

A NORTON CRITICAL EDITION

Virginia Woolf

ORLANDO

AUTHORITATIVE TEXT
BACKGROUND AND CONTEXTS
CRITICISM

Edited by

MADELYN DETLOFF
MIAMI UNIVERSITY

W. W. NORTON & COMPANY
Independent Publishers Since 1923

W. W. Norton & Company has been independent since its founding in 1923, when William Warder Norton and Mary D. Herter Norton first published lectures delivered at the People's Institute, the adult education division of New York City's Cooper Union. The firm soon expanded its program beyond the Institute, publishing books by celebrated academics from America and abroad. By mid-century, the two major pillars of Norton's publishing program—trade books and college texts—were firmly established. In the 1950s, the Norton family transferred control of the company to its employees, and today—with a staff of five hundred and hundreds of trade, college, and professional titles published each year—W. W. Norton & Company stands as the largest and oldest publishing house owned wholly by its employees.

Manufacturing by Maple Press
Book design by Antonina Krass
Production manager: Brenda Manzanedo

Library of Congress Control Number: 2024950794

ISBN: 978-1-324-04436-9

W. W. Norton & Company, Inc., 500 Fifth Avenue, New York, NY 10110
    www.wwnorton.com
W. W. Norton & Company Ltd., 15 Carlisle Street, London W1D 3BS

1 2 3 4 5 6 7 8 9 0

For Theresa Raniere, née Conroy

Contents

Introduction

Like its protagonist, *Orlando* is many things—a mock-biography; a satire of British literary history; a tribute to a friend's beloved home soon to be relinquished; an ode to a lover abroad; a keepsake of a love affair trending from passion to friendship; a critical commentary on social structures that make monarchies, peerages, and empires appear just and inevitable; an exposé of restrictive and often nonsensical gender roles; and even a playful homage to a lover's shapely legs. Attempting to hierarchize one aspect of the novel over another says more about the reader's interests than the writer's. Virginia Woolf would not be averse to that practice, just mindful. In her 1932 essay "How Should One Read a Book?" Woolf writes, "The only advice, indeed, that one person can give another about reading is to take no advice, to follow your own instincts, to use your own reason, to come to your own conclusions."[1] Similarly, in "Craftsmanship," her 1937 radio broadcast for the BBC program *Words Fail Me*, Woolf says that words "hate anything that stamps them with one meaning or confines them to one attitude, for it is their nature to change. . . . It is because the truth they try to catch is many-sided and they convey it by being themselves many-sided, flashing this way, then that."[2] This Norton Critical Edition of *Orlando* is designed to invite readers to revel in the novel's similarly multidimensional, elusive, and often fantastical truths. Attentive to Woolf's advice that we all must follow our own instincts when encountering a text, I've nevertheless provided a few signposts below that may help readers navigate Orlando's romp through centuries of life and love.

Virginia Woolf and Family

Virginia Woolf, born Adeline Virginia Stephen, was a prolific writer and innovative thinker who lived from 1882 to 1941, primarily in London, England. She grew up in a large, blended family consisting of two half sisters, two half brothers, and three full siblings—Thoby, Vanessa

---

1. Virginia Woolf, "How Should One Read a Book," in *The Second Common Reader*, ed. Andrew McNeillie (New York: Harcourt Brace Jovanovich, 1986), 258.
2. Virginia Woolf, "Craftsmanship," in *The Death of the Moth and Other Essays*, ed. Leonard Woolf (New York: Harcourt Brace and Company, 1942), 206.

Bell, and Adrian. Woolf wrote intimately about her late-Victorian upbringing in the posthumously published memoirs collected in *Moments of Being*. Her girlhood was rife with traumatic experiences, such as molestation by her half brothers and the deaths of her mother, half sister, father, and older brother by the time she was twenty-four.

Woolf was a self-described "daughter of an educated man" (as she would come to define her social class in *Three Guineas*), and as such had access to a rigorous informal education, although as a girl she was not allowed to attend school as her brothers were.[3] She read freely from the extensive library of her father, Sir Leslie Stephen, and began ongoing lessons in Greek and Latin as a teenager. In her memoirs Woolf describes her father as a prototypical Victorian paterfamilias—dignified and accomplished in public, moody and dependent on unpaid female emotional labor in private. He was a well-known and well-respected man of letters, serving as editor of the *Cornhill Magazine* and the *Dictionary of National Biography*. His example no doubt provided Woolf with plenty of material to draw on for her parody in *Orlando* of both biography and literary criticism.

The maternal side of Woolf's family was similarly well connected in Victorian artistic circles, as Woolf's mother, Julia Prinsep (Duckworth) Stephen (née Jackson), was the niece of pioneering photographer Julia Margaret Cameron. As a young woman, Julia Jackson spent much time at Little Holland House, an eclectic ménage bustling with artists and writers such as Alfred, Lord Tennyson; Robert Browning; William Thackeray; Edward Burne-Jones; and G. F. Watts.[4] In 1923 Woolf began writing a farcical play, *Freshwater*, about her great-aunt Julia Margaret Cameron's circle of friends.[5] (This satire of Victorian salon culture[6] was ultimately revised and staged privately for Woolf's Bloomsbury friends in 1935 and published posthumously in 1976.) Despite Woolf's satire of it in both *Orlando* and *Freshwater*, Woolf and her siblings took part in their own version of avant-garde salon culture through the conviviality and creative energy of the Bloomsbury Group, which included notable authors, artists, and intellectuals such as herself, Vanessa Bell, Lytton Strachey, Roger Fry, John Maynard Keynes, T. S. Eliot, Leonard Woolf, Duncan Grant, David Garnett, Dora Carrington, Clive Bell, and E. M. Forster.[7]

3. Virginia Woolf, *Three Guineas* (New York: Harcourt, 1966), 4.
4. See the entry for "Prinsep Family" in Mark Hussey's indispensable *Virginia Woolf A–Z: The Essential Reference to Her Life and Writings* (New York: Oxford UP, 1995), 218.
5. Virginia Woolf, *Freshwater: A Comedy*, ed. Lucio P. Ruotolo (New York: Harcourt Brace Jovanovich, 1976).
6. From the French name for "living room," a salon refers to a regular gathering of artists or intellectuals at someone's home for witty conversation about art, philosophy, life, and culture.
7. For more information on Woolf's position in the Bloomsbury Group, see Christine Froula, *Virginia Woolf and the Bloomsbury Avant-Garde* (New York: Columbia UP, 2005).

Vita Sackville-West and Knole

Although Woolf was married to writer and political theorist Leonard Woolf (1880–1969), she, like many of her counterparts in the Bloomsbury Group, was not exactly straight.[8] She had erotic feelings for women and consummated a passionate affair with the author and aristocrat (Victoria Mary) Vita Sackville-West (1892–1962), who herself was in an open (and what we today might call polyamorous) marriage with diplomat Harold Nicolson. *Orlando* is dedicated to Sackville-West, and the character Orlando is based on her, superimposed via speculative fiction onto centuries of Sackville ancestors who mingled with royalty, held many high offices, and garnered numerous noble titles while maintaining a home base on the estate of Knole in Kent, England.

Arguably the coprotagonist of *Orlando*, Knole was owned by the Sackville family from 1603 until 1946, when Vita's uncle, the 4th Lord Sackville, gave Knole to the National Trust.[9] While many details of Orlando's wild and lusty adventures have the larger-than-life force of hyperbole, Woolf's lavish depiction of the enormous house is perhaps the only thing that is not exaggerated. Knole was reputed to be a "calendar house" with 365 rooms, 52 staircases, and 12 entrances, although according to the National Trust, the building was not originally designed with that idea in mind. Presently the house has more rooms than days in a year, with "seven acres of roofs and . . . around 400 rooms."[1] Vita Sackville-West grew up in Knole, which her father inherited, but she herself was not legally permitted to inherit the estate upon his death in 1928. As a manor tied to a hereditary peerage, the inheritance of Knole was governed by the dictates of male primogeniture.[2] Thus Vita was prevented from inheriting her family home simply because she was a woman. The novel, published nine months after Vita's father died, bears witness to that fundamental unfairness.

Gender, Heteronormativity, and Social Status

In *A Room of One's Own* (a 1929 book based on lectures Woolf gave at Newnham and Girton Colleges at Cambridge University the year prior), Woolf is particularly critical of the treatment of women under

8. For more on what we would now call the queer subculture of Bloomsbury, see *Queer Bloomsbury*, ed. Brenda S. Helt and Madelyn Detloff (Edinburgh: Edinburgh UP, 2016).
9. A nonprofit agency that oversees the preservation of many places of historic, natural, and cultural importance in the UK.
1. "Explore the showrooms at Knole," *The National Trust*, "Knole" [website].
2. Male primogeniture is still the case for hereditary peerages in the UK as of June 2024, although the preference for male heirs was removed from laws of succession to the British monarchy by the Succession to the Crown Act of 2013, and a bill to allow female succession to hereditary peerages was proposed in the House of Commons during the 2023–24 session.

British patriarchal law. Noting the stark difference between how women were depicted in early modern literature (during a time when most writers were men) and how women actually lived, Woolf writes:

> Imaginatively, she is of the highest importance; practically she is completely insignificant. She pervades poetry from cover to cover; she is all but absent from history. . . . Some of the most inspired words, some of the most profound thoughts in literature fall from her lips; in real life she could hardly read, could scarcely spell, and was the property of her husband.[3]

As Woolf notes in *Three Guineas*, it was not until the late nineteenth century, with the passage of laws such as the Married Women's Property Acts of 1870 and 1882, that women could hope to keep the money they had earned or inherited in their own right and gain financial and intellectual independence from their husbands, brothers, or fathers.

As someone raised a nobleman with money and property, Orlando is oblivious to the legal and social impediments to women's independence and flourishing until her return to England in the eighteenth century as a woman. Able to compare her previous life as a man to her new life as a woman, Orlando begins to realize how much more restricted the scope of her actions and rights as a person have become.[4] In the myriad lawsuits meant to determine whether she was "alive or dead, man or woman, Duke or nonentity," Orlando's new gender status is tantamount to social death: "The chief charges against her were (1) that she was dead, and therefore could not hold any property whatsoever; (2) that she was a woman, which amounts to much the same thing" (91). Orlando's legal position is only slightly mitigated in the Victorian age via heterosexual marriage, a condition that Woolf caricatures as both compulsory (through the invasive image of the aggressively mandatory wedding band) and self-parodying (through Orlando and Shel's instant engagement, before they even learn each other's names) (133). The bathos of this courtship scene suggests that, for Woolf at least, the heteronormative marriage plot is a little too overdone to be taken seriously.

British History

The opening scene of the novel, depicting a boyish Orlando whacking the preserved skull of a long-dead, presumably North African opponent of one of his ancestors, sets up Woolf's parody of British history and the sorts of events (war, conquest, pillage) and people

3. Virginia Woolf, *A Room of One's Own* (New York: Harcourt Brace and Company, 1981 [1929]), 43–44.
4. I follow the practice indicated by Woolf's fictional biographer by using "he" pronouns to refer to Orlando before the section in Chapter III where Orlando wakes up as a woman, and "she" pronouns to refer to Orlando afterwards. See page 75 in this volume.

(ruling class, mostly white, men) typically featured in the annals of history. The youthful Orlando's solitary swordplay establishes his lineage at the same time that the narrative associates that lineage with generations of bloodshed: "Orlando's fathers had ridden in fields of asphodel, and stony fields, and fields watered by strange rivers, and they had struck many heads of many colours off many shoulders, and brought them back to hang from the rafters" (9). Knole—the structure that begins and ends the story and overlooks acres of land that Orlando's relatives own—serves as the marker of Orlando's nobility. The skulls (symbolically or actually) hanging in its rafters remind us that the great house's grandeur was made possible by centuries of violent conquest. Orlando's attempt at gentlemanly fair play—"fastening [the skull] with some chivalry almost out of reach" without factoring in that it is already dead, unable to fight back, and literally tied up—suggests that "chivalry" might be a cover story for less-than-noble behavior. The opening scene thus provides the first instance of the novel's frequent deployment of dramatic irony in its depiction of Orlando, who, especially during his life as a man, is often the last to know when he is acting the fool.

Woolf's practice of entwining playful historical allusions with glimpses of their sordid underside continues in her depiction of a sixteenth-century frost fair at which Orlando meets his heartbreaking love, the Russian princess Sasha. In her depiction of the frost fair, Woolf draws on historical accounts from the seventeenth century, such as Thomas Dekker's 1608 pamphlet, "The Great Frost," and accounts of the "Hard Frost" of 1684. Alvin Snider describes the frequency and character of historical frost fairs, noting that "in the seventeenth century alone, records exist for frost fairs upon the Thames for 1608, 1609, 1620, 1648–49, and so on."[5] The "Hard Frost" of 1684 would have taken place after Orlando's encounter with Sasha is set, but Snider's summary of historical accounts of the hard frost resonates with Woolf's fantastical account of the "Great Frost" in *Orlando*. According to Snider,

> Stalls extended on the river from the Temple Stairs to the Barge House in Southwark so that merchants could take advantage of the booming trade. Eye-witness accounts mention the hawkers, the bull and bear baiting, coaches, cooks' shops, taverns, and other signs of urban life usually located on shore. Crowds turned the Thames into Smithfield or Bartholomew Fair, and bawds, whores, pickpockets, and other denizens of the street mingled with the crowds.[6]

5. Alvin Snider, "Hard Frost 1684," *Journal for Early Modern Cultural Studies* 8.2 (Fall–Winter, 2008): 20. See also p. 198 in this volume.
6. Snider, "Hard Frost," 20.

Orlando includes such spectacles, while illuminating what lies beneath them: "But while the country people suffered the extremity of want, and the trade of the country was at a standstill, London enjoyed a carnival of the utmost brilliancy" (20). On the surface of the ice the nobles frolic and feast, while beneath the ice workers, such as a frozen apple seller, are petrified in the act of their labor. The nobles can literally see this through the ice—"'Twas a sight King James specially liked to look upon, and he would bring a troupe of courtiers to gaze with him"—yet they remain obtuse to the suffering just below the surface of their merriment (21). With this juxtaposition, Woolf illustrates a point that she articulates more directly in *A Room of One's Own*—that traditional history, with its focus on great men, wars, and extraordinary events, overlooks the everyday events and ordinary people that provide its foundation.[7]

Meta-Biography

While it is certainly possible to read *Orlando* as a historically informed roman à clef—discovering the clever inside jokes and correspondences between the main characters and real-life persons in Woolf's or Sackville-West's lives—it is also possible to read the novel as an extended commentary on the practice of biography.[8] Woolf was interested in the limits of what biography could or could not say. In "The Art of Biography" (1939), Woolf discusses the "conditions" the genre imposes on the writer, as well as social pressures to censor or self-censor unflattering details about one's subject: "Suppose for example, the man of genius was immoral, ill-tempered, and threw the boots at the maid's head. The widow would say, 'Still I loved him—he was the father of my children; and the public, who love his books, must on no account be disillusioned. Cover up; omit.'"[9] The pressure to "cover up; omit" was one of the unsubtle constraints of the genre during much of Woolf's lifetime, and Orlando's fictional biographer is fittingly far from subtle in dramatizing that pressure as a comic showdown between the "gods" of the biographer "Truth, Candour, and Honesty" and the allegorical "ladies" representing "Purity," "Chastity," and "Modesty" (73). "Truth" wins by drowning

---

7. In *A Room of One's Own*, Woolf bemoans the lack of information about ordinary people, especially ordinary women, in typical historical accounts. "What one wants . . . is a mass of information; at what age did she marry; how many children had she as a rule; what was her house like; had she a room to herself . . . the life of the average Elizabethan woman must be scattered about somewhere, could one collect it and make a book of it" (45).

8. For an extended discussion of *Orlando* as a form of queer feminist biography, see Melanie Micir, *The Passion Projects: Modernist Women, Intimate Archives, Unfinished Lives* (Princeton: Princeton UP, 2019).

9. Virginia Woolf, "The Art of Biography," in *The Death of the Moth and Other Essays*, ed. Leonard Woolf (New York: Harcourt Brace and Company, 1942), 188. Originally published in the *Atlantic* (April 1939): 506–10.

out the prudish ladies with its trumpet blasts. But its overpowering force may be too easy, too confident in its victory to leave room for the elusive quality of life that a professional, seemingly objective, description of "just the facts" might miss.

In the opening pages of her own unfinished memoir, Woolf contemplates this difficulty:

> Here I come to one of the memoir writer's difficulties—one of the many reasons why, though I read so many, so many are failures. They leave out the person to whom things happened. The reason is that it is so difficult to describe any human being. So they say: "This is what happened," but they do not say what the person was like to whom it happened. And the events mean very little unless we know first to whom they happened.[1]

As it is for the memoir writer, the biographer's task of presenting a "true" picture of a person is trickier than the "gods" of biography might admit. The biographer, Woolf contends, "has the right to all the facts that are available."[2] And yet, she notes, "These facts are not like the facts of science—once they are discovered, always the same. They are subject to changes of opinion; opinions change as the times change."[3] A biographer can nevertheless take changing perceptions into account by providing contextual information, or what the theorist Michel Foucault would call a "genealogy" of received ideas surrounding a person's identity or actions during the time that they lived.[4] We can do this for Woolf, for example, by suggesting that while "Sapphist" was a term she used to describe Vita Sackville-West, today we might call such a person bisexual or polyamorous. Similarly, Radclyffe Hall, whose censorship trial for *The Well of Loneliness* Woolf and Sackville-West attended in 1928,[5] used the term "invert" to describe the novel's protagonist, although today we would eschew the clinical term and consider Stephen Gordon a transmasculine person. Historical and cultural contexts don't alter the person, but they do have the capacity to alter the *story* of the person, or the meaning given to the facts of a person's life.

Orlando's fictional biographer is therefore aware that Orlando's shift in status from living as a man to living as a woman will be interpreted differently by entities with differing motives and/or understandings of gender. Soon after the triumph of the trumpeters of "THE TRUTH!" the biographer breaks the fourth wall of biography

---

1. Virginia Woolf, *A Sketch of the Past*, in *Moments of Being*, 2nd ed., ed. Jeanne Schulkind (New York: Harcourt Brace and Company, 1985), 65.
2. Woolf, "The Art of Biography," 194.
3. Woolf, "The Art of Biography," 194.
4. On genealogy, see Michel Foucault, "Nietzsche, Genealogy, History," in *Language, Counter-Memory, Practice: Selected Essays and Interviews*, ed. Donald F. Bouchard, trans. Bouchard and Sherry Simon (Ithaca: Cornell UP, 2019), 139–64.
5. See pp. 204–08 in this volume.

(in one of the many moments of metanarrative or meta-biography in the text) and addresses the reader:

> We may take advantage of this pause in the narrative to make certain statements. Orlando had become a woman—there is no denying it. But in every other respect, Orlando remained precisely as he had been. . . . The change seemed to have been accomplished painlessly and completely and in such a way that Orlando herself showed no surprise at it. Many people, taking this into account, and holding that such a change of sex is against nature, have been at great pains to prove (1) that Orlando had always been a woman, (2) that Orlando is at this moment a man. Let biologists and psychologists determine. It is enough for us to state the simple fact; Orlando was a man till the age of thirty; when he became a woman and has remained so ever since. (75–76)

In the midst of such a fantastical life story, the restraint with which the biographer describes Orlando's change is telling. This reticence is not the same as the censorious demands of Purity, Chastity, and Modesty, for the biographer is not covering anything up, but rather refusing to engage in what Foucault would later describe as "*scientia sexualis*"— probing disciplines such as psychoanalysis, sexology, and/or comparative anatomy—to extract some deeper, usually pathological, meaning beneath the "simple fact" of Orlando's gender.[6] Instead, the reader is told the only pertinent details: He was a man. She is now a woman. Neither Orlando nor her biographer needs to produce a reason. In the words of activist organization Queer Nation: "Get used to it."

A refusal to dissect one's subject's inner workings to discover what one has already presumed to be there is not the same as laying a shroud over the inner life of the subject. A simple recital of events and occurrences would "leave out the person to whom things happened," as Woolf notes in her memoirs. Orlando's biographer parodies such an approach in recounting the year that Orlando sits at her desk writing the final draft of "The Oak Tree":

> It was now November. After November, comes December. Then January, February, March, and April. After April comes May. June, July, August follow. Next is September. Then October, and so, behold, here we are back at November again, with a whole year accomplished.
>
> This method of writing biography, though it has its merits, is a little bare. (141)

The biographer's dilemma in this instance is that the "authorities," presumably scholars and biographers like Sir Leslie Stephen, deem

---

6. Michel Foucault, *The History of Sexuality*, vol. I, trans. Robert Hurley (New York: Random House, 1990), 53–73.

that "life" is the only proper subject for biography, but "life, the same authorities have decided, has nothing whatever to do with sitting still in a chair and thinking" (143). Woolf's critical swipe at the "authorities" of biography echoes her criticism of the "materialist" novelists of the present day in her essay "Modern Fiction." Novelists such as Arnold Bennett and John Galsworthy, Woolf argues, strove to make their novels lifelike and plausible, but their focus on details and generic conventions caused them to trade life for realism:

> Life is not a series of gig lamps symmetrically arranged; life is a luminous halo, a semi-transparent envelope surrounding us from the beginning of consciousness to the end. Is it not the task of the novelist to convey this varying, this unknown and uncircumscribed spirit, whatever aberration and complexity it may display, with as little mixture of the alien and external as possible?[7]

Following suit, "The Present Day" chapter of *Orlando* attempts to convey Orlando's "varying . . . unknown and uncircumscribed spirit" to the reader in a narrative style that is far looser, more typically "Woolfian," than the previous five chapters. Orlando is trailed by the biographer as she does errands, lunches, drives like a boss from London to Kent, and experiences the multiplicity of selves that intrude upon her consciousness by virtue of memory and shifting attention. There are no "gig lamps symmetrically arranged" in Orlando's journey because there is no symmetry in it, only the expansion and contraction of time as Orlando experiences it. In this sense, Orlando's biographer has finally arrived at a method that is faithful to their subject, but like Orlando, not conventionally so.

Backgrounds, Contexts, and Criticism

The secondary material that accompanies this text has been chosen to represent some of the key strands of criticism on the text without presuming to present *the* authoritative take on a novel that purposely eludes a single or even unified interpretation. The Backgrounds and Contexts section samples positive and negative reviews of *Orlando* written by Woolf's contemporaries. The novelist Elizabeth Bowen, a slightly younger friend of Woolf's, provides retrospective context for the novel's immediate critical reception in her "Afterword" to a 1960 edition of the novel.

The Criticism section is divided in two. The first part includes the work of scholars who provide historical and cultural contexts for reading *Orlando*. Jane de Gay provides insight into Woolf's parodic critique of what she saw as Victorian overemphasis on the "spirit of

---

7. Virginia Woolf, "Modern Fiction," in *The Common Reader: First Series*, ed. Andrew McNeillie (New York: Harcourt, Inc., 1984), 150.

the age" in literary history. Abby Bardi examines the stereotyping practice of exoticizing Romani people (using the "Gypsy" trope) in nineteenth-century British literature and suggests that *Orlando* draws on that tradition when representing Orlando's gender transition. Julie Vandivere illuminates the historical contexts of the novel's spotlight on British cultural standards regarding heteronormative legitimacy, race, and inheritance.

The second part of the Criticism section provides a selection of readings that analyze several dimensions of Woolf's erudite and witty observations about the intricacy and social significance of gender and sexuality norms. Brenda Helt offers a careful reading of Woolf's representations of androgyny and bisexuality, suggesting that Woolf's understanding of sexual and gender identity was capacious and flexible, and therefore at odds with more essentialist conceptions popularized at the time by sexology and by later readers who projected either heteronormative or homonormative identities onto Orlando and/or Woolf. Margaret Homans carefully outlines the thorny questions (about identity, representation, and accountability to contemporary trans communities) that arise when readers attempt to reread *Orlando* as a transgender text. Homans, as do many critics seeking to situate *Orlando* vis-à-vis trans writing, cites Pamela Caughie's thought-provoking essay comparing *Orlando* with Lili Elbe's *Man Into Woman*.[8] Caughie's essay is excerpted here under her original prepublication title, "Time's Queer Force: Modernist Life Writing in the Era of Transsexualism." Caughie reads *Orlando* as a "transgenre" text that engages fruitfully with modernist conceptions of temporality as well as emerging public, literary, and medical discourses regarding "transsexualism" (what we might today call trans or transgender identity) in the early twentieth century. Adding another layer to a complex conversation, Gwen Rose offers a trans-centered perspective on both the novel and critical attempts to read *Orlando* as a trans narrative, suggesting instead that the novel's depiction of gender change can't be said to represent a trans narrative because Orlando lacks the requisite desire to reject his (at the time) assigned gender before he becomes a woman. (The conversation becomes even more complex when one adds Paul B. Preciado's 2023 film, referenced below, to the mix.) Finally, my own essay on the nuances of "camp" and gender performance in *Orlando* and its later adaptations draws on long associations between camp, drag, and what Susan Sontag called "love of human nature."[9] *Orlando* is, in

8. Lili Elbe, *Man Into Woman: A Comparative Scholarly Edition*, ed. Pamela L. Caughie and Sabine Meyer (New York: Bloomsbury Academic, 2020). Originally published in Danish in 1931.

9. Susan Sontag, "Notes on Camp," in *Against Interpretation* (New York: Picador, 2001), 291.

my view, playful, serious, hyperbolic, and an adoring critique—
which are all features of camp.

In sum, the secondary material is meant to provide an introduction to the vibrant, growing body of scholarship on *Orlando* that is
too expansive to be contained in one volume. I hope that readers will
approach the small sample included in the secondary materials as an
invitation to continue exploring.

Orlando's *Afterlives*

Orlando was a publishing success for the Hogarth Press, which
Virginia and Leonard Woolf owned and operated. According to
Suzanne Raitt and Ian Blyth, the British edition of the text had to
be reprinted twice (three impressions totaling over 11,000 books)
within a year, and American sales of the novel exceeded 13,000 by
January 1929.[1] Some of Woolf's contemporaries found the text too
whimsical and not up to the experimental literary standards of
Woolf's previous novels *Jacob's Room*, *Mrs. Dalloway*, and *To the
Lighthouse* (see Bowen, p. 193, in this volume). Others, such as Arnold
Bennett, who called the book "a very odd volume," seem to be clueless (or pretend to be clueless?) about the novel's sapphic open secret.
Others, including Vita Sackville-West, were delighted by the novel's
dazzling energy. *Orlando* has remained in print ever since 1928, and
has enjoyed a resurgence since the late twentieth century, when
LGBTQ+ studies and queer theory gained more traction in aca-
deme. Since that time, the novel has made it to both stage and screen.
In 1992, filmmaker Sally Potter wrote and directed a popular film
adaptation of the novel, starring Tilda Swinton as Orlando, Billy Zane
as Shelmerdine, and Quentin Crisp as Queen Elizabeth I.[2] Paul B.
Preciado's 2023 documentary *Orlando, My Political Biography* draws on
Woolf's novel to amplify contemporary trans and nonbinary voices.[3]
Sarah Ruhl's stage adaptation of *Orlando* was first performed in 2010.[4]
Woolf's and Sackville-West's letters to each other have also been published and adapted for both media.[5] Nothing quite surpasses the original, however. Nearly a century after Woolf conceived *Orlando*, the
novel continues (to paraphrase Horace) to delight and instruct.

1. Suzanne Raitt and Ian Blyth, "Introduction" to *Orlando: A Biography, The Cambridge
   Edition of the Works of Virginia Woolf* (New York: Cambridge UP, 2018), lxv–lxix.
2. Sally Potter, *Orlando*, based on the novel by Virginia Woolf, dir. Sally Potter, prod.
   Christopher Sheppard, Adventure Pictures, 1992.
3. Paul B. Preciado, *Orlando, My Political Biography*, dir. Paul B. Preciado, prod. 24
   Images, ARTE, Les Films du Poisson, 2023.
4. Sarah Ruhl, *Orlando (Adapted from the Original by Virginia Woolf)*. First produced at
   Classic Stage Company in New York City in September 2010, dir. Rebecca Taichman.
5. Virginia Woolf and Vita Sackville-West, *Love Letters*, with an "Introduction" by Alison
   Bechdel (New York: Vintage, 2021). Eileen Atkins, *Vita and Virginia* (New York:
   Samuel French Ltd. 1995). Eileen Atkins and Chanya Button, *Vita and Virginia*,
   dir. Chanya Button, distributed by IFC films, 2018.

A Note on the Text

The text of *Orlando* in this volume is that of the first UK edition, published by Hogarth Press on October 11, 1928. Woolf included two footnotes in the original. These have been reproduced using symbols rather than numbers to differentiate them from informational notes included for this Norton Critical Edition. Woolf authorized a US limited edition, published by Crosby Gaige on October 2, 1928, and a US trade edition, published by Harcourt, Brace on October 18, 1928.[1] I've chosen the first UK edition of *Orlando* as the definitive text of the novel, as Virginia and Leonard Woolf were the publishers of the UK edition and had editorial control over the process. Furthermore, as Alison M. Scott notes in her careful study of the corrections Woolf made to different sets of UK and US proofs, "the text which received the most corrections latest in the production process, is the British edition published by the Hogarth Press" (289).[2] I have retained UK spellings and the punctuation idiosyncrasies of the Hogarth edition regarding the placement of quotation marks. Finally, for a careful outline of the publication history of *Orlando*, see Suzanne Raitt and Ian Blyth's "Introduction" to *Orlando: A Biography, The Cambridge Edition of the Works of Virginia Woolf* (New York: Cambridge UP, 2018). Raitt and Blyth's meticulous explanatory notes and introduction have been extremely helpful in preparing the present text, and I am indebted to their scholarship as well as the scholarship of the General Editors of the *Cambridge Edition of the Works of Virginia Woolf*, Jane Goldman, Susan Sellers, and Bryony Randall.

---

1. The US limited release of October 2nd was designed to be a collectors' edition at the urging of Crosby Gaige, a printer of high-priced limited editions. Gaige visited Woolf in May 1928 to persuade her to publish a run of 800 signed copies with his firm. Woolf later regretted the decision, and the edition was not successful. For more on the Crosby Gaige edition, see Lise Jaillant, "'Flowers for the Living': Crosby Gaige and Modernist Limited Editions," *Publishing Modernist Fiction and Poetry*, ed. Lise Jaillant (Edinburgh: Edinburgh UP, 2019), 154–172.
2. See Alison M. Scott, "'Tantalising Fragments': The Proofs of Virginia Woolf's *Orlando*," *The Papers of the Bibliographical Society of America* 88.3 (September 1994): 279–351. For a discussion of some of the changes Woolf made between the manuscript and the proof stage, see Madeline Moore, "*Orlando*: An Edition of the Manuscript," *Twentieth-Century Literature* 25.3/4 (Autumn–Winter, 1979): 303–55.

Acknowledgments

This work would not be possible without the generous and erudite community of Virginia Woolf scholars in the International Virginia Woolf Society and beyond. Among the long list of people I've been grateful to for companionship, criticism, and inspiration over more than twenty-five years of reading, discussing, critiquing, and admiring Virginia Woolf are: Brenda Silver, Bonnie Kime Scott, Christine Froula, Jeannette McVicker, Mark Hussey, Vara Neverow, Jane Goldman, Kathryn Simpson, Jane de Gay, Leslie Hankins, Brenda Helt, Diana Royer, Beth Rigel Daugherty, Eileen Barrett, Karen Levenback, Drew Shannon, Melba Cuddy-Keane, Erica Delsandro, Kristin Czarnecki, Paula Maggio, Gabrielle McIntire, Ben Hagen, Catherine Hollis, Ann Martin, Jeanne Dubino, Celia Marshik, Julie Vandivere, Anne Fernald, Jodie Medd, Jessica Berman, Derek Ryan, Kimberley Coates, Laura Marcus, Georgia Johnston, and Susan Stanford Friedman. I owe my gratitude to my editors at W. W. Norton—Kylie Yamauchi, Carol Bemis, and Thea Goodrich—who have been gracious and erudite. For their support and comradeship, I thank my colleagues in the Miami University English and Global and Intercultural Studies departments. Lauren Van Atta and Conner Moore provided me with invaluable research assistance tracking down resources and helping transcribe a clean copy of the Hogarth first edition of *Orlando*. Amy Toland, Assistant to the Chair Extraordinaire, made my life and work so much easier because she was unfailingly on the ball. Special thanks to Stefanie Dunning, Liz Wardle, Anita Mannur, Theresa Kulbaga, Jason Palmeri, Elaine Miller, Erin Edwards, Jen Cohen, and Cathy Wagner for friendship and support during very tough times. MVP-level thanks to Mary Jean Corbett, who belongs on my list of Woolf scholars and my list of friends for whom I'm thankful. Dr. Corbett deserves her own line for her friendship and loyalty; impeccable editorial eye (these semicolons are for you, MJC); and her intellectual, professional, and life advice. I wouldn't have made it through the past two years without my siblings Mary, Pete, and Liz, who have been a lifeline as we navigate difficult waters together. And finally, my love and gratitude to Gaile Pohlhaus Jr., my partner in life and feminist thought. If I ever were to write a 300-page novel about a brilliant and quirky adventurer poet, it would be about you.

Figure 1. Orlando as a boy. British Library, London, UK. From the British Library archive / Bridgeman Images.

The Text of
ORLANDO
A BIOGRAPHY

TO
V. SACKVILLE WEST[1]

---

1. (Victoria Mary) Vita Sackville-West. See p. xi above.

PREFACE

Many friends have helped me in writing this book. Some are dead and so illustrious that I scarcely dare name them, yet no one can read or write without being perpetually in the debt of Defoe, Sir Thomas Browne, Sterne, Sir Walter Scott, Lord Macaulay, Emily Brontë, De Quincey, and Walter Pater,—to name the first that come to mind. Others are alive, and though perhaps as illustrious in their own way, are less formidable for that very reason. I am specially indebted to Mr. C. P. Sanger, without whose knowledge of the law of real property this book could never have been written. Mr. Sydney-Turner's wide and peculiar erudition has saved me, I hope, some lamentable blunders. I have had the advantage—how great I alone can estimate—of Mr. Arthur Waley's knowledge of Chinese. Madame Lopokova (Mrs. J. M. Keynes) has been at hand to correct my Russian. To the unrivalled sympathy and imagination of Mr. Roger Fry I owe whatever understanding of the art of painting I may possess. I have, I hope, profited, in another department by the singularly penetrating, if severe, criticism of my nephew Mr. Julian Bell. Miss M. K. Snowdon's indefatigable researches in the archives of Harrogate and Cheltenham were none the less arduous for being vain. Other friends have helped me in ways too various to specify. I must content myself with naming Mr. Angus Davidson; Mrs. Cartwright; Miss Janet Case; Lord Berners (whose knowledge of Elizabethan music has proved invaluable); Mr. Francis Birrell; my brother, Dr. Adrian Stephen; Mr. F. L. Lucas; Mr. and Mrs. Desmond Maccarthy; that most inspiriting of critics, my brother-in-law, Mr. Clive Bell; Mr. G. H. Rylands; Lady Colefax; Miss Nellie Boxall; Mr. J. M. Keynes; Mr. Hugh Walpole; Miss Violet Dickinson; the Hon. Edward Sackville West; Mr. and Mrs. St. John Hutchinson; Mr. Duncan Grant; Mr. and Mrs. Stephen Tomlin; Mr. and Lady Ottoline Morrell; my mother-in-law, Mrs. Sidney Woolf; Mr. Osbert Sitwell; Madame Jacques Raverat; Colonel Cory Bell; Miss Valerie Taylor; Mr. J. T. Sheppard; Mr. and Mrs. T. S. Eliot; Miss Ethel Sands; Miss Nan Hudson; my nephew Mr. Quentin Bell (an old and valued collaborator in fiction); Mr. Raymond Mortimer; Lady Gerald Wellesley; Mr. Lytton Strachey; the Viscountess Cecil; Miss Hope Mirrlees; Mr. E. M. Forster; the Hon. Harold Nicolson; and my sister, Vanessa Bell—but the list threatens to grow too long and is already far too distinguished. For while it rouses in me memories of the pleasantest kind it will inevitably wake expectations in the reader which the book itself can only disappoint. Therefore I will conclude by thanking the officials of the British Museum and Record Office for their wonted courtesy; my niece Miss Angelica Bell, for a service which none but she could have rendered; and my husband for the patience with which he has invariably helped my researches and for the profound historical knowledge to which these pages owe whatever degree of accuracy they may attain. Finally, I would thank, had I not lost his name and address, a gentleman in America, who has generously and gratuitously corrected the punctuation, the botany, the entomology, the geography, and the chronology of previous works of mine and will, I hope, not spare his services on the present occasion.

CONTENTS

ILLUSTRATIONS

CHAPTER I

HE—for there could be no doubt of his sex, though the fashion of the time did something to disguise it—was in the act of slicing at the head of a Moor[1] which swung from the rafters. It was the colour of an old football, and more or less the shape of one, save for the sunken cheeks and a strand or two of coarse, dry hair, like the hair on a cocoanut. Orlando's father, or perhaps his grandfather, had struck it from the shoulders of a vast Pagan who had started up under the moon in the barbarian fields of Africa; and now it swung, gently, perpetually, in the breeze which never ceased blowing through the attic rooms of the gigantic house of the lord who had slain him.

Orlando's fathers had ridden in fields of asphodel, and stony fields, and fields watered by strange rivers, and they had struck many heads of many colours off many shoulders, and brought them back to hang from the rafters. So too would Orlando, he vowed. But since he was sixteen only, and too young to ride with them in Africa or France, he would steal away from his mother and the peacocks in the garden and go to his attic room and there lunge and plunge and slice the air with his blade. Sometimes he cut the cord so that the skull bumped on the floor and he had to string it up again, fastening it with some chivalry almost out of reach so that his enemy grinned at him through shrunk, black lips triumphantly. The skull swung to and fro, for the house, at the top of which he lived, was so vast that there seemed trapped in it the wind itself, blowing this way, blowing that way, winter and summer. The green arras with the hunters on it moved perpetually. His fathers had been noble since they had been at all. They came out of the northern mists wearing coronets on their heads. Were not the bars of darkness in the room, and the yellow pools which chequered the floor, made by the sun falling through the stained glass of a vast coat of arms in the window? Orlando stood now in the midst of the yellow body of an heraldic leopard. When he put his hand on the window-sill to push the window open, it was instantly coloured red, blue, and yellow like a butterfly's wing. Thus, those who like symbols, and have a turn for the deciphering of them, might observe that though the shapely legs,[2] the handsome body, and the well-set shoulders were all of them decorated with various tints of heraldic light, Orlando's face, as he threw

---

1. A person from North Africa, presumably of Muslim faith. For a discussion of how the term "Moor" would have been understood vis-à-vis race and religion, see Julie Vandivere in this volume, pp. 227–48.
2. This is the first of many references to Orlando's "shapely" legs—a flirtatious inside joke between Woolf and Vita Sackville-West, whose legs Virginia thought "exquisite" (*Letters of Virginia Woolf*, to Jacques Raverat [#1520] Dec. 26, 1924).

the window open, was lit solely by the sun itself. A more candid, sullen face it would be impossible to find. Happy the mother who bears, happier still the biographer who records the life of such a one! Never need she vex herself, nor he invoke the help of novelist or poet. From deed to deed, from glory to glory, from office to office he must go, his scribe following after, till they reach whatever seat it may be that is the height of their desire. Orlando, to look at, was cut out precisely for some such career. The red of the cheeks was covered with peach down; the down on the lips was only a little thicker than the down on the cheeks. The lips themselves were short and slightly drawn back over teeth of an exquisite and almond whiteness. Nothing disturbed the arrowy nose in its short, tense flight; the hair was dark, the ears small, and fitted closely to the head. But, alas, that these catalogues of youthful beauty cannot end without mentioning forehead and eyes. Alas, that people are seldom devoid of all three; for directly we glance at Orlando standing by the window, we must admit that he had eyes like drenched violets, so large that the water seemed to have brimmed in them and widened them; and a brow like the swelling of a marble dome pressed between the two blank medallions which were his temples. Directly we glance at eyes and forehead, thus do we rhapsodise. Directly we glance at eyes and forehead, we have to admit a thousand disagreeables which it is the aim of every good biographer to ignore. Sights disturbed him, like that of his mother, a very beautiful lady in green walking out to feed the peacocks with Twitchett, her maid, behind her; sights exalted him—the birds and the trees; and made him in love with death—the evening sky, the homing rooks; and so, mounting up the spiral stairway into his brain—which was a roomy one—all these sights, and the garden sounds too, the hammer beating, the wood chopping, began that riot and confusion of the passions and emotions which every good biographer detests. But to continue—Orlando slowly drew in his head, sat down at the table, and, with the half-conscious air of one doing what they do every day of their lives at this hour, took out a writing book labelled "Æthelbert: A Tragedy in Five Acts", and dipped an old stained goose quill in the ink.

Soon he had covered ten pages and more with poetry. He was fluent, evidently, but he was abstract. Vice, Crime, Misery were the personages of his drama; there were Kings and Queens of impossible territories; horrid plots confounded them; noble sentiments suffused them; there was never a word said as he himself would have said it, but all was turned with a fluency and sweetness which, considering his age—he was not yet seventeen—and that the sixteenth century had still some years of its course to run, were remarkable enough. At last, however, he came to a halt. He was describing, as all young poets are for ever describing, nature, and in order to match the shade of green precisely he looked (and here he showed more audacity than most) at the thing itself,[3] which happened to be a laurel bush growing beneath the window. After that, of course, he could write no more. Green in nature is one thing, green in literature another. Nature and letters seem to have a natural antipathy; bring them together and they tear each other to pieces. The shade of green Orlando now saw spoilt his rhyme and split his metre. Moreover, nature has tricks of her own. Once look out of a window at bees among flowers, at a yawning dog, at the sun setting, once think "how many more suns shall I see set", etc, etc. (the thought is too well known to be worth writing out) and one drops the pen, takes one's cloak, strides out of the room, and catches one's foot on a painted chest as one does so. For Orlando was a trifle clumsy.

He was careful to avoid meeting anyone. There was Stubbs, the gardener, coming along the path. He hid behind a tree till he had passed. He let himself out at a little gate in the garden wall. He skirted all stables, kennels, breweries, carpenters' shops, wash-houses, places where they make tallow candles, kill oxen, forge horse-shoes, stitch jerkins—for the house was a town ringing with men at work at their various crafts—and gained the ferny path leading uphill through the park unseen. There is perhaps a kinship among qualities; one draws another along with it; and the biographer should here call attention to the fact that this clumsiness is often mated with a love of solitude. Having stumbled over a chest, Orlando naturally loved solitary places, vast views, and to feel himself for ever and ever and ever alone.

So, after a long silence, "I am alone", he breathed at last, opening his lips for the first time in this record. He had walked very quickly uphill through ferns and hawthorn bushes, startling deer and wild birds, to a place crowned by a single oak tree. It was very high, so high indeed that nineteen English counties could be seen beneath; and on clear days thirty or perhaps forty, if the weather was very fine. Sometimes one could see the English Channel, wave reiterating upon wave. Rivers could be seen and pleasure boats gliding on them; and galleons setting out to sea; and armadas with puffs of smoke from which came the dull thud of cannon firing; and forts on the coast; and castles among the meadows; and here a watch tower; and there a fortress; and again some vast mansion like that of Orlando's father, massed like a town in the valley circled by walls. To the east there were the spires of London and the smoke of the city; and perhaps on the very sky line, when the wind was in the right

---

3. In her essay "Modern Fiction," published in revised form in *The Common Reader: First Series* (1925), Woolf emphasizes the writer's duty to depict life with "courage and sincerity" (150).

quarter, the craggy top and serrated edges of Snowdon[4] herself showed mountainous among the clouds. For a moment Orlando stood counting, gazing, recognising. That was his father's house; that his uncle's. His aunt owned those three great turrets among the trees there. The heath was theirs and the forest; the pheasant and the deer, the fox, the badger, and the butterfly.

He sighed profoundly, and flung himself—there was a passion in his movements which deserves the word—on the earth at the foot of the oak tree. He loved, beneath all this summer transiency, to feel the earth's spine beneath him; for such he took the hard root of the oak tree to be; or, for image followed image, it was the back of a great horse that he was riding; or the deck of a tumbling ship—it was anything indeed, so long as it was hard, for he felt the need of something which he could attach his floating heart to; the heart that tugged at his side; the heart that seemed filled with spiced and amorous gales every evening about this time when he walked out. To the oak tree he tied it and as he lay there, gradually the flutter in and about him stilled itself; the little leaves hung, the deer stopped; the pale summer clouds stayed; his limbs grew heavy on the ground; and he lay so still that by degrees the deer stepped nearer and the rooks wheeled round him and the swallows dipped and circled and the dragon-flies shot past, as if all the fertility and amorous activity of a summer's evening were woven web-like about his body.

After an hour or so—the sun was rapidly sinking, the white clouds had turned red, the hills were violet, the woods purple, the valleys black—trumpet sounded. Orlando leapt to his feet. The shrill sound came from the valley. It came from a dark spot down there; a spot compact and mapped out; a maze; a town, yet girt about with walls; it came from the heart of his own great house in the valley, which, dark before, even as he looked and the single trumpet duplicated and reduplicated itself with other shriller sounds, lost its darkness and became pierced with lights. Some were small hurrying lights, as if servants dashed along corridors to answer summonses; others were high and lustrous lights, as if they burnt in empty banqueting-halls made ready to receive guests who had not come; and others dipped and waved and sank and rose, as if held in the hands of troops of serving men, bending, kneeling, rising, receiving, guarding, and escorting with all dignity indoors a great Princess alighting from her chariot. Coaches turned and wheeled in the courtyard. Horses tossed their plumes. The Queen had come.[5]

---

4. Mt. Snowdon is the highest peak in Wales and the highest mountain in the British Isles outside of Scotland. It is located approximately 250 miles to the west of Knole.
5. Queen Elizabeth I of England (1533–1603).

Orlando looked no more. He dashed downhill. He let himself in at a wicket gate. He tore up the winding staircase. He reached his room. He tossed his stockings to one side of the room, his jerkin to the other. He dipped his head. He scoured his hands. He pared his finger nails. With no more than six inches of looking-glass and a pair of old candles to help him, he had thrust on crimson breeches, lace collar, waistcoat of taffeta, and shoes with rosettes on them as big as double dahlias in less than ten minutes by the stable clock. He was ready. He was flushed. He was excited. But he was terribly late.

By short cuts known to him, he made his way now through the vast congeries of rooms and staircases to the banqueting-hall, five acres distant on the other side of the house. But half-way there, in the back quarters where the servants lived, he stopped. The door of Mrs. Stewkley's sitting-room stood open—she was gone, doubtless, with all her keys to wait upon her mistress. But there, sitting at the servant's dinner table with a tankard beside him and paper in front of him, sat a rather fat, rather shabby man; whose ruff was a thought dirty, and whose clothes were of hodden brown. He held a pen in his hand, but he was not writing. He seemed in the act of rolling some thought up and down, to and fro in his mind till it gathered shape or momentum to his liking. His eyes, globed and clouded like some green stone of curious texture, were fixed. He did not see Orlando. For all his hurry, Orlando stopped dead. Was this a poet? Was he writing poetry? "Tell me", he wanted to say, "everything in the whole world"—for he had the wildest, most absurd, extravagant ideas about poets and poetry—but how speak to a man who does not see you? who sees ogres, satyrs, perhaps the depths of the sea instead? So Orlando stood gazing while the man turned his pen in his fingers, this way and that way; and gazed and mused; and then, very quickly, wrote half-a-dozen lines and looked up. Whereupon Orlando, overcome with shyness, darted off and reached the banqueting-hall only just in time to sink upon his knees and, hanging his head in confusion, to offer a bowl of rose water to the great Queen herself.

Such was his shyness that he saw no more of her than her ringed hand in water; but it was enough. It was a memorable hand; a thin hand with long fingers always curling as if round orb or sceptre; a nervous, crabbed, sickly hand; a commanding hand too; a hand that had only to raise itself for a head to fall; a hand, he guessed, attached to an old body that smelt like a cupboard in which furs are kept in camphor; which body was yet caparisoned in all sorts of brocades and gems; and held itself very upright though perhaps in pain from sciatica; and never flinched though strung together by a thousand fears; and the Queen's eyes were light yellow. All this he felt as the great rings flashed in the water and then something pressed his hair—which, perhaps, accounts for his seeing nothing more likely to be of use to a historian. And in truth, his mind was such a welter of opposites—of the night and the blazing candles, of the shabby poet and the great Queen, of silent fields and the clatter of serving men—that he could see nothing; or only a hand.

By the same showing, the Queen herself can have seen only a head. But if it is possible from a hand to deduce a body, informed with all the attributes of a great Queen, her crabbedness, courage, frailty, and terror, surely a head can be as fertile, looked down upon from a chair of state by a lady whose eyes were always, if the waxworks at the Abbey are to be trusted, wide open. The long, curled hair, the dark head bent so reverently, so innocently before her, implied a pair of the finest legs that a young nobleman has ever stood upright upon; and violet eyes; and a heart of gold; and loyalty and manly charm—all qualities which the old woman loved the more the more they failed her. For she was growing old and worn and bent before her time. The sound of cannon was always in her ears. She saw always the glistening poison drop and the long stiletto. As she sat at table she listened; she heard the guns in the Channel; she dreaded—was that a curse, was that a whisper? Innocence, simplicity, were all the more dear to her for the dark background she set them against. And it was that same night, so tradition has it, when Orlando was sound asleep, that she made over formally, putting her hand and seal finally to the parchment, the gift of the great monastic house that had been the Archbishop's and then the King's to Orlando's father.[6]

Orlando slept all night in ignorance. He had been kissed by a queen without knowing it. And perhaps, for women's hearts are intricate, it was his ignorance and the start he gave when her lips touched him that kept the memory of her young cousin (for they had blood in common) green in her mind. At any rate, two years of this quiet country life had not passed, and Orlando had written no more perhaps than twenty tragedies and a dozen histories and a score of sonnets when a message came that he was to attend the Queen at Whitehall.

"Here", she said, watching him advance down the long gallery towards her, "comes my innocent!" (There was a serenity about him always which had the look of innocence when, technically, the word was no longer applicable.)

"Come!" she said. She was sitting bolt upright beside the fire. And she held him a foot's pace from her and looked him up and down.

---

6. According to the chronological table in Sackville-West's *Knole and the Sackvilles* (which Woolf read before completing *Orlando*), Queen Elizabeth I granted Knole to Thomas Sackville, Lord Buckhurst, First Earl of Dorset in 1586. See *Knole and the Sackvilles* (vii).

Was she matching her speculations the other night with the truth now visible? Did she find her guesses justified? Eyes, mouth, nose, breast, hips, hands—she ran them over; her lips twitched visibly as she looked; but when she saw his legs she laughed out loud. He was the very image of a noble gentleman. But inwardly? She flashed her yellow hawk's eyes upon him as if she would pierce his soul. The young man withstood her gaze blushing only a damask rose as became him. Strength, grace, romance, folly, poetry, youth—she read him like a page. Instantly she plucked a ring from her finger (the joint was swollen rather) and as she fitted it to his, named him her Treasurer and Steward; next hung about him chains of office; and bidding him bend his knee, tied round it at the slenderest part the jewelled order of the Garter. Nothing after that was denied him. When she drove in state he rode at her carriage door. She sent him to Scotland on a sad embassy to the unhappy Queen.[7] He was about to sail for the Polish wars when she recalled him. For how could she bear to think of that tender flesh torn and that curly head rolled in the dust? She kept him with her. At the height of her triumph when the guns were booming at the Tower and the air was thick enough with gunpowder to make one sneeze and the huzzas of the people rang beneath the windows, she pulled him down among the cushions where her women had laid her (she was so worn and old) and made him bury his face in that astonishing composition—she had not changed her dress for a month—which smelt for all the world, he thought, recalling his boyish memory, like some old cabinet at home where his mother's furs were stored. He rose, half suffocated from the embrace. "This", she breathed, "is my victory!"—even as a rocket roared up and dyed her cheeks scarlet.

For the old woman loved him. And the Queen, who knew a man when she saw one, though not, it is said, in the usual way, plotted for him a splendid ambitious career. Lands were given him, houses assigned him. He was to be the son of her old age; the limb of her infirmity; the oak tree on which she leant her degradation. She croaked out these promises and strange domineering tendernesses (they were at Richmond[8] now) sitting bolt upright in her stiff brocades by the fire which, however high they piled it, never kept her warm.

Meanwhile, the long winter months drew on. Every tree in the Park was lined with frost. The river ran sluggishly. One day when the snow was on the ground and the dark panelled rooms were full of shadows and the stags were barking in the Park, she saw in the mirror, which she kept for fear of spies always by her, through the door, which she kept for fear of murderers always open, a boy—could

---

7. Mary, Queen of Scots, who was executed in 1587 by order of Queen Elizabeth I.
8. Richmond Palace, a royal residence favored by Queen Elizabeth I.

it be Orlando?—kissing a girl—who in the Devil's name was the brazen hussy? Snatching at her golden-hilted sword she struck violently at the mirror. The glass crashed; people came running; she was lifted and set in her chair again; but she was stricken after that and groaned much, as her days wore to an end, of man's treachery.

It was Orlando's fault perhaps; yet, after all, are we to blame Orlando? The age was the Elizabethan; their morals were not ours; nor their poets; nor their climate; nor their vegetables even. Everything was different. The weather itself, the heat and cold of summer and winter, was, we may believe, of another temper altogether. The brilliant amorous day was divided as sheerly from the night as land from water. Sunsets were redder and more intense; dawns were whiter and more auroral. Of our crepuscular half-lights and lingering twilights they knew nothing. The rain fell vehemently, or not at all. The sun blazed or there was darkness. Translating this to the spiritual regions as their wont is, the poets sang beautifully how roses fade and petals fall. The moment is brief they sang; the moment is over; one long night is then to be slept by all. As for using the artifices of the greenhouse or conservatory to prolong or preserve these fresh pinks and roses, that was not their way. The withered intricacies and ambiguities of our more gradual and doubtful age were unknown to them. Violence was all. The flower bloomed and faded. The sun rose and sank. The lover loved and went. And what the poets said in rhyme, the young translated into practice. Girls were roses, and their seasons were short as the flowers'. Plucked they must be before nightfall; for the day was brief and the day was all. Thus, if Orlando followed the leading of the climate, of the poets, of the age itself, and plucked his flower in the window-seat even with the snow on the ground and the Queen vigilant in the corridor, we can scarcely bring ourselves to blame him. He was young; he was boyish; he did but as nature bade him do. As for the girl, we know no more than Queen Elizabeth herself did what her name was. It may have been Doris, Chloris, Delia, or Diana, for he made rhymes to them all in turn; equally, she may have been a court lady, or some serving maid. For Orlando's taste was broad; he was no lover of garden flowers only; the wild and the weeds even had always a fascination for him.

Here, indeed, we lay bare rudely, as a biographer may, a curious trait in him, to be accounted for, perhaps, by the fact that a certain grandmother of his had worn a smock and carried milkpails. Some grains of the Kentish or Sussex earth were mixed with the thin, fine fluid which came to him from Normandy. He held that the mixture of brown earth and blue blood was a good one. Certain it is that he had always a liking for low company, especially for that of lettered people whose wits so often keep them under, as if there were the sympathy of blood between them. At this season of his life, when his head brimmed with rhymes and he never went to bed without striking off some conceit, the cheek of an innkeeper's daughter seemed fresher and the wit of a gamekeeper's niece seemed quicker than those of the ladies at Court. Hence, he began going frequently to Wapping[9] Old Stairs and the beer gardens at night, wrapped in a grey cloak to hide the star at his neck and the garter at his knee. There, with a mug before him, among the sanded alleys and bowling greens and all the simple architecture of such places, he listened to sailors' stories of hardship and horror and cruelty on the Spanish main; how some had lost their toes, others their noses—for the spoken story was never so rounded or so finely coloured as the written. Especially he loved to hear them volley forth their songs of the Azores, while the parrakeets, which they had brought from those parts, pecked at the rings in their ears, tapped with their hard acquisitive beaks at the rubies on their fingers, and swore as vilely as their masters. The women were scarcely less bold in their speech and less free in their manners than the birds. They perched on his knee, flung their arms round his neck and, guessing that something out of the common lay hid beneath his duffle cloak, were quite as eager to come at the truth of the matter as Orlando himself.

Nor was opportunity lacking. The river was astir early and late with barges, wherries,[1] and craft of all description. Every day sailed to sea some fine ship bound for the Indies; now and again another blackened and ragged with hairy unknown men on board crept painfully to anchor. No one missed a boy or girl if they dallied a little on the water after sunset; or raised an eyebrow if gossip had seen them sleeping soundly among the treasure sacks safe in each other's arms. Such indeed was the adventure that befel Orlando, Sukey, and the Earl of Cumberland. The day was hot; their loves had been active; they had fallen asleep among the rubies. Late that night the Earl, whose fortunes were much bound up in the Spanish ventures, came to check the booty alone with a lantern. He flashed the light on a barrel. He started back with an oath. Twined about the cask two spirits lay sleeping. Superstitious by nature, and his conscience laden with many a crime, the Earl took the couple—they were wrapped in a red cloak, and Sukey's bosom was almost as white as the eternal snows of Orlando's poetry—for a phantom sprung from the graves of drowned sailors to upbraid him. He crossed himself. He vowed repentance. The row of alms houses still standing in the Sheen Road is the visible fruit of that moment's panic. Twelve poor old women of the parish to-day drink tea and to-night bless his Lordship for a

9. A neighborhood in the eastern part of London on the Thames River.
1. A long, low-profiled boat designed to transport cargo up and down rivers.

roof above their heads; so that illicit love in a treasure ship—but we omit the moral.

Soon, however, Orlando grew tired, not only of the discomfort of this way of life, and of the crabbed streets of the neighbourhood, but of the primitive manners of the people. For it has to be remembered that crime and poverty had none of the attraction for the Elizabethans that they have for us. They had none of our modern shame of book learning; none of our belief that to be born the son of a butcher is a blessing and to be unable to read a virtue; no fancy that what we call "life" and "reality" are somehow connected with ignorance and brutality; nor, indeed, any equivalent for these two words at all. It was not to seek "life" that Orlando went among them; not in quest of "reality" that he left them. But when he had heard a score of times how Jakes had lost his nose and Sukey her honour—and they told the stories admirably, it must be admitted—he began to be a little weary of the repetition, for a nose can only be cut off in one way and maidenhood lost in another—or so it seemed to him—whereas the arts and the sciences had a diversity about them which stirred his curiosity profoundly. So, always keeping them in happy memory, he left off frequenting the beer gardens and the skittle alleys, hung his grey cloak in his wardrobe, let his star shine at his neck and his garter twinkle at his knee, and appeared once more at the Court of King James.[2] He was young, he was rich, he was handsome. No one could have been received with greater acclamation than he was.

It is certain indeed that many ladies were ready to show him their favours. The names of three at least were freely coupled with his in marriage—Clorinda, Favilla, Euphrosyne—so he called them in his sonnets.

To take them in order; Clorinda was a sweet-mannered gentle lady enough;—indeed Orlando was greatly taken with her for six months and a half; but she had white eyelashes and could not bear the sight of blood. A hare brought up roasted at her father's table turned her faint. She was much under the influence of the Priests too, and stinted[3] her underlinen in order to give to the poor. She took it on her to reform Orlando of his sins, which sickened him, so that he drew back from the marriage, and did not much regret it when she died soon after of the small-pox.

Favilla, who comes next, was of a different sort altogether. She was the daughter of a poor Somersetshire gentleman; who, by sheer assiduity and the use of her eyes had worked her way up at court,

---

2. James Stuart, James VI of Scotland and James I of England. He succeeded Queen Elizabeth I to the throne upon her death in 1603.
3. Kept an inadequate supply of.

where her address in horsemanship, her fine instep, and her grace
in dancing won the admiration of all. Once, however, she was so ill-
advised as to whip a spaniel that had torn one of her silk stockings
(and it must be said in justice that Favilla had few stockings and
those for the most part of drugget[4]) within an inch of its life beneath
Orlando's window. Orlando, who was a passionate lover of animals,
now noticed that her teeth were crooked, and the two front turned
inward, which, he said, is a sure sign of a perverse and cruel disposition in woman, and so broke the engagement that very night for ever.

The third, Euphrosyne,[5] was by far the most serious of his flames.
She was by birth one of the Irish Desmonds and had therefore a
family tree of her own as old and deeply rooted as Orlando's itself.
She was fair, florid, and a trifle phlegmatic. She spoke Italian well,
had a perfect set of teeth in the upper jaw, though those on the lower
were slightly discoloured. She was never without a whippet or spaniel at her knee; fed them with white bread from her own plate; sang
sweetly to the virginals; and was never dressed before mid-day owing
to the extreme care she took of her person. In short, she would have
made a perfect wife for such a nobleman as Orlando, and matters
had gone so far that the lawyers on both sides were busy with covenants, jointures, settlements, messages, tenements, and whatever
is needed before one great fortune can mate with another when,
with the suddenness and severity that then marked the English climate, came the Great Frost.

The Great Frost was, historians tell us, the most severe that has
ever visited these islands. Birds froze in mid-air and fell like stones
to the ground. At Norwich a young countrywoman started to cross
the road in her usual robust health and was seen by the onlookers
to turn visibly to powder and be blown in a puff of dust over the roofs
as the icy blast struck her at the street corner. The mortality among
sheep and cattle was enormous. Corpses froze and could not be
drawn from the sheets. It was no uncommon sight to come upon a
whole herd of swine frozen immovable upon the road. The fields
were full of shepherds, ploughmen, teams of horses, and little bird-
scaring boys all struck stark in the act of the moment, one with his
hand to his nose, another with the bottle to his lips, a third with a
stone raised to throw at the raven who sat, as if stuffed, upon the
hedge within a yard of him. The severity of the frost was so extraordinary that a kind of petrifaction sometimes ensued; and it was

4. Coarse wool cloth.
5. The title of a collection of poetry with contributions by several Bloomsbury Group
   members (Leonard Woolf, Lytton Strachey, Clive Bell, Walter Lamb, and Saxon
   Sydney-Turner) shortly after they graduated from Cambridge University. Woolf's
   choice of the name Euphrosyne for a "fair, florid, and a trifle phlegmatic" person is
   likely an inside joke poking fun at her (now older and more distinguished) husband and
   close friends.

commonly supposed that the great increase of rocks in some parts of Derbyshire was due to no eruption, for there was none, but to the solidification of unfortunate wayfarers who had been turned literally to stone where they stood. The Church could give little help in the matter, and though some landowners had these relics blessed, the most part preferred to use them either as landmarks, scratching-posts for sheep, or, when the form of the stone allowed, drinking troughs for cattle, which purposes they serve, admirably for the most part, to this day.

But while the country people suffered the extremity of want, and the trade of the country was at a standstill, London enjoyed a carnival of the utmost brilliancy. The Court was at Greenwich, and the new King seized the opportunity that his coronation gave him to curry favour with the citizens. He directed that the river, which was frozen to a depth of twenty feet and more for six or seven miles on either side, should be swept, decorated and given all the semblance of a park or pleasure ground, with arbours, mazes, alleys, drinking booths, etc., at his expense. For himself and the courtiers, he reserved a certain space immediately opposite the Palace gates; which, railed off from the public only by a silken rope, became at once the centre of the most brilliant society in England. Great statesmen, in their beards and ruffs, despatched affairs of state under the crimson awning of the Royal Pagoda. Soldiers planned the conquest of the Moor and the downfall of the Turk in striped arbours surmounted by plumes of ostrich feathers. Admirals strode up and down the narrow pathways, glass in hand, sweeping the horizon and telling stories of the north-west passage and the Spanish Armada. Lovers dallied upon divans spread with sables. Frozen roses fell in showers when the Queen and her ladies walked abroad. Colored balloons hovered motionless in the air. Here and there burnt vast bonfires of cedar and oak wood, lavishly salted, so that the flames were of green, orange, and purple fire. But however fiercely they burnt, the heat was not enough to melt the ice which, though of singular transparency, was yet of the hardness of steel. So clear indeed was it that there could be seen, congealed at a depth of several feet, here a porpoise, there a flounder. Shoals of eels lay motionless in a trance, but whether their state was one of death or merely of suspended animation which the warmth would revive puzzled the philosophers. Near London Bridge, where the river had frozen to a depth of some twenty fathoms, a wrecked wherry boat was plainly visible, lying on the bed of the river where it had sunk last autumn, overladen with apples. The old bumboat[6] woman, who was carrying her fruit to market on the Surrey side, sat there in her plaids and farthingales

---

6. A small boat used by vendors to carry provisions for sale to larger boats.

with her lap full of apples, for all the world as if she were about to
serve a customer, though a certain blueness about the lips hinted
the truth. 'Twas a sight King James specially liked to look upon, and
he would bring a troupe of courtiers to gaze with him. In short,
nothing could exceed the brilliancy and gaiety of the scene by day.
But it was at night that the carnival was at its merriest. For the
frost continued unbroken; the nights were of perfect stillness; the
moon and stars blazed with the hard fixity of diamonds, and to the
fine music of flute and trumpet the courtiers danced.

Orlando, it is true, was none of those who tread lightly the coran-
toe and lavolta;[7] he was clumsy and a little absent-minded. He much
preferred the plain dances of his own country, which he had danced
as a child to these fantastic foreign measures. He had indeed just
brought his feet together about six in the evening of the seventh of
January at the finish of some such quadrille or minuet when he
beheld, coming from the pavilion of the Muscovite Embassy, a figure,
which, whether boy's or woman's, for the loose tunic and trousers
of the Russian fashion served to disguise the sex, filled him with
the highest curiosity. The person, whatever the name or sex, was
about middle height, very slenderly fashioned, and dressed entirely
in oyster-coloured velvet, trimmed with some unfamiliar greenish-
coloured fur. But these details were obscured by the extraordinary
seductiveness which issued from the whole person. Images, metaphors
of the most extreme and extravagant twined and twisted in his mind.
He called her a melon, a pineapple, an olive tree, an emerald, and a
fox in the snow all in the space of three seconds; he did not know
whether he had heard her, tasted her, seen her, or all three together.
(For though we must pause not a moment in the narrative we may
here hastily note that all his images at this time were simple in the
extreme to match his senses and were mostly taken from things he
had liked the taste of as a boy. But if his senses were simple they
were at the same time extremely strong. To pause therefore and
seek the reasons of things is out of the question.) . . . A melon, an
emerald, a fox in the snow—so he raved, so he stared. When the
boy, for alas, a boy it must be—no woman could skate with such
speed and vigour—swept almost on tiptoe past him, Orlando was
ready to tear his hair with vexation that the person was of his own
sex, and thus all embraces were out of the question. But the skater
came closer. Legs, hands, carriage, were a boy's, but no boy ever
had a mouth like that; no boy had those breasts; no boy had eyes
which looked as if they had been fished from the bottom of the sea.
Finally, coming to a stop and sweeping a curtsey with the utmost
grace to the King, who was shuffling past on the arm of some

7. Popular early modern dances.

Lord-in-waiting, the unknown skater came to a standstill. She was not a handsbreadth off. She was a woman. Orlando stared; trembled; turned hot; turned cold; longed to hurl himself through the summer air; to crush acorns beneath his feet; to toss his arms with the beech trees and the oaks. As it was, he drew his lips up over his small white teeth; opened them perhaps half an inch as if to bite; shut them as if he had bitten. The Lady Euphrosyne hung upon his arm.

The stranger's name, he found, was the Princess Marousha Stanilovska Dagmar Natasha Iliana Romanovitch,[8] and she had come in the train of the Muscovite Ambassador, who was her uncle perhaps, or perhaps her father, to attend the coronation. Very little was known of the Muscovites. In their great beards and furred hats they sat almost silent; drinking some black liquid which they spat out now and then upon the ice. None spoke English, and French with which some at least were familiar was then little spoken at the English Court.

It was through this accident that Orlando and the Princess became acquainted. They were seated opposite each other at the great table spread under a huge awning for the entertainment of the notables. The Princess was placed between two young Lords, one Lord Francis Vere and the other the young Earl of Moray. It was laughable to see the predicament she soon had them in, for though both were fine lads in their way, the babe unborn had as much knowledge of the French tongue as they had. When at the beginning of dinner the Princess turned to the Earl and said, with a grace which ravished his heart, "Je crois avoir fait la connaissance d'un gentilhomme qui vous était apparenté en Pologne l'été dernier",[9] or "La beauté des dames de la cour d'Angleterre me met dans le ravissement. On ne peut voir une dame plus gracieuse que votre reine, ni une coiffure plus belle que la sienne",[1] both Lord Francis and the Earl showed the highest embarrassment. The one helped her largely to horse-radish sauce, the other whistled to his dog and made him beg for a marrow bone. At this the Princess could no longer contain her laughter, and Orlando, catching her eyes across the boars' heads and stuffed peacocks, laughed too. He laughed, but the laugh on his lips froze in wonder. Whom had he loved, what had he loved, he asked himself in a tumult of emotion, until now? An old woman, he answered, all skin and bone. Red-cheeked trulls too many to mention. A puling

---

8. In a letter to Sackville-West, Woolf hints that the princess/Sasha is modeled on Violet Trefusis, with whom Sackville-West had a serious and ultimately scandalous affair: "Tomorrow I begin the chapter which describes Violet and you meeting on the ice. The whole thing has to be gone into thoroughly" (*Letters*, vol. 3 [#1821] Oct. 13, 1927, p. 420).
9. I think I met a gentleman of your family in Poland last summer (French).
1. The ladies of the English Court ravish me with their beauty. Never have I seen so graceful a lady as your Queen or so fine a head dress as she wears (French).

nun. A hard-bitten cruel-mouthed adventuress. A nodding mass of lace and ceremony. Love had meant to him nothing but sawdust and cinders. The joys he had had of it tasted insipid in the extreme. He marvelled how he could have gone through with it without yawning. For as he looked the thickness of his blood melted; the ice turned to wine in his veins; he heard the waters flowing and the birds singing; spring broke over the hard wintry landscape; his manhood woke; he grasped a sword in his hand; he charged a more daring foe than Pole or Moor; he dived in deep water; he saw the flower of danger growing in a crevice; he stretched his hand—in fact he was rattling off one of his most impassioned sonnets when the Princess addressed him, "Would you have the goodness to pass the salt?"

He blushed deeply.

"With all the pleasure in the world, Madame," he replied, speaking French with a perfect accent. For, heaven be praised, he spoke the tongue as his own; his mother's maid had taught him. Yet perhaps it would have been better for him had he never learnt that tongue; never answered that voice; never followed the light of those eyes. . . .

The Princess continued. Who were those bumpkins, she asked him, who sat beside her with the manners of stablemen? What was the nauseating mixture they had poured on her plate? Did the dogs eat at the same table with the men in England? Was that figure of fun at the end of the table with her hair rigged up like a Maypole (comme une grande perche mal fagotée)[2] really the Queen? And did the King always slobber like that? And which of those popinjays was George Villiers?[3] Though these questions rather discomposed Orlando at first, they were put with such archness and drollery that he could not help but laugh; and as he saw from the blank faces of the company that nobody understood a word, he answered her as freely as she asked him, speaking, as she did, in perfect French.

Thus began an intimacy between the two which soon became the scandal of the Court.

Soon it was observed Orlando paid the Muscovite far more attention than mere civility demanded. He was seldom far from her side, and their conversation, though unintelligible to the rest, was carried on with such animation, provoked such blushes and laughter, that the dullest could guess the subject. Moreover, the change in Orlando himself was extraordinary. Nobody had ever seen him so animated. In one night he had thrown off his boyish clumsiness; he was changed from a sulky stripling,[4] who could not enter a ladies' room without sweeping half the ornaments from the table, to a

2. Literally "like a big, badly dressed pole" (French).
3. First Duke of Buckingham, a favorite of James I and possibly his lover. "Popinjay" is a derisive term for a vain, extravagantly dressed person.
4. A young man.

nobleman, full of grace and manly courtesy. To see him hand the Muscovite (as she was called) to her sledge, or offer her his hand for the dance, or catch the spotted kerchief which she had let drop, or discharge any other of those manifold duties which the supreme lady exacts and the lover hastens to anticipate was a sight to kindle the dull eyes of age, and to make the quick pulse of youth beat faster. Yet over it all hung a cloud. The old men shrugged their shoulders. The young tittered between their fingers. All knew that Orlando was betrothed to another. The Lady Margaret O'Brien O'Dare O'Reilly Tyrconnel (for that was the proper name of Euphrosyne of the Sonnets) wore Orlando's splendid sapphire on the second finger of her left hand. It was she who had the supreme right to his attentions. Yet she might drop all the handkerchiefs in her wardrobe (of which she had many scores) upon the ice and Orlando never stooped to pick them up. She might wait twenty minutes for him to hand her to her sledge, and in the end have to be content with the services of her Blackamoor.[5] When she skated, which she did rather clumsily, no one was at her elbow to encourage her, and, if she fell, which she did rather heavily, no one raised her to her feet and dusted the snow from her petticoats. Although she was naturally phlegmatic, slow to take offence, and more reluctant than most people to believe that a mere foreigner could oust her from Orlando's affections, still even the Lady Margaret herself was brought at last to suspect that something was brewing against her peace of mind.

Indeed, as the days passed, Orlando took less and less care to hide his feelings. Making some excuse or other, he would leave the company as soon as they had dined, or steal away from the skaters, who were forming sets for a quadrille.[6] Next moment it would be seen that the Muscovite was missing too. But what most outraged the Court, and stung it in its tenderest part, which is its vanity, was that the couple was often seen to slip under the silken rope, which railed off the Royal enclosure from the public part of the river and to disappear among the crowd of common people. For suddenly the Princess would stamp her foot and cry, "Take me away. I detest your English mob," by which she meant the English Court itself. She could stand it no longer. It was full of prying old women, she said, who stared in one's face, and of bumptious young men who trod on one's toes. They smelt bad. Their dogs ran between her legs. It was like being in a cage. In Russia they had rivers ten miles broad on which one could gallop six horses abreast all day long without meeting a soul. Besides, she wanted to see the Tower, the Beefeaters, the

---

5. In the early 17th century this term would have referred to a dark-skinned person from Africa or of African descent.

6. A multi-couple dance popular in the 18th century. The dance's inclusion here is an anachronism.

Heads on Temple Bar, and the jewellers' shops in the city. Thus, it came about that Orlando took her to the city, showed her the Beefeaters and the rebels' heads, and bought her whatever took her fancy in the Royal Exchange. But this was not enough. Each increasingly desired the other's company in privacy all day long where there were none to marvel or to stare. Instead of taking the road to London, therefore, they turned the other way about and were soon beyond the crowd among the frozen reaches of the Thames where, save for sea birds and some old country woman hacking at the ice in a vain attempt to draw a pailful of water or gathering what sticks or dead leaves she could find for firing, not a living soul ever came their way. The poor kept closely to their cottages, and the better sort, who could afford it, crowded for warmth and merriment to the city.

Hence, Orlando and Sasha, as he called her for short, and because it was the name of a white Russian fox he had had as a boy—a creature soft as snow, but with teeth of steel, which bit him so savagely that his father had it killed—hence, they had the river to themselves. Hot with skating and with love they would throw themselves down in some solitary reach, where the yellow osiers[7] fringed the bank, and wrapped in a great fur cloak Orlando would take her in his arms, and know, for the first time, he murmured, the delights of love. Then, when the ecstasy was over and they lay lulled in a swoon on the ice, he would tell her of his other loves, and how, compared with her, they had been of wood, of sackcloth, and of cinders. And laughing at his vehemence, she would turn once more in his arms and give him, for love's sake, one more embrace. And then they would marvel that the ice did not melt with their heat, and pity the poor old woman who had no such natural means of thawing it, but must hack at it with a chopper of cold steel. And then, wrapped in their sables, they would talk of everything under the sun; of sights and travels; of Moor and Pagan; of this man's beard and that woman's skin; of a rat that fed from her hand at table; of the arras that moved always in the hall at home; of a face; of a feather. Nothing was too small for such converse, nothing was too great.

Then, suddenly Orlando would fall into one of his moods of melancholy; the sight of the old woman hobbling over the ice might be the cause of it, or nothing; and would fling himself face downwards on the ice and look into the frozen waters and think of death. For the philosopher is right who says that nothing thicker than a knife's blade separates happiness from melancholy; and he goes on to opine that one is twin fellow to the other; and draws from this the conclusion that all extremes of feeling are allied to madness; and so bids us take refuge in the true Church (in his view the Anabaptist), which

7. A type of willow.

is the only harbour, port, anchorage, etc., he said, for those tossed on this sea.

"All ends in death," Orlando would say, sitting upright, his face clouded with gloom. (For that was the way his mind worked now, in violent see-saws from life to death, stopping at nothing in between, so that the biographer must not stop either, but must fly as fast as he can and so keep pace with the unthinking passionate foolish actions and sudden extravagant words in which, it is impossible to deny, Orlando at this time of his life indulged.)

"All ends in death," Orlando would say, sitting upright on the ice. But Sasha who after all had no English blood in her but was from Russia where the sunsets are longer, the dawns less sudden, and sentences often left unfinished from doubt as to how best to end them—Sasha stared at him, perhaps sneered at him, for he must have seemed a child to her, and said nothing. But at length the ice grew cold beneath them, which she disliked, so pulling him to his feet again, she talked so enchantingly, so wittily, so wisely (but unfortunately always in French, which notoriously loses its flavour in translation) that he forgot the frozen waters or night coming or the old woman or whatever it was, and would try to tell her—plunging and splashing among a thousand images which had gone as stale as the women who inspired them—what she was like. Snow, cream, marble, cherries, alabaster, golden wire? None of these. She was like a fox, or an olive tree; like the waves of the sea when you look down upon them from a height; like an emerald; like the sun on a green hill which is yet clouded—like nothing he had seen or known in England. Ransack the language as he might, words failed him. He wanted another landscape, and another tongue, English was too frank, too candid, too honeyed a speech for Sasha. For in all she said, however open she seemed and voluptuous, there was something hidden; in all she did, however daring, there was something concealed. So the green flame seems hidden in the emerald, or the sun prisoned in a hill. The clearness was only outward; within was a wandering flame. It came; it went; she never shone with the steady beam of an Englishwoman—here, however, remembering the Lady Margaret and her petticoats, Orlando ran wild in his transports and swept her over the ice, faster, faster, vowing that he would chase the flame, dive for the gem, and so on and so on, the words coming on the pants of his breath with the passion of a poet whose poetry is half pressed out of him by pain.

But Sasha was silent. When Orlando had done telling her that she was a fox, an olive tree, or a green hill-top, and had given her the whole history of his family; how their house was one of the most ancient in Britain; how they had come from Rome with the Caesars and had the right to walk down the Corso (which is the chief street in Rome) under a tasselled palanquin,[8] which he said is a privilege reserved only for those of imperial blood (for there was an orgulous[9] credulity about him which was pleasant enough), he would pause and ask her, Where was her own house? What was her father? Had she brothers? Why was she here alone with her uncle? Then, some-how, though she answered readily enough, an awkwardness would come between them. He suspected at first that her rank was not as high as she would like; or that she was ashamed of the savage ways of her people, for he had heard that the women in Muscovy wear beards and the men are covered with fur from the waist down; that both sexes are smeared with tallow to keep the cold out, tear meat with their fingers and live in huts where an English noble would scruple to keep his cattle; so that he forbore to press her. But on reflection, he concluded that her silence could not be for that rea-son; she herself was entirely free from hair on the chin; she dressed in velvet and pearls, and her manners were certainly not those of a woman bred in a cattle-shed.

What, then, did she hide from him? The doubt underlying the tre-mendous force of his feelings was like a quicksand beneath a mon-ument which shifts suddenly and makes the whole pile shake. The agony would seize him suddenly. Then he would blaze out in such wrath that she did not know how to quiet him. Perhaps she did not want to quiet him; perhaps his rages pleased her and she provoked them purposely—such is the curious obliquity of the Muscovitish temperament.

To continue the story—skating farther than their wont that day they reached that part of the river where the ships had anchored and been frozen in midstream. Among them was the ship of the Musco-vite Embassy flying its double-headed black eagle from the main mast, which was hung with many-coloured icicles several yards in length. Sasha had left some of her clothing on board, and suppos-ing the ship to be empty they climbed on deck and went in search of it. Remembering certain passages in his own past, Orlando would not have marvelled had some good citizens sought this refuge before them; and so it turned out. They had not ventured far when a fine young man started up from some business of his own behind a coil of rope and saying, apparently, for he spoke Russian, that he was one of the crew and would help the Princess to find what she wanted, lit a lump of candle and disappeared with her into the lower parts of the ship.

8. A covered chair or bench situated on top of two long, parallel poles, each of which would have been lifted and conveyed by servants.
9. Proud or haughty.

Time went by, and Orlando, wrapped in his own dreams, thought only of the pleasures of life; of his jewel; of her rarity; of means for making her irrevocably and indissolubly his own. Obstacles there were and hardships to be overcome. She was determined to live in Russia, where there were frozen rivers and wild horses and men, she said, who gashed each other's throats open. It is true that a landscape of pine and snow, habits of lust and slaughter, did not entice him. Nor was he anxious to cease his pleasant country ways of sport and tree-planting; relinquish his office; ruin his career; shoot the reindeer instead of the rabbit; drink vodka instead of canary, and slip a knife up his sleeve—for what purpose, he knew not. Still, all this and more than all this he would do for her sake. As for his marriage with the Lady Margaret, fixed though it was for this day sennight,[1] the thing was so palpably absurd that he scarcely gave it a thought. Her kinsmen would abuse him for deserting a great lady; his friends would deride him for ruining the finest career in the world for a Cossack woman and a waste of snow—it weighed not a straw in the balance compared with Sasha herself. On the first dark night they would fly. They would take ship to Russia. So he pondered; so he plotted as he walked up and down the deck.

He was recalled, turning westward, by the sight of the sun, slung like an orange on the cross of St. Paul's. It was blood-red and sinking rapidly. It must be almost evening. Sasha had been gone this hour and more. Seized instantly with those dark forebodings which shadowed even his most confident thoughts of her, he plunged the way he had seen them go into the hold of the ship; and, after stumbling among chests and barrels in the darkness, was made aware by a faint glimmer in a corner that they were seated there. For one second, he had a vision of them; saw Sasha seated on the sailor's knee; saw her bend towards him; saw them embrace before the light was blotted out in a red cloud by his rage. He blazed into such a howl of anguish that the whole ship echoed. Sasha threw herself between them, or the sailor would have been stifled before he could draw his cutlass. Then a deadly sickness came over Orlando, and they had to lay him on the floor and give him brandy to drink before he revived. And then, when he had recovered and was sat upon a heap of sacking on deck, Sasha hung over him, passing before his dizzied eyes softly, sinuously, like the fox that had bit him, now cajoling, now denouncing, so that he came to doubt what he had seen. Had not the candle guttered; had not the shadows moved? The box was heavy, she said; the man was helping her to move it. Orlando believed her one moment—for who can be sure that his rage has not painted what he most dreads to find?—the next was the more violent with anger

1. A week (seven nights).

Figure 2. The Russian Princess as a Child. © 2024 Artists Rights Society (ARS), New York / DACS, London. British Library, London, UK. From the British Library archive / Bridgeman Images.

at her deceit. Then Sasha herself turned white; stamped her foot on deck; said she would go that night, and called upon her Gods to destroy her, if she, a Romanovitch, had lain in the arms of a common seaman. Indeed, looking at them together (which he could hardly bring himself to do) Orlando was outraged by the foulness of his imagination that could have painted so frail a creature in the paws of that hairy sea brute. The man was huge; stood six feet four in his stockings; wore common wire rings in his ears; and looked like a dray horse upon which some wren or robin had perched in flight. So he yielded; believed her; and asked her pardon. Yet, when they were going down the ships side, lovingly again, Sasha paused with her hand on the ladder, and called back to the tawny wide-cheeked monster a volley of Russian greetings, jests, or endearments, not a word of which Orlando could understand. But there was something in her tone (it might be the fault of the Russian consonants) that reminded Orlando of a scene some nights since, when he had come upon her in secret gnawing a candle-end in a corner, which she had picked from the floor. True, it was pink; it was gilt; and it was from the King's table; but it was tallow, and she gnawed it. Was there not, he thought, handing her on to the ice, something rank in her, something coarse flavoured, something peasant born? And he fancied her at forty grown unwieldy though she was now slim as a reed, and lethargic though she was now blithe as a lark. But again as they skated towards London such suspicions melted in his breast, and he felt as if he had been hooked by a great fish through the nose and rushed through the waters unwillingly, yet with his own consent.

It was an evening of astonishing beauty. As the sun sank, all the domes, spires, turrets, and pinnacles of London rose in inky blackness against the furious red sunset clouds. Here was the fretted cross at Charing; there the dome of St. Paul's;[2] there the massy square of the Tower buildings; there like a grove of trees stripped of all leaves save a knob at the end were the heads on the pikes at Temple Bar. Now the Abbey windows were lit up and burnt like a heavenly, many-coloured shield (in Orlando's fancy); now all the west seemed a golden window with troops of angels (in Orlando's fancy again) passing up and down the heavenly stairs perpetually. All the time they seemed to be skating on fathomless depths of air, so blue the ice had become; and so glassy smooth was it that they sped quicker and quicker to the city with the white gulls circling about them, and cutting in the air with their wings the very same sweeps that they cut on the ice with their skates.

2. At the time of James I, St. Paul's would not have had a dome. The cathedral burned down in the Great Fire of London in 1666. It was rebuilt in 1668–1711 under the direction of Sir Christopher Wren (1632–1723). The iconic dome of the new building was completed in 1708.

Sasha, as if to reassure him, was tenderer than usual and even more delightful. Seldom would she talk about her past life, but now she told him how, in winter in Russia, she would listen to the wolves howling across the steppes, and thrice, to show him, she barked like a wolf. Upon which he told her of the stags in the snow at home, and how they would stray into the great hall for warmth and be fed by an old man with porridge from a bucket. And then she praised him; for his love of beasts; for his gallantry; for his legs. Ravished with her praises and shamed to think how he had maligned her by fancying her on the knees of a common sailor and grown fat and lethargic at forty, he told her that he could find no words to praise her; yet instantly bethought him how she was like the spring and green grass and rushing waters, and seizing her more tightly than ever, he swung her with him half across the river so that the gulls and the cormorants swung too. And halting at length, out of breath, she said, panting slightly, that he was like a million-candled Christmas tree (such as they have in Russia) hung with yellow globes; incandescent; enough to light a whole street by; (so one might translate it) for what with his glowing cheeks, his dark curls, his black and crimson cloak, he looked as if he were burning with his own radiance, from a lamp lit within.

All the colour, save the red of Orlando's cheeks, soon faded. Night came on. As the orange light of sunset vanished it was succeeded by an astonishing white glare from the torches, bonfires, flaming cressets, and other devices by which the river was lit up and the strangest transformation took place. Various churches and noblemen's palaces, whose fronts were of white stone showed in streaks and patches as if floating on the air. Of St. Paul's, in particular, nothing was left but a gilt Cross. The Abbey appeared like the grey skeleton of a leaf. Everything suffered emaciation and transformation. As they approached the carnival, they heard a deep note like that struck on a tuning-fork which boomed louder and louder until it became an uproar. Every now and then a great shout followed a rocket into the air. Gradually they could discern little figures breaking off from the vast crowd and spinning hither and thither like gnats on the surface of a river. Above and around this brilliant circle like a bowl of darkness pressed the deep black of a winter's night. And then into this darkness there began to rise with pauses, which kept the expectation alert and the mouth open, flowering rockets; crescents; serpents; a crown. At one moment the woods and distant hills showed green as on a summer's day; the next all was winter and blackness again.

By this time Orlando and the Princess were close to the Royal enclosure and found their way barred by a great crowd of the common people, who were pressing as near to the silken rope as they dared. Loth to end their privacy and encounter the sharp eyes that were on the watch for them, the couple lingered there, shouldered by apprentices; tailors; fishwives; horse dealers; cony catchers;[3] starving scholars; maid-servants in their whimples;[4] orange girls; ostlers; sober citizens; bawdy tapsters; and a crowd of little ragamuffins such as always haunt the outskirts of a crowd, screaming and scrambling among people's feet—all the riff-raff of the London streets indeed was there, jesting and jostling, here casting dice, telling fortunes, shoving, tickling, pinching; here uproarious, there glum; some of them with mouths gaping a yard wide; others as little reverent as daws[5] on a house-top; all as variously rigged out as their purse or stations allowed; here in fur and broadcloth; there in tatters with their feet kept from the ice only by a dishclout bound about them. The main press of people, it appeared, stood opposite a booth or stage something like our Punch and Judy show[6] upon which some kind of theatrical performance was going forward. A black man was waving his arms and vociferating. There was a woman in white laid upon a bed.[7] Rough though the staging was, the actors running up and down a pair of steps and sometimes tripping, and the crowd stamping their feet and whistling, or when they were bored, tossing a piece of orange peel on to the ice which a dog would scramble for, still the astonishing, sinuous melody of the words stirred Orlando like music. Spoken with extreme speed and a daring agility of tongue which reminded him of the sailors singing in the beer gardens at Wapping, the words even without meaning were as wine to him. But now and again a single phrase would come to him over the ice which was as if torn from the depths of his heart. The frenzy of the Moor seemed to him his own frenzy, and when the Moor suffocated the woman in her bed it was Sasha he killed with his own hands.

At last the play was ended. All had grown dark. The tears streamed down his face. Looking up into the sky there was nothing but blackness there too. Ruin and death, he thought, cover all. The life of man ends in the grave. Worms devour us.

> Methinks it should be now a huge eclipse
> Of sun and moon, and that the affrighted globe
> Should yawn—[8]

Even as he said this a star of some pallor rose in his memory. The night was dark; it was pitch dark; but it was such a night as this that they had waited for; it was on such a night as this that they had

---

3. Scam artists.
4. A woman's headcovering of white fabric draped over the head, forehead, and neck.
5. Jackdaw, a variety of crow.
6. A traditional British puppet show often staged outdoors in a boothlike portable theater.
7. The play being enacted is a version of William Shakespeare's *Othello*. See n. 9, p. 48.
8. Shakespeare, *Othello* 5.2.123–25.

planned to fly. He remembered everything. The time had come. With a burst of passion he snatched Sasha to him, and hissed in her ear "Jour de ma vie!"[9] It was their signal. At midnight they would meet at an inn near Blackfriars. Horses waited there. Everything was in readiness for their flight. So they parted, she to her tent, he to his. It still wanted an hour of the time.

Long before midnight Orlando was in waiting. The night was of so inky a blackness that a man was on you before he could be seen, which was all to the good, but it was also of the most solemn stillness so that a horse's hoof, or a child's cry, could be heard at a distance of half a mile. Many a time did Orlando, pacing the little courtyard, hold his heart at the sound of some nag's steady footfall on the cobbles, or at the rustle of a woman's dress. But the traveller was only some merchant, making home belated; or some woman of the quarter whose errand was nothing so innocent. They passed, and the street was quieter than before. Then those lights which burnt downstairs in the small, huddled quarters where the poor of the city lived moved up to the sleeping-rooms, and then, one by one, were extinguished. The street lanterns in these purlieus were few at most; and the negligence of the night watchman often suffered them to expire long before dawn. The darkness then became even deeper than before. Orlando looked to the wicks of his lantern, saw to the saddle girths; primed his pistols; examined his holsters; and did all these things a dozen times at least till he could find nothing more needing his attention. Though it still lacked some twenty minutes to midnight, he could not bring himself to go indoors to the inn parlour, where the hostess was still serving sack and the cheaper sort of canary wine[1] to a few seafaring men, who would sit there trolling their ditties, and telling their stories of Drake, Hawkins, and Grenville,[2] till they toppled off the benches and rolled asleep on the sanded floor. The darkness was more compassionate to his swollen and violent heart. He listened to every footfall; speculated on every sound. Each drunken shout and each wail from some poor wretch laid in the straw or in other distress cut his heart to the quick, as if it boded ill omen to his venture. Yet, he had no fear for Sasha. Her courage made nothing of the adventure. She would come alone, in her cloak and trousers, booted like a man. Light as her footfall was, it would hardly be heard, even in this silence.

9. Day of my life (French).
1. A sweet, fortified wine from the Spanish-occupied Canary Islands.
2. Sir Francis Drake (1540–1596), a British nobleman and explorer. Sir Richard Grenville (1542–1591), commander of the British navy ship the *Revenge*; he was famous for a valiant but losing sea battle against the Spanish armada in 1591. Sir John Hawkins (1532–1595), British explorer and slave trader who served as Rear Admiral for Britain during the British navy's 1588 defeat of the Spanish armada.

So he waited in the darkness. Suddenly he was struck in the face by a blow, soft, yet heavy, on the side of his cheek. So strung with expectation was he, that he started and put his hand to his sword. The blow was repeated a dozen times on forehead and cheek. The dry frost had lasted so long that it took him a minute to realise that these were raindrops falling; the blows were the blows of the rain. At first, they fell slowly, deliberately, one by one. But soon the six drops became sixty; then six hundred; then ran themselves together in a steady spout of water. It was as if the hard and consolidated sky poured itself forth in one profuse fountain. In the space of five minutes Orlando was soaked to the skin.

Hastily putting the horses under cover, he sought shelter beneath the lintel of the door whence he could still observe the courtyard. The air was thicker now than ever, and such a steaming and droning rose from the downpour that no footfall of man or beast could be heard above it. The roads, pitted as they were with great holes, would be under water and perhaps impassable. But of what effect this would have upon their flight he scarcely thought. All his senses were bent upon gazing along the cobbled pathway—gleaming in the light of the lantern—for Sasha's coming. Sometimes, in the darkness, he seemed to see her wrapped about with rain strokes. But the phantom vanished. Suddenly, with an awful and ominous voice, a voice full of horror and alarm which raised every hair of anguish in Orlando's soul, St. Paul's struck the first stroke of midnight. Four times more it struck remorselessly. With the superstition of a lover, Orlando had made out that it was on the sixth stroke that she would come. But the sixth stroke echoed away, and the seventh came and the eighth, and to his apprehensive mind they seemed notes first heralding and then proclaiming death and disaster. When the twelfth struck he knew that his doom was sealed. It was useless for the rational part of him to reason; she might be late; she might be prevented; she might have missed her way. The passionate and feeling heart of Orlando knew the truth. Other clocks struck, jangling one after another. The whole world seemed to ring with the news of her deceit and his derision. The old suspicions subterraneously at work in him rushed forth from concealment openly. He was bitten by a swarm of snakes, each more poisonous than the last. He stood in the doorway in the tremendous rain without moving. As the minutes passed, he sagged a little at the knees. The downpour rushed on. In the thick of it, great guns seemed to boom. Huge noises as of the tearing and rending of oak trees could be heard. There were also wild cries and terrible inhuman groanings. But Orlando stood there immovable till Paul's clock struck two, and then, crying aloud with an awful irony, and all his teeth showing, "Jour de ma vie!" he dashed the lantern to the ground, mounted his horse and galloped he knew not where.

Some blind instinct, for he was past reasoning, must have driven him to take the river bank in the direction of the sea. For when the dawn broke, which it did with unusual suddenness, the sky turning a pale yellow and the rain almost ceasing, he found himself on the banks of the Thames off Wapping. Now a sight of the most extraordinary nature met his eyes. Where, for three months and more, there had been solid ice of such thickness that it seemed permanent as stone, and a whole gay city had been stood on its pavement, was now a race of turbulent yellow waters. The river had gained its freedom in the night. It was as if a sulphur spring (to which view many philosophers inclined) had risen from the volcanic regions beneath and burst the ice asunder with such vehemence that it swept the huge and massy fragments furiously apart. The mere look of the water was enough to turn one giddy. All was riot and confusion. The river was strewn with icebergs. Some of these were as broad as a bowling green and as high as a house; others no bigger than a man's hat, but most fantastically twisted. Now would come down a whole convoy of ice blocks sinking everything that stood in their way. Now, eddying and swirling like a tortured serpent, the river would seem to be hurtling itself between the fragments and tossing them from bank to bank, so that they could be heard smashing against the piers and pillars. But what was the most awful and inspiring of terror was the sight of the human creatures who had been trapped in the night and now paced their twisting and precarious islands in the utmost agony of spirit. Whether they jumped into the flood or stayed on the ice their doom was certain. Sometimes quite a cluster of these poor creatures would come down together, some on their knees, others suckling their babies. One old man seemed to be reading aloud from a holy book. At other times, and his fate perhaps was the most dreadful, a solitary wretch would stride his narrow tenement alone. As they swept out to sea, some could be heard crying vainly for help, making wild promises to amend their ways, confessing their sins and vowing altars and wealth if God would hear their prayers. Others were so dazed with terror that they sat immovable and silent looking steadfastly before them. One crew of young watermen or post-boys, to judge by their liveries, roared and shouted the lewdest tavern songs, as if in bravado, and were dashed against a tree and sunk with blasphemies on their lips. An old nobleman—for such his furred gown and golden chain proclaimed him—went down not far from where Orlando stood, calling vengeance upon the Irish rebels, who, he cried with his last breath, had plotted this devilry. Many perished clasping some silver pot or other treasure to their breasts; and at least a score of poor wretches were drowned by their own cupidity, hurling themselves from the bank into the flood rather than let a gold goblet escape them, or see before their eyes the disappearance of some furred gown. For furniture, valuables, possessions of all sorts were carried away on the icebergs. Among other strange sights was to be seen a cat suckling its young; a table laid sumptuously for a supper of twenty; a couple in bed; together with an extraordinary number of cooking utensils.

Dazed and astounded, Orlando could do nothing for some time but watch the appalling race of waters as it hurled itself past him. At last, seeming to recollect himself, he clapped spurs to his horse and galloped hard along the river bank in the direction of the sea. Rounding a bend of the river, he came opposite that reach where, not two days ago, the ships of the Ambassadors had seemed immovably frozen. Hastily, he made count of them all; the French; the Spanish; the Austrian; the Turk. All still floated, though the French had broken loose from her moorings, and the Turkish vessel had taken a great rent in her side and was fast filling with water. But the Russian ship was nowhere to be seen. For one moment Orlando thought it must have foundered; but, raising himself in his stirrups and shading his eyes, which had the sight of a hawk's, he could just make out the shape of a ship on the horizon. The black eagles were flying from the mast head. The ship of the Muscovite Embassy was standing out to sea.

Flinging himself from his horse, he made, in his rage, as if he would breast the flood. Standing knee-deep in water he hurled at the faithless woman all the insults that have ever been the lot of her sex. Faithless, mutable, fickle, he called her; devil, adulteress, deceiver; and the swirling waters took his words, and tossed at his feet a broken pot and a little straw.

CHAPTER II

THE biographer is now faced with a difficulty which it is better perhaps to confess than to gloss over. Up to this point in telling the story of Orlando's life, documents, both private and historical, have made it possible to fulfil the first duty of a biographer, which is to plod, without looking to right or left, in the indelible footprints of truth; unenticed by flowers; regardless of shade; on and on methodically till we fall plump into the grave and write *finis* on the tombstone above our heads. But now we come to an episode which lies right across our path, so that there is no ignoring it. Yet it is dark, mysterious, and undocumented so that there is no explaining it. Volumes might be written in interpretation of it; whole religious systems founded upon the signification of it. Our simple duty is to state the facts as far as they are known, and so let the reader make of them what he may.

In the summer of that disastrous winter which saw the frost, the flood, the deaths of many thousands, and the complete downfall of Orlando's hopes—for he was exiled from Court; in deep disgrace with the most powerful nobles of his time; the Irish house of Desmond was justly enraged; the King had already trouble enough with the Irish not to relish this further addition—in that summer Orlando retired to his great house in the country and there lived in complete solitude. One June morning—it was Saturday the 18th—he failed to rise at his usual hour, and when his groom went to call him he was found fast asleep. Nor could he be awakened. He lay as if in a trance, without perceptible breathing; and though dogs were set to bark under his window; cymbals, drums, bones beaten perpetually in his room; a gorse[1] bush put under his pillow; and mustard plasters[2] applied to his feet, still he did not wake, take food, or show any sign of life for seven whole days. On the seventh day he woke at his usual time (a quarter before eight, precisely) and turned the whole posse of caterwauling wives and village soothsayers out of his room; which was natural enough; but what was strange was that he showed no consciousness of any such trance, but dressed himself and sent for his horse as if he had woken from a single night's slumber. Yet some change, it was suspected, must have taken place in the chambers of his brain, for though he was perfectly rational and seemed graver and more sedate in his ways than before, he appeared to have an imperfect recollection of his past life. He would listen when people spoke of the great frost or the skating or the carnival, but he never gave any sign, except by passing his hand across his brow as if to wipe away some cloud, of having witnessed them himself. When the events of the past six months were discussed, he seemed not so much distressed as puzzled, as if he were troubled by confused memories of some time long gone or were trying to recall stories told him by another. It was observed that if Russia was mentioned or Princesses or ships, he would fall into a gloom of an uneasy kind and get up and look out of the window or call one of the dogs to him, or take a knife and carve a piece of cedar wood. But the doctors were hardly wiser then than they are now, and after prescribing rest and exercise, starvation and nourishment, society and solitude, that he should lie in bed all day and ride forty miles between lunch and dinner, together with the usual sedatives and irritants, diversified, as the fancy took them, with possets of newt's slobber on rising, and draughts of peacock's gall on going to bed, they left him to himself, and gave it as their opinion that he had been asleep for a week.

1. A spiny shrub.
2. Traditional remedy consisting of mustard soaked into a patch or bandage and placed topically on the skin to ease inflammation or congestion.

But if sleep it was, of what nature, we can scarcely refrain from asking, are such sleeps as these? Are they remedial measures—trances in which the most galling memories, events that seem likely to cripple life for ever, are brushed with a dark wing which rubs their harshness off and gilds them, even the ugliest and basest, with a lustre, an incandescence? Has the finger of death to be laid on the tumult of life from time to time lest it rend us asunder? Are we so made that we have to take death in small doses daily or we could not go on with the business of living? And then what strange powers are these that penetrate our most secret ways and change our most treasured possessions without our willing it? Had Orlando, worn out by the extremity of his suffering, died for a week, and then come to life again? And if so, of what nature is death and of what nature life? Having waited well over half an hour for an answer to these questions, and none coming, let us get on with the story.

Now Orlando gave himself up to a life of extreme solitude. His disgrace at Court and the violence of his grief were partly the reason of it, but as he made no effort to defend himself and seldom invited anyone to visit him (though he had many friends who would willingly have done so) it appeared as if to be alone in the great house of his fathers suited his temper. Solitude was his choice. How he spent his time, nobody quite knew. The servants, of whom he kept a full retinue, though much of their business was to dust empty rooms and to smooth the coverlets of beds that were never slept in, watched, in the dark of the evening, as they sat over their cakes and ale, a light passing along the galleries, through the banqueting-halls, up the staircases, into the bedrooms, and knew that their master was perambulating the house alone. None dared follow him, for the house was haunted by a great variety of ghosts, and the extent of it made it easy to lose one's way and either fall down some hidden staircase or open a door which, should the wind blow it to, would shut upon one for ever—accidents of no uncommon occurrence, as the frequent discovery of the skeletons of men and animals in attitudes of great agony made evident. Then the light would be lost altogether, and Mrs. Grimsditch, the housekeeper, would say to Mr. Dupper, the chaplain, how she hoped his Lordship had not met with some bad accident. Mr. Dupper would opine that his Lordship was on his knees, no doubt, among the tombs of his ancestors in the Chapel, which was in the Billiard Table Court, half a mile away on the south side. For he had sins on his conscience, Mr. Dupper was afraid; upon which Mrs. Grimsditch would retort, rather sharply, that so had most of us; and Mrs. Stewkley and Mrs. Field and old Nurse Carpenter would all raise their voices in his Lordship's praise; and the grooms and the stewards would swear that it was a thousand pities to see so fine a nobleman moping about the house when he might be hunting the fox or chasing the deer; and even the little laundry maids and scullery maids, the Judys and the Faiths, who were handing round the tankards and cakes, would pipe up their testimony to his Lordship's gallantry; for never was there a kinder gentleman, or one more free with those little pieces of silver which serve to buy a knot of ribbon or put a posy in one's hair; until even the Blackamoor whom they called Grace Robinson by way of making a Christian woman of her, understood what they were at, and agreed that his Lordship was a handsome, pleasant, darling gentleman in the only way she could, that is to say by showing all her teeth at once in a broad grin. In short, all his serving men and women held him in high respect, and cursed the foreign Princess (but they called her by a coarser name than that) who had brought him to this pass.

But though it was probably cowardice, or love of hot ale, that led Mr. Dupper to imagine his Lordship safe among the tombs so that he need not go in search of him, it may well have been that Mr. Dupper was right, Orlando now took a strange delight in thoughts of death and decay, and, after pacing the long galleries and ballrooms with a taper in his hand, looking at picture after picture as if he sought the likeness of somebody whom he could not find, would mount into the family pew and sit for hours watching the banners stir and the moonlight waver with a bat or death's head moth to keep him company. Even this was not enough for him, but he must descend into the crypt where his ancestors lay, coffin piled upon coffin, for ten generations together. The place was so seldom visited that the rats had made free with the lead work, and now a thigh bone would catch at his cloak as he passed, or he would crack the skull of some old Sir Malise as it rolled beneath his foot. It was a ghastly sepulchre; dug deep beneath the foundations of the house as if the first Lord of the family, who had come from France with the Conqueror, had wished to testify how all pomp is built upon corruption; how the skeleton lies beneath the flesh; how we that dance and sing above must lie below; how the crimson velvet turns to dust; how the ring (here Orlando, stooping his lantern, would pick up a gold circle lacking a stone, that had rolled into a corner) loses its ruby and the eye which was so lustrous shines no more. "Nothing remains of all these Princes", Orlando would say, indulging in some pardonable exaggeration of their rank, "except one digit," and he would take a skeleton hand in his and bend the joints this way and that. "Whose hand was it?" he went on to ask. "The right or the left? The hand of man or woman, of age or youth? Had it urged the war horse, or plied the needle? Had it plucked the rose, or grasped cold steel? Had it——" but here either his invention failed him or, what is more likely, provided him with so many instances of what a hand can do that he shrank, as his wont was, from the cardinal labour of composition, which is excision, and he put it with the other bones, thinking how there was a writer called Thomas Browne,[3] a Doctor of Norwich, whose writing upon such subjects took his fancy amazingly.

So, taking his lantern and seeing that the bones were in order, for though romantic, he was singularly methodical and detested nothing so much as a ball of string on the floor, let alone the skull of an ancestor; he returned to that curious, moody pacing down the galleries, looking for something among the pictures, which was interrupted at length by a veritable spasm of sobbing, at the sight of a Dutch snow scene by an unknown artist. Then it seemed to him that life was not worth living any more. Forgetting the bones of his ancestors and how life is founded on a grave, he stood there shaken with sobs, all for the desire of a woman in Russian trousers, with slanting eyes, a pouting mouth, and pearls about her neck. She had gone. She had left him. He was never to see her again. And so he sobbed. And so he found his way back to his own rooms; and Mrs. Grimsditch, seeing the light in the window, put the tankard from her lips and said Praise be to God, his Lordship was safe in his room again; for she had been thinking all this while that he was foully murdered.

Orlando now drew his chair up to the table; opened the works of Sir Thomas Browne and proceded to investigate the delicate articulation of one of the doctor's longest and most marvellously contorted cogitations.

For though these are not matters on which a biographer can profitably enlarge it is plain enough to those who have done a reader's part in making up from bare hints dropped here and there the whole boundary and circumference of a living person; can hear in what we only whisper a living voice; can see, often when we say nothing about it, exactly what he looked like; know without a word to guide them precisely what he thought—and it is for readers such as these that we write—it is plain then to such a reader that Orlando was strangely compounded of many humours—of melancholy, of indolence, of passion, of love of solitude, to say nothing of all those contortions and subtleties of temper which were indicated on the first page, when he slashed at a dead nigger's[4] head; cut it down; hung it

3. See Woolf, "Sir Thomas Browne," in *The Essays of Virginia Woolf*, vol. 3 (368–72). The essay is a reprint of Woolf's June 28, 1923, review in the *Times Literary Supplement* of *Religio Medici; Hydrotaphia. Urn Burial: or a discourse of the sepulchral urns lately found in Norfolk;* and of *The Garden of Cyrus. Or the Quincuncial lozenge, or network plantation of the ancients artificially, naturally, mystically consider'd* (Waltham St. Lawrence, Berkshire: Golden Cockerel Press, 1923). Originally published as Thomas Browne, *Hydriotaphia, Urn Burial, or, a Discourse of the Sepulchral Urns lately found in Norfolk* (London: Hen Brome, 1658).

4. In her writing Woolf occasionally used this term, a sample of the casual racist language she and most of her white English peers took for granted at the time of *Orlando's* writing. In this instance Woolf's shift from the term "Moor" in the Elizabethan opening of *Orlando* (p. 9) to this particular racial epithet also signals a shift in the historical setting from Chapter I to Chapter II, which is set in the mid-17th century, when English

chivalrously out of his reach again and then betook himself to the window-seat with a book. The taste for books was an early one. As a child he was sometimes found at midnight by a page still reading. They took his taper away, and he bred glow-worms to serve his purpose. They took the glow-worms away, and he almost burnt the house down with a tinder. To put it in a nutshell, leaving the novelist to smooth out the crumpled silk and all its implications, he was a noble-man afflicted with a love of literature. Many people of his time, still more of his rank, escaped the infection and were thus free to run or ride or make love at their own sweet will. But some were early infected by a germ said to be bred of the pollen of the asphodel and to be blown out of Greece and Italy; which was of so deadly a nature that it would shake the hand as it was raised to strike, cloud the eye as it sought its prey, and make the tongue stammer as it declared its love. It was the fatal nature of this disease to substitute a phantom for reality, so that Orlando, to whom fortune had given every gift—plate, linen, houses, men-servants, carpets, beds in profusion—had only to open a book for the whole vast accumulation to turn to mist. The nine acres of stone which were his house vanished; one hundred and fifty indoor servants disappeared; his eighty riding horses became invisible; it would take too long to count the carpets, sofas, trappings, china, plate, cruets, chafing dishes and other movables often of beaten gold, which evaporated like so much sea mist under the miasma. So it was, and Orlando would sit by himself, reading, a naked man.

The disease gained rapidly upon him now in his solitude. He would read often six hours into the night; and when they came to him for orders about the slaughtering of cattle or the harvesting of wheat, he would push away his folio and look as if he did not under-stand what was said to him. This was bad enough and wrung the hearts of Hall, the falconer, of Giles, the groom, of Mrs. Grims-ditch, the housekeeper, of Mr. Dupper, the chaplain. A fine gentleman like that, they said, had no need of books. Let him leave books, they said, to the palsied or the dying. But worse was to come. For once the disease of reading has laid hold upon the system it weakens it so that it falls an easy prey to that other scourge which dwells in the inkpot and festers in the quill. The wretch takes to writing. And while this is bad enough in a poor man, whose only property is a chair and a table set beneath a leaky roof—for he has not much to lose, after all—the plight of a rich man, who has houses and

---

involvement in the transatlantic slave trade was at its height. For more on Woolf and race, see Vandivere in this volume (pp. 231–40); Jane Marcus, *Hearts of Darkness: White Women Write Race* (New Brunswick, NJ: Rutgers UP, 2004), 24–85; and Madelyn Detloff, *The Value of Virginia Woolf* (New York: Cambridge UP, 2016), 71–92.

cattle, maid-servants, asses and linen, and yet writes books, is piti-
able in the extreme. The flavour of it all goes out of him; he is rid-
dled by hot irons; gnawed by vermin. He would give every penny he
has (such is the malignity of the germ) to write one little book and
become famous; yet all the gold in Peru will not buy him the
treasure of a well-turned line. So he falls into consumption and
sickness, blows his brains out, turns his face to the wall. It matters
not in what attitude they find him. He has passed through the gates
of Death and known the flames of Hell.

Happily, Orlando was of a strong constitution and the disease (for
reasons presently to be given) never broke him down as it has broken many of his peers. But he was deeply smitten with it, as the
sequel shows. For when he had read for an hour or so in Sir Thomas
Browne, and the bark of the stag and the call of the night watchman showed that it was the dead of night and all safe asleep, he
crossed the room, took a silver key from his pocket and unlocked
the doors of a great inlaid cabinet which stood in the corner. Within
were some fifty drawers of cedar wood and upon each was a paper
neatly written in Orlando's hand. He paused, as if hesitating which
to open. One was inscribed "The Death of Ajax", another "The Birth
of Pyramus", another "Iphigenia in Aulis", another "The Death of Hip-
polytus", another "Meleager", another "The Return of Odysseus",—
in fact there was scarcely a single drawer that lacked the name
of some mythological personage at a crisis of his career. In each
drawer lay a document of considerable size all written over in Orlando's hand. The truth was that Orlando had been afflicted thus for
many years. Never had any boy begged apples as Orlando begged
paper; nor sweetmeats as he begged ink. Stealing away from talk and
games, he had hidden himself behind curtains, in priest's holes, or
in the cupboard behind his mother's bedroom which had a great hole
in the floor and smelt horribly of starling's dung, with an inkhorn in
one hand, a pen in another, and on his knee a roll of paper. Thus
had been written, before he was turned twenty-five, some forty-seven
plays, histories, romances, poems; some in prose, some in verse;
some in French, some in Italian; all romantic, and all long. One he
had had printed by John Ball of the Feathers and Coronet opposite
St. Paul's Cross, Cheapside; but though the sight of it gave him
extreme delight, he had never dared show it even to his mother, since
to write, much more to publish, was, he knew, for a nobleman an
inexpiable disgrace.

Now, however, that it was the dead of night and he was alone, he
chose from this repository one thick document called "Xenophila a
Tragedy" or some such title, and one thin one, called simply "The
Oak Tree" (this was the only monosyllabic title among the lot), and
then he approached the inkhorn, fingered the quill, and made other

such passes as those addicted to this vice begin their rites with. But he paused.

As this pause was of extreme significance in his history, more so, indeed, than many acts which bring men to their knees and make rivers run with blood, it behoves us to ask why he paused; and to reply, after due reflection, that it was for some such reason as this. Nature, who has played so many queer tricks upon us, making us so unequally of clay and diamonds, of rainbow and granite, and stuffed them into a case, often of the most incongruous, for the poet has a butcher's face and the butcher a poet's; nature, who delights in muddle and mystery, so that even now (the first of November 1927) we know not why we go upstairs, or why we come down again, our most daily movements are like the passage of a ship on an unknown sea, and the sailors at the mast-head ask, pointing their glasses to the horizon; Is there land or is there none? to which, if we are prophets, we make answer "Yes"; if we are truthful we say "No"; nature, who has so much to answer for besides the perhaps unwieldy length of this sentence, has further complicated her task and added to our confusion by providing not only a perfect rag-bag of odds and ends within us—a piece of a policeman's trousers lying cheek by jowl with Queen Alexandra's wedding veil—but has contrived that the whole assortment shall be lightly stitched together by a single thread. Memory is the seamstress, and a capricious one at that. Memory runs her needle in and out, up and down, hither and thither. We know not what comes next, or what follows after. Thus, the most ordinary movement in the world, such as sitting down at a table and pulling the inkstand towards one, may agitate a thousand odd, disconnected fragments, now bright, now dim, hanging and bobbing and dipping and flaunting, like the underlinen of a family of fourteen on a line in a gale of wind. Instead of being a single, downright, bluff piece of work of which no man need feel ashamed, our commonest deeds are set about with a fluttering and fickering of wings, a rising and falling of lights. Thus it was that Orlando, dipping his pen in the ink, saw the mocking face of the lost Princess and asked himself a million questions instantly which were as arrows dipped in gall. Where was she; and why had she left him? Was the Ambassador her uncle or her lover? Had they plotted? Was she forced? Was she married? Was she dead?—all of which so drove their venom into him that, as if to vent his agony somewhere, he plunged his quill so deep into the inkhorn that the ink spirted over the table, which act, explain it how one may (and no explanation perhaps is possible—Memory is inexplicable), at once substituted for the face of the Princess a face of a very different sort. But whose was it, he asked himself? And he had to wait, perhaps half a minute, looking at the new picture which lay on top of the old, as one lantern slide is half seen through the next, before he could say to himself, "This is the face of that rather fat, shabby man who sat in Twitchett's room ever so many years ago when old Queen Bess came here to dine; and I saw him," Orlando continued, catching at another of those little coloured rags, "sitting at the table, as I peeped in on my way downstairs, and he had the most amazing eyes," said Orlando, "that ever were, but who the devil was he?" Orlando asked, for here Memory added to the forehead and eyes, first, a coarse, grease-stained ruffle, then a brown doublet, and finally a pair of thick boots such as citizens wear in Cheapside. "Not a Nobleman; not one of us," said Orlando (which he would not have said aloud, for he was the most courteous of gentlemen; but it shows what an effect noble birth has upon the mind and incidentally how difficult it is for a nobleman to be a writer), "a poet, I dare say." By all the laws, Memory, having disturbed him sufficiently, should now have blotted the whole thing out completely, or have fetched up something so idiotic and out of keeping—like a dog chasing a cat or an old woman blowing her nose into a red cotton handkerchief—that, in despair of keeping pace with her vagaries, Orlando should have struck his pen in earnest against his paper. (For we can, if we have the resolution, turn the hussy, Memory, and all her ragtag and bobtail out of the house.) But Orlando paused. Memory still held before him the image of a shabby man with big, bright eyes. Still he looked, still he paused. It is these pauses that are our undoing. It is then that sedition enters the fortress and our troops rise in insurrection. Once before he had paused, and love with its horrid rout, its shawms, its cymbals,[5] and its heads with gory locks[6] torn from the shoulders had burst in. From love he had suffered the tortures of the damned. Now, again, he paused, and into the breach thus made, leapt Ambition, the harridan, and Poetry, the witch, and Desire of Fame, the strumpet; all joined hands and made of his heart their dancing ground. Standing upright in the solitude of his room, he vowed that he would be the first poet of his race and bring immortal lustre upon his name. He said (reciting the names and exploits of his ancestors) that Sir Boris had fought and killed the Paynim; Sir Gawain, the Turk; Sir Miles, the Pole; Sir Andrew, the Frank; Sir Richard, the Austrian; Sir Jordan, the Frenchman; and Sir Herbert, the Spaniard. But of all that killing and campaigning, that drinking and love-making, that spending and hunting and riding and eating, what remained? A skull; a finger. Whereas,

5. Small finger cymbals were used for dances and outdoor music in early modern Europe. *Shawms*: Early modern double-reed instruments similar to oboes but larger.
6. Susanne Raitt and Ian Blythe attribute Woolf's reference to "gory locks" to the ghost of Banquo in Shakespeare's *Macbeth* 3.4 (374). The image also conjures the myth of Medusa, whose head was cut off by Perseus during a trial given to him by Polydectes, an unrequited lover of Perseus' mother.

he said, turning to the page of Sir Thomas Browne, which lay open upon the table—and again he paused. Like an incantation rising from all parts of the room, from the night wind and the moonlight, rolled the divine melody of those words which, lest they should out-stare this page, we will leave where they lie entombed, not dead, embalmed rather, so fresh is their colour, so sound their breathing— and Orlando, comparing that achievement with those of his ances-tors, cried out that they and their deeds were dust and ashes, but this man and his words were immortal.

He soon perceived, however, that the battles which Sir Miles and the rest had waged against armed knights to win a kingdom, were not half so arduous as this which he now undertook to win immor-tality against the English language. Anyone moderately familiar with the rigours of composition will not need to be told the story in detail; how he wrote and it seemed good; read and it seemed vile; corrected and tore up; cut out; put in; was in ecstasy; in despair; had his good nights and bad mornings; snatched at ideas and lost them; saw his book plain before him and it vanished; acted his people's parts as he ate; mouthed them as he walked; now cried; now laughed; vacil-lated between this style and that; now preferred the heroic and pompous; next the plain and simple; now the vales of Tempe; then the fields of Kent or Cornwall; and could not decide whether he was the divinest genius or the greatest fool in the world.

It was to settle this last question that he decided, after many months of such feverish labour, to break the solitude of years and communicate with the outer world. He had a friend in London, one Giles Isham of Norfolk, who, though of gentle birth, was acquainted with writers and could doubtless put him in touch with some mem-ber of that blessed, indeed sacred, fraternity. For, to Orlando in the state he was now in, there was a glory about a man who had written a book and had it printed, which outshone all the glories of blood and state. To his imagination it seemed as if even the bodies of those instinct with such divine thoughts must be transfigured. They must have aureoles for hair, incense for breath, and roses must grow between their lips—which was certainly not true either of himself or Mr. Dupper. He could think of no greater happiness than to be allowed to sit behind a curtain and hear them talk. Even the imag-ination of that bold and various discourse made the memory of what he and his courtier friends used to talk about—a dog, a horse, a woman, a game of cards—seem brutish in the extreme. He bethought him with pride that he had always been called a scholar, and sneered at for his love of solitude and books. He had never been apt at pretty phrases. He would stand stock still, blush, and stride like a grenadier in a ladies' drawing-room. He had twice fallen; in sheer abstraction, from his horse. He had broken Lady Winchilsea's

fan once while making a rhyme. Eagerly recalling these and other
instances of his unfitness for the life of society, an ineffable hope;
that all the turbulence of his youth, his clumsiness, his blushes, his
long walks, and his love of the country proved that he himself
belonged to the sacred race rather than to the noble—was by birth
a writer, rather than an aristocrat—possessed him. For the first time
since the night of the great flood he was happy.

He now commissioned Mr. Isham of Norfolk to deliver to Mr.
Nicholas Greene[7] of Clifford's Inn a document which set forth
Orlando's admiration for his works (for Nick Greene was a very
famous writer at that time) and his desire to make his acquaintance;
which he scarcely dared ask; for he had nothing to offer in return;
but if Mr. Nicholas Greene would condescend to visit him, a coach
and four would be at the corner of Fetter Lane at whatever hour
Mr. Greene chose to appoint, and bring him safely to Orlando's
house. One may fill up the phrases which then followed; and figure
Orlando's delight when, in no long time, Mr. Greene signified his
acceptance of the Noble Lord's invitation; took his place in the coach
and was set down in the hall to the south of the main building punc-
tually at seven o'clock on Monday, April the twenty-first.

Many Kings, Queens, and Ambassadors had been received there;
Judges had stood there in their ermine. The loveliest ladies of the
land had come there; and the sternest warriors. Banners hung there
which had been at Flodden and at Agincourt. There were displayed
the painted coats of arms with their lions and their leopards and
their coronets. There were the long tables where the gold and silver
plate was stood; and there the vast fireplaces of wrought Italian marble where nightly a whole oak tree, with its million leaves and its
nests of rook and wren, was burnt to ashes. Nicholas Greene, the
poet stood there now, plainly dressed in his slouched hat and black
doublet, carrying in one hand a small bag.

That Orlando as he hastened to greet him was slightly disappointed was inevitable. The poet was not above middle height; was
of a mean figure; was lean and stooped somewhat, and, stumbling
over the mastiff on entering, the dog bit him. Moreover, Orlando
for all his knowledge of mankind was puzzled where to place him.
There was something about him which belonged neither to servant,
squire, or noble. The head with its rounded forehead and beaked
nose was fine, but the chin receded. The eyes were brilliant, but the
lips hung loose and slobbered. It was the expression of the face as a

---

7. Nicholas Greene is an amalgam of several lesser-known playwrights and poets, including Robert Greene, a popular early modern playwright who reputedly wrote a disparag-
   ing attack on Shakespeare. Nick Greene also appears in *A Room of One's Own* (1929)
   as the actor-manager who takes in Woolf's fictional Judith Shakespeare and impreg-
   nates her (48).

whole, however, that was disquieting. There was none of that stately composure which makes the faces of the nobility so pleasing to look at; nor had it anything of the dignified servility of a well-trained domestic's face; it was a face seamed, puckered, and drawn together. Poet though he was, it seemed as if he were more used to scold than to flatter; to quarrel than to coo; to scramble than to ride; to struggle than to rest; to hate than to love. This, too, was shown by the quickness of his movements; and by something fiery and suspicious in his glance. Orlando was somewhat taken aback. But they went to dinner.

Here, Orlando, who usually took such things for granted, was, for the first time, unaccountably ashamed of the number of his servants and of the splendour of his table. Stranger still, he bethought him with pride—for the thought was generally distasteful—of that great grandmother Moll who had milked the cows. He was about somehow to allude to this humble woman and her milk-pails, when the poet forestalled him by saying that it was odd, seeing how common the name of Greene was; that the family had come over with the Conqueror and was of the highest nobility in France. Unfortunately, they had come down in the world and done little more than leave their name to the royal borough of Greenwich. Further talk of the same sort, about lost castles, coats of arms, cousins who were baronets in the north, intermarriage with noble families in the west, how some Greens spelt the name with an e at the end, and others without, lasted till the venison was on the table. Then Orlando contrived to say something of Grandmother Moll and her cows, and had eased his heart a little of its burden by the time the wild fowl were before them. But it was not until the Malmsey was passing freely that Orlando dared mention what he could not help thinking a more important matter than the Greens or the cows; that is to say the sacred subject of poetry. At the first mention of the word, the poet's eyes flashed fire; he dropped the fine gentleman airs he had worn; thumped his glass on the table, and launched into one of the longest, most intricate, most passionate, and bitterest stories that Orlando had ever heard, save from the lips of a jilted woman, about a play of his; another poet; and a critic. Of the nature of poetry itself, Orlando only gathered that it was harder to sell than prose, and though the lines were shorter took longer in the writing. So the talk went on with ramifications interminable, until Orlando ventured to hint that he had himself been so rash as to write—but here the poet leapt from his chair. A mouse had squeaked in the wainscot,[8] he said. The truth was, he explained, that his nerves were in a state where a mouse's squeak upset them for a fortnight. Doubtless the

---

8. Decorative wooden paneling generally covering the lower half of a wall.

house was full of vermin, but Orlando had not heard them. The poet then gave Orlando the full story of his health for the past ten years or so. It had been so bad that one could only marvel that he still lived. He had had the palsy, the gout, the ague, the dropsy, and the three sorts of fever in succession; added to which he had an enlarged heart, a great spleen, and a diseased liver. But, above all, he had, he told Orlando, sensations in his spine which defied description. There was one knob about the third from the top which burnt like fire; another about the second from the bottom which was cold as ice. Sometimes he woke with a brain like lead; at others it was as if a thousand wax tapers were alight and people were throwing fireworks inside him. He could feel a rose leaf through his mattress, he said; and knew his way almost about London by the feel of the cobbles. Altogether he was a piece of machinery so finely made and so curiously put together (here he raised his hand as if unconsciously, and indeed it was of the finest shape imaginable) that it confounded him to think that he had only sold five hundred copies of his poem, but that of course was largely due to the conspiracy against him. All he could say, he concluded, banging his fist upon the table, was that the art of poetry was dead in England.

How that could be with Shakespeare, Marlowe, Ben Jonson, Browne, Donne,[9] all now writing or just having written, Orlando, reeling off the names of his favourite heroes, could not think.

Greene laughed sardonically. Shakespeare, he admitted, had written some scenes that were well enough; but he had taken them chiefly from Marlowe. Marlowe was a likely boy, but what could you say of a lad who died before he was thirty? As for Browne, he was for writing poetry in prose, and people soon got tired of such conceits as that. Donne was a mountebank who wrapped up his lack of meaning in hard words. The gulls were taken in; but the style would be out of fashion twelve months hence. As for Ben Jonson—Ben Jonson was a friend of his and he never spoke ill of his friends.

No, he concluded, the great age of literature is past; the great age of literature was the Greek; the Elizabethan age was inferior in every respect to the Greek. In such ages men cherished a divine ambition which he might call La Gloire (he pronounced it Glawr, so that Orlando did not at first catch his meaning). Now all young writers were in the pay of the booksellers and poured out any trash that would sell. Shakespeare was the chief offender in this way and

9. William Shakespeare (1564–1616), considered by many (including Woolf) to be one of the greatest English playwrights. Christopher (Kit) Marlowe (1564–1593), English playwright and literary rival of Shakespeare. Ben Jonson (1572–1637), English playwright and friend of Shakespeare. Sir Thomas Browne (1605–1682), English author (see n. 3, p. 40). John Donne (1572–1631), English poet famous for his sonnets and innovative extended metaphors called "metaphysical conceits."

Shakespeare was already paying the penalty. Their own age, he said, was marked by precious conceits and wild experiments—neither of which the Greeks would have tolerated for a moment. Much though it hurt him to say it—for he loved literature as he loved his life—he could see no good in the present and had no hope of the future. Here he poured himself out another glass of wine.

Orlando was shocked by these doctrines; yet could not help observing that the critic himself seemed by no means downcast. On the contrary, the more he denounced his own time, the more complacent he became. He could remember, he said, a night at the Cock Tavern in Fleet Street when Kit Marlowe was there and some others. Kit was in high feather, rather drunk, which he easily became, and in a mood to say silly things. He could see him now, brandishing his glass at the company and hiccoughing out, "Stap my vitals, Bill" (this was to Shakespeare), "there's a great wave coming and you're on the top of it," by which he meant, Greene explained, that they were trembling on the verge of a great age in English literature, and that Shakespeare was to be a poet of some importance. Happily for himself, he was killed two nights later in a drunken brawl, and so did not live to see how this prediction turned out. "Poor foolish fellow," said Greene, "to go and say a thing like that. A great age, forsooth— the Elizabethan a great age!"

"So, my dear Lord," he continued, settling himself comfortably in his chair and rubbing the wine-glass between his fingers, "we must make the best of it, cherish the past and honour those writers—there are still a few left of 'em—who take antiquity for their model and write, not for pay but for Glawr." (Orlando could have wished him a better accent.) "Glawr", said Greene, "is the spur of noble minds. Had I a pension of three hundred pounds a year paid quarterly, I would live for Glawr alone. I would lie in bed every morning reading Cicero. I would imitate his style so that you couldn't tell the difference between us. That's what I call fine writing," said Greene; "that's what I call Glawr. But it's necessary to have a pension to do it."

By this time Orlando had abandoned all hope of discussing his own work with the poet; but this mattered the less as the talk now got upon the lives and characters of Shakespeare, Ben Jonson, and the rest, all of whom Greene had known intimately and about whom he had a thousand anecdotes of the most amusing kind to tell, Orlando had never laughed so much in his life. These, then, were his gods! Half were drunken and all were amorous. Most of them quarrelled with their wives; not one of them was above a lie or an intrigue of the most paltry kind. Their poetry was scribbled down on the backs of washing bills held to the heads of printer's devils at the street door. Thus Hamlet went to press; thus Lear; thus Othello. No wonder, as Greene said, that these plays show the faults they do.

The rest of the time was spent in carousings and junketings in taverns and in beer gardens, when things were said that passed belief for wit, and things were done that made the utmost frolic of the courtiers seem pale in comparison. All this Greene told with a spirit that roused Orlando to the highest pitch of delight. He had a power of mimicry that brought the dead to life, and could say the finest things of books provided they were written three hundred years ago.

So time passed; and Orlando felt for his guest a strange mixture of liking and contempt, of admiration and pity, as well as something too indefinite to be called by any one name, but had something of fear in it and something of fascination. He talked incessantly about himself, yet was such good company that one could listen to the story of his ague for ever. Then he was so witty; then he was so irreverent; then he made so free with the names of God and Woman; then he was so full of queer crafts and had such strange lore in his head; could make salad in three hundred different ways; knew all that could be known of the mixing of wines; played half-a-dozen musical instruments, and was the first person, and perhaps the last, to toast cheese in the great Italian fireplace. That he did not know a geranium from a carnation, an oak from a birch tree, a mastiff from a greyhound, a teg[1] from a ewe, wheat from barley, plough land from fallow; was ignorant of the rotation of the crops; thought oranges grew under ground and turnips on trees; preferred any townscape to any landscape;—all this and much more amazed Orlando, who had never met anybody of his kind before. Even the maids, who despised him, tittered at his jokes, and the men-servants, who loathed him, hung about to hear his stories. Indeed, the house had never been so lively as now that he was there—all of which gave Orlando a great deal to think about, and caused him to compare this way of life with the old. He recalled the sort of talk he had been used to about the King of Spain's apoplexy or the mating of a bitch; he bethought him how the day passed between the stables and the dressing closet; he remembered how the Lords snored over their wine and hated anybody who woke them up. He bethought him how active and valiant they were in body; how slothful and timid in mind. Worried by these thoughts, and unable to strike a proper balance, he came to the conclusion that he had admitted to his house a plaguey spirit of unrest that would never suffer him to sleep sound again.

At the same moment, Nick Greene came to precisely the opposite conclusion. Lying in bed of a morning on the softest pillows between the smoothest sheets and looking out of his oriel window upon turf which for three centuries had known neither dandelion nor dock weed, he thought that unless he could somehow make his escape,

1. A young female sheep before it gives birth for the first time.

he should be smothered alive. Getting up and hearing the pigeons coo, dressing and hearing the fountains fall, he thought that unless he could hear the drays roar upon the cobbles of Fleet Street, he would never write another line. If this goes on much longer, he thought, hearing the footman mend the fire and spread the table with silver dishes next door, I shall fall asleep and (here he gave a prodigious yawn) sleeping die.

So he sought Orlando in his room, and explained that he had not been able to sleep a wink all night because of the silence. (Indeed, the house was surrounded by a park fifteen miles in circumference and a wall ten feet high.) Silence, he said, was of all things the most oppressive to his nerves. He would end his visit, by Orlando's leave, that very morning. Orlando felt some relief at this, yet also a great reluctance to let him go. The house, he thought, would seem very dull without him. On parting (for he had never yet liked to mention the subject), he had the temerity to press his play upon the Death of Hercules upon the poet and ask his opinion of it. The poet took it; muttered something about Glawr and Cicero, which Orlando cut short by promising to pay the pension quarterly; whereupon Greene, with many protestations of affection, jumped into the coach and was gone.

The great hall had never seemed so large, so splendid, or so empty as the chariot rolled away. Orlando knew that he would never have the heart to make toasted cheese in the Italian fireplace again. He would never have the wit to crack jokes about Italian pictures; never have the skill to mix punch as it should be mixed; a thousand good quips and cranks would be lost to him. Yet what a relief to be out of the sound of that querulous voice, what a luxury to be alone once more, so he could not help reflecting, as he unloosed the mastiff which had been tied up these six weeks because it never saw the poet without biting him.

Nick Greene was set down at the corner of Fetter Lane that same afternoon, and found things going on much as he had left them. Mrs. Greene, that is to say, was giving birth to a baby in one room; Tom Fletcher was drinking gin in another. Books were tumbled all about the floor; dinner—such as it was—was set on a dressing-table where the children had been making mud pies. But this, Greene felt, was the atmosphere for writing; here he could write, and write he did. The subject was made for him. A noble Lord at home. A visit to a Nobleman in the country—his new poem was to have some such title as that. Seizing the pen with which his little boy was tickling the cat's ears, and dipping it in the egg-cup which served for ink-pot, Greene dashed off a very spirited satire there and then. It was so done to a turn that no one could doubt that the young Lord who was roasted was Orlando; his most private sayings and doings, his enthusiasms and follies, down to the very colour of his hair and the foreign way he had of rolling his r's, were there to the life. And if there had been any doubt about it, Greene clinched the matter by introducing, with scarcely any disguise, passages from that aristocratic tragedy, the Death of Hercules, which he found as he expected, wordy and bombastic in the extreme.

The pamphlet, which ran at once into several editions, and paid the expenses of Mrs. Greene's tenth lying-in, was soon sent by friends who take care of such matters to Orlando himself. When he had read it, which he did with deadly composure from start to finish, he rang for the footman; delivered the document to him at the end of a pair of tongs; bade him drop it in the filthiest heart of the foulest midden on the estate. Then, when the man was turning to go he stopped him, "Take the swiftest horse in the stable," he said, "ride for dear life to Harwich. There embark upon a ship which you will find bound for Norway. Buy for me from the King's own kennels the finest elk-hounds of the Royal strain, male and female. Bring them back without delay, For", he murmured, scarcely above his breath as he turned to his books, "I have done with men."

The footman, who was perfectly trained in his duties, bowed and disappeared. He fulfilled his task so efficiently that he was back that day three weeks, leading in his hand a leash of the finest elk-hounds, one of whom, a female, gave birth that very night under the dinner-table to a litter of eight fine puppies. Orlando had them brought to his bed-chamber.

"For", he said, "I have done with men."
Nevertheless, he paid the pension quarterly.

Thus, at the age of thirty, or thereabouts, this young Nobleman had not only had every experience that life has to offer, but had seen the worthlessness of them all. Love and ambition, women and poets were all equally vain. Literature was a farce. The night after reading Greene's Visit to a Nobleman in the Country, he burnt in a great conflagration fifty-seven poetical works, only retaining "The Oak Tree", which was his boyish dream and very short. Two things alone remained to him in which he now put any trust: dogs and nature; an elk-hound and a rose bush. The world, in all its variety, life in all its complexity, had shrunk to that. Dogs and a bush were the whole of it. So feeling quit of a vast mountain of illusion, and very naked in consequence, he called his hounds to him and strode through the Park.

So long had he been secluded, writing and reading, that he had half forgotten the amenities of nature, which in June can be great. When he reached that high mound whence on fine days half of England with a slice of Wales and Scotland thrown in can be seen, he flung himself under his favourite oak tree and felt that if he need never speak to another man or woman so long as he lived; if his dogs did not develop the faculty of speech; if he never met a poet or a Princess again, he might make out what years remained to him in tolerable content.

Here he came then, day after day, week after week, month after month, year after year. He saw the beech trees turn golden and the young ferns unfurl; he saw the moon sickle and then circular; he saw—but probably the reader can imagine the passage which should follow and how every tree and plant in the neighbourhood is described first green, then golden; how moons rise and suns set; how spring follows winter and autumn summer; how night succeeds day and day night; how there is first a storm and then fine weather; how things remain much as they are for two or three hundred years or so, except for a little dust and a few cobwebs which one old woman can sweep up in half an hour; a conclusion which, one cannot help feeling, might have been reached more quickly by the simple statement that "Time passed" (here the exact amount could be indicated in brackets) and nothing whatever happened?[2]

But Time, unfortunately, though it makes animals and vegetables bloom and fade with amazing punctuality, has no such simple effect upon the mind of man. The mind of man, moreover, works with equal strangeness upon the body of time. An hour, once it lodges in the queer element of the human spirit, may be stretched to fifty or a hundred times its clock length; on the other hand, an hour may be accurately represented on the timepiece of the mind by one second. This extraordinary discrepancy between time on the clock and time in the mind is less known than it should be and deserves fuller investigation. But the biographer, whose interests are, as we have said, highly restricted, must confine himself to one simple statement: when a man has reached the age of thirty, as Orlando now had, time when he is thinking becomes inordinately long; time when he is doing becomes inordinately short. Thus Orlando gave his orders and did the business of his vast estates in a flash; but directly he was alone on the mound under the oak tree, the seconds began to round and fill until it seemed as if they would never fall. They filled themselves, moreover, with the strangest variety of objects. For not only did he find himself confronted by problems which have puzzled the wisest of men, such as What is love? What friendship? What truth? but directly he came to think about them, his whole past, which seemed to him of extreme length and variety, rushed into the falling second, swelled it a dozen times its natural size, coloured it a thousand tints, and filled it with all the odds and ends in the universe.

In such thinking (or by whatever name it should be called) he spent months and years of his life. It would be no exaggeration to

2. This sentence is a playful allusion to the middle section, "Time Passes," of Woolf's *To the Lighthouse* (1927).

say that he would go out after breakfast a man of thirty and come home to dinner a man of fifty-five at least. Some weeks added a century to his age, others no more than three seconds at most. Altogether, the task of estimating the length of human life (of the animals' we presume not to speak) is beyond our capacity, for directly we say that it is ages long, we are reminded that it is briefer than the fall of a rose leaf to the ground. Of the two forces which alternately, and what is more confusing still, at the same moment, dominate our unfortunate numbskulls—brevity and diuturnity[3]—Orlando was sometimes under the influence of the elephant-footed deity, then of the gnatwinged fly. Life seemed to him of prodigious length. Yet even so, it went like a flash. But even when it stretched longest and the moments swelled biggest and he seemed to wander alone in deserts of vast eternity, there was no time for the smoothing out and deciphering of those thickly scored parchments which thirty years among men and women had rolled tight in his heart and brain. Long before he had done thinking about Love (the oak tree had put forth its leaves and shaken them to the ground a dozen times in the process) Ambition would jostle it off the field, to be replaced by Friendship or Literature. And as the first question had not been settled—What is Love?—back it would come at the least provocation or none, and hustle Books or Metaphors or What one lives for into the margin, there to wait till they saw their chance to rush into the field again. What made the process still longer was that it was profusely illustrated, not only with pictures, as that of old Queen Elizabeth, laid on her tapestry couch in rose-coloured brocade with an ivory snuff-box in her hand and a gold-hilted sword by her side, but with scents—she was strongly perfumed—and with sounds; the stags were barking in Richmond Park that winter's day. And so, the thought of love would be all ambered over with snow and winter; with log fires burning; with Russian women, gold swords, and the bark of stags; with old King James' slobbering and fireworks and sacks of treasure in the holds of Elizabethan sailing ships. Every single thing, once he tried to dislodge it from its place in his mind, he found thus cumbered with other matter like the lump of glass which, after a year at the bottom of the sea, is grown about with bones and dragon-flies, and coins and the tresses of drowned women.

"Another metaphor by Jupiter!" he would exclaim as he said this (which will show the disorderly and circuitous way in which his mind worked and explain why the oak tree flowered and faded so often before he came to any conclusion about Love). "And what's the point of it?" he would ask himself. "Why not say simply in so many words——" and then he would try to think for half an hour,—or was

3. Duration, or the quality of being long-lasting.

it two years and a half?—how to say simply in so many words what love is. "A figure like that is manifestly untruthful," he argued, "for no dragon-fly, unless under very exceptional circumstances, could live at the bottom of the sea. And if literature is not the Bride and Bedfellow of Truth, what is she? Confound it all," he cried, "why say Bedfellow when one's already said Bride? Why not simply say what one means and leave it?"

So then he tried saying the grass is green and the sky is blue and so to propitiate the austere spirit of poetry whom still, though at a great distance, he could not help reverencing. "The sky is blue," he said, "the grass is green." Looking up, he saw that, on the contrary, the sky is like the veils which a thousand Madonnas have let fall from their hair; and the grass fleets and darkens like a flight of girls fleeing the embraces of hairy satyrs from enchanted woods. "Upon my word," he said (for he had fallen into the bad habit of speaking aloud), "I don't see that one's more true than another. Both are utterly false." And he despaired of being able to solve the problem of what poetry is and what truth is and fell into a deep dejection.

And here we may profit by a pause in his soliloquy to reflect how odd it was to see Orlando stretched there on his elbow on a June day and to reflect that this fine fellow with all his faculties about him and a healthy body, witness cheeks and limbs—a man who never thought twice about heading a charge or fighting a duel—should be so subject to the lethargy of thought, and rendered so susceptible by it, that when it came to a question of poetry, or his own competence in it, he was as shy as a little girl behind her mother's cottage door. In our belief, Greene's ridicule of his tragedy hurt him as much as the Princess' ridicule of his love. But to return—

Orlando went on thinking. He kept looking at the grass and at the sky and trying to bethink him what a true poet, who has his verses published in London, would say about them. Memory meanwhile (whose habits have already been described) kept steady before his eyes the face of Nicholas Greene, as if that sardonic loose-lipped man, treacherous as he had proved himself, were the Muse in person, and it was to him that Orlando must do homage. So Orlando, that summer morning, offered him a variety of phrases, some plain, others figured, and Nick Greene kept shaking his head and sneering and muttering something about Glawr and Cicero and the death of poetry in our time. At length, starting to his feet (it was now winter and very cold) Orlando swore one of the most remarkable oaths of his lifetime, for it bound him to a servitude than which none is stricter. "I'll be blasted", he said, "if I ever write another word, or try to write another word, to please Nick Greene or the Muse. Bad, good, or indifferent, I'll write, from this day forward, to please myself"; and here he made as if he were tearing a whole budget of papers across and tossing them in the face of that sneering loose-lipped man. Upon which, as a cur ducks if you stoop to shy a stone at him, Memory ducked her effigy of Nick Greene out of sight; and substituted for it—nothing whatever.

But Orlando, all the same, went on thinking. He had indeed much to think of. For when he tore the parchment across, he tore, in one rending, the scrolloping,[4] emblazoned scroll which he had made out in his own favour in the solitude of his room appointing himself, as the King appoints Ambassadors, the first poet of his race, the first writer of his age, conferring eternal immortality upon his soul and granting his body a grave among laurels and the intangible banners of a people's reverence perpetually. Eloquent as this all was, he now tore it up and threw it in the dustbin. "Fame", he said, "is like" (and since there was no Nick Greene to stop him, he went on to revel in images of which we will choose only one or two of the quietest) "a braided coat which hampers the limbs; a jacket of silver which curbs the heart; a painted shield which covers a scarecrow," etc. etc. The pith of his phrases was that while fame impedes and constricts, obscurity wraps about a man like a mist; obscurity is dark, ample, and free; obscurity lets the mind take its way unimpeded. Over the obscure man is poured the merciful suffusion of darkness. None knows where he goes or comes. He may seek the truth and speak it; he alone is free; he alone is truthful; he alone is at peace. And so he sank into a quiet mood, under the oak tree, the hardness of whose roots, exposed above the ground, seemed to him rather comfortable than otherwise.

Sunk for a long time in profound thoughts as to the value of obscurity, and the delight of having no name, but being like a wave which returns to the deep body of the sea; thinking how obscurity rids the mind of the irk of envy and spite; how it sets running in the veins the free waters of generosity and magnanimity; and allows giving and taking without thanks offered or praise given; which must have been the way of all great poets, he supposed (though his knowledge of Greek was not enough to bear him out), for, he thought, Shakespeare must have written like that, and the church builders built like that, anonymously, needing no thanking or naming, but only their work in the daytime and a little ale perhaps at night—"What an admirable life this is," he thought, stretching his limbs out under the oak tree. "And why not enjoy it this very moment?" The thought struck him like a bullet. Ambition dropped like a plummet. Rid of the heart-burn of rejected love, and of vanity rebuked, and all the other stings and pricks which the nettle-bed of life had burnt upon him when ambitious of fame, but could no longer inflict upon one careless of glory, he opened his eyes, which had been wide open all

4. Excessively ornamented.

the time, but had seen only thoughts, and saw, lying in the hollow beneath him, his house.

There it lay in the early sunshine of spring. It looked a town rather than a house, but a town built, not hither and thither, as this man wished or that, but circumspectly, by a single architect with one idea in his head. Courts and buildings, grey, red, plum colour, lay orderly and symmetrical; the courts were some of them oblong and some square; in this was a fountain; in that a statue; the buildings were some of them low, some pointed; here was a chapel, there a belfry; spaces of the greenest grass lay in between and clumps of cedar trees and beds of bright flowers; all were clasped—yet so well set out was it that it seemed that every part had room to spread itself fittingly— by the roll of a massive wall; while smoke from innumerable chimneys curled perpetually into the air. This vast, yet ordered building, which could house a thousand men and perhaps two thousand horses, was built, Orlando thought, by workmen whose names are unknown. Here have lived, for more centuries than I can count, the obscure generations of my own obscure family. Not one of these Richards, Johns, Annes, Elizabeths has left a token of himself behind him, yet all, working together with their spades and their needles, their love-making and their child-bearing, have left this.

Never had the house looked more noble and humane.

Why, then, had he wished to raise himself above them? For it seemed vain and arrogant in the extreme to try to better that anonymous work of creation; the labours of those vanished hands. Better was it to go unknown and leave behind you an arch, a potting shed, a wall where peaches ripen, than to burn like a meteor and leave no dust. For after all, he said, kindling as he looked at the great house on the greensward below, the unknown lords and ladies who lived there never forgot to set aside something for those who come after; for the roof that will leak; for the tree that will fall. There was always a warm corner for the old shepherd in the kitchen; always food for the hungry; always their goblets were polished, though they lay sick; and their windows were lit though they lay dying. Lords though they were, they were content to go down into obscurity with the molecatcher and the stone-mason. Obscure noblemen, forgotten builders—thus he apostrophised them with a warmth that entirely gainsaid such critics as called him cold, indifferent, slothful (the truth being that a quality often lies just on the other side of the wall from where we seek it)—thus he apostrophised his house and race in terms of the most moving eloquence; but when it came to the peroration—and what is eloquence that lacks a peroration?—he fumbled. He would have liked to have ended with a flourish to the effect that he would follow in their footsteps and add another stone to their building. Since, however, the building already covered nine acres, to add even a single stone seemed superfluous. Could one mention furniture in a peroration? Could one speak of chairs and tables and mats to lie beside people's beds? For whatever the peroration wanted, that was what the house stood in need of. Leaving his speech unfinished for the moment, he strode down hill again resolved henceforward to devote himself to the furnishing of the mansion. The news—that she was to attend him—instantly brought tears to the eyes of good old Mrs. Grimsditch, now grown somewhat old. Together they perambulated the house.

The towel horse in the King's bedroom ("and that was King Jamie, my Lord," she said, hinting that it was many a day since a King had slept under their roof; but the odious Parliament days were over and there was now a Crown in England again) lacked a leg; there were no stands to the ewers[5] in the little closet leading into the waiting room of the Duchess's page; Mr. Greene had made a stain on the carpet with his nasty pipe smoking, which she and Judy, for all their scrubbing, had never been able to wash out. Indeed, when Orlando came to reckon up the matter of furnishing with rosewood chairs and cedar-wood cabinets, with silver basins, china bowls, and Persian carpets, every one of the three hundred and sixty-five bedrooms which the house contained,[6] he saw that it would be no light one; and if some thousands of pounds of his estate remained over, these would do little more than hang a few galleries with tapestry, set the dining hall with fine, carved chairs and provide mirrors of solid silver and chairs of the same metal (for which he had an inordinate passion) for the furnishing of the royal bedchambers.

He now set to work in earnest, as we can prove beyond a doubt if we look at his ledgers. Let us glance at an inventory of what he bought at this time, with the expenses totted up in the margin— but these we omit.

"To fifty pairs of Spanish blankets, ditto curtains of crimson and white taffeta; the valence to them of white satin embroidered with crimson and white silk. . . .

"To seventy yellow satin chairs and sixty stools, suitable with their buckram covers to them all. . . .

"To sixty seven walnut tree tables. . . .

"To seventeen dozen boxes containing each dozen five dozen of Venice glasses. . . .

---

5. Large jugs suitable for pouring water.
6. Woolf's numbers are not exact here, but they convey the expansiveness of Knole. According to the National Trust, the organization that serves as conservator of many aristocratic estates in the UK, "There's a popular myth (heavily promoted by Sackville-West) that Knole is a calendar house—with 365 rooms, 52 staircases, 12 entrances and seven courtyards. While a fascinating idea, sadly this isn't the case. The reality is the house was not designed and built in a single phase but is the accumulation of several stages of construction. The house itself encompasses seven acres of roofs and contains around 400 rooms."

"To one hundred and two mats, each thirty yards long. . . .

"To ninety seven cushions of crimson damask laid with silver parchment lace and footstools of cloth of tissue and chairs suitable. . . .

"To fifty branches for a dozen lights apiece. . . ."

Already—it is an effect lists have upon us—we are beginning to yawn. But if we stop, it is only that the catalogue is tedious, not that it is finished. There are ninety-nine pages more of it and the total sum disbursed ran into many thousands—that is to say millions of our money. And if his day was spent like this, at night again, Lord Orlando might be found reckoning out what it would cost to level a million molehills, if the men were paid tenpence an hour; and again, how many hundredweight of nails at 5½d. a gill[7] were needed to repair the fence round the park, which was fifteen miles in circumference. And so on and so on.

The tale, we say, is tedious, for one cupboard is much like another, and one molehill not much different from a million. Some pleasant journeys it cost him; and some fine adventures. As, for instance, when he set a whole city of blind women near Bruges to stitch hangings for a silver canopied bed; and the story of his adventure with a Moor in Venice of whom he bought (but only at the sword's point) his lacquered cabinet, might, in other hands, prove worth the telling. Nor did the work lack variety; for here would come, drawn by teams from Sussex, great trees, to be sawn across and laid along the gallery for flooring; and then a chest from Persia, stuffed with wool and sawdust, from which, at last, he would take a single plate, or one topaz ring.

At length, however, there was no room in the galleries for another table; no room on the tables for another cabinet; no room in the cabinet for another rose-bowl; no room in the bowl for another handful of potpourri; there was no room for anything anywhere; in short the house was furnished. In the garden snowdrops, crocuses, hyacinths, magnolias, roses, lilies, asters, the dahlia in all its varieties, pear trees and apple trees and cherry trees and mulberry trees, with an enormous quantity of rare and flowering shrubs, of trees evergreen and perennial, grew so thick on each other's roots that there was no plot of earth without its bloom, and no stretch of sward without its shade. In addition, he had imported wild fowl with gay plumage; and two Malay bears, the surliness of whose manners concealed, he was certain, trusty hearts.

All now was ready; and when it was evening and the innumerable silver sconces were lit and the light airs which for ever moved about the galleries stirred the blue and green arras, so that it looked as if

---

7. Five and a half pence (pennies) for approximately half a cup.

the huntsmen were riding and Daphne flying; when the silver shone
and lacquer glowed and wood kindled; when the carved chairs held
their arms out and dolphins swam upon the walls with mermaids
on their backs; when all this and much more than all this was complete and to his liking, Orlando walked through the house with his
elk hounds following and felt content. He had matter now, he
thought, to fill out his peroration. Perhaps it would be well to begin
the speech all over again. Yet, as he paraded the galleries he felt that
still something was lacking. Chairs and tables, however richly gilt
and carved, sofas, resting on lions' paws with swans' necks curving
under them, beds even of the softest swansdown are not by themselves enough. People sitting in them, people lying in them improve
them amazingly. Accordingly Orlando now began a series of very
splendid entertainments to the nobility and gentry of the neighbourhood. The three hundred and sixty-five bedrooms were full for a
month at a time. Guests jostled each other on the fifty-two staircases. Three hundred servants bustled about the pantries. Banquets
took place almost nightly. Thus, in a very few years, Orlando had
worn the nap off his velvet, and spent the half of his fortune; but he
had earned the good opinion of his neighbours, held a score of
offices in the county, and was annually presented with perhaps a
dozen volumes dedicated to his Lordship in rather fulsome terms
by grateful poets. For though he was careful not to consort with writers at that time and kept himself always aloof from ladies of foreign
blood, still, he was excessively generous both to women and to poets,
and both adored him.

But when the feasting was at its height and his guests were at their
revels, he was apt to take himself off to his private room alone. There
when the door was shut, and he was certain of privacy, he would
have out an old writing book, stitched together with silk stolen from
his mother's workbox, and labelled in a round schoolboy hand, "The
Oak Tree, A Poem". In this he would write till midnight chimed and
long after. But as he scratched out as many lines as he wrote in, the
sum of them was often, at the end of the year, rather less than at
the beginning, and it looked as if in the process of writing the poem
would be completely unwritten. For it is for the historian of letters
to remark that he had changed his style amazingly. His floridity was
chastened; his abundance curbed; the age of prose was congealing
those warm fountains. The very landscape outside was less stuck
about with garlands and the briars themselves were less thorned and
intricate. Perhaps the senses were a little duller and honey and cream
less seductive to the palate. Also that the streets were better drained
and the houses better lit had its effect upon the style, it cannot be
doubted.

One day he was adding a line or two with enormous labour to "The Oak Tree, A Poem", when a shadow crossed the tail of his eye. It was no shadow, he soon saw, but the figure of a very tall lady in riding hood and mantle crossing the quadrangle on which his room looked out. As this was the most private of the courts, and the lady was a stranger to him, Orlando marvelled how she had got there. Three days later the same apparition appeared again; and on Wednesday noon appeared once more. This time, Orlando was determined to follow her, nor apparently was she afraid to be found, for she slackened her steps as he came up and looked him full in the face. Any other woman thus caught in a Lord's private grounds would have been afraid; any other woman with that face, headdress, and aspect would have thrown her mantilla across her shoulders to hide it. For this lady resembled nothing so much as a hare; a hare startled, but obdurate; a hare whose timidity is overcome by an immense and foolish audacity; a hare that sits upright and glowers at its pursuer with great, bulging eyes; with ears erect but quivering, with nose pointed, but twitching. This hare, moreover, was six feet high and wore a headdress into the bargain of some antiquated kind which made her look still taller. Thus confronted, she stared at Orlando with a stare in which timidity and audacity were most strangely combined.

First, she asked him, with a proper, but somewhat clumsy curtsey, to forgive her her intrusion. Then, rising to her full height again, which must have been something over six feet two, she went on to say—but with such a cackle of nervous laughter, so much tee-heeing and haw-hawing that Orlando thought she must have escaped from a lunatic asylum—that she was the Archduchess Harriet Griselda of Finster-Aarhorn and Scand-op-Boom in the Roumanian territory. She desired above all things to make his acquaintance, she said. She had taken lodging over a baker's shop at the Park Gates. She had seen his picture and it was the image of a sister of hers who was— here she guffawed—long since dead. She was visiting the English court. The Queen was her Cousin. The King was a very good fellow but seldom went to bed sober. Here she tee-heed and haw-hawed again. In short, there was nothing for it but to ask her in and give her a glass of wine.

Indoors, her manners regained the hauteur natural to a Romanian Archduchess; and had she not shown a knowledge of wines rare in a lady, and made some observations upon firearms and the customs of sportsmen in her country, which were sensible enough, the talk would have lacked spontaneity. Jumping to her feet at last, she announced that she would call the following day, swept another prodigious curtsy and departed. The following day, Orlando rode out. The next, he turned his back; on the third he drew his curtain.

On the fourth it rained, and as he could not keep a lady in the wet, nor was altogether averse to company, he invited her in and asked her opinion whether a suit of armour, which belonged to an ancestor of his, was the work of Jacobi or of Topp. He inclined to Topp. She held another opinion—it matters very little which. But it is of some importance to the course of our story that, in illustrating her argument, which had to do with the working of the tie pieces, the Archduchess Harriet took the golden shin case and fitted it to Orlando's leg.

That he had a pair of the shapeliest legs that any Nobleman has ever stood upright upon has already been said.

Perhaps something in the way she fastened the ankle buckle; or her stooping posture; or Orlando's long seclusion; or the natural sympathy which is between the sexes; or the Burgundy; or the fire—any of these causes may have been to blame; for certainly blame there is on one side or another, when a Nobleman of Orlando's breeding, entertaining a lady in his house, and she his elder by many years, with a face a yard long and staring eyes, dressed somewhat ridiculously too, in a mantle and riding cloak though the season was warm—blame there is when such a Nobleman is so suddenly and violently overcome by passion of some sort that he has to leave the room.

But what sort of passion, it may well be asked, could this be? And the answer is double faced as Love herself. For Love—but leaving Love out of the argument for a moment, the actual event was this:

When the Archduchess Harriet Griselda stooped to fasten the buckle, Orlando heard, suddenly and unaccountably, far off the beating of Love's wings. The distant stir of that soft plumage roused in him a thousand memories of rushing waters, of loveliness in the snow and faithlessness in the flood; and the sound came nearer; and he blushed and trembled; and he was moved as he had thought never to be moved again; and he was ready to raise his hands and let the bird of beauty alight upon his shoulders, when—horror!—a creaking sound like that the crows make tumbling over the trees began to reverberate; the air seemed dark with coarse black wings; voices croaked; bits of straw, twigs, and feathers dropped; and there pitched down upon his shoulders the heaviest and foulest of the birds; which is the vulture. Thus he rushed from the room and sent the footman to see the Archduchess Harriet to her carriage.

For Love, to which we may now return, has two faces; one white, the other black; two bodies; one smooth, the other hairy. It has two hands, two feet, two tails, two, indeed, of every member and each one is the exact opposite of the other. Yet, so strictly are they joined together that you cannot separate them. In this case, Orlando's love

Figure 3. The Archduchess Harriet. British Library, London, UK. From
the British Library archive / Bridgeman Images.

began her flight towards him with her white face turned, and her smooth and lovely body outwards. Nearer and nearer she came wafting before her airs of pure delight. All of a sudden (at the sight of the Archduchess presumably) she wheeled about, turned the other way round; showed herself black, hairy, brutish; and it was Lust the vulture, not Love, the Bird of Paradise, that flopped, foully and disgustingly, upon his shoulders. Hence he ran; hence he fetched the footman,

But the harpy is not so easily banished as all that. Not only did the Archduchess continue to lodge at the Baker's, but Orlando was haunted every day and night by phantoms of the foulest kind. Vainly, it seemed, had he furnished his house with silver and hung the walls with arras, when at any moment a dung-bedraggled fowl could settle upon his writing table. There she was, flopping about among the chairs; he saw her waddling ungracefully across the galleries. Now, she perched, top heavy upon a fire screen. When he chased her out, back she came and pecked at the glass till she broke it.

Thus realising that his home was uninhabitable, and that steps must be taken to end the matter instantly, he did what any other young man would have done in his place, and asked King Charles to send him as Ambassador Extraordinary to Constantinople.[8] The King was walking in Whitehall. Nell Gwyn[9] was on his arm. She was pelting him with hazel nuts. 'Twas a thousand pities, that amorous lady sighed, that such a pair of legs should leave the country.

Howbeit, the Fates were hard; she could do no more than toss one kiss over her shoulder before Orlando sailed.

CHAPTER III

IT is, indeed, highly unfortunate, and much to be regretted that at this stage of Orlando's career, when he played a most important part in the public life of his country, we have least information to go upon. We know that he discharged his duties to admiration—witness his Bath and his Dukedom. We know that he had a finger in some of the most delicate negotiations between King Charles and the Turks—to that, treaties in the vault of the Record Office bear testimony. But the revolution which broke out during his period of office, and the fire which followed, have so damaged or destroyed all those

8. In 1930 Constantinople was officially renamed Istanbul. Woolf briefly visited Constantinople with her siblings in 1906 and recorded her impressions in her journal. See *Virginia Woolf, A Passionate Apprentice: The Early Journals 1897–1909*, ed. Mitchell A. Leaska (New York: Harcourt, Brace, Jovanovich, 1990), 347–64.
9. The mistress of King Charles II, who reigned from the Restoration of 1660 to 1685. Orlando's fictional biographer completely passes over the English Civil War (1642–51) and Interregnum (1649–60).

papers from which any trustworthy record could be drawn, that what we can give is lamentably incomplete. Often the paper was scorched a deep brown in the middle of the most important sentence. Just when we thought to elucidate a secret that has puzzled historians for a hundred years, there was a hole in the manuscript big enough to put your finger through. We have done our best to piece out a meagre summary from the charred fragments that remain; but often it has been necessary to speculate, to surmise, and even to use the imagination.

Orlando's day was passed, it would seem, somewhat in this fashion. About seven, he would rise, wrap himself in a long Turkish cloak, light a cheroot, and lean his elbows on the parapet. Thus he would stand, gazing at the city beneath him, apparently entranced. At this hour the mist would lie so thick that the domes of Santa Sofia[1] and the rest would seem to be afloat; gradually the mist would uncover them; the bubbles would be seen to be firmly fixed; there would be the river; there the Galata Bridge;[2] there the green-turbaned pilgrims without eyes or noses, begging alms; there the pariah dogs picking up offal; there the shawled women; there the innumerable donkeys; there men on horses carrying long poles. Soon, the whole town would be astir with the cracking of whips, the beating of gongs, cryings to prayer, lashing of mules, and rattle of brass-bound wheels, while sour odours, made from bread fermenting and incense, and spice, rose even to the heights of Pera itself and seemed the very breath of the strident multicolored and barbaric population.

Nothing, he reflected, gazing at the view which was now sparkling in the sun, could well be less like the counties of Surrey and Kent or the towns of London and Tunbridge Wells. To the right and left rose in bald and stony prominence the inhospitable Asian mountains, to which the arid castle of a robber chief or two might hang; but parsonage there was none, nor manor house, nor cottage, nor oak, elm, violet, ivy, or wild eglantine. There were no hedges for ferns to grow on, and no fields for sheep to graze. The houses were white as egg-shells and as bald. That he, who was English root and fibre, should yet exult to the depths of his heart in this wild panorama, and gaze and gaze at those passes and far heights planning journeys

1. Or Hagia Sophia. The original building was constructed in the 6th century C.E., first serving as an Eastern Orthodox Christian cathedral, then becoming a mosque under the Ottoman Empire. It was converted to a secular museum under the first president of the Republic of Turkey, Mustafa Kemal Atatürk, and was recently reconverted to the Great Holy Mosque of Ayasofya. See Ziad Jamaleddine, "Hagia Sophia Past and Future," *Places Journal*, August 2020. Accessed 4 July 2023.
2. The first Galata Bridge, connecting the European part of Istanbul with the Asian part of Istanbul, was built in 1845, although the Galata Tower would have been a prominent feature in the landscape during the 17th century.

there alone on foot where only the goat and shepherd had gone
before; should feel a passion of affection for the bright, unseason-
able flowers, love the unkempt, pariah dogs beyond even his elk
hounds at home, and snuff the acrid, sharp smell of the streets
eagerly into his nostrils, surprised him. He wondered if, in the season of the Crusades, one of his ancestors had taken up with a Circassian peasant woman; thought it possible; fancied a certain darkness
in his complexion; and, going indoors again, withdrew to his bath.

An hour later, properly scented, curled, and anointed, he would
receive visits from secretaries and other high officials carrying, one
after another, red boxes which yielded only to his own golden key.
Within were papers of the highest importance, of which only fragments, here a flourish, there a seal firmly attached to a piece of burnt
silk, now remain. Of their contents then, we cannot speak, but can
only testify that Orlando was kept busy, what with his wax and seals,
his various coloured ribbons which had to be diversely attached, his
engrossing of titles and making of flourishes round capital letters,
till luncheon came—a splendid meal of perhaps thirty courses.

After luncheon, lackeys announced that his coach and six was at
the door, and he went, preceded by purple Janissaries[3] running on
foot and waving great ostrich feather fans above their heads, to call
upon the other ambassadors and dignitaries of state. The ceremony
was always the same. On reaching the courtyard, the Janissaries
struck with their fans upon the main portal, which immediately few
open revealing a large chamber, splendidly furnished. Here were
seated two figures, generally of the opposite sexes. Profound bows
and curtseys were exchanged. In the first room, it was permissible
only to mention the weather. Having said that it was fine or wet, hot
or cold, the Ambassador then passed on to the next chamber, where
again, two figures rose to greet him. Here it was only permissible to
compare Constantinople as a place of residence with London; and
the Ambassador naturally said that he preferred Constantinople, and
his hosts naturally said, though they had not seen it, that they preferred London. In the next chamber, King Charles's and the Sultan's
healths had to be discussed at some length. In the next were discussed the Ambassador's health and that of his host's wife, but more
briefly. In the next the Ambassador complimented his host upon his
furniture, and the host complimented the Ambassador upon his
dress. In the next, sweet meats were offered, the host deploring their
badness, the Ambassador extolling their goodness. The ceremony
ended at length with the smoking of a hookah and the drinking of
a glass of coffee; but though the motions of smoking and drinking

---

3. Turkish soldiers who served as part of the Sultan's guard.

Figure 4. Orlando as Ambassador. British Library, London, UK. From the British Library archive / Bridgeman Images.

were gone through punctiliously there was neither tobacco in the pipe nor coffee in the glass, as, had either smoke or drink been real, the human frame would have sunk beneath the surfeit. For, no sooner had the Ambassador despatched one such visit, than another had to be undertaken. The same ceremonies were gone through in precisely the same order six or seven times over at the houses of the other great officials, so that it was often late at night before the Ambassador reached home. Though Orlando performed these tasks to admiration and never denied that they are, perhaps, the most important part of a diplomatist's duties, he was undoubtedly fatigued by them, and often depressed to such a pitch of gloom that he preferred to take his dinner alone with his dogs. To them, indeed, he might be heard talking in his own tongue. And sometimes, it is said, he would pass out of his own gates late at night so disguised that the sentries did not know him. Then he would mingle with the crowd on the Galata Bridge; or stroll through the bazaars; or throw aside his shoes and join the worshippers in the Mosques. Once, when it was given out that he was ill of a fever, shepherds, bringing their goats to market, reported that they had met an English Lord on the mountain top and heard him praying to his God. This was thought to be Orlando himself, and his prayer was, no doubt, a poem said aloud, for it was known that he still carried about with him, in the bosom of his cloak, a much scored manuscript; and servants, listening at the door, heard the Ambassador chanting something in an odd, sing-song voice when he was alone.

It is with fragments such as these that we must do our best to make up a picture of Orlando's life and character at this time. There exist, even to this day, rumours, legends, anecdotes of a floating and unauthenticated kind about Orlando's life in Constantinople—(we have quoted but a few of them) which go to prove that he possessed, now that he was in the prime of life, the power to stir the fancy and rivet the eye which will keep a memory green long after all that more durable qualities can do to preserve it is forgotten. The power is a mysterious one compounded of beauty, birth, and some rarer gift, which we may call glamour and have done with it. "A million candles", as Sasha had said, burnt in him without his being at the trouble of lighting a single one. He moved like a stag, without any need to think about his legs. He spoke in his ordinary voice and echo beat a silver gong. Hence rumours gathered round him. He became the adored of many women and some men. It was not necessary that they should speak to him or even that they should see him; they conjured up before them especially when the scenery was romantic, or the sun was setting, the figure of a noble gentleman in silk stockings. Upon the poor and uneducated, he had the same power as upon

the rich. Shepherds, gipsies,[4] donkey drivers, still sing songs about
the English Lord "who dropped his emeralds in the well", which
undoubtedly refer to Orlando, who once, it seems, tore his jewels
from him in a moment of rage or intoxication and flung them in a
fountain; whence they were fished by a page boy. But this romantic
power, it is well known, is often associated with a nature of extreme
reserve. Orlando seems to have made no friends. As far as is known,
he formed no attachments. A certain great lady came all the way
from England in order to be near him, and pestered him with her
attentions, but he continued to discharge his duties so indefatigably
that he had not been Ambassador at the Horn more than two years
and a half before King Charles signified his intention of raising him
to the highest rank in the peerage. The envious said that this was
Nell Gwyn's tribute to the memory of a leg. But, as she had seen
him once only, and was then busily engaged in pelting her royal master with nutshells, it is likely that it was his merits that won him his
Dukedom, not his calves.

Here we must pause, for we have reached a moment of great significance in his career. For the conferring of the Dukedom was the
occasion of a very famous, and indeed, much disputed incident,
which we must now describe, picking our way among burnt papers
and little bits of tape as best we may. It was at the end of the great
fast of Ramadan that the Order of the Bath and the patent of nobility arrived in a frigate commanded by Sir Adrian Scrope; and
Orlando made this the occasion for an entertainment more splendid than any that has been known before or since in Constantinople. The night was fine; the crowd immense, and the windows of the
Embassy brilliantly illuminated. Again, details are lacking, for the
fire had its way with all such records, and has left only tantalising
fragments which leave the most important points obscure. From the
diary of John Fenner Brigge, however, an English naval officer, who
was among the guests, we gather that people of all nationalities
"were packed like herrings in a barrel" in the courtyard. The crowd
pressed so unpleasantly close that Brigge soon climbed into a Judas
tree, the better to observe the proceedings. The rumour had got
about among the natives (and here is additional proof of Orlando's
mysterious power over the imagination) that some kind of miracle
was to be performed. "Thus," writes Brigge (but his manuscript is
full of burns and holes, some sentences being quite illegible), "when
the rockets began to soar into the air, there was considerable

---

4. Woolf uses the terms "gypsy" and "gipsies" (now considered pejorative terms) to refer to
the Roma people or the Romany, an ethnic group of people who tend to be itinerant.
See Abby Bardi in this volume (pp. 220–27) for further analysis of the exoticization of
the Roma people in literature.

uneasiness among us lest the native population should be seized . . .
fraught with unpleasant consequences to all . . . English ladies in
the company, I own that my hand went to my cutlass. Happily," he
continues in his somewhat long-winded style, "these fears seemed,
for the moment, groundless and, observing the demeanour of the
natives . . . I came to the conclusion that this demonstration of
our skill in the art of pyrotechny was valuable, if only because it
impressed upon them . . . the superiority of the British. . . . Indeed,
the sight was one of indescribable magnificence. I found myself alternately praising the Lord that he had permitted . . . and wishing that
my poor, dear mother. . . . By the Ambassador's orders, the long windows, which are so imposing a feature of Eastern architecture, for
though ignorant in many ways . . . were thrown wide; and within,
we could see a tableau vivant or theatrical display in which English
ladies and gentlemen . . . represented a masque the work of one. . . .
The words were inaudible, but the sight of so many of our country-
men and women; dressed with the highest elegance and distinction . . .
moved me to emotions of which I am certainly not ashamed, though
unable. . . . I was intent upon observing the astonishing conduct of
Lady —— which was of a nature to fasten the eyes of all upon her, and
to bring discredit upon her sex and country, when"—unfortunately
a branch of the Judas tree broke; Lieutenant Brigge fell to the
ground, and the rest of the entry records only his gratitude to Providence (who plays a very large part in the diary) and the exact nature
of his injuries.

Happily, Miss Penelope Hartopp, daughter of the General of that
name, saw the scene from inside and carries on the tale in a letter,
much defaced too, which ultimately reached a female friend at Tunbridge Wells. Miss Penelope was no less lavish in her enthusiasm
than the gallant officer. "Ravishing," she exclaims ten times on one
page, "wondrous . . . utterly beyond description . . . gold plate . . .
candelabras . . . negroes in plush breeches . . . pyramids of ice . . .
fountains of negus[5] . . . jellies made to represent His Majesty's
ships . . . swans made to represent water lilies . . . birds in golden
cages . . . gentlemen in slashed crimson velvet . . . Ladies' head-
dresses *at least* six foot high . . . musical boxes. . . . Mr. Peregrine
said I looked *quite* lovely which I only repeat to you, my dearest,
because I know. . . . Oh! how I longed for you all! . . . surpassing anything we have seen at the Pantiles . . . oceans to drink . . . some
gentlemen overcome . . . Lady Betty ravishing. . . . Poor Lady Bon-
ham made the unfortunate mistake of sitting down without a chair
beneath her. . . . Gentlemen all very gallant . . . wished a thousand
times for you and dearest Betsy. . . . But the sight of all others, the

---

5. A hot drink featuring port, lemon, and spices.

cynosure of all eyes . . . as all admitted, for none could be so vile as
to deny it, was the Ambassador himself. Such a leg! Such a countenance!! Such princely manners!!! To see him come into the room!
To see him go out again! And something *interesting* in the expression, which makes one feel, one scarcely knows why, that he has *suffered*! They say a lady was the cause of it. The heartless monster!!!
How can one of our reputed tender sex have had the effrontery!!!
He is unmarried, and half the ladies in the place are wild for love of
him. . . . A thousand, thousand kisses to Tom, Gerry, Peter, and
dearest Mew" [presumably her cat].

From the Gazette of the time, we gather that "as the clock struck
twelve, the Ambassador appeared on the centre Balcony which was
hung with priceless rugs. Six Turks of the Imperial Body Guard, each
over six foot in height, held torches to his right and left. Rockets rose
into the air at his appearance, and a great shout went up from the
people, which the Ambassador acknowledged, bowing deeply, and
speaking a few words of thanks in the Turkish language, which it
was one of his accomplishments to speak with fluency. Next, Sir
Adrian Scrope, in the full dress of a British Admiral advanced;
the Ambassador knelt on one knee; the Admiral placed the Collar
of the Most Noble Order of the Bath round his neck, then pinned
the Star to his breast; after which another gentleman of the diplo-
matic corps advancing in a stately manner placed on his shoulders
the ducal robes, and handed him on a crimson cushion, the ducal
coronet."

At length, with a gesture of extraordinary majesty and grace, first
bowing profoundly, then raising himself proudly erect, Orlando took
the golden circlet of strawberry leaves and placed it, with a gesture
which none that saw it ever forgot, upon his brows. It was at this
point that the first disturbance began. Either the people had expected
a miracle—some say a shower of gold was prophesied to fall from
the skies—which did not happen; or this was the signal chosen for
the attack to begin; nobody seems to know; but as the coronet settled
on Orlando's brows a great uproar rose. Bells began ringing; the
harsh cries of the prophets were heard above the shouts of the
people; many Turks fell flat to the ground and touched the earth
with their foreheads. A door burst open. The natives pressed into
the banqueting rooms. Women shrieked. A certain lady, who was
said to be dying for love of Orlando, seized a candelabra and dashed
it to the ground: What might not have happened, had it not been
for the presence of Sir Adrian Scope and a squad of British bluejackets, nobody can say. But the Admiral ordered the bugles to be
sounded; a hundred bluejackets stood instantly at attention; the disorder was quelled, and quiet, at least for the time being, fell upon
the scene.

So far, we are on the firm, if rather narrow, ground of ascertained truth. But nobody has ever known exactly what took place later that night. The testimony of the sentries and others seems, however; to prove that the Embassy was empty of company, and shut up for the night in the usual way by two A.M. The Ambassador was seen to go to his room, still wearing the insignia of his rank, and shut the door. Some say he locked it, which was against his custom. Others maintain that they heard music of a rustic kind, such as shepherds play, later that night in the courtyard under the Ambassador's window. A washer-woman, who was kept awake by a toothache, said that she saw a man's figure, wrapped in a cloak or dressing gown, come out upon the balcony. Then, she said, a woman, much muffled, but apparently of the peasant class, was drawn up by means of a rope which the man let down to her on to the balcony. There, the washer-woman said, they embraced passionately 'like lovers', and went into the room together, drawing the curtains so that no more could be seen.

Next morning, the Duke, as we must now call him, was found by his secretaries sunk in profound slumber amid bed clothes that were much tumbled. The room was in some disorder, his coronet having rolled on the floor, and his cloak and garter being flung all of a heap on a chair. The table was littered with papers. No suspicion was felt at first, as the fatigues of the night had been great. But when afternoon came and he still slept, a doctor was summoned. He applied remedies which had been used on the previous occasion, plasters, nettles, emetics, etc., but without success. Orlando slept on. His secretaries then thought it their duty to examine the papers on the table. Many were scribbled over with poetry, in which frequent mention was made of an oak tree. There were also various state papers and others of a private nature concerning the management of his estates in England. But at length they came upon a document of far greater significance. It was nothing less, indeed, than a deed of marriage, drawn up, signed, and witnessed between his Lordship, Orlando, Knight of the Garter, etc., etc., etc., and Rosina Pepita,[6] a

---

6. A reference to Vita Sackville-West's maternal grandmother Josefa Durán y Ortega, who was a Spanish and Romani dancer (Pepita is a nickname for Josefa). The convoluted family history on Vita's maternal side is described in her *Pepita* (New York: Doubleday, Doran, and Co., 1937). Vita's grandparents' relationship and the legal complications that followed are also outlined at the outset of Victoria Glendinning's biography *Vita: A Biography of Vita Sackville-West* (New York: Quill, 1983). In brief, Vita's grandfather, Lionel Sackville-West, 2nd Lord Sackville, and Josefa were lovers but reputedly not married to each other. Josefa was legally married to another man, Juan Antonio de Oliva, at the time she became involved with Vita's grandfather. Whether the first marriage or the contested claim of a second marriage between Josefa and Lionel could be proved to be legal through documents (such as the one left among Orlando's scattered papers) would become significant later when the succession of Knole and the Sackville peerage became a legal dispute in the late 19th and early 20th centuries.

dancer, father unknown, but reputed a gipsy; mother also unknown but reputed a seller of old iron in the market-place over against the Galata Bridge. The secretaries looked at each other in dismay. And still Orlando slept. Morning and evening they watched him, but, save that his breathing was regular and his cheeks still flushed their habitual deep rose, he gave no sign of life. Whatever science or ingenuity could do to waken him they did. But still he slept.

On the seventh day of his trance (Thursday, May the 10th) the first shot was fired of that terrible and bloody insurrection of which Lieutenant Brigge had detected the first symptoms. The Turks rose against the Sultan, set fire to the town, and put every foreigner they could find, either to the sword or to the bastinado. A few English managed to escape; but, as might have been expected, the gentlemen of the British Embassy preferred to die in defence of their red boxes, or, in extreme cases, to swallow bunches of keys rather than let them fall into the hands of the Infidel. The rioters broke into Orlando's room, but seeing him stretched to all appearance dead they left him untouched, and only robbed him of his coronet and the robes of the Garter. And now again obscurity descends, and would indeed that it were deeper! Would, we almost have it in our hearts to exclaim, that it were so deep that we could see nothing whatever through its opacity! Would that we might here take the pen and write Finis to our work! Would that we might spare the reader what is to come and say to him in so many words; Orlando died and was buried. But here, alas, Truth, Candour, and Honesty, the austere Gods who keep watch and ward by the inkpot of the biographer, cry No! Putting their silver trumpets to their lips they demand in one blast, Truth! And again they cry Truth! and sounding yet a third time in concert they peal forth, The Truth and nothing but the Truth!

At which—Heaven be praised for it affords us a breathing space— the doors gently open, as if a breath of the gentlest and holiest zephyr had wafted them apart, and three figures enter. First, comes our Lady of Purity; whose brows are bound with fillets of the whitest lamb's wool; whose hair is as an avalanche of the driven snow; and in whose hand reposes the white quill of a virgin goose. Following her, but with a statelier step, comes our Lady of Chastity; on whose brow is set like a turret of burning but unwasting fire a diadem of icicles; her eyes are pure stars, and her fingers, if they touch you, freeze you to the bone. Close behind her, sheltering indeed in the shadow of her more stately sisters, comes our Lady of Modesty, frailest and fairest of the three; whose face is only shown as the young moon shows when it is thin and sickle shaped and half hidden among clouds. Each advances towards the centre of the room where Orlando still lies sleeping; and with gestures at once appealing and commanding, *Our Lady of Purity* speaks first:

"I am the guardian of the sleeping fawn; the snow is dear to me; and the moon rising; and the silver sea. With my robes I cover the speckled hen's eggs and the brindled sea shell; I cover vice and poverty. On all things frail or dark or doubtful, my veil descends. Wherefore, speak not, reveal not. Spare, O spare!"

Here the trumpets peal forth.

"Purity Avaunt! Begone Purity!"

Then *Our Lady Chastity* speaks:

"I am she whose touch freezes and whose glance turns to stone. I have stayed the star in its dancing, and the wave as it falls. The highest Alps are my dwelling place; and when I walk, the lightnings flash in my hair; where my eyes fall, they kill. Rather than let Orlando wake, I will freeze him to the bone. Spare, O spare!"

Here the trumpets peal forth.

"Chastity Avaunt! Begone Chastity!"

Then *Our Lady of Modesty* speaks, so low that one can hardly hear:

"I am she that men call Modesty. Virgin I am and ever shall be. Not for me the fruitful fields and the fertile vineyard. Increase is odious to me; and when the apples burgeon or the flocks breed, I run, I run; I let my mantle fall. I do not see. My hair covers my eyes. Spare, O spare!"

Again the trumpets peal forth:

"Modesty Avaunt! Begone Modesty!"

With gestures of grief and lamentation the three sisters now join hands and dance slowly, tossing their veils and singing as they go:

"Truth come not out from your horrid den. Hide deeper, fearful Truth. For you flaunt in the brutal gaze of the sun things that were better unknown and undone; you unveil the shameful; the dark you make clear, Hide! Hide! Hide!"

Here they make as if to cover Orlando with their draperies. The trumpets, meanwhile, still blare forth,

"The Truth and nothing but the Truth."

At this the sisters try to cast their veils over the mouths of the trumpets so as to muffle them, but in vain, for now all the trumpets blare forth together,

"Horrid Sisters, go!"

The sisters become distracted and wail in unison, still circling and flinging their veils up and down.

"It has not always been so! But men want us no longer; the women detest us. We go; we go. I (*Purity says this*) to the hen roost. I (*Chastity says this*) to the still unravished heights of Surrey. I (*Modesty says this*) to any cosy nook where there are ivy and curtains in plenty."

"For there, not here (all speak together joining hands and making gestures of farewell and despair towards the bed where Orlando lies sleeping) dwell still in nest and boudoir, office and lawcourt those who love us; those who honour us, virgins and city men; lawyers and doctors; those who prohibit; those who deny; those who reverence without knowing why; those who praise without understanding; the still very numerous (Heaven be praised) tribe of the respectable; who prefer to see not; desire to know not; love the darkness; those still worship us, and with reason; for we have given them Wealth, Prosperity, Comfort, Ease. To them we go, you we leave. Come, Sisters, come! This is no place for us here."

They retire in haste, waving their draperies over their heads, as if to shut out something that they dare not look upon and close the door behind them.

We are, therefore, now left entirely alone in the room with the sleeping Orlando and the trumpeters. The trumpeters, ranging themselves side by side in order, blow one terrific blast:—

"THE TRUTH!"

at which Orlando woke.

He stretched himself. He rose. He stood upright in complete nakedness before us, and while the trumpets pealed Truth! Truth! Truth! we have no choice left but confess—he was a woman.

❋   ❋   ❋   ❋   ❋

The sound of the trumpets died away and Orlando stood stark naked. No human being, since the world began, has ever looked more ravishing. His form combined in one the strength of a man and a woman's grace. As he stood there, the silver trumpets prolonged their note, as if reluctant to leave the lovely sight which their blast had called forth; and Chastity, Purity, and Modesty, inspired, no doubt, by Curiosity, peeped in at the door and threw a garment like a towel at the naked form which, unfortunately, fell short by several inches. Orlando looked himself up and down in a long looking-glass, without showing any signs of discomposure, and went, presumably, to his bath.

We may take advantage of this pause in the narrative to make certain statements. Orlando had become a woman—there is no denying it. But in every other respect, Orlando remained precisely as he had been. The change of sex, though it altered their future, did nothing whatever to alter their identity. Their faces remained, as their portraits prove, practically the same. His memory—but in future we must, for convention's sake, say 'her' for 'his', and 'she' for 'he'—her memory then, went back through all the events of her past life without encountering any obstacle. Some slight haziness there may have been, as if a few dark drops had fallen into the clear pool of memory; certain things had become a little dimmed; but that was all. The change seemed to have been accomplished painlessly and completely and in such a way that Orlando herself showed no surprise at it. Many people, taking this into account, and holding that such a change of sex is against nature, have been at great pains to prove (1) that Orlando had always been a woman, (2) that Orlando is at this moment a man. Let biologists and psychologists determine. It is enough for us to state the simple fact; Orlando was a man till the age of thirty; when he became a woman and has remained so ever since.

But let other pens treat of sex and sexuality; we quit such odious subjects as soon as we can. Orlando had now washed, and dressed herself in those Turkish coats and trousers which can be worn indifferently by either sex; and was forced to consider her position. That it was precarious and embarrassing in the extreme must be the first thought of every reader who has followed her story with sympathy. Young, noble, beautiful, she had woken to find herself in a position than which we can conceive none more delicate for a young lady of rank. We should not have blamed her had she rung the bell, screamed, or fainted. But Orlando showed no such signs of perturbation. All her actions were deliberate in the extreme, and might indeed have been thought to show tokens of premeditation. First, she carefully examined the papers on the table; took such as seemed to be written in poetry, and secreted them in her bosom; next she called her Seleuchi hound, which had never left her bed all these days, though half famished with hunger, fed and combed him; then stuck a pair of pistols in her belt; finally wound about her person several strings of emeralds and pearls of the finest orient which had formed part of her Ambassadorial wardrobe. This done, she leant out of the window, gave one low whistle, and descended the shattered and bloodstained staircase, now strewn with the litter of wastepaper baskets, treaties, despatches, seals, sealing wax, etc., and so entered the courtyard. There, in the shadow of a giant fig tree, waited an old gipsy on a donkey. He led another by the bridle. Orlando swung her leg over it; and thus, attended by a lean dog, riding a donkey, in company of a gipsy, the Ambassador of Great Britain at the Court of the Sultan left Constantinople.

They rode for several days and nights and met with a variety of adventures, some at the hands of men, some at the hands of nature, in all of which Orlando acquitted herself with courage. Within a week they reached the high ground outside Broussa, which was then the chief camping ground of the gipsy tribe to which Orlando had allied herself. Often she had looked at those mountains from her balcony at the Embassy; often had longed to be there; and to find oneself where one has longed to be always, to a reflective mind, gives food for thought. For some time, however, she was too well pleased with the change to spoil it by thinking. The pleasure of having no documents to seal or sign, no flourishes to make, no calls to pay, was enough. The gipsies followed the grass; when it was grazed down, on they moved again. She washed in streams if she washed at all; no boxes, red, blue, or green, were presented to her; there was not a key, let alone a golden key, in the whole camp; as for 'visiting', the word was unknown. She milked the goats; she collected brushwood; she stole a hen's egg now and then, but always put a coin or a pearl in place of it; she herded cattle; she stripped vines; she trod the grape; she filled the goat-skin and drank from it; and when she remembered how, at about this time of day, she should have been making the motions of drinking and smoking over an empty coffee-cup and a pipe which lacked tobacco, she laughed aloud, cut herself another hunch of bread, and begged for a puff from old Rustum's pipe, filled though it was with cow dung.

The gipsies, with whom it is obvious that she must have been in secret communication before the revolution, seem to have looked upon her as one of themselves[7] (which is always the highest compliment a people can pay), and her dark hair and dark complexion bore out the belief that she was, by birth, one of them and had been snatched by an English Duke from a nut tree when she was a baby and taken to that barbarous land where people live in houses because they are too feeble and diseased to stand the open air. Thus, though in many ways inferior to them, they were willing to help her to become more like them; taught her their arts of cheese-making and basket-weaving, their science of stealing and bird-snaring, and were even prepared to consider letting her marry among them.

But Orlando had contracted in England some of the customs or diseases (whatever you choose to consider them) which cannot, it seems, be expelled. One evening, when they were all sitting round the camp fire and the sunset was blazing over the Thessalian hills, Orlando exclaimed:

"How good to eat!"

(The gipsies have no word for 'beautiful'. This is the nearest.)[8]

All the young men and women burst out laughing uproariously. The sky good to eat, indeed! The elders, however, who had seen more of foreigners than they had, became suspicious. They noticed that Orlando often sat for whole hours doing nothing whatever, except look here and then there; they would come upon her on some hill-top staring straight in front of her, no matter whether the goats were

---

7. See n. 6 on p. 72.
8. Whether Woolf thought this the case or not, the Romani language does have a word, *shukar*, that translates to beautiful.

grazing or straying. They began to suspect that she had other beliefs than their own, and the older men and women thought it probable that she had fallen into the clutches of the vilest and cruellest among all the Gods, which is Nature.[9] Nor were they far wrong. The English disease, a love of Nature, was inborn in her, and here, where Nature was so much larger and more powerful than in England, she fell into its hands as she had never done before. The malady is too well known, and has been, alas, too often described to need describing afresh, save very briefly. There were mountains; there were valleys; there were streams. She climbed the mountains; roamed the valleys; sat on the banks of the streams. She likened the hills to ramparts, to the breasts of doves, and the flanks of kine. She compared the flowers to enamel and the turf to Turkey rugs worn thin. Trees were withered hags, and sheep were grey boulders. Everything, in fact, was something else. She found the tarn on the mountain-top and almost threw herself in to seek the wisdom she thought lay hid there; and when, from the mountain-top, she beheld far off, across the Sea of Marmara, the plains of Greece, and made out (her eyes were admirable) the Acropolis with a white streak or two which must, she thought, be the Parthenon, her soul expanded with her eyeballs, and she prayed that she might share the majesty of the hills, know the serenity of the plains, etc. etc., as all such believers do. Then, looking down, the red hyacinth, the purple iris wrought her to cry out in ecstasy at the goodness, the beauty of nature; raising her eyes again, she beheld the eagle soaring, and imagined its raptures and made them her own. Returning home, she saluted each star, each peak, and each watch-fire as if they signalled to her alone; and at last, when she flung herself upon her mat in the gipsies' tent, she could not help bursting out again, How good to eat! How good to eat! (For it is a curious fact that though human beings have such imperfect means of communication, that they can only say 'good to eat' when they mean 'beautiful' and the other way about, they will yet endure ridicule and misunderstanding rather than keep any experience to themselves.) All the young gipsies laughed. But Rustum el Sadi, the old man who had brought Orlando out of Constantinople on his donkey, sat silent. He had a nose like a scimitar; his cheeks were furrowed as if from the age-long descent of iron hail; he was brown and keen-eyed, and as he sat tugging at his hookah he observed Orlando narrowly. He had the deepest suspicion that her God was Nature. One day he found her in tears. Interpreting this to mean that her God had punished her, he told her that he was not

---

9. Orlando's intense love of nature is perhaps an allusion to Sackville-West's poem *The Land*, which won the Hawthornden Prize in 1926, a period of time when the affair between Woolf and her was intensifying.

surprised. He showed her the fingers of his left hand, withered by the frost; he showed her his right foot, crushed where a rock had fallen. This, he said, was what her God did to men. When she said, "But so beautiful", using the English word, he shook his head; and when she repeated it he was angry. He saw that she did not believe what he believed, and that was enough, wise and ancient as he was, to enrage him.

This difference of opinion disturbed Orlando, who had been perfectly happy until now. She began to think, was Nature beautiful or cruel; and then she asked herself what this beauty was; whether it was in things themselves, or only in herself; so she went on to the nature of reality, which led her to truth, which in its turn led to Love, Friendship, Poetry (as in the days on the high mound at home); which meditations, since she could impart no word of them, made her long, as she had never longed before, for pen and ink.

"Oh! if only I could write!" she cried (for she had the odd conceit of those who write that words written are shared). She had no ink; and but little paper. But she made ink from berries and wine; and finding a few margins and blank spaces in the manuscript of "The Oak Tree", managed, by writing a kind of shorthand, to describe the scenery in a long, blank version poem, and to carry on a dialogue with herself about this Beauty and Truth concisely enough. This kept her extremely happy for hours on end. But the gipsies became suspicious. First, they noticed that she was less adept than before at milking and cheese-making; next, she often hesitated before replying; and once a gipsy boy who had been asleep, woke in a terror feeling her eyes upon him. Sometimes this constraint would be felt by the whole tribe, numbering some dozens of grown men and women. It sprang from the sense they had (and their senses are very sharp and much in advance of their vocabulary) that whatever they were doing crumbled like ashes in their hands. An old woman making a basket, a boy skinning a sheep, would be singing or crooning contentedly at their work, when Orlando would come into the camp, fling herself down by the fire and gaze into the flames. She need not even look at them, and yet they felt, here is someone who doubts; (we make a rough-and-ready translation from the gipsy language) here is someone who does not do the thing for the sake of doing; nor looks for looking's sake; here is someone who believes neither in sheep-skin nor basket; but sees (here they looked apprehensively about the tent) something else. Then a vague but most unpleasant feeling would begin to work in the boy and in the old woman. They broke their withys;[1] they cut their fingers. A great rage filled them. They wished Orlando would leave the tent and never come near

---

1. Willow branches.

them again. Yet she was of a cheerful and willing disposition, they owned; and one of her pearls was enough to buy the finest herd of goats in Broussa.

Slowly, she began to feel that there was some difference between her and the gipsies which made her hesitate sometimes to marry and settle down among them for ever. At first she tried to account for it by saying that she came of an ancient and civilised race, whereas these gipsies were an ignorant people, not much better than savages. One night when they were questioning her about England she could not help with some pride describing the house where she was born, how it had 365 bedrooms and had been in the possession of her family for four or five hundred years. Her ancestors were earls, or even dukes, she added. At this she noticed again that the gipsies were uneasy; but not angry as before when she had praised the beauty of nature. Now they were courteous, but concerned as people of fine breeding are when a stranger has been made to reveal his low birth or poverty. Rustum followed her out of the tent alone and said that she need not mind if her father were a Duke, and possessed all the bedrooms and furniture that she described. They would none of them think the worse of her for that. Then she was seized with a shame that she had never felt before. It was clear that Rustum and the other gipsies thought a descent of four or five hundred years only the meanest possible. Their own families went back at least two or three thousand years. To the gipsy whose ancestors had built the Pyramids centuries before Christ was born, the genealogy of Howards and Plantagenets was no better and no worse than that of the Smiths and the Joneses: both were negligible. Moreover, where the shepherd boy had a lineage of such antiquity, there was nothing specially memorable or desirable in ancient birth; vagabonds and beggars all shared it. And then, though he was too courteous to speak openly, it was clear that the gipsy thought that there was no more vulgar ambition than to possess bedrooms by the hundred (they were on top of a hill as they spoke; it was night; the mountains rose around them) when the whole earth is ours. Looked at from the gipsy point of view, a Duke, Orlando understood, was nothing but a profiteer or robber who snatched land and money from people who rated these things of little worth, and could think of nothing better to do than to build three hundred and sixty-five bedrooms when one was enough, and none was even better than one. She could not deny that her ancestors had accumulated field after field; house after house; honour after honour; yet had none of them been saints or heroes, or great benefactors of the human race. Nor could she counter the argument (Rustum was too much of a gentleman to press it, but she understood) that any man who did now what her ancestors had done three or four hundred years ago would be denounced—and by her own family most loudly—for a vulgar upstart, an adventurer, a *nouveau riche*.

She sought to answer such arguments by the familiar if oblique method of finding the gipsy life itself rude and barbarous; and so, in a short time, much bad blood was bred between them. Indeed, such differences of opinion are enough to cause bloodshed and revolution. Towns have been sacked for less, and a million martyrs have suffered at the stake rather than yield an inch upon any of the points here debated. No passion is stronger in the breast of man than the desire to make others believe as he believes. Nothing so cuts at the root of his happiness and fills him with rage as the sense that another rates low what he prizes high. Whigs and Tories, Liberal party and Labour party—for what do they battle except their own prestige? It is not love of truth but desire to prevail that sets quarter against quarter and makes parish desire the downfall of parish. Each seeks peace of mind and subserviency rather than the triumph of truth and the exaltation of virtue—but these moralities belong, and should be left to the historian, since they are as dull as ditch water.

"Four hundred and seventy-six bedrooms mean nothing to them," sighed Orlando.

"She prefers a sunset to a flock of goats," said the gipsies.

What was to be done, Orlando could not think. To leave the gipsies and become once more an Ambassador seemed to her intolerable. But it was equally impossible to remain for ever where there was neither ink nor writing paper, neither reverence for the Talbots nor respect for a multiplicity of bedrooms. So she was thinking, one fine morning on the slopes of Mount Athos, when minding her goats. And then Nature, in whom she trusted, either played her a trick or worked a miracle—again, opinions differ too much for it to be possible to say which. Orlando was gazing rather disconsolately at the steep hill-side in front of her. It was now midsummer, and if we must compare the landscape to anything, it would have been to a dry bone; to a sheep's skeleton; to a gigantic skull picked white by a thousand vultures. The heat was intense, and the little fig tree under which Orlando lay only served to print patterns of fig-leaves upon her light burnous.[2]

Suddenly a shadow, though there was nothing to cast a shadow, appeared on the bald mountain-side opposite. It deepened quickly and soon a green hollow showed where there had been barren rock before. As she looked, the hollow deepened and widened, and a great park-like space opened in the flank of the hill. Within, she could see an undulating and grassy lawn; she could see oak trees dotted here and there; she could see the thrushes hopping among the branches.

2. A long, hooded cloak of Arab origin.

She could see the deer stepping delicately from shade to shade, and could even hear the hum of insects and the gentle sighs and shivers of a summer's day in England. After she had gazed entranced for some time, snow began falling; soon the whole landscape was covered and marked with violet shades instead of yellow sunlight. Now she saw heavy carts coming along the roads, laden with tree trunks, which they were taking, she knew, to be sawn for firewood; and then there appeared the roofs and belfries and towers and courtyards of her own home. The snow was falling steadily, and she could now hear the slither and flop which it made as it slid down the roof and fell to the ground. The smoke went up from a thousand chimneys. All was so clear and minute that she could see a daw pecking for worms in the snow. Then, gradually, the violet shadows deepened and closed over the carts and the lawns and the great house itself. All was swallowed up. Now there was nothing left of the grassy hollow, and instead of the green lawns was only the blazing hill-side which a thousand vultures seemed to have picked bare. At this, she burst into a passion of tears, and striding back to the gipsies' camp, told them that she must sail for England the very next day.

It was happy for her that she did so. Already the young men had plotted her death. Honour, they said, demanded it, for she did not think as they did. Yet they would have been sorry to cut her throat; and welcomed the news of her departure. An English merchant ship, as luck would have it, was already under sail in the harbour about to return to England; and Orlando, by breaking off another pearl from her necklace, not only paid her passage but had some banknotes left over in her wallet. These she would have liked to present to the gipsies. But they despised wealth she knew; and she had to content herself with embraces, which on her part were sincere.

CHAPTER IV

WITH some of the guineas[1] left from the sale of the tenth pearl of her string, Orlando had bought herself a complete outfit of such clothes as women then wore, and it was in the dress of a young Englishwoman of rank that she now sat on the deck of the *Enamoured Lady*. It is a strange fact, but a true one, that up to this moment she had scarcely given her sex a thought. Perhaps the Turkish trousers which she had hitherto worn had done something to distract her thoughts; and the gipsy women, except in one or two important particulars, differ very little from the gipsy men. At any rate, it was not until she felt the coil of skirts about her legs and the Captain

---

1. A guinea was a gold coin worth a little over a pound in the 18th century.

offered, with the greatest politeness, to have an awning spread for her on deck, that she realised with a start the penalties and the privileges of her position. But that start was not of the kind that might have been expected.

It was not caused, that is to say, simply and solely by the thought of her chastity and how she could preserve it. In normal circumstances a lovely young woman alone would have thought of nothing else; the whole edifice of female government is based on that foundation stone; chastity is their jewel, their centrepiece, which they run mad to protect, and die when ravished of. But if one has been a man for thirty years or so, and an Ambassador into the bargain, if one has held a Queen in one's arms and one or two other ladies, if report be true, of less exalted rank, if one has married a Rosina Pepita, and so on, one does not perhaps give such a very great start about that. Orlando's start was of a very complicated kind, and not to be summed up in a trice. Nobody, indeed, ever accused her of being one of those quick wits who run to the end of things in a minute. It took her the entire length of the voyage to moralise out the meaning of her start, and so, at her own pace, we will follow her.

"Lord," she thought, when she had recovered from her start, stretching herself out at length under her awning, "this is a pleasant, lazy way of life, to be sure. But", she thought, giving her legs a kick, "these skirts are plaguey things to have about one's heels. Yet the stuff (flowered paduasoy)[2] is the loveliest in the world. Never have I seen my own skin (here she laid her hand on her knee) look to such advantage as now. Could I, however, leap overboard and swim in clothes like these? No! Therefore, I should have to trust to the protection of a blue-jacket.[3] Do I object to that? Now do I?" she wondered, here encountering the first knot in the smooth skein of her argument.

Dinner came before she had untied it, and then it was the Captain himself—Captain Nicholas Benedict Bartolus, a sea-captain of distinguished aspect, who did it for her as he helped her to a slice of corned beef.

"A little of the fat, Ma'am?" he asked. "Let me cut you just the tiniest little slice the size of your finger nail." At those words a delicious tremor ran through her frame. Birds sang; the torrents rushed. It recalled the feeling of indescribable pleasure with which she had first seen Sasha, hundred of years ago. Then she had pursued, now she fed. Which is the greater ecstasy? The man's or the woman's? And are they not perhaps the same? No, she thought, this is the

2. A corded silk fabric that was fashionable in the 18th century.
3. An enlisted sailor in the British navy.

most delicious (thanking the Captain but refusing), to refuse, and
see him frown. Well, she would, if he wished it, have the very thinnest, smallest shiver in the world. This was the most delicious of all,
to yield and see him smile. "For nothing", she thought, regaining her
couch on deck, and continuing the argument, "is more heavenly
than to resist and to yield; to yield and to resist. Surely it throws the
spirit into such a rapture as nothing else can. So that I'm not sure",
she continued, "that I won't throw myself overboard, for the mere
pleasure of being rescued by a blue-jacket after all."

(It must be remembered that she was like a child entering into
possession of a pleasaunce[4] or toy cupboard; her arguments would
not commend themselves to mature women, who have had the run
of it all their lives.)

"But what used we young fellows in the cockpit of the *Marie Rose*
to say about a woman who threw herself overboard for the pleasure
of being rescued by a blue-jacket?" she said. "We had a word for
them. Ah! I have it. . . ." (But we must omit that word; it was disrespectful in the extreme and passing strange on a lady's lips.) "Lord!
Lord!" she cried again at the conclusion of her thoughts, "must I then
begin to respect the opinion of the other sex, however monstrous I
think it? If I wear skirts, if I can't swim, if I have to be rescued by a
blue-jacket, by God!" she cried, "I must!" Upon which a gloom fell
over her. Candid by nature, and averse to all kinds of equivocation,
to tell lies bored her. It seemed to her a roundabout way of going to
work. Yet, she reflected, the flowered paduasoy—the pleasure of
being rescued by a blue-jacket if these were only to be obtained by
roundabout ways, roundabout one must go, she supposed. She
remembered how, as a young man, she had insisted that women must
be obedient, chaste, scented, and exquisitely apparelled. "Now I shall
have to pay in my own person for those desires," she reflected; "for
women are not (judging by my own short experience of the sex) obedient, chaste, scented, and exquisitely apparelled by nature. They
can only attain these graces, without which they may enjoy none of
the delights of life, by the most tedious discipline. There's the hairdressing," she thought, "that alone will take an hour of my morning; there's looking in the looking-glass, another hour; there's staying
and lacing; there's washing and powdering; there's changing from
silk to lace and from lace to paduasoy; there's being chaste year in
year out. . . ." Here she tossed her foot impatiently, and showed an
inch or two of calf. A sailor on the mast, who happened to look down
at the moment, started so violently that he missed his footing and
only saved himself by the skin of his teeth. "If the sight of my ankles
means death to an honest fellow who, no doubt, has a wife and

4. A garden designed to be pleasing.

family to support, I must, in all humanity, keep them covered,"
Orlando thought. Yet her legs were among her chiefest beauties. And
she fell to thinking what an odd pass we have come to when all a
woman's beauty has to be kept covered lest a sailor may fall from a
mast-head. "A pox on them!" she said, realising for the first time
what, in other circumstances, she would have been taught as a child,
that is to say, the sacred responsibilities of womanhood.

"And that's the last oath I shall ever be able to swear," she thought;
"once I set foot on English soil. And I shall never be able to crack a
man over the head, or tell him he lies in his teeth, or draw my sword
and run him through the body, or sit among my peers, or wear a
coronet, or walk in procession, or sentence a man to death, or lead
an army, or prance down Whitehall[5] on a charger, or wear seventy-
two different medals on my breast. All I can do, once I set foot on
English soil, is to pour out tea and ask my lords how they like it.
D'you take sugar? D'you take cream?" And mincing out the words,
she was horrified to perceive how low an opinion she was forming
of the other sex, the manly, to which it had once been her pride to
belong. "To fall from a mast-head", she thought, "because you see
a woman's ankles; to dress up like a Guy Fawkes[6] and parade the
streets, so that women may praise you; to deny a woman teaching
lest she may laugh at you; to be the slave of the frailest chit in petticoats, and yet to go about as if you were the Lords of creation.—
Heavens!" she thought, "what fools they make of us—what fools we
are!" And here it would seem from some ambiguity in her terms that
she was censuring both sexes equally, as if she belonged to neither;
and indeed, for the time being, she seemed to vacillate; she was man;
she was woman; she knew the secrets, shared the weaknesses of
each. It was a most bewildering and whirligig state of mind to be in.
The comforts of ignorance seemed utterly denied her. She was a
feather blown on the gale. Thus it is no great wonder, as she pitted
one sex against the other, and found each alternately full of the most
deplorable infirmities, and was not sure to which she belonged—it
was no great wonder that she was about to cry out that she would
return to Turkey and become a gipsy again when the anchor fell with
a great splash into the sea; the sails came tumbling on deck, and
she perceived (so sunk had she been in thought that she had seen
nothing for several days) that the ship was anchored off the coast of

5. Both a street and a neighborhood in London where the main government offices of the
   UK are located.
6. One of the conspirators who attempted to blow up Parliament on November 5, 1605.
   The UK tradition of lighting bonfires and parading with effigies of Guy Fawkes on Guy
   Fawkes Day remains to this day. In her book *Three Guineas* (1938), Woolf pokes fun at
   the proclivities of highborn men who wear fancy outfits despite hypocritically chastis-
   ing women for wearing extravagant clothing.

Figure 5. Orlando on her return to England. British Library, London, UK. From the British Library archive / Bridgeman Images.

Italy. The Captain at once sent to ask the honour of her company ashore with him in the long-boat.

When she returned the next morning, she stretched herself on her couch under the awning and arranged her draperies with the greatest decorum about her ankles.

"Ignorant and poor as we are compared with the other sex," she thought, continuing the sentence which she had left unfinished the other day, "armoured with every weapon as they are, while they debar us even from a knowledge of the alphabet" (and from these opening words it is plain that something had happened during the night to give her a push towards the female sex, for she was speaking more as a woman speaks than as a man, yet with a sort of content after all), "still—they fall from the mast-head." Here she gave a yawn and fell asleep. When she woke, the ship was sailing before a fair breeze so near the shore that towns on the cliffs' edge seemed only kept from slipping into the water by the interposition of some great rock or the twisted roots of some ancient olive tree. The scent of oranges wafted from a million trees, heavy with the fruit, reached her on deck. A score of blue dolphins, twisting their tails, leapt high now and again into the air. Stretching her arms out (arms, she had learnt already, have no such fatal effects as legs), she thanked Heaven that she was not prancing down Whitehall on a war-horse, nor even sentencing a man to death. "Better is it", she thought, "to be clothed with poverty and ignorance, which are the dark garments of the female sex; better to leave the rule and discipline of the world to others; better be quit of martial ambition, the love of power, and all the other manly desires if so one can more fully enjoy the most exalted raptures known to the human spirit, which are", she said aloud, as her habit was when deeply moved, "contemplation, solitude, love."

"Praise God that I'm a woman!"[7] she cried, and was about to run into the extreme folly—than which none is more distressing in woman or man either—of being proud of her sex, when she paused over the singular word, which, for all we can do to put it in its place, has crept in at the end of the last sentence: Love. "Love," said Orlando. Instantly—such is its impetuosity—love took a human shape—such is its pride. For where other thoughts are content to remain abstract, nothing will satisfy this one but to put on flesh and blood, mantilla and petticoats, hose and jerkin. And as all Orlando's loves had been women, now, through the culpable laggardry of the human frame to adapt itself to convention, though she herself

7. This may be an allusion to the Orthodox Jewish tradition of men beginning the morning with a prayer that includes the line "Shelo Asani Isha," which roughly translates to "Praise God that I was not born a woman" (Hebrew).

was a woman, it was still a woman she loved; and if the consciousness of being of the same sex had any effect at all, it was to quicken
and deepen those feelings which she had had as a man. For now a
thousand hints and mysteries became plain to her that were then
dark. Now, the obscurity, which divides the sexes and lets linger
innumerable impurities in its gloom, was removed, and if there is
anything in what the poet says about truth and beauty, this affection gained in beauty what it lost in falsity. At last, she cried, she
knew Sasha as she was, and in the ardour of this discovery, and in
the pursuit of all those treasures which were now revealed, she was
so rapt and enchanted that it was as if a cannon ball had exploded
at her ear when a man's voice said, "Permit me, Madam," a man's
hand raised her to her feet; and the fingers of a man with a three-
masted sailing ship tattooed on the middle finger pointed to the
horizon.

"The cliffs of England, Ma'am," said the Captain, and he raised
the hand which had pointed at the sky to the salute. Orlando now
gave a second start, even more violent than the first.

"Christ Jesus!" she cried.

Happily, the sight of her native land after long absence excused
both start and exclamation, or she would have been hard put to it to
explain to Captain Bartolus the raging and conflicting emotions
which now boiled within her. How tell him that she, who now trembled on his arm, had been a Duke and an Ambassador? How explain
to him that she, who had been lapped like a lily in folds of paduasoy, had hacked heads off, and lain with loose women among treasure
sacks in the holds of pirate ships on summer nights when the tulips
were abloom and the bees buzzing off Wapping Old Stairs? Not even
to herself could she explain the giant start she gave, as the resolute
right hand of the sea-captain indicated the cliffs of the British
Islands.

"To refuse and to yield," she murmured, "how delightful; to pursue and to conquer, how august; to perceive and to reason, how sublime." Not one of these words so coupled together seemed to her
wrong; nevertheless, as the chalky cliffs loomed nearer, she felt culpable; dishonoured; unchaste, which, for one who had never given
the matter a thought, was strange. Closer and closer they drew, till
the samphire[8] gatherers, hanging half-way down the cliff, were
plain to the naked eye. And watching them, she felt, scampering
up and down within her, like some derisive ghost who in another
instant will pick up her skirts and flaunt out of sight, Sasha the
lost, Sasha the memory, whose reality she had proved just now so

8. Rock samphire is a vegetable, also known in North America as sea beans. It grows on
   coastal rocks in the British Isles and is hazardous to gather.

surprisingly—Sasha, she felt, mopping and mowing and making all sorts of disrespectful gestures towards the cliffs and the samphire gatherers; and when the sailors began chanting, "So good-bye and adieu to you, Ladies of Spain", the words echoed in Orlando's sad heart, and she felt that however much landing there meant comfort, meant opulence, meant consequence and state (for she would doubtless pick up some noble Prince and reign, his consort, over half Yorkshire), still, if it meant conventionality, meant slavery, meant deceit, meant denying her love, fettering her limbs, pursing her lips, and restraining her tongue, then she would turn about with the ship and set sail once more for the gipsies.

Among the hurry of these thoughts, however, there now rose, like a dome of smooth, white marble, something which, whether fact or fancy, was so impressive to her fevered imagination that she settled upon it as one has seen a swarm of vibrant dragon-flies alight, with apparent satisfaction, upon the glass bell which shelters some tender vegetable. The form of it, by the hazard of fancy, recalled that earliest, most persistent memory—the man with the big forehead in Twitchett's sitting-room, the man who sat writing, or rather looking, but certainly not at her, for he never seemed to see her poised there in all her finery, lovely boy though she must have been, she could not deny it—and whenever she thought of him, the thought spread round it, like the risen moon on turbulent waters, a sheet of silver calm. Now her hand went to her bosom (the other was still in the Captain's keeping), where the pages of her poem were hidden safe. It might have been a talisman that she kept there. The distraction of sex, which hers was, and what it meant, subsided; she thought now only of the glory of poetry, and the great lines of Marlowe, Shakespeare, Ben Jonson, Milton began booming and reverberating, as if a golden clapper beat against a golden bell in the cathedral tower which was her mind. The truth was that the image of the marble dome which her eyes had first discovered so faintly that it suggested a poet's forehead and thus started a flock of irrelevant ideas, was no figment, but a reality; and as the ship advanced down the Thames before a favouring gale, the image with all its associations gave place to the truth, and revealed itself as nothing more and nothing less than the dome of a vast cathedral rising among a fretwork of white spires.

"St. Paul's," said Captain Bartolus, who stood by her side. "The Tower of London," he continued. "Greenwich Hospital, erected in memory of Queen Mary by her husband, his late majesty, William the Third. Westminster Abbey. The Houses of Parliament." As he spoke, each of these famous buildings rose to view. It was a fine September morning. A myriad of little water-craft plied from bank to bank. Rarely has a gayer, or more interesting, spectacle presented

itself to the gaze of a returned traveller. Orlando hung over the prow,
absorbed in wonder. Her eyes had been used too long to savages and
nature not to be entranced by these urban glories. That, then, was
the dome of St. Paul's which Mr. Wren had built during her absence.
Near by, a shock of golden hair burst from a pillar—Captain Bartolus
was at her side to inform her that that was the Monument;[9] there
had been a plague and a fire during her absence, he said. Do what
she would to restrain them, the tears came to her eyes, until,
remembering that it is becoming in a woman to weep, she let them
flow. Here, she thought, had been the great carnival. Here, where
the waves slapped briskly, had stood the Royal Pavilion. Here she
had first met Sasha. About here (she looked down into the sparkling
waters) one had been used to see the frozen bumboat woman with
her apples on her lap. All that splendour and corruption was gone.
Gone, too, was the dark night, the monstrous downpour, the violent surges of the flood. Here, where yellow icebergs had raced circling with a crew of terror-stricken wretches on top, a covey of swans
floated, orgulous, undulant, superb. London itself had completely
changed since she had last seen it. Then, she remembered, it had
been a huddle of little black, beetle-browed houses. The heads of
rebels had grinned on pikes at Temple Bar. The cobbled pavements
had reeked of garbage and ordure. Now, as the ship sailed past Wapping, she caught glimpses of broad and orderly thoroughfares. Stately
coaches drawn by teams of well-fed horses stood at the doors of
houses whose bow windows, whose plate glass, whose polished knock-
ers, testified to the wealth and modest dignity of the dwellers within.
Ladies in flowered silk (she put the Captain's glass to her eye)
walked on raised footpaths. Citizens in broidered coats took snuff
at street corners under lamp-posts. She caught sight of a variety of
painted signs swinging in the breeze and could form a rapid notion
from what was painted on them of the tobacco, of the stuff, of the
silk, of the gold, of the silver ware, of the gloves, of the perfumes,
and of a thousand other articles which were sold within. Nor could
she do more as the ship sailed to its anchorage by London Bridge
than glance at coffee-house windows where, on balconies, since the
weather was fine, a great number of decent citizens sat at ease, with
china dishes in front of them, clay pipes by their sides, while one
among them read from a news sheet, and was frequently interrupted
by the laughter or the comments of the others. Were these taverns,
were these wits, were these poets? she asked of Captain Bartolus,
who obligingly informed her that even now—if she turned her head a
little to the left and looked along the line of his first finger—so—they

9. The Monument to the Great Fire of London, erected in 1671 to commemorate the fire
   that devastated the city in 1666.

were passing the Cocoa Tree, where,—yes, there he was—one might
see Mr. Addison taking his coffee; the other two gentlemen—"there,
Ma'am, a little to the right of the lamp-post, one of 'em humped,
t'other much the same as you or me"—Were Mr. Dryden and
Mr. Pope.† "Sad dogs," said the Captain, by which he meant that they
were Papists, "but men of parts, none the less," he added, hurrying
aft to superintend the arrangements for landing.

"Addison, Dryden, Pope,"[1] Orlando repeated as if the words were
an incantation. For one moment she saw the high mountains above
Broussa, the next, she had set her foot upon her native shore.

But now Orlando was to learn how little the most tempestuous flutter of excitement avails against the iron countenance of the law;
how harder than the stones of London Bridge it is, and than the lips
of a cannon more severe. No sooner had she returned to her home
in Blackfriars than she was made aware by a succession of Bow Street
runners and other grave emissaries from the Law Courts that she was
a party to three major suits which had been preferred against her during her absence, as well as innumerable minor litigations, some aris-
ing out of, others depending on them. The chief charges against her
were (1) that she was dead, and therefore could not hold any property whatsoever; (2) that she was a woman, which amounts to much
the same thing; (3) that she was an English Duke who had married
one Rosina Pepita, a dancer; and had had by her three sons, which
sons now declaring that their father was deceased, claimed that all
his property descended to them.[2] Such grave charges as these
would, of course, take time and money to dispose of. All her estates
were put in Chancery and her titles pronounced in abeyance while
the suits were under litigation. Thus it was in a highly ambiguous
condition, uncertain whether she was alive or dead, man or woman,
Duke or nonentity, that she posted down to her country seat, where,
pending the legal judgment, she had the Law's permission to reside
in a state of incognito or incognita, as the case might turn out to be.

It was a fine evening in December when she arrived and the snow
was falling and the violet shadows were slanting much as she had
seen them from the hill-top at Broussa. The great house lay more

---

† The Captain must have been mistaken, as a reference to any text-book of literature will
   show; but the mistake was a kindly one, and so we let it stand [Woolf's note].
1. Alexander Pope (1688–1744), 18th century poet and satirist who wrote the mock-
   heroic long poem *The Rape of the Lock*. Joseph Addison (1672–1719), writer and states-
   man; he founded *The Spectator*, a popular 18th-century periodical. John Dryden (b.
   1659), a famous Restoration dramatist, died in 1700, hence Woolf's footnote about the
   captain's error.
2. An allusion to a 1910 lawsuit to determine the rightful inheritors of Knole. Glendinning
   describes the lawsuit in her biography of Sackville-West, *Vita*, p. 35. Woolf includes a
   critique here of the law of primogeniture, which rendered women unable to inherit
   their family's estate.

like a town than a house, brown and blue, rose and purple in the
snow, with all its chimneys smoking busily as if inspired with a life
of their own. She could not restrain a cry as she saw it there tran-
quil and massive, couched upon the meadows. As the yellow coach
entered the park and came bowling along the drive between the
trees, the red deer raised their heads as if expectantly, and it was
observed that instead of showing the timidity natural to their kind,
they followed the coach and stood about the courtyard when it drew
up. Some tossed their antlers, others pawed the ground as the step
was let down and Orlando alighted. One, it is said, actually knelt in
the snow before her. She had not time to reach her hand towards
the knocker before both wings of the great door were flung open,
and there, with lights and torches held above their heads, were
Mrs. Grimsditch, Mr. Dupper, and a whole retinue of servants come
to greet her. But the orderly procession was interrupted first by the
impetuosity of Canute, the elk-hound, who threw himself with such
ardour upon his mistress that he almost knocked her to the ground;
next, by the agitation of Mrs. Grimsditch, who, making as if to curtsey, was overcome with emotion and could do no more than gasp
Milord! Milady! Milady! Milord! until Orlando comforted her with
a hearty kiss upon both her cheeks. After that, Mr. Dupper began
to read from a parchment, but the dogs barking, the huntsmen winding their horns, and the stags, who had come into the courtyard in
the confusion, baying the moon, not much progress was made, and
the company dispersed within after crowding about their Mistress,
and testifying in every way to their great joy at her return.

No one showed an instant's suspicion that Orlando was not the
Orlando they had known. If any doubt there was in the human mind
the action of the deer and the dogs would have been enough to dispel it,
for the dumb creatures, as is well known, are far better judges both
of identity and character than we are. Moreover, said Mrs. Grimsditch,
over her dish of china tea, to Mr. Dupper that night, if her Lord was
a Lady now, she had never seen a lovelier one, nor was there a penny
piece to choose between them; one was as well-favoured as the other;
they were as like as two peaches on one branch; which, said Mrs.
Grimsditch, becoming confidential, she had always had her suspicions (here she nodded her head very mysteriously), which it was no
surprise to her (here she nodded her head very knowingly), and for
her part, a very great comfort; for what with the towels wanting
mending and the curtains in the chaplain's parlour being moth-
eaten round the fringes, it was time they had a Mistress among them.

"And some little masters and mistresses to come after her," Mr.
Dupper added, being privileged by virtue of his holy office to speak
his mind on such delicate matters as these.

So, while the old servants gossiped in the servants' hall, Orlando took a silver candle in her hand and roamed once more through the halls, the galleries, the courts, the bedrooms; saw loom down at her again the dark visage of this Lord Keeper, that Lord Chamberlain, among her ancestors; sat now in this chair of state, now reclined on that canopy of delight; observed the arras, how it swayed; watched the huntsmen riding and Daphne flying; bathed her hand, as she had loved to do as a child, in the yellow pool of light which the moonlight made falling through the heraldic Leopard in the window; slid along the polished planks of the gallery, the other side of which was rough timber; touched this silk, that satin; fancied the carved dolphins swam; brushed her hair with King James' silver brush; buried her face in the pot-pourri, which was made as the Conqueror had taught them many hundred years ago and from the same roses; looked at the garden and imagined the sleeping crocuses, the dormant dahlias; saw the frail nymphs gleaming white in the snow and the great yew hedges, thick as a house, black behind them; saw the orangeries and the giant medlars;—all this she saw, and each sight and sound, rudely as we write it down, filled her heart with such a lust and balm of joy, that at length, tired out, she entered the Chapel and sank into the old red arm-chair in which her ancestors used to hear service. There she lit a cheroot ('twas a habit she had brought back from the East) and opened the Prayer Book.

It was a little book bound in velvet, stitched with gold, which had been held by Mary Queen of Scots on the scaffold, and the eye of faith could detect a brownish stain, said to be made of a drop of the Royal blood. But what pious thoughts it roused in Orlando, what evil passions it soothed asleep, who dare say, seeing that of all communions this with the deity is the most inscrutable? Novelist, poet, historian all falter with their hand on that door; nor does the believer himself enlighten us, for is he more ready to die than other people, or more eager to share his goods? Does he not keep as many maids and carriage horses as the rest? and yet with it all, holds a faith he says which should make goods a vanity and death desirable. In the Queen's prayer-book, along with the blood-stain, was also a lock of hair and a crumb of pastry; Orlando now added to these keepsakes a flake of tobacco, and so, reading and smoking, was moved by the humane jumble of them all—the hair, the pastry, the blood-stain, the tobacco—to such a mood of contemplation as gave her a reverent air suitable in the circumstances, though she had, it is said, no traffic with the usual God. Nothing, however, can be more arrogant, though nothing is commoner than to assume that of Gods there is only one, and of religions none but the speaker's. Orlando, it seemed, had a faith of her own. With all the religious ardour in the world, she now reflected upon her sins and the imperfections that had crept into her spiritual state. The letter S, she reflected, is the serpent in the poet's Eden. Do what she would there were still too many of these sinful reptiles in the first stanzas of "The Oak Tree". But 'S' was nothing, in her opinion, compared with the termination 'ing'. The present participle is the Devil himself, she thought (now that we are in the place for believing in Devils). To evade such temptations is the first duty of the poet, she concluded, for as the ear is the antechamber to the soul, poetry can adulterate and destroy more surely than lust or gunpowder. The poet's, then, is the highest office of all, she continued. His words reach where others fall short. A silly song of Shakespeare's has done more for the poor and the wicked than all the preachers and philanthropists in the world. No time, no devotion, can be too great, therefore, which makes the vehicle of our message less distorting. We must shape our words till they are the thinnest integument for our thoughts. Thoughts are divine, etc. Thus it is obvious that she was back in the confines of her own religion which time had only strengthened in her absence, and was rapidly acquiring the intolerance of belief.

"I am growing up," she thought, taking her taper at last. "I am losing some illusions," she said, shutting Queen Mary's book, "perhaps to acquire others," and she descended among the tombs where the bones of her ancestors lay.

But even the bones of her ancestors, Sir Miles, Sir Gervase, and the rest, had lost something of their sanctity since Rustum el Sadi had waved his hand that night in the Asian mountains. Somehow the fact that only three or four hundred years ago these skeletons had been men with their way to make in the world like any modern upstart, and that they had made it by acquiring houses and offices, garters and ribbands, as any other upstart does, while poets, perhaps, and men of great mind and breeding had preferred the quietude of the country, for which choice they paid the penalty by extreme poverty, and now hawked broadsheets in the Strand, or herded sheep in the fields, filled her with remorse. She thought of the Egyptian pyramids and what bones lie beneath them as she stood in the crypt; and the vast, empty hills which lie above the Sea of Marmara seemed, for the moment, a finer dwelling-place than this many-roomed mansion in which no bed lacked its quilt and no silver dish its silver cover.

"I am growing up," she thought, taking her taper. "I am losing my illusions, perhaps to acquire new ones," and she paced down the long gallery to her bedroom. It was a disagreeable process, and a troublesome. But it was interesting, amazingly, she thought, stretching her legs out to her log fire (for no sailor was present), and she reviewed, as if it were an avenue of great edifices, the progress of her own self along her own past.

How she had loved sound when she was a boy, and thought the volley of tumultuous syllables from the lips the finest of all poetry. Then—it was the effect of Sasha and her disillusionment perhaps—into this high frenzy was let fall some black drop, which turned her rhapsody to sluggishness. Slowly there had opened within her something intricate and many-chambered, which one must take a torch to explore, in prose not verse; and she remembered how passionately she had studied that doctor at Norwich, Browne, whose book was at her hand there. She had formed here in solitude after her affair with Greene, or tried to form, for Heaven knows these growths are agelong in coming, a spirit capable of resistance.[3] "I will write," she had said, "what I enjoy writing"; and so had scratched out twenty-six volumes. Yet still, for all her travels and adventures and profound thinkings and turnings this way and that, she was only in process of fabrication. What the future might bring, Heaven only knew. Change was incessant, and change perhaps would never cease. High battlements of thought, habits that had seemed durable as stone, went down like shadows at the touch of another mind and left a naked sky and fresh stars twinkling in it. Here she went to the window, and in spite of the cold could not help unlatching it. She leant out into the damp night air. She heard a fox bark in the woods, and the clutter of a pheasant trailing through the branches. She heard the snow slither and flop from the roof to the ground. "By my life," she exclaimed, "this is a thousand times better than Turkey. Rustum," she cried, as if she were arguing with the gipsy (and in this new power of bearing an argument in mind and continuing it with someone who was not there to contradict she showed again the development of her soul), "you were wrong. This is better than Turkey. Hair, pastry, tobacco—of what odds and ends are we compounded," she said (thinking of Queen Mary's prayer-book). "What a phantasmagoria the mind is and meeting-place of dissemblables! At one moment we deplore our birth and state and aspire to an ascetic exaltation; the next we are overcome by the smell of some old garden path and weep to hear the thrushes sing." And so bewildered as usual by the multitude of things which

3. Victorian poet and literary critic Matthew Arnold, who much like the character of Nick Greene in this novel, thought that his own age was not replete with great poetry and argued that Britain after the Restoration had a need for "fit prose." Orlando's desire for precision in her writing is therefore a reflection of the age, at least as it is presented in the British literary history of Woolf's time. In his 1880 essay "The Study of Poetry," Arnold writes, "We are to regard Dryden as the puissant and glorious founder, Pope as the splendid high priest, of our age of prose and reason, of our excellent and indispensable eighteenth century."

call for explanation and imprint their message without leaving any hint as to their meaning, she threw her cheroot out of the window and went to bed.

Next morning, in pursuance of these thoughts, she had out her pen and paper, and started afresh upon "The Oak Tree", for to have ink and paper in plenty when one has made do with berries and margins is a delight not to be conceived. Thus she was now striking out a phrase in the depths of despair, now in the heights of ecstasy writing one in, when a shadow darkened the page. She hastily hid her manuscript.

As her window gave on to the most central of the courts, as she had given orders that she would see no one, as she knew no one and was herself legally unknown, she was first surprised at the shadow, then indignant at it, then (when she looked up and saw what caused it) overcome with merriment. For it was a familiar shadow, a grotesque shadow, the shadow of no less a personage than the Archduchess Harriet Griselda of Finster-Aarhorn and Scand-op-Boom in the Roumanian territory. She was loping across the court in her old black riding-habit and mantle as before. Not a hair of her head was changed. This then was the woman who had chased her from England! This was the eyrie[4] of that obscene vulture—this the fatal fowl herself! At the thought that she had fled all the way to Turkey to avoid her seductions (now become excessively flat), Orlando laughed aloud. There was something inexpressibly comic in the sight. She resembled, as Orlando had thought before, nothing so much as a monstrous hare. She had the staring eyes, the lank cheeks, the high headdress of that animal. She stopped now, much as a hare sits erect in the corn when thinking itself unobserved, and stared at Orlando, who stared back at her from the window. After they had stared like this for a certain time, there was nothing for it but to ask her in, and soon the two ladies were exchanging compliments while the Archduchess struck the snow from her mantle.

"A plague on women," said Orlando to herself, going to the cupboard to fetch a glass of wine, "they never leave one a moment's peace. A more ferreting, inquisiting, busybodying set of people don't exist. It was to escape this Maypole that I left England, and now"—here she turned to present the Archduchess with the salver, and behold—in her place stood a tall gentleman in black. A heap of clothes lay in the fender. She was alone with a man.

Recalled thus suddenly to a consciousness of her sex, which she had completely forgotten, and of his, which was now remote enough to be equally upsetting, Orlando felt seized with faintness.

"La!" she cried, putting her hand to her side, "how you frighten me!"

---

4. A large nest.

"Gentle creature," cried the Archduchess, falling on one knee and at the same time pressing a cordial to Orlando's lips, "forgive me for the deceit I have practised on you!"

Orlando sipped the wine and the Archduke knelt and kissed her hand.

In short, they acted the parts of man and woman for ten minutes with great vigour and then fell into natural discourse. The Archduchess (but she must in future be known as the Archduke) told his story—that he was a man and always had been one; that he had seen a portrait of Orlando and fallen hopelessly in love with him; that to compass his ends, he had dressed as a woman and lodged at the Baker's shop; that he was desolated when he fled to Turkey; that he had heard of her change and hastened to offer his services (here he teed and heed intolerably). For to him, said the Archduke Harry, she was and would ever be the Pink, the Pearl, the Perfection of her sex. The three p's would have been more persuasive if they had not been interspersed with tee-hees and haw-haws of the strangest kind. "If this is love," said Orlando to herself, looking at the Archduke on the other side of the fender, and now from the woman's point of view, "there is something highly ridiculous about it."

Falling on his knees, the Archduke Harry made the most passionate declaration of his suit. He told her that he had something like twenty million ducats in a strong box at his castle. He had more acres than any nobleman in England. The shooting was excellent: he could promise her a mixed bag of ptarmigan and grouse such as no English moor, or Scotch either, could rival. True, the pheasants had suffered from the gape in his absence, and the does had slipped their young, but that could be put right, and would be with her help when they lived in Roumania together.

As he spoke, enormous tears formed in his rather prominent eyes and ran down the sandy tracts of his long and lanky cheeks.

That men cry as frequently and as unreasonably as women, Orlando knew from her own experience as a man; but she was beginning to be aware that women should be shocked when men display emotion in their presence, and so, shocked she was.

The Archduke apologised. He commanded himself sufficiently to say that he would leave her now, but would return on the following day for his answer.

That was a Tuesday. He came on Wednesday; he came on Thursday; he came on Friday; and he came on Saturday. It is true that each visit began, continued, or concluded with a declaration of love, but in between there was much room for silence. They sat on either side of the fireplace and sometimes the Archduke knocked over the fire-irons and Orlando picked them up again. Then the Archduke would bethink him how he had shot an elk in Sweden, and Orlando would ask, was it a very big elk, and the Archduke would say that it was not as big as the reindeer which he had shot in Norway; and Orlando would ask, had he ever shot a tiger, and the Archduke would say he had shot an albatross, and Orlando would say (half hiding her yawn) was an albatross as big as an elephant, and the Archduke would say—something very sensible, no doubt, but Orlando heard it not, for she was looking at her writing-table, out of the window, at the door. Upon which the Archduke would say, "I adore you", at the very same moment that Orlando said "Look, it's beginning to rain", at which they were both much embarrassed, and blushed scarlet, and could neither of them think what to say next. Indeed, Orlando was at her wit's end what to talk about and had she not bethought her of a game called Fly Loo, at which great sums of money can be lost with very little expense of spirit, she would have had to marry him, she supposed; for how else to get rid of him she knew not. By this device, however, and it was a simple one, needing only three lumps of sugar and a sufficiency of flies, the embarrassment of conversation was overcome and the necessity of marriage avoided. For now, the Archduke would bet her five hundred pounds to a tester that a fly would settle on this lump and not on that. Thus, they would have occupation for a whole morning watching the flies (who were naturally sluggish at this season and often spent an hour or so circling round the ceiling) until at length some fine blue-bottle made his choice and the match was won. Many hundreds of pounds changed hands between them at this game, which the Archduke, who was a born gambler, swore was every bit as good as horse racing, and vowed he could play at for ever. But Orlando soon began to weary.

"What's the good of being a fine young woman in the prime of life", she asked, "if I have to pass all my mornings watching blue-bottles with an Archduke?"

She began to detest the sight of sugar; flies made her dizzy. Some way out of the difficulty there must be, she supposed, but she was still awkward in the arts of her sex, and as she could no longer knock a man over the head or run him through the body with a rapier, she could think of no better method than this. She caught a blue-bottle, gently pressed the life out of it (it was half dead already, or her kindness for the dumb creatures would not have permitted it) and secured it by a drop of gum arabic to a lump of sugar. While the Archduke was gazing at the ceiling, she deftly substituted this lump for the one she had laid her money on, and crying "Loo Loo!" declared that she had won her bet. Her reckoning was that the Archduke, with all his knowledge of sport and horse-racing, would detect the fraud and, as to cheat at Loo is the most heinous of crimes, and men have been banished from the society of mankind to that of apes in the tropics for ever because of it, she calculated that he would be manly enough to refuse to have anything further to do with her. But she misjudged the simplicity of the amiable nobleman. He was no nice judge of flies. A dead fly looked to him much the same as a living one. She played the trick twenty times on him and he paid her over £17,250 (which is about £40,885: 6: 8[5] of our own money) before Orlando cheated so grossly that even he could be deceived no longer. When he realised the truth at last, a painful scene ensued. The Archduke rose to his full height. He coloured scarlet. Tears rolled down his cheeks one by one. That she had won a fortune from him was nothing—she was welcome to it; that she had deceived him was something—it hurt him to think her capable of it; but that she had cheated at Loo was everything. To love a woman who cheated at play was, he said, impossible. Here he broke down completely. Happily, he said, recovering slightly, there were no witnesses. She was, after all, only a woman, he said. In short, he was preparing in the chivalry of his heart to forgive her and had bent to ask her pardon for the violence of his language, when she cut the matter short, as he stooped his proud head, by dropping a small toad between his skin and his shirt.

In justice to her, it must be said that she would infinitely have preferred a rapier. Toads are clammy things to conceal about one's person a whole morning. But if rapiers are forbidden, one must have recourse to toads. Moreover toads and laughter between them sometimes do what cold steel cannot. She laughed. The Archduke blushed. She laughed. The Archduke cursed. She laughed. The Archduke slammed the door.

"Heaven be praised!" cried Orlando still laughing. She heard the sound of chariot wheels driven at a furious pace down the courtyard. She heard them rattle along the road. Fainter and fainter the sound became. Now it faded away altogether.

"I am alone," said Orlando, aloud since there was no one to hear.

That silence is more profound after noise still wants the confirmation of science. But that loneliness is more apparent directly after one has been made love to, many women would take their oath. As the sound of the Archduke's chariot wheels died away, Orlando felt drawing further from her and further from her an Archduke (she did not mind that), a fortune (she did not mind that), a title (she did not mind that), the safety and circumstance of married life (she did not mind that), but life she heard going from her, and a lover. "Life and a lover," she murmured; and going to her writing-table she dipped her pen in the ink and wrote:

5. 40,855 pounds, six shillings, and eight pence.

"Life and a lover"—a line which did not scan and made no sense with what went before—something about the proper way of dipping sheep to avoid the scab. Reading it over she blushed and repeated,

"Life and a lover." Then laying her pen aside she went into her bedroom, stood in front of her mirror, and arranged her pearls about her neck. Then since pearls do not show to advantage against a morning gown of sprigged cotton, she changed to a dove grey taffeta; thence to one of peach bloom; thence to a wine-coloured brocade. Perhaps a dash of powder was needed, and if her hair were disposed—so—about her brow, it might become her. Then she slipped her feet into pointed slippers, and drew an emerald ring upon her finger. "Now," she said when all was ready and lit the silver sconces on either side of the mirror. What woman would not have kindled to see what Orlando saw then burning in the snow—for all about the looking-glass were snowy lawns, and she was like a fire, a burning bush, and the candle flames about her head were silver leaves; or again, the glass was green water, and she a mermaid, slung with pearls, a siren in a cave, singing so that oarsmen leant from their boats and fell down, down to embrace her; so dark, so bright, so hard, so soft, was she, so astonishingly seductive that it was a thousand pities that there was no one there to put it in plain English, and say outright, "Damn it, Madam, you are loveliness incarnate," which was the truth. Even Orlando (who had no conceit of her person) knew it, for she smiled the involuntary smile which women smile when their own beauty, which seems not their own, forms like a drop falling or a fountain rising and confronts them all of a sudden in the glass—this smile she smiled and then she listened for a moment and heard only the leaves blowing and the sparrows twittering, and then she sighed, "Life, a lover," and then she turned on her heel with extraordinary rapidity; whipped her pearls from her neck, stripped the satins from her back, stood erect in the neat black silk knickerbockers of an ordinary nobleman, and rang the bell. When the servant came, she told him to order a coach and six to be in readiness instantly. She was summoned by urgent affairs to London. Within an hour of the Archduke's departure, off she drove.

And as she drove, we may seize the opportunity, since the landscape was of a simple English kind which needs no description, to draw the reader's attention more particularly than we could at the moment to one or two remarks which have slipped in here and there in the course of the narrative. For example, it may have been observed that Orlando hid her manuscripts when interrupted.[6] Next, that she

---

6. In *A Room of One's Own*, written in the same year that *Orlando* was published, Woolf contends that middle-class women writers would have had to write in the drawing

looked long and intently in the glass; and now, as she drove to London, one might notice her starting and suppressing a cry when the horses galloped faster than she liked. Her modesty as to her writing, her vanity as to her person, her fears for her safety all seems to hint that what was said a short time ago about there being no change in Orlando the man and Orlando the woman, was ceasing to be altogether true. She was becoming a little more modest, as women are, of her brains, and a little more vain, as women are, of her person. Certain susceptibilities were asserting themselves, and others were diminishing. The change of clothes had, some philosophers will say, much to do with it. Vain trifles as they seem, clothes have, they say, more important offices than merely to keep us warm. They change our view of the world and the world's view of us. For example, when Captain Bartolus saw Orlando's skirt, he had an awning stretched for her immediately, pressed her to take another slice of beef, and invited her to go ashore with him in the long-boat. These compliments would certainly not have been paid her had her skirts, instead of flowing, been cut tight to her legs in the fashion of breeches. And when we are paid compliments, it behoves us to make some return. Orlando curtseyed; she complied; she flattered the good man's humours as she would not have done had his neat breeches been a woman's skirts, and his braided coat a woman's satin bodice. Thus, there is much to support the view that it is clothes that wear us and not we them; we may make them take the mould of arm or breast, but they mould our hearts, our brains, our tongues to their liking. So, having now worn skirts for a considerable time, a certain change was visible in Orlando, which is to be found if the reader will look at page 86, even in her face. If we compare the picture of Orlando as a man with that of Orlando as a woman we shall see that though both are undoubtedly one and the same person, there are certain changes. The man has his hand free to seize his sword, the woman must use hers to keep the satins from slipping from her shoulders. The man looks the world full in the face, as if it were made for his uses and fashioned to his liking. The woman takes a sidelong glance at it, full of subtlety, even of suspicion. Had they both worn the same clothes, it is possible that their outlook might have been the same.

That is the view of some philosophers and wise ones, but on the whole, we incline to another. The difference between the sexes is, happily, one of great profundity. Clothes are but a symbol of

---

room and thus be subject to constant interruption. Moreover, they would have been socialized to hide the fact that they were writing: "Jane Austen hid her manuscripts or covered them with a piece of blotting-paper" (67). Orlando was wealthy and not of the middle class, but as an unmarried woman at the time, she would have had to keep up the appearance of respectability, and writing was not considered a respectable occupation for a woman.

something hid deep beneath. It was a change in Orlando herself that dictated her choice of a woman's dress and of a woman's sex. And perhaps in this she was only expressing rather more openly than usual—openness indeed was the soul of her nature—something that happens to most people without being thus plainly expressed. For here again, we come to a dilemma. Different though the sexes are, they intermix.[7] In every human being a vacillation from one sex to the other takes place, and often it is only the clothes that keep the male or female likeness, while underneath the sex is the very opposite of what it is above. Of the complications and confusions which thus result everyone has had experience; but here we leave the general question and note only the odd effect it had in the particular case of Orlando herself.

For it was this mixture in her of man and woman, one being uppermost and then the other, that often gave her conduct an unexpected turn. The curious of her own sex would argue, for example, if Orlando was a woman, how did she never take more than ten minutes to dress? And were not her clothes chosen rather at random, and sometimes worn rather shabby? And then they would say, still, she has none of the formality of a man, or a man's love of power. She is excessively tender-hearted. She could not endure to see a donkey beaten or a kitten drowned. Yet again, they noted, she detested household matters, was up at dawn and out among the fields in summer before the sun had risen. No farmer knew more about the crops than she did. She could drink with the best and liked games of hazard. She rode well and drove six horses at a gallop over London Bridge. Yet again, though bold and active as a man, it was remarked that the sight of another in danger brought on the most womanly palpitations. She would burst into tears on slight provocation. She was unversed in geography and found mathematics intolerable and held some caprices which are more common among women than men, as for instance, that to travel south is to travel downhill. Whether, then, Orlando was most man or woman, it is difficult to say and cannot now be decided. For her coach was now rattling on the cobbles. She had reached her home in the city. The steps were being let down; the iron gates were being opened. She was entering her father's house at Blackfriars, which, though fashion was fast deserting that end of the town, was still a pleasant, roomy mansion, with gardens running down to the river, and a pleasant grove of nut trees to walk in.

---

7. Woolf suggests a similar idea in *A Room of One's Own*, "in each of us, two powers preside, one male, one female; and in the man's brain, the man predominates over the woman, and in the woman's brain, the woman over the man. The normal and comfortable state of being is that when the two live in harmony together, spiritually cooperating" (98). See also p. 200 in this volume.

Here she took up her lodging and began instantly to look about her for what she had come in search of—that is to say, life and a lover. About the first there might be some doubt; the second she found without the least difficulty two days after her arrival. It was a Tuesday that she came to town. On Thursday she went for a walk in the Mall, as was then the habit of persons of quality. She had not made more than a turn or two of the avenue before she was observed by a little knot of vulgar people who go there to spy upon their betters. As she came past them, a common woman carrying a child at her breast stepped forward, peered familiarly into Orlando's face, and cried out, "Lawk upon us, if it ain't the Lady Orlando!" Her companions came crowding round, and Orlando found herself in a moment the centre of a mob of staring citizens and tradesmen's wives, all eager to gaze upon the heroine of the celebrated lawsuit. Such was the interest that the case excited in the minds of the common people. She might, indeed, have found herself gravely discommoded by the pressure of the crowd—she had forgotten that ladies are not supposed to walk in public places alone—had not a tall gentleman at once stepped forward and offered her the protection of his arm. It was the Archduke. She was overcome with distress and yet with some amusement at the sight. Not only had this magnanimous nobleman forgiven her, but in order to show that he took her levity with the toad in good part, he had procured a jewel made in the shape of that reptile which he pressed upon her with a repetition of his suit as he handed her to her coach.

What with the crowd, what with the Duke, what with the jewel, she drove home in the vilest temper imaginable. Was it impossible then to go for a walk without being half-suffocated, presented with a toad set in emeralds, and asked in marriage by an Archduke? She took a kinder view of the case next day when she found on her breakfast table half a dozen billets from some of the greatest ladies in the land—Lady Suffolk, Lady Salisbury, Lady Chesterfield, Lady Tavistock, and others who reminded her in the politest manner of old alliances between their families and her own, and desired the honour of her acquaintance. Next day, which was a Saturday, many of these great ladies waited on her in person. On Tuesday, about noon, their footmen brought cards of invitation to various routs, dinners, and assemblies in the near future; so that Orlando was launched without delay, and with some splash and foam at that, upon the waters of London society.

To give a truthful account of London society at that or indeed at any other time, is beyond the powers of the biographer or the historian. Only those who have little need of the truth, and no respect for it—the poets and the novelists—can be trusted to do it, for this is one of the cases where the truth does not exist. Nothing exists.

The whole thing is a miasma—a mirage. To make our meaning plain—Orlando would come home from one of these routs at three or four in the morning with cheeks like a Christmas tree and eyes like stars. She would untie a lace, pace the room a score of times, untie another lace, stop, and pace the room again. Often the sun would be blazing over Southwark chimneys before she could persuade herself to get into bed, and there she would lie, pitching and tossing, laughing and sighing for an hour or longer before she slept at last. And what was all this stir about? Society. And what had society said or done to throw a reasonable lady into such an excitement? In plain language, nothing. Rack her memory as she would, next day Orlando could never remember a single word to magnify into the name something. Lord O. had been gallant. Lord A. polite. The Marquis of C. charming. Mr. M. amusing. But when she tried to recollect in what their gallantry, politeness, charm, or wit had consisted, she was bound to suppose her memory at fault, for she could not name a thing. It was the same always. Nothing remained over the next day, yet the excitement of the moment was intense. Thus we are forced to conclude that society is one of those brews such as skilled housekeepers serve hot about Christmas time, whose flavour depends upon the proper mixing and stirring of a dozen different ingredients. Take one out, and it is in itself insipid. Take away Lord O., Lord A., Lord C., or Mr. M. and separately each is nothing. Stir them all together and they combine to give off the most intoxicating of flavours, the most seductive of scents. Yet this intoxication, this seductiveness, entirely evade our analysis. At one and the same time, therefore, society is everything and society is nothing. Society is the most powerful concoction in the world and society has no existence whatsoever. Such monsters the poets and the novelists alone can deal with; with such something-nothings their works are stuffed out to prodigious size; and to them with the best will in the world we are content to leave it.

Following the example of our predecessors, therefore, we will only say that society in the reign of Queen Anne[8] was of unparalleled brilliance. To have the entry there was the aim of every well-bred person. The graces were supreme. Fathers instructed their sons, mothers their daughters. No education was complete for either sex which did not include the science of deportment, the art of bowing and curtseying, the management of the sword and the fan, the care of the teeth, the conduct of the leg, the flexibility of the knee, the proper methods of entering and leaving the room, with a thousand

8. Queen Anne, Queen of England, Scotland, and Ireland (1702–07) and, after the Acts of Union between Scotland and England, Queen of Great Britain and Ireland (1707–14).

etceteras, such as will immediately suggest themselves to anybody who has himself been in society. Since Orlando had won the praise of Queen Elizabeth for the way she handed a bowl of rose water as a boy, it must be supposed that she was sufficiently expert to pass muster. Yet it is true that there was an absent mindedness about her which sometimes made her clumsy; she was apt to think of poetry when she should have been thinking of taffeta; her walk was a little too much of a stride for a woman, perhaps, and her gestures, being abrupt, might endanger a cup of tea on occasion.

Whether this slight disability was enough to counterbalance the splendour of her bearing, or whether she inherited a drop too much of that black humour which ran in the veins of all her race, certain it is that she had not been in the world more than a score of times before she might have been heard to ask herself, had there been anybody but her spaniel Pippin to hear her, "What the devil is the matter with me?" The occasion was Tuesday, the 16th of June 1712; she had just returned from a great ball at Arlington House; the dawn was in the sky, and she was pulling off her stockings. "I don't care if I never meet another soul as long as I live," cried Orlando, bursting into tears. Lovers she had in plenty, but life, which is, after all, of some importance in its way, escaped her. "Is this", she asked—but there was none to answer, "is this", she finished her sentence all the same, "what people call life?" The spaniel raised her forepaw in token of sympathy. The spaniel licked Orlando with her tongue. Orlando stroked the spaniel with her hand. Orlando kissed the spaniel with her lips. In short, there was the truest sympathy between them that can be between a dog and its mistress, and yet it cannot be denied that the dumbness of animals is a great impediment to the refinements of intercourse. They wag their tails; they bow the front part of the body and elevate the hind; they roll, they jump, they paw, they whine, they bark, they slobber, they have all sorts of ceremonies and artifices of their own, but the whole thing is of no avail, since speak they cannot. Such was her quarrel, she thought, setting the dog gently on to the floor, with the great people at Arlington House. They, too, wag their tails, bow, roll, jump, paw, and slobber, but talk they cannot. "All these months that I've been out in the world", said Orlando, pitching one stocking across the room, "I've heard nothing but what Pippin might have said. I'm cold. I'm happy. I'm hungry. I've caught a mouse. I've buried a bone. Please kiss my nose." And it was not enough.

How, in so short a time, she had passed from intoxication to disgust we will only seek to explain by supposing that this mysterious composition which we call society, is nothing absolutely good or bad in itself, but has a spirit in it, volatile but potent, which either makes you drunk when you think it, as Orlando thought it, delightful, or gives you a headache when you think it, as Orlando thought it, repulsive. That the faculty of speech has much to do with it either way, we take leave to doubt. Often a dumb hour is the most ravishing of all; brilliant wit can be tedious beyond description. But to the poets we leave it, and so on with our story.

Orlando threw the second stocking after the first and went to bed dismally enough, determined that she would forswear society for ever. But again as it turned out, she was too hasty in coming to her conclusions. For the very next morning she woke to find, among the usual cards of invitation upon her table, one from a certain great Lady, the Countess of R. Having determined overnight that she would never go into society again, we can only explain Orlando's behaviour—she sent a messenger hot-foot to R—— House to say that she would attend her Ladyship with all the pleasure in the world— by the fact that she was still suffering from the effect of three honeyed words dropped into her ear on the deck of the *Enamoured Lady* by Captain Nicholas Benedict Bartolus as they sailed down the Thames. Addison, Dryden, Pope, he had said, pointing to the Cocoa Tree, and Addison, Dryden, Pope had chimed in her head like an incantation ever since.[9] Who can credit such folly? but so it was. All her experience with Nick Greene had taught her nothing. Such names still exercised over her the most powerful fascination. Something, perhaps, we must believe in, and as Orlando, we have said, had no belief in the usual divinities she bestowed her credulity upon great men—yet with a distinction. Admirals, soldiers, statesmen, moved her not at all. But the very thought of a great writer stirred her to such a pitch of belief that she almost believed him to be invisible. Her instinct was a sound one. One can only believe entirely, perhaps, in what one cannot see. The little glimpse she had of these great men from the deck of the ship was of the nature of a vision. That the cup was china, or the gazette paper, she doubted. When Lord O. said one day that he had dined with Dryden the night before, she flatly disbelieved him. Now, the Lady R.'s reception room had the reputation of being the antechamber to the presence room of genius; it was the place where men and women met to swing censers and chant hymns to the bust of genius in a niche in the wall. Sometimes the God himself vouchsafed his presence for a moment. Intellect alone admitted the suppliant, and nothing (so the report ran) was said inside that was not witty.

It was thus with great trepidation that Orlando entered the room. She found a company already assembled in a semicircle round the fire. Lady R., an oldish lady, of dark complexion, with a black lace

9. For more on Woolf's critique of the "great men" of literary history, see Jane de Gay in this volume (pp. 211–20).

mantilla on her head, was seated in a great arm-chair in the centre. Thus being somewhat deaf, she could control the conversation on both sides of her. On both sides of her sat men and women of the highest distinction. Every man, it was said, had been a Prime Minister and every woman, it was whispered, had been the mistress of a king. Certain it is that all were brilliant, and all were famous. Orlando took her seat with a deep reverence in silence. . . . After three hours, she curtseyed profoundly and left.

But what, the reader may ask with some exasperation, happened in between? In three hours, such a company must have said the wittiest, the profoundest, the most interesting things in the world. So it would seem indeed. But the fact appears to be that they said nothing. It is a curious characteristic which they share with all the most brilliant societies that the world has seen. Old Madame du Deffand and her friends talked for fifty years without stopping. And of it all, what remains? Perhaps three witty sayings. So that we are at liberty to suppose either that nothing was said, or that nothing witty was said, or that the fraction of three witty sayings lasted eighteen thousand two hundred and fifty nights, which does not leave a liberal allowance of wit for any one of them.

The truth would seem to be—if we dare use such a word in such a connection—that all these groups of people lie under an enchantment. The hostess is our modern Sibyl. She is a witch who lays her guests under a spell. In this house they think themselves happy; in that witty; in a third profound. It is all an illusion (which is nothing against it, for illusions are the most valuable and necessary of all things, and she who can create one is among the world's greatest benefactors), but as it is notorious that illusions are shattered by conflict with reality, so no real happiness, no real wit, no real profundity are tolerated where the illusion prevails. This serves to explain why Madame du Deffand said no more than three witty things in the course of fifty years. Had she said more, her circle would have been destroyed. The witticism, as it left her lips, bowled over the current conversation as a cannon ball lays low the violets and the daisies. When she made her famous 'mot de Saint Denis' the very grass was singed. Disillusionment and desolation followed. Not a word was uttered. "Spare us another such, for Heaven's sake, Madame!" her friends cried with one accord. And she obeyed. For almost seventeen years she said nothing memorable and all went well. The beautiful counterpane of illusion lay unbroken on her circle as it lay unbroken on the circle of Lady R. The guests thought that they were happy, thought that they were witty, thought that they were profound, and, as they thought this, other people thought it still more strongly; and so it got about that nothing was more delightful than one of Lady R.'s assemblies; everyone envied those who were admitted;

those who were admitted envied themselves because other people envied them; and so there seemed no end to it—except that which we have now to relate.

For about the third time Orlando went there a certain incident occurred. She was still under the illusion that she was listening to the most brilliant epigrams in the world, though, as a matter of fact, old General C. was only saying, at some length, how the gout had left his left leg and gone to his right, while Mr. L. interrupted when any proper name was mentioned, "R.? Oh! I know Billy R. as well as I know myself. S.? My dearest friend. T.? Stayed with him a fort-night in Yorkshire"—which, such is the force of illusion, sounded like the wittiest repartee, the most searching comment upon human life, and kept the company in a roar; when the door opened and a little gentleman entered whose name Orlando did not catch. Soon a curiously disagreeable sensation came over her. To judge from their faces, the rest began to feel it as well. One gentleman said there was a draught. The Marchioness of C. feared a cat must be under the sofa. It was as if their eyes were being slowly opened after a pleas-ant dream and nothing met them but a cheap wash-stand and a dirty counterpane. It was as if the fumes of some delicious wine were slowly leaving them. Still the General talked and still Mr. L. remem-bered. But it became more and more apparent how red the Gener-al's neck was, how bald Mr. L.'s head was. As for what they said—nothing more tedious and trivial could be imagined. Every-body fidgeted and those who had fans yawned behind them. At last Lady R. rapped with hers upon the arm of her great chair. Both gen-tlemen stopped talking.

Then the little gentleman said,

He said next,

He said finally,[†]

Here, it cannot be denied, was true wit, true wisdom, true pro-fundity. The company was thrown into complete dismay. One such saying was bad enough; but three, one after another, on the same evening! No society could survive it.

"Mr. Pope," said old Lady R. in a voice trembling with sarcastic fury, "you are pleased to be witty." Mr. Pope flushed red. Nobody spoke a word. They sat in dead silence some twenty minutes. Then, one by one, they rose and slunk from the room. That they would ever come back after such an experience was doubtful. Link-boys could be heard calling their coaches all down South Audley Street. Doors were slammed and carriages drove off. Orlando found herself near Mr. Pope on the staircase. His lean and misshapen frame was shaken

---

[†] These sayings are too well known to require repetition, and besides, they are all to be found in his published works [Woolf's note].

by a variety of emotions. Darts of malice, rage, triumph, wit, and terror (he was shaking like a leaf) shot from his eyes. He looked like some squat reptile set with a burning topaz in its forehead. At the same time, the strangest tempest of emotion seized now upon the luckless Orlando. A disillusionment so complete as that inflicted not an hour ago leaves the mind rocking from side to side. Everything appears ten times more bare and stark than before. It is a moment fraught with the highest danger for the human spirit. Women turn nuns and men priests in such moments. In such moments, rich men sign away their wealth; and happy men cut their throats with carving knives. Orlando would have done all willingly, but there was a rasher thing still for her to do, and this she did. She invited Mr. Pope to come home with her.

For if it is rash to walk into a lion's den unarmed, rash to navigate the Atlantic in a rowing boat, rash to stand on one foot on the top of St. Paul's, it is still more rash to go home alone with a poet. A poet is Atlantic and lion in one. While one drowns us the other gnaws us. If we survive the teeth, we succumb to the waves. A man who can destroy illusions is both beast and flood. Illusions are to the soul what atmosphere is to the earth. Roll up that tender air and the plant dies, the colour fades. The earth we walk on is a parched cinder, it is marl we tread and fiery cobbles scorch our feet. By the truth we are undone. Life is a dream. 'Tis waking that kills us. He who robs us of our dreams robs us of our life—(and so on for six pages if you will, but the style is tedious and may well be dropped.)[1]

On this showing, however, Orlando should have been a heap of cinders by the time the chariot drew up at her house in Blackfriars. That she was still flesh and blood, though certainly exhausted, is entirely due to a fact to which we drew attention earlier in the narrative. The less we see the more we believe. Now the streets that lie between Mayfair and Blackfriars were at that time very imperfectly lit. True, the lightning was a great improvement upon that of the Elizabethan age. Then the benighted traveller had to trust to the stars or the red flame of some night watchman to save him from the gravel pits at Park Lane or the oak woods where swine rootled in the Tottenham Court Road. But even so it wanted much of our modern efficiency. Lamp-posts lit with oil-lamps occurred every two hundred yards or so, but between lay a considerable stretch of pitch darkness. Thus for ten minutes Orlando and Mr. Pope would be in blackness; and then for about half a minute again in the light. A very strange state of mind was thus bred in Orlando. As the light faded,

---

1. Here Woolf is employing the rhetorical devices of the mock heroic, a style for which Alexander Pope was famous. His 1712 poem *Rape of the Lock* mocks British high society, especially women's role in it.

she began to feel steal over her the most delicious balm. "This is
indeed a very great honour for a young woman, to be driving with
Mr. Pope," she began to think, looking at the outline of his nose. "I
am the most blessed of my sex. Half an inch from me—indeed, I
feel the knot of his knee ribbons pressing against my thigh—is the
greatest wit in Her Majesty's dominions. Future ages will think of
us with curiosity and envy me with fury." Here came the lamppost
again. "What a foolish wretch I am!" she thought. "There is no such
thing as fame and glory. Ages to come will never cast a thought on
me or on Mr. Pope either. What's an 'age', indeed? What are 'we'?"
and their progress through Berkeley Square seemed the groping of
two blind ants, momentarily thrown together without interest or
concern in common, across a blackened desert. She shivered. But
here again was darkness. Her illusion revived. "How noble his brow
is," she thought (mistaking a hump on a cushion for Mr. Pope's forehead in the darkness). "What a weight of genius lives in it! What
wit, wisdom, and truth—what a wealth of all those jewels, indeed,
for which people are ready to barter their lives! Yours is the only light
that burns for ever. But for you the human pilgrimage would be performed in utter darkness"; (here the coach gave a great lurch as it
fell into a rut in Park Lane) "without genius we should be upset and
undone. Most august, most lucid of beams,"—thus she was apostro-
phising the hump on the cushion when they drove beneath one of
the street lamps in Berkeley Square and she realized her mistake.
Mr. Pope had a forehead no bigger than another man's. "Wretched
man," she thought, "How you have deceived me! I took that hump
for your forehead. When one sees you plain, how ignoble, how despi-
cable you are! Deformed and weakly, there is nothing to venerate in
you, much to pity, most to despise."

Again they were in darkness and her anger became modified
directly she could see nothing but the poet's knees.

"But it is I that am a wretch," she reflected, once they were in complete obscurity again, "for base as you may be, am I not still baser?
It is you who nourish and protect me, you who scare the wild beast,
frighten the savage, make me clothes of the silkworm's wool, and
carpet of the sheep's. If I want to worship, have you not provided
me with an image of yourself and set it in the sky? Are not evidences
of your care everywhere? How humble, how grateful, how docile,
should I not be, therefore? Let it be all my joy to serve, honour, and
obey you."

Here they reached the big lamp-post at the corner of what is now
Piccadilly Circus. The light blazed in her eyes, and she saw, besides
some degraded creatures of her own sex, two wretched pigmies on
a stark desert land. Both were naked, solitary, and defenceless.
The one was powerless to help the other. Each had enough to do to

look after itself. Looking Mr. Pope full in the face, "It is equally vain", she thought, "for you to think you can protect me, or for me to think I can worship you. The light of truth beats upon us without shadow, and the light of truth is damnably unbecoming to us both."

All this time, of course, they went on talking agreeably, as people of birth and education use, about the Queen's temper and the Prime Minister's gout, while the coach went from light to darkness down the Haymarket, along the Strand, up Fleet Street, and reached, at length, her house in Blackfriars. For some time the dark spaces between the lamps had been becoming brighter and the lamps themselves less bright—that is to say, the sun was rising, and it was in the equable but confused light of a summer's morning in which everything is seen but nothing is seen distinctly that they alighted, Mr. Pope handing Orlando from her carriage and Orlando curtseying Mr. Pope to precede her into her mansion with the most scrupulous attention to the rites of the Graces.

From the foregoing passage, however, it must not be supposed that genius (but the disease is now stamped out in the British Isles, the late Lord Tennyson, it is said, being the last person to suffer from it) is constantly alight, for then we should see everything plain and perhaps should be scorched to death in the process. Rather it resembles the lighthouse in its working, which sends one ray and then no more for a time; save that genius is much more capricious in its manifestations and may flash six or seven beams in quick succession (as Mr. Pope did that night) and then lapse into darkness for a year or for ever. To steer by its beams is therefore impossible, and when the dark spell is on them men of genius are, it is said, much like other people.

It was happy for Orlando, though at first disappointing, that this should be so, for she now began to live much in the company of men of genius. Nor were they so different from the rest of us as one might have supposed. Addison, Pope, Swift,[2] proved, she found, to be fond of tea. They liked arbours. They collected little bits of coloured glass. They adored grottos. Rank was not distasteful to them. Praise was delightful. They wore plum-coloured suits one day and grey another. Mr. Swift had a fine malacca cane.[3] Mr. Addison scented his handkerchiefs. Mr. Pope suffered with his head. A piece of gossip did not come amiss. Nor were they without their jealousies. (We are jotting down a few reflections that came to Orlando higgledy-piggledy.) At first, she was annoyed with herself for noticing such trifles, and kept

2. Jonathan Swift (1667–1745), Irish satirist and dean of St. Patrick's Cathedral in Dublin, known for writing *Gulliver's Travels*, *A Tale of a Tub*, and "A Modest Proposal."
3. A fine cane made of rattan wood from trees native to Sumatra.

a book in which to write down their memorable sayings, but the page remained empty. All the same, her spirits revived, and she took to tearing up her cards of invitation to great parties; kept her evenings free; began to look forward to Mr. Pope's visit, to Mr. Addison's, to Mr. Swift's—and so on and so on. If the reader will here refer to the *Rape of the Lock*, to the *Spectator*, to *Gulliver's Travels*, he will understand precisely what these mysterious words may mean. Indeed, biographers and critics might save themselves all their labours if readers would only take this advice. For when we read:

> Whether the Nymph shall break Diana's Law,
> Or some frail China Jar receive a Flaw,
> Or stain her Honour, or her new Brocade,
> Forget her Pray'rs or miss a Masquerade,
> Or lose her Heart, or Necklace, at a Ball.

—we know as if we heard him how Mr. Pope's tongue flickered like a lizard's, how his eyes flashed, how his hand trembled, how he loved, how he lied, how he suffered. In short, every secret of a writer's soul, every experience of his life, every quality of his mind is written large in his works, yet we require critics to explain the one and biographers to expound the other. That time hangs heavy on people's hands is the only explanation of the monstrous growth.

So, now that we have read a page or two of the *Rape of the Lock*, we know exactly why Orlando was so much amused and so much frightened and so very bright-cheeked and bright-eyed that afternoon.

Mrs. Nelly then knocked at the door to say that Mr. Addison waited on her Ladyship. At this, Mr. Pope got up with a wry smile, made his congee, and limped off. In came Mr. Addison. Let us, as he takes his seat, read the following passage from the *Spectator*:

"I consider woman as a beautiful, romantic animal, that may be adorned with furs and feathers, pearls and diamonds, ores and silks. The lynx shall cast its skin at her feet to make her a tippet, the peacock, parrot and swan shall pay contributions to her muff; the sea shall be searched for shells, and the rocks for gems, and every part of nature furnish out its share towards the embellishment of a creature that is the most consummate work of it. All this, I shall indulge them in, but as for the petticoat I have been speaking of, I neither can, nor will allow it."

We hold that gentleman, cocked hat and all, in the hollow of our hands. Look once more into the crystal. Is he not clear to the very wrinkle in his stocking? Does not every ripple and curve of his wit lie exposed before us, and his benignity and his timidity and his urbanity and the fact that he would marry a Countess and die very respectably in the end? All is clear. And when Mr. Addison has said his say, there is a terrific rap at the door, and Mr. Swift, who had these arbitrary ways with him, walks in unannounced. One moment, where is *Gulliver's Travels*? Here it is! Let us read a passage from the voyage to the Houyhnhnms:

"I enjoyed perfect Health of Body and Tranquillity of Mind; I did not find the Treachery or Inconstancy of a Friend, nor the Injuries of a secret or open Enemy. I had no occasion of bribing, flattering or pimping, to procure the Favour of any great Man or of his Minion. I wanted no Fence against Fraud or Oppression; Here was neither Physician to destroy my Body, nor Lawyer to ruin my Fortune; No Informer to watch my Words, and Actions, or forge Accusations against me for Hire: Here were no Gibers, Censurers, Backbiters, Pickpockets, Highwaymen, House-breakers, Attorneys, Bawds, Buffoons, Gamesters, Politicians, Wits, splenetick tedious Talkers. . . ."

But stop, stop your iron pelt of words, lest you flay us all alive, and yourself too! Nothing can be plainer than that violent man. He is so coarse and yet so clean; so brutal, yet so kind; scorns the whole world, yet talks baby language to a girl, and will die, can we doubt it? in a madhouse.[4]

So Orlando poured out tea for them all; and sometimes, when the weather was fine, she carried them down to the country with her, and feasted them royally in the Round Parlour, which she had hung with their pictures all in a circle, so that Mr. Pope could not say that Mr. Addison came before him, or the other way about. They were very witty, too (but their wit is all in their books), and taught her the most important part of style, which is the natural run of the voice in speaking—a quality which none that has not heard it can imitate, not Greene even, with all his skill; for it is born of the air and breaks like a wave on the furniture, and rolls and fades away, and is never to be recaptured, least of all by those who prick up their ears, half a century later, and try. They taught her this, merely by the cadence of their voices in speech; so that her style changed somewhat, and she wrote some very pleasant, witty verses and characters in prose. And so she lavished her wine on them and put bank-notes, which they took very kindly, beneath their plates at dinner, and accepted their dedications, and thought herself highly honoured by the exchange.

---

4. There are different speculations about what illnesses Jonathan Swift may have had later in his life. Most accounts agree that he suffered a devastating stroke in the last years of his life and in 1742 he was deemed unable to care for himself and put under guardianship. He bequeathed a large sum of money to found St. Patrick's Hospital, what we would now call a psychiatric hospital. See for example JMS Pearce, "The Legacy and Maladies of Jonathan Swift," *Hektoen International: A Journal of Medical Humanities* (Fall 2019), online.

Thus time ran on, and Orlando could often be heard saying to herself with an emphasis which might, perhaps, make the hearer a little suspicious, "Upon my soul, what a life this is!" (For she was still in search of that commodity.) But circumstances soon forced her to consider the matter more narrowly.

One day she was pouring out tea for Mr. Pope while, as anyone can tell from the verses quoted above, he sat very bright-eyed, observant, and all crumpled up in a chair by her side.

"Lord," she thought, as she raised the sugar tongs, "how women in ages to come will envy me! And yet——" she paused; for Mr. Pope needed her attention. And yet—let us finish her thought for her—when anybody says "How future ages will envy me", it is safe to say that they are extremely uneasy at the present moment. Was this life quite so exciting, quite so flattering, quite so glorious as it sounds when the memoir writer has done his work upon it? For one thing, Orlando had a positive hatred of tea; for another, the intellect, divine as it is, and all-worshipful, has a habit of lodging in the most seedy of carcases, and often, alas, acts the cannibal among the other faculties so that often, where the Mind is biggest, the Heart, the Senses, Magnanimity, Charity, Tolerance, Kindliness, and the rest of them scarcely have room to breathe. Then the high opinion poets have of themselves; then the low one they have of others; then the enmities, injuries, envies, and repartees in which they are constantly engaged; then the volubility with which they impart them; then the rapacity with which they demand sympathy for them; all this, one may whisper, lest the wits may overhear us, makes pouring out tea a more precarious and, indeed, arduous occupation than is generally allowed. Added to which (we whisper again lest the women may overhear us), there is a little secret which men share among them; Lord Chesterfield whispered it to his son with strict injunctions to secrecy, "Women are but children of a larger growth. . . . A man of sense only trifles with them, plays with them, humours and flatters them", which, since children always hear what they are not meant to, and sometimes, even, grow up, may have somehow leaked out, so that the whole ceremony of pouring out tea is a curious one. A woman knows very well that, though a wit sends her his poems, praises her judgment, solicits her criticism, and drinks her tea, this by no means signifies that he respects her opinions, admires her understanding, or will refuse, though the rapier is denied him, to run her through the body with his pen. All this, we say, whisper it as low as we can, may have leaked out by now; so that even with the cream jug suspended and the sugar tongs distended the ladies may fidget a little, look out of the window a little, yawn a little, and so let the sugar fall with a great plop—as Orlando did now—into Mr. Pope's tea. Never was any mortal so ready to suspect an insult or so quick to avenge one as Mr. Pope. He turned to Orlando and presented her instantly with the rough draught of a certain famous line in the "Characters of Women". Much polish was afterwards bestowed on it, but even in the original it was striking enough. Orlando received it with a curtsey. Mr. Pope left her with a bow. Orlando, to cool her cheeks, for really she felt as if the little man had struck her, strolled in the nut grove at the bottom of the garden. Soon the cool breezes did their work. To her amazement she found that she was hugely relieved to find herself alone. She watched the merry boatloads rowing up the river. No doubt the sight put her in mind of one or two incidents in her past life. She sat herself down in profound meditation beneath a fine willow tree. There she sat till the stars were in the sky. Then she rose, turned, and went into the house, where she sought her bedroom and locked the door. Now she opened a cupboard in which hung still many of the clothes she had worn as a young man of fashion, and from among them she chose a black velvet suit richly trimmed with Venetian lace. It was a little out of fashion, indeed, but it fitted her to perfection and dressed in it she looked the very figure of a noble Lord. She took a turn or two before the mirror to make sure that her petticoats had not lost her the freedom of her legs, and then let herself secretly out of doors.

It was a fine night early in April. A myriad stars mingling with the light of a sickle moon, which again was enforced by the street lamps, made a light infinitely becoming to the human countenance and to the architecture of Mr. Wren. Everything appeared in its tenderest form, yet, just as it seemed on the point of dissolution, some drop of silver sharpened it to animation. Thus it was that talk should be, thought Orlando (indulging in foolish reverie); that society should be, that friendship should be, that love should be. For, Heaven knows why, just as we have lost faith in human intercourse some random collocation of barns and trees or a haystack and a waggon presents us with so perfect a symbol of what is unattainable that we begin the search again.

She entered Leicester Square as she made these observations. The buildings had an airy yet formal symmetry not theirs by day. The canopy of the sky seemed most dexterously washed in to fill up the outline of roof and chimney. A young woman who sat dejectedly with one arm drooping by her side, the other reposing in her lap, on a seat beneath a plane tree in the middle of the square seemed the very figure of grace, simplicity, and desolation. Orlando swept her hat off to her in the manner of a gallant paying his addresses to a lady of fashion in a public place. The young woman raised her head. It was of the most exquisite shapeliness. The young woman raised her eyes. Orlando saw them to be of a lustre such as is sometimes seen on teapots but rarely in a human face. Through this silver glaze the young woman looked up at him (for a man he was to her) appealing, hoping, trembling, fearing. She rose; she accepted his arm. For—need we stress the point?—she was of the tribe which nightly burnishes their wares, and sets them in order on the common counter to wait the highest bidder. She led Orlando to the room in Gerrard Street which was her lodging. To feel her hanging lightly yet like a suppliant on her arm, roused in Orlando all the feelings which become a man. She looked, she felt, she talked like one. Yet, having been so lately a woman herself, she suspected that the girl's timidity and her hesitating answers and the very fumbling with the key in the latch and the fold of her cloak and the droop of her wrist were all put on to gratify her masculinity. Upstairs they went, and the pains which the poor creature had been at to decorate her room and hide the fact that she had no other deceived Orlando not a moment. The deception roused her scorn; the truth roused her pity. One thing showing through the other bred the oddest assortment of feeling, so that she did not know whether to laugh or to cry. Meanwhile Nell, as the girl called herself, unbuttoned her gloves; carefully concealed the left-hand thumb, which wanted mending; then drew behind a screen, where, perhaps, she rouged her cheeks, arranged her clothes, fixed a new kerchief round her neck—all the time prattling as women do, to amuse her lover, though Orlando could have sworn, from the tone of her voice, that her thoughts were elsewhere. When all was ready, out she came, prepared—but here Orlando could stand it no longer. In the strangest torment of anger, merriment, and pity she flung off all disguise and admitted herself a woman.

At this, Nell burst into such a roar of laughter as might have been heard across the way.

"Well, my dear," she said, when she had somewhat recovered, "I'm by no means sorry to hear it. For the plain Dunstable[5] of the matter is" (and it was remarkable how soon, on discovering that they were of the same sex, her manner changed and she dropped her plaintive, appealing ways), "the plain Dunstable of the matter is, that I'm not in the mood for the society of the other sex to-night. Indeed, I'm in the devil of a fix." Whereupon, drawing up the fire and stirring a bowl of punch, she told Orlando the whole story of her life. Since it is Orlando's life that engages us at present, we need not relate the adventures of the other lady, but it is certain that Orlando had never known the hours speed faster or more merrily, though Mistress Nell had not a particle of wit about her, and when the name of Mr. Pope came up in talk asked innocently if he were connected

5. A phrase that connotes direct, straightforward speech.

with the perruque[6] maker of that name in Jermyn Street. Yet, to Orlando, such is the charm of ease and the seduction of beauty, this poor girl's talk, larded though it was with the commonest expressions of the street corners, tasted like wine after the fine phrases she had been used to, and she was forced to the conclusion that there was something in the sneer of Mr. Pope, in the condescension of Mr. Addison, and in the secret of Lord Chesterfield which took away her relish for the society of wits, deeply though she must continue to respect their works.

These poor creatures, she ascertained, for Nell brought Prue, and Prue Kitty, and Kitty Rose, had a society of their own of which they now elected her a member. Each would tell the story of the adventures which had landed her in her present way of life. Several were the natural daughters of earls and one was a good deal nearer than she should have been to the King's person. None was too wretched or too poor but to have some ring or handkerchief in her pocket which stood her in lieu of pedigree. So they would draw round the punch-bowl which Orlando made it her business to furnish generously, and many were the fine tales they told and many the amusing observations they made, for it cannot be denied that when women get together—but hist—they are always careful to see that the doors are shut and that not a word of it gets into print. All they desire is— but hist again—is that not a man's step on the stair? All they desire, we were about to say when the gentleman took the very words out of our mouths. Women have no desires, says this gentleman, coming into Nell's parlour; only affectations. Without desires (she has served him and he is gone) their conversation cannot be of the slightest interest to anyone. "It is well known", says Mr. S. W., "that when they lack the stimulus of the other sex, women can find nothing to say to each other. When they are alone, they do not talk, they scratch." And since they cannot talk together and scratching cannot continue without interruption and it is well known (Mr. T. R. has proved it) "that women are incapable of any feeling of affection for their own sex and hold each other in the greatest aversion", what can we suppose that women do when they seek out each other's society?

As that is not a question that can engage the attention of a sensible man, let us, who enjoy the immunity of all biographers and historians from any sex whatever, pass it over, and merely state that Orlando professed great enjoyment in the society of her own sex, and leave it to the gentlemen to prove, as they are very fond of doing, that this is impossible.

6. A kind of wig.

But to give an exact and particular account of Orlando's life at
this time becomes more and more out of the question. As we peer
and grope in the ill-lit, ill-paved, ill-ventilated courtyards that lay
about Gerrard Street and Drury Lane at that time, we seem now to
catch sight of her and then again to lose it. The task is made still
more difficult by the fact that she found it convenient at this time
to change frequently from one set of clothes to another.[7] Thus she
often occurs in contemporary memoirs as "Lord" So-and-so, who
was in fact her cousin; her bounty is ascribed to him, and it is he
who is said to have written the poems that were really hers. She had,
it seems, no difficulty in sustaining the different parts, for her sex
changed far more frequently than those who have worn only one set
of clothing can conceive; nor can there be any doubt that she reaped
a twofold harvest by this device; the pleasures of life were increased
and its experiences multiplied. For the probity of breeches she
exchanged the seductiveness of petticoats and enjoyed the love of
both sexes equally.

So then one may sketch her spending her morning in a China
robe[8] of ambiguous gender among her books; then receiving a client
or two (for she had many scores of suppliants) in the same garment;
then she would take a turn in the garden and clip the nut trees—
for which knee-breeches were convenient; then she would change
into a flowered taffeta which best suited a drive to Richmond and a
proposal of marriage from some great nobleman; and so back again
to town, where she would don a snuff-coloured gown like a lawyer's
and visit the courts to hear how her cases were doing,—for her fortune was wasting hourly and the suits seemed no nearer consummation than they had been a hundred years ago; and so, finally,
when night came, she would more often than not become a nobleman complete from head to toe and walk the streets in search of
adventure.

Returning from some of these junketings—of which there were
many stories told at the time, as, that she fought a duel, served on
one of the King's ships as a captain, was seen to dance naked on a
balcony, and fled with a certain lady to the Low Countries where
the lady's husband followed them—but of the truth or otherwise of
these stories, we express no opinion—returning from whatever her
occupation may have been, she made a point sometimes of passing
beneath the windows of a coffee house, where she could see the wits
without being seen, and thus could fancy from their gestures what

7. Sackville-West dressed up in men's clothes and adopted the persona of "Julian" while
   conducting her passionate affair with Trefusis. See Glendinning, 95.
8. A mid-length silk robe of Asian design.

wise, witty, or spiteful things they were saying without hearing a word of them; which was perhaps an advantage; and once she stood half an hour watching three shadows on the blind drinking tea together in a house in Bolt Court.

Never was any play so absorbing. She wanted to cry out, Bravo! Bravo! For, to be sure, what a fine drama it was—what a page torn from the thickest volume of human life. There was the little shadow with the pouting lips, fidgeting this way and that on his chair, uneasy, petulant, officious; there was the bent female shadow, crooking a finger in the cup to feel how deep the tea was, for she was blind; and there was the Roman-looking rolling shadow in the big arm-chair—he who twisted his fingers so oddly and jerked his head from side to side and swallowed down the tea in such vast gulps. Dr. Johnson, Mr. Boswell, and Mrs. Williams,[9]—those were the shadows' names. So absorbed was she in the sight, that she forgot to think how other ages would have envied her, though it seems probable that on this occasion they would. She was content to gaze and gaze. At length Mr. Boswell rose. He saluted the old woman with tart asperity. But with what humility did he not abase himself before the great Roman shadow, who now rose to its full height and rock-ing somewhat as he stood there rolled out the most magnificent phrases that ever left human lips; so Orlando thought them, though she never heard a word that any of the three shadows said as they sat there drinking tea.

At length she came home one night after one of these saunter-ings and mounted to her bedroom. She took off her laced coat and stood there in shirt and breeches looking out of the window. There was something stirring in the air which forbade her to go to bed. A white haze lay over the town, for it was a frosty night in midwinter and a magnificent vista lay all round her. She could see St. Paul's, the Tower, Westminster Abbey, with all the spires and domes of the city churches, the smooth bulk of its banks, the opulent and ample curves of its halls and meeting-places. On the north rose the smooth, shorn heights of Hampstead, and in the west the streets and squares of Mayfair shone out in one clear radiance. Upon this serene and orderly prospect the stars looked down, glittering, positive, hard, from a cloudless sky. In the extreme clearness of the atmosphere the line of every roof, the cowl of every chimney was perceptible; even

9. Anna Williams (1706–1783), a Welsh poet who became part of Samuel Johnson's house-hold in the 1740s after cataracts and a failed cataract surgery contributed to her increasing visual impairment. Samuel Johnson (1709–1784), a writer famous for the publication of one of the first comprehensive dictionaries of the English language in 1755. James Boswell (1740–1795), a friend of Johnson's known primarily for his biogra-phy of Johnson, *Life of Samuel Johnson* (1791).

the cobbles in the streets showed distinct one from another, and Orlando could not help comparing this orderly scene with the irregular and huddled purlieus which had been the city of London in the reign of Queen Elizabeth. Then, she remembered, the city, if such one could call it, lay crowded, a mere huddle and conglomeration of houses, under her windows at Blackfriars. The stars reflected themselves in deep pits of stagnant water which lay in the middle of the streets. A black shadow at the corner where the wine shop used to stand was, as likely as not, the corpse of a murdered man. She could remember the cries of many a one wounded in such night brawlings, when she was a little boy, held to the diamond-paned window in her nurse's arms. Troops of ruffians, men and women, unspeakably interlaced, lurched down the streets, trolling out wild songs with jewels flashing in their ears, and knives gleaming in their fists. On such a night as this the impermeable tangle of the forests on Highgate and Hampstead would be outlined, writhing in contorted intricacy against the sky. Here and there, on one of the hills which rose above London, was a stark gallows tree, with a corpse nailed to rot or parch on its cross; for danger and insecurity, lust and violence, poetry and filth swarmed over the tortuous Elizabethan highways and buzzed and stank—Orlando could remember even now the smell of them on a hot night—in the little rooms and narrow pathways of the city. Now—she leant out of her window—all was light, order, and serenity. There was the faint rattle of a coach on the cobbles. She heard the far-away cry of the night watchman—"Just twelve o'clock on a frosty morning". No sooner had the words left his lips than the first stroke of midnight sounded. Orlando then for the first time noticed a small cloud gathered behind the dome of St. Paul's. As the strokes sounded, the cloud increased, and she saw it darken and spread with extraordinary speed. At the same time a light breeze rose and by the time the sixth stroke of midnight had struck the whole of the eastern sky was covered with an irregular moving darkness, though the sky to the west and north stayed clear as ever. Then the cloud spread north. Height upon height above the city was engulfed by it. Only Mayfair, with all its lights shining, burnt more brilliantly than ever by contrast. With the eighth stroke, some hurrying tatters of cloud sprawled over Piccadilly. They seemed to mass themselves and to advance with extraordinary rapidity towards the west end. As the ninth, tenth, and eleventh strokes struck, a huge blackness sprawled over the whole of London. With the twelfth stroke of midnight, the darkness was complete. A turbulent welter of cloud covered the city. All was darkness; all was doubt; all was confusion. The Eighteenth century was over; the Nineteenth century had begun.

CHAPTER V

THE great cloud which hung, not only over London, but over the whole of the British Isles on the first day of the nineteenth century stayed, or rather, did not stay, for it was buffeted about constantly by blustering gales, long enough to have extraordinary consequences upon those who lived beneath its shadow. A change seemed to have come over the climate of England. Rain fell frequently, but only in fitful gusts, which were no sooner over than they began again. The sun shone, of course, but it was so girt about with clouds and the air was so saturated with water, that its beams were discoloured and purples, oranges, and reds of a dull sort took the place of the more positive landscapes of the eighteenth century. Under this bruised and sullen canopy the green of the cabbages was less intense, and the white of the snow was muddied. But what was worse, damp now began to make its way into every house—damp, which is the most insidious of all enemies, for while the sun can be shut out by blinds, and the frost roasted by a hot fire, damp steals in while we sleep; damp is silent, imperceptible, ubiquitous. Damp swells the wood, furs the kettle, rusts the iron, rots the stone. So gradual is the process, that it is not until we pick up some chest of drawers, or coal scuttle, and the whole thing drops to pieces in our hands, that we suspect even that the disease is at work.

Thus, stealthily and imperceptibly, none marking the exact day or hour of the change, the constitution of England was altered and nobody knew it. Everywhere the effects were felt. The hardy country gentleman, who had sat down gladly to a meal of ale and beef in a room designed, perhaps by the brothers Adam, with classic dignity, now felt chilly. Rugs appeared; beards were grown; trousers were fastened tight under the instep. The chill which he felt in his legs the country gentleman soon transferred to his house; furniture was muffled; walls and tables were covered; nothing was left bare. Then a change of diet became essential. The muffin was invented and the crumpet. Coffee supplanted the after-dinner port, and, as coffee led to a drawing-room in which to drink it, and a drawing-room to glass cases, and glass cases to artificial flowers, and artificial flowers to mantelpieces, and mantelpieces to pianofortes, and pianofortes to drawing-room ballads, and drawing-room ballads (skipping a stage or two) to innumerable little dogs, mats, and china ornaments, the home—which had become extremely important—was completely altered.

Outside the house—it was another effect of the damp—ivy grew in unparalleled profusion. Houses that had been of bare stone were smothered in greenery. No garden, however formal its original design, lacked a shrubbery, a wilderness, a maze. What light

penetrated to the bedrooms where children were born was naturally of an obfusc[1] green, and what light penetrated to the drawing-
rooms where grown men and women lived came through curtains of
brown and purple plush. But the change did not stop at outward
things. The damp struck within. Men felt the chill in their hearts;
the damp in their minds. In a desperate effort to snuggle their feelings into some sort of warmth one subterfuge was tried after
another. Love, birth, and death were all swaddled in a variety of
fine phrases. The sexes drew further and further apart. No open
conversation was tolerated. Evasions and concealments were sedu-
lously practised on both sides. And just as the ivy and the evergreen
rioted in the damp earth outside, so did the same fertility show
itself within. The life of the average woman was a succession of
childbirths. She married at nineteen and had fifteen or eighteen
children by the time she was thirty; for twins abounded. Thus the
British Empire came into existence; and thus—for there is no stopping damp; it gets into the inkpot as it gets into the woodwork—
sentences swelled, adjectives multiplied, lyrics became epics, and
little trifles that had been essays a column long were now encyclo-
paedias in ten or twenty volumes. But Eusebius Chubb shall be our
witness to the effect this all had upon the mind of a sensitive man
who could do nothing to stop it. There is a passage towards the end
of his memoirs where he describes how, after writing thirty-five folio
pages one morning 'all about nothing' he screwed the lid on his inkpot and went for a turn in his garden. Soon he found himself
involved in the shrubbery. Innumerable leaves creaked and glis-
tened above his head. He seemed to himself "to crush the mould of
a million more under his feet". Thick smoke exuded from a damp
bonfire at the end of the garden. He reflected that no fire on earth
could ever hope to consume that vast vegetable encumbrance.
Wherever he looked, vegetation was rampant. Cucumbers "came
scrolloping across the grass to his feet". Giant cauliflowers tow-
ered deck above deck till they rivalled, to his disordered imagination, the elm trees themselves. Hens laid incessantly eggs of no
special tint. Then, remembering with a sigh his own fecundity and
his poor wife Jane, now in the throes of her fifteenth confinement
indoors, how, he asked himself, could he blame the fowls? He
looked upwards into the sky. Did not heaven itself, or that great
frontispiece of heaven, which is the sky, indicate the assent, indeed,
the instigation of the heavenly hierarchy? For there, winter or
summer, year in year out, the clouds turned and tumbled, like
whales, he pondered, or elephants rather; but no, there was no escaping the simile which was pressed upon him from a thousand airy

1. Dark or obscure.

acres; the whole sky itself as it spread wide above the British Isles was nothing but a vast feather bed; and the undistinguished fecundity of the garden, the bedroom and the henroost was copied there. He went indoors, wrote the passage quoted above, laid his head in a gas oven, and when they found him later he was past revival.

While this went on in every part of England, it was all very well for Orlando to mew herself in her house at Blackfriars and pretend that the climate was the same; that one could still say what one liked and wear knee-breeches or skirts as the fancy took one. Even she, at length, was forced to acknowledge that times were changed. One afternoon in the early part of the century she was driving through St. James's Park in her old panelled coach when one of those sunbeams, which occasionally, though not often, managed to come to earth, struggled through, marbling the clouds with strange prismatic colours as it passed. Such a sight was sufficiently strange after the clear and uniform skies of the eighteenth century to cause her to pull the window down and look at it. The puce and flamingo clouds made her think with a pleasurable anguish, which proves that she was insensibly afflicted with the damp already, of dolphins dying in Ionian seas. But what was her surprise when, as it struck the earth, the sunbeam seemed to call forth, or to light up, a pyramid, hecatomb, or trophy (for it had something of a banquet-table air)—a conglomeration at any rate of the most heterogeneous and ill-assorted objects, piled higgledy-piggledy in a vast mound where the statue of Queen Victoria now stands! Draped about a vast cross of fretted and floriated gold were widow's weeds and bridal veils; hooked on to other excrescences were crystal palaces, bassinettes, military helmets, memorial wreaths, trousers, whiskers, wedding cakes, cannon, Christmas trees, telescopes, extinct monsters, globes, maps, elephants, and mathematical instruments—the whole supported like a gigantic coat of arms on the right side by a female figure clothed in flowing white; on the left, by a portly gentleman wearing a frockcoat and sponge-bag trousers. The incongruity of the objects, the association of the fully clothed and the partly draped, the garishness of the different colours and their plaid-like juxtapositions afflicted Orlando with the most profound dismay. She had never, in all her life, seen anything at once so indecent, so hideous, and so monumental. It might, and indeed it must be, the effect of the sun on the water-logged air; it would vanish with the first breeze that blew; but for all that, it looked, as she drove past, as if it were destined to endure for ever. Nothing, she felt, sinking back into the corner of her coach, no wind, rain, sun, or thunder, could ever demolish that garish erection. Only the noses would mottle and the trumpets would rust; but there they would remain, pointing east, west, south, and north, eternally. She looked back as her coach swept up Constitution Hill. Yes, there it was, still beaming placidly in a light which—she pulled her watch out of her fob—was, of course, the light of twelve o'clock mid-day. None other could be so prosaic, so matter-of-fact, so impervious to any hint of dawn or sunset, so seemingly calculated to last for ever. She was determined not to look again. Already she felt the tides of her blood run sluggishly. But what was more peculiar, a blush, vivid and singular, overspread her cheeks as she passed Buckingham Palace and her eyes seemed forced by a superior power down upon her knees. Suddenly she saw with a start that she was wearing black breeches. She never ceased blushing till she had reached her country house, which, considering the time it takes four horses to trot thirty miles, will be taken, we hope, as a signal proof of her chastity.

Once there, she followed what had now become the most imperious need of her nature and wrapped herself as well as she could in a damask quilt which she snatched from her bed. She explained to the Widow Bartholomew (who had succeeded good old Grimsditch as housekeeper) that she felt chilly.

"So do we all, m'lady," said the Widow, heaving a profound sigh. "The walls is sweating," she said, with a curious, lugubrious complacency, and sure enough, she had only to lay her hand on the oak panels for the finger-prints to be marked there. The ivy had grown so profusely that many windows were now sealed up. The kitchen was so dark that they could scarcely tell a kettle from a cullender. A poor black cat had been mistaken for coals and shovelled on the fire. Most of the maids were already wearing three or four red-flannel petticoats, though the month was August.

"But is it true, m'lady," the good woman asked, hugging herself, while the golden crucifix heaved on her bosom, "that the Queen, bless her, is wearing a what d'you call it, a ——," the good woman hesitated and blushed.

"A crinoline," Orlando helped her out with it (for the word had reached Blackfriars). Mrs. Bartholomew nodded. The tears were already running down her cheeks, but as she wept she smiled. For it was pleasant to weep. Were they not all of them weak women? wearing crinolines the better to conceal the fact; the great fact; the only fact; but, nevertheless, the deplorable fact; which every modest woman did her best to deny until denial was impossible; the fact that she was about to bear a child? to bear fifteen or twenty children indeed, so that most of a modest woman's life was spent, after all, in denying what, on one day at least of every year, was made obvious.

"The muffins is keepin' 'ot", said Mrs. Bartholomew, mopping up her tears, "in the liberry."

And wrapped in a damask bed quilt, to a dish of muffins Orlando now sat down.

"The muffins is keepin' 'ot in the liberry"—Orlando minced out the horrid cockney phrase in Mrs. Bartholomew's refined cockney accents as she drank—but no, she detested the mild fluid—her tea. It was in this very room, she remembered, that Queen Elizabeth had stood astride the fireplace with a flagon of beer in her hand, which she suddenly dashed on the table when Lord Burghley tactlessly used the imperative instead of the subjunctive. "Little man, little man,"— Orlando could hear her say—"is 'must' a word to be addressed to princes?" And down came the flagon on the table: there was the mark of it still.

But when Orlando leapt to her feet, as the mere thought of that great Queen commanded, the bed quilt tripped her up, and she fell back in her arm-chair with a curse. To-morrow she would have to buy twenty yards or more of black bombazine, she supposed, to make a skirt. And then (here she blushed), she would have to buy a crino-line, and then (here she blushed) a bassinette, and then another crin-oline, and so on. . . . The blushes came and went with the most exquisite iteration of modesty and shame imaginable. One might see the spirit of the age blowing, now hot, now cold, upon her cheeks. And if the spirit of the age blew a little unequally, the crinoline being blushed for before the husband, her ambiguous position must excuse her (even her sex was still in dispute) and the irregular life she had lived before.

At length the colour on her cheeks resumed its stability and it seemed as if the spirit of the age—if such indeed it were—lay dor-mant for a time. Then Orlando felt in the bosom of her shirt as if for some locket or relic of lost affection, and drew out no such thing, but a roll of paper, sea-stained, blood-stained, travel-stained—the manuscript of her poem, "The Oak Tree". She had carried this about with her for so many years now, and in such hazardous circum-stances, that many of the pages were stained, some were torn, while the straits she had been in for writing paper when with the gipsies, had forced her to overscore the margins and cross the lines till the manuscript looked like a piece of darning most conscientiously car-ried out. She turned back to the first page and read the date, 1586, written in her own boyish hand. She had been working at it for close on three hundred years now. It was time to make an end. Mean-while she began turning and dipping and reading and skipping and thinking as she read, how very little she had changed all these years. She had been a gloomy boy, in love with death, as boys are; and then she had been amorous and florid; and then she had been sprightly and satirical; and sometimes she had tried prose and sometimes she had tried drama. Yet through all these changes she had remained, she reflected, fundamentally the same. She had the same brooding meditative temper, the same love of animals and nature, the same passion for the country and the seasons.

"After all," she thought, getting up and going to the window, "nothing has changed. The house, the garden are precisely as they were. Not a chair has been moved, not a trinket sold. There are the same walks, the same lawns, the same trees, and the same pool, which, I dare say, has the same carp in it. True, Queen Victoria is on the throne and not Queen Elizabeth, but what difference. . . ."

No sooner had the thought taken shape, than, as if to rebuke it, the door was flung wide and in marched Basket, the butler, followed by Bartholomew, the housekeeper, to clear away tea. Orlando, who had just dipped her pen in the ink, and was about to indite some reflection upon the eternity of all things, was much annoyed to be impeded by a blot, which spread and meandered round her pen. It was some infirmity of the quill, she supposed; it was split or dirty. She dipped it again. The blot increased. She tried to go on with what she was saying; no words came. Next she began to decorate the blot with wings and whiskers, till it became a round-headed monster, something between a bat and a wombat. But as for writing poetry with Basket and Bartholomew in the room, it was impossible. No sooner had she said "Impossible" than, to her astonishment and alarm, the pen began to curve and caracole with the smoothest possible fluency. Her page was written in the neatest sloping Italian hand with the most insipid verse she had ever read in her life:

> I am myself but a vile link
>   Amid life's weary chain,
> But I have spoken hallow'd words,
>   Oh, do not say in vain!
>
> Will the young maiden, when her tears,
>   Alone in moonlight shine,
> Tears for the absent and the loved,
>   Murmur—[2]

she wrote without a stop as Bartholomew and Basket grunted and groaned about the room, mending the fire, picking up the muffins.

Again she dipped her pen and off it went—

---

2. An excerpt from "Lines of Life," a poem by Letitia Elizabeth Landon (1802–1838). The Hogarth Press published a book about Landon in 1928, the same year that *Orlando* was published. See D. E. Enfield, *L.E.L.: A Mystery of the Thirties* (London: Hogarth Press, 1928).

> She was so changed, the soft carnation cloud
> Once mantling o'er her cheek like that which eve
> Hangs o'er the sky, glowing with roseate hue,
> Had faded into paleness, broken by
> Bright burning blushes, torches of the tomb,[3]

but here, by an abrupt movement she spilt the ink over the page and blotted it from human sight she hoped for ever. She was all of a quiver, all of a stew. Nothing more repulsive could be imagined than to feel the ink flowing thus in cascades of involuntary inspiration. What had happened to her? Was it the damp, was it Bartholomew, was it Basket, what was it? she demanded. But the room was empty. No one answered her, unless the dripping of the rain in the ivy could be taken for an answer.

Meanwhile, she became conscious, as she stood at the window, of an extraordinary tingling and vibration all over her, as if she were made of a thousand wires upon which some breeze or errant fingers were playing scales. Now her toes tingled; now her marrow. She had the queerest sensations about the thigh bones. Her hairs seemed to erect themselves. Her arms sang and twanged as the telegraph wires would be singing and twanging in twenty years or so. But all this agitation seemed at length to concentrate in her hands; and then in one hand, and then in one finger of that hand, and then finally to contract itself so that it made a ring of quivering sensibility about the second finger of the left hand. And when she raised it to see what caused this agitation, she saw nothing—nothing but the vast solitary emerald which Queen Elizabeth had given her. And was that not enough? she asked. It was of the finest water. It was worth ten thousand pounds at least. The vibration seemed, in the oddest way (but remember we are dealing with some of the darkest manifestations of the human soul) to say No, that is not enough; and, further, to assume a note of interrogation, as though it were asking, what did it mean, this hiatus, this strange oversight? till poor Orlando felt positively ashamed of the second finger of her left hand without in the least knowing why. At this moment, Bartholomew came in to ask which dress she would lay out for dinner, and Orlando, whose senses were much quickened, instantly glanced at Bartholomew's left hand, and instantly perceived what she had never noticed before—a thick ring of rather jaundiced yellow circling the third finger where her own was bare.

"Let me look at your ring, Bartholomew," she said, stretching her hand to take it.

---

3. An excerpt from another Landon poem, "Fragment."

At this, Bartholomew made as if she had been struck in the breast by a rogue. She started back a pace or two, clenched her hand and flung it away from her with a gesture that was noble in the extreme. "No," she said, with resolute dignity, her Ladyship might look if she pleased, but as for taking off her wedding ring, not the Archbishop nor the Pope nor Queen Victoria on her throne could force her to do that. Her Thomas had put it on her finger twenty-five years, six months, three weeks ago; she had slept in it; worked in it; washed in it; prayed in it; and proposed to be buried in it. In fact, Orlando understood her to say, but her voice was much broken with emotion, that it was by the gleam on her wedding ring that she would be assigned her station among the angels and its lustre would be tarnished for ever if she let it out of her keeping for a second.

"Heaven help us," said Orlando, standing at the window and watching the pigeons at their pranks, "what a world we live in! What a world to be sure!" Its complexities amazed her. It now seemed to her that the whole world was ringed with gold. She went in to dinner. Wedding rings abounded. She went to church. Wedding rings were everywhere. She drove out. Gold, or pinchbeck,[4] thin, thick, plain, smooth, they glowed dully on every hand. Rings filled the jewellers' shops, not the flashing pastes and diamonds of Orlando's recollection, but simple bands without a stone in them. At the same time, she began to notice a new habit among the town people. In the old days, one would meet a boy trifling with a girl under a hawthorn hedge frequently enough. Orlando had flicked many a couple with the tip of her whip and laughed and passed on. Now, all that was changed. Couples trudged and plodded in the middle of the road indissolubly linked together. The woman's right hand was invariably passed through the man's left and her fingers were firmly gripped by his. Often it was not till the horses' noses were on them that they budged, and then, though they moved it was all in one piece, heavily, to the side of the road. Orlando could only suppose that some new discovery had been made about the race; that they were somehow stuck together, couple after couple, but who had made it, and when, she could not guess. It did not seem to be Nature. She looked at the doves and the rabbits and the elk-hounds and she could not see that Nature had changed her ways or mended them, since the time of Elizabeth at least. There was no indissoluble alliance among the brutes that she could see. Could it be Queen Victoria then, or Lord Melbourne? Was it from them that the great discovery of marriage proceeded? Yet the Queen, she pondered, was said to be fond of dogs, and Lord Melbourne, she had heard, was said to be fond of women. It was strange—it was distasteful; indeed, there was something in

---

4. An alloy used to produce relatively inexpensive jewelry that looked like gold.

this indissolubility of bodies which was repugnant to her sense of decency and sanitation. Her ruminations, however, were accompanied by such a tingling and twangling of the afflicted finger that she could scarcely keep her ideas in order. They were languishing and ogling like a housemaid's fancies. They made her blush. There was nothing for it but to buy one of those ugly bands and wear it like the rest. This she did, slipping it, overcome with shame, upon her finger in the shadow of a curtain; but without avail. The tingling persisted more violently, more indignantly than ever. She did not sleep a wink that night. Next morning when she took up the pen to write, either she could think of nothing, and the pen make one large lachrymose blot after another, or it ambled off, more alarmingly still, into mellifluous fluencies about early death and corruption, which were worse than no thinking at all. For it would seem—her case proved it—that we write, not with the fingers, but with the whole person. The nerve which controls the pen winds itself about every fibre of our being, threads the heart, pierces the liver. Though the seat of her trouble seemed to be the left hand, she could feel herself poisoned through and through, and was forced at length to consider the most desperate of remedies, which was to yield completely and submissively to the spirit of the age, and take a husband.

That this was much against her natural temperament has been sufficiently made plain. When the sound of the Archduke's chariot wheels died away, the cry that rose to her lips was "Life! A Lover!" not "Life! A Husband!" and it was in pursuit of this aim that she had gone to town and run about the world as has been shown in the previous chapter. Such is the indomitable nature of the spirit of the age, however, that it batters down anyone who tries to make stand against it far more effectually than those who bend its own way. Orlando had inclined herself naturally to the Elizabethan spirit, to the Restoration spirit, to the spirit of the eighteenth century, and had in consequence scarcely been aware of the change from one age to the other. But the spirit of the nineteenth century was antipathetic to her in the extreme, and thus it took her and broke her, and she was aware of her defeat at its hands as she had never been before. For it is probable that the human spirit has its place in time assigned to it; some are born of this age, some of that; and now that Orlando was grown a woman, a year or two past thirty indeed, the lines of her character were fixed, and to bend them the wrong way was intolerable.

So she stood mournfully at the drawing-room window (Bartholomew had so christened the library) dragged down by the weight of the crinoline which she had submissively adopted. It was heavier and more drab than any dress she had yet worn. None had ever so impeded her movements. No longer could she stride through

the garden with her dogs, or run lightly to the high mound and fling
herself beneath the oak tree. Her skirts collected damp leaves and
straw. The plumed hat tossed on the breeze. The thin shoes were
quickly soaked and mud-caked. Her muscles had lost their pliancy.
She became nervous lest there should be robbers behind the wainscot and afraid, for the first time in her life, of ghosts in the corridors. All these things inclined her, step by step, to submit to the new
discovery, whether Queen Victoria's or another's, that each man and
each woman has another allotted to it for life, whom it supports, by
whom it is supported, till death them do part. It would be a comfort, she felt to lean; to sit down; yes, to lie down; never, never, never
to get up again. Thus did the spirit work upon her, for all her past
pride, and as she came sloping down the scale of emotion to this
lowly and unaccustomed lodging-place, those twanglings and tin-
glings which had been so captious and so interrogative modulated
into the sweetest melodies, till it seemed as if angels were plucking
harp-strings with white fingers and her whole being was pervaded
by a seraphic harmony.

But whom could she lean upon? She asked that question of the
wild autumn winds. For it was now October and wet as usual. Not
the Archduke; he had married a very great lady and had hunted
hares in Roumania these many years now; nor Mr. M.; he was
become a Catholic; nor the Marquis of C.; he made sacks in Botany
Bay; nor the Lord O.; he had long been food for fishes. One way or
another, all her old cronies were gone now, and the Nells and the
Kits of Drury Lane, much though she favoured them, scarcely did
to lean upon.

"Whom", she asked, casting her eyes upon the revolving clouds,
clasping her hands as she knelt on the window-sill, and looking the
very image of appealing womanhood as she did so, "can I lean upon?"
Her words formed themselves, her hands clasped themselves, invol-
untarily, just as her pen had written of its own accord. It was not
Orlando who spoke, but the spirit of the age. But whichever it was,
nobody answered it. The rooks were tumbling pell-mell among the
violet clouds of autumn. The rain had stopped at last and there was
an iridescence in the sky which tempted her to put on her plumed
hat and her little stringed shoes and stroll out before dinner.

"Everyone is mated except myself," she mused, as she trailed
disconsolately across the courtyard. There were the rooks; Canute
and Pippin even—transitory as their alliances were, still each this
evening seemed to have a partner. "Whereas, I, who am mistress of
it all," Orlando thought, glancing as she passed at the innumerable
emblazoned windows of the hall, "am single, am mateless, am alone."

Such thoughts had never entered her head before. Now they bore
her down unescapably. Instead of thrusting the gate open, she tapped

with a gloved hand for the porter to unfasten it for her. One must lean on someone, she thought, if it is only on a porter; and half wished to stay behind and help him to grill his chop on a bucket of fiery coals, but was too timid to ask it. So she strayed out into the park alone, faltering at first and apprehensive lest there might be poachers or gamekeepers or even errand-boys to marvel that a great lady should walk alone.

At every step she glanced nervously lest some male form should be hiding behind a furze bush or some savage cow be lowering its horns to toss her. But there were only the rooks flaunting in the sky. A steel-blue plume from one of them fell among the heather. She loved wild birds' feathers. She had used to collect them as a boy. She picked it up and stuck it in her hat. The air blew upon her spirit somewhat and revived it. As the rooks went whirling and wheeling above her head and feather after feather fell gleaming through the purplish air, she followed them, her long cloak floating behind her, over the moor, up the hill. She had not walked so far for years. Six feathers had she picked from the grass and drawn between her finger tips and pressed to her lips to feel their smooth, glinting plumage, when she saw, gleaming on the hill-side, a silver pool, mysterious as the lake into which Sir Bedivere flung the sword of Arthur. A single feather quivered in the air and fell into the middle of it. Then, some strange ecstasy came over her. Some wild notion she had of following the birds to the rim of the world and flinging herself on the spongy turf and there drinking forgetfulness, while the rooks' hoarse laughter sounded over her. She quickened her pace; she ran; she tripped; the tough heather roots flung her to the ground. Her ankle was broken. She could not rise. But there she lay content. The scent of the bog myrtle and the meadow-sweet was in her nostrils. The rooks' hoarse laughter was in her ears. "I have found my mate," she murmured. "It is the moor. I am nature's bride," she whispered, giving herself in rapture to the cold embraces of the grass as she lay folded in her cloak in the hollow by the pool. "Here will I lie. (A feather fell upon her brow.) I have found a greener laurel than the bay. My forehead will be cool always. These are wild birds' feathers— the owl's, the nightjar's. I shall dream wild dreams. My hands shall wear no wedding ring," she continued, slipping it from her finger. "The roots shall twine about them. Ah!" she sighed, pressing her head luxuriously on its spongy pillow, "I have sought happiness through many ages and not found it; fame and missed it; love and not known it; life—and behold, death is better. I have known many men and many women," she continued; "none have I understood. It is better that I should lie at peace here with only the sky above me— as the gipsy told me years ago. That was in Turkey." And she looked straight up into the marvellous golden foam into which the clouds

Figure 6. Orlando about the year 1840. © 2024 Artists Rights Society (ARS), New York / DACS, London. British Library, London, UK. From the British Library archive / Bridgeman Images.

had churned themselves, and saw next moment a track in it, and camels passing in single file through the rocky desert among clouds of red dust; and then, when the camels had passed, there were only mountains, very high and full of clefts and with pinnacles of rock, and she fancied she heard goat bells ringing in their passes, and in their folds were fields of irises and gentian. So the sky changed and her eyes slowly lowered themselves down and down till they came to the rain-darkened earth and saw the great hump of the South Downs, flowing in one wave along the coast; and where the land parted, there was the sea, the sea with ships passing; and she fancied she heard a gun far out at sea, and thought at first, "That's the Armada", and then thought "No, it's Nelson", and then remembered how those wars were over and the ships were busy merchant ships; and the sails on the winding river were those of pleasure boats. She saw, too, cattle sprinkled on the dark fields, sheep and cows, and she saw the lights coming here and there in farm-house windows, and lanterns moving among the cattle as the shepherd went his rounds and the cowman; and then the lights went out and the stars rose and tangled themselves about the sky. Indeed, she was falling asleep with the wet feathers on her face and her ear pressed to the ground when she heard, deep within, some hammer on an anvil, or was it a heart beating? Tick-tock, tick-tock, so it hammered, so it beat, the anvil, or the heart in the middle of the earth; until, as she listened, she thought it changed to the trot of a horse's hoofs; one, two, three, four, she counted; then she heard a stumble; then, as it came nearer and nearer, she could hear the crack of a twig and the suck of the wet bog in its hoofs. The horse was almost on her. She sat upright. Towering dark against the yellow-slashed sky of dawn, with the plovers rising and falling about him, she saw a man on horseback. He started. The horse stopped.

"Madam," the man cried, leaping to the ground, "you're hurt!"

"I'm dead, sir!" she replied.

A few minutes later, they became engaged.

The morning after, as they sat at breakfast, he told her his name. It was Marmaduke Bonthrop Shelmerdine, Esquire.

"I knew it!" she said, for there was something romantic and chivalrous, passionate, melancholy, yet determined about him which went with the wild, dark-plumed name—a name which had, in her mind, the steel-blue gleam of rooks' wings, the hoarse laughter of their caws, the snake-like twisting descent of their feathers in a silver pool, and a thousand other things which will be described presently.

"Mine is Orlando," she said. He had guessed it. For if you see a ship in full sail coming with the sun on it proudly sweeping across the Mediterranean from the South Seas, one says at once, "Orlando", he explained.

In fact, though their acquaintance had been so short, they had guessed, as always happens between lovers, everything of any importance about each other in two seconds at the utmost, and it now remained only to fill in such unimportant details as what they were called; where they lived; and whether they were beggars or people of substance. He had a castle in the Hebrides, but it was ruined, he told her. Gannets feasted in the banqueting hall. He had been a soldier and a sailor, and had explored the East. He was on his way now to join his brig at Falmouth, but the wind had fallen and it was only when the gale blew from the South-west that he could put out to sea. Orlando looked hastily from the breakfast-room window at the gilt leopard on the weather vane. Mercifully its tail pointed due east and was steady as a rock. "Oh! Shel, don't leave me!" she cried. "I'm passionately in love with you," she said. No sooner had the words left her mouth than an awful suspicion rushed into both their minds simultaneously,

"You're a woman, Shel!" she cried.

"You're a man, Orlando!" he cried.[5]

Never was there such a scene of protestation and demonstration as then took place since the world began. When it was over and they were seated again she asked him, what was this talk of a South-west gale? Where was he bound for?

"For the Horn," he said briefly, and blushed. (For a man had to blush as a woman had, only at rather different things.) It was only by dint of great pressure on her side and the use of much intuition that she gathered that his life was spent in the most desperate and splendid of adventures—which is to voyage round Cape Horn in the teeth of a gale. Masts had been snapped off; sails torn to ribbons (she had to drag the admission from him). Sometimes the ship had sunk, and he had been left the only survivor on a raft with a biscuit.

"It's about all a fellow can do nowadays," he said sheepishly, and helped himself to great spoonfuls of strawberry jam. The vision which she had thereupon of this boy (for he was little more) sucking peppermints, for which he had a passion, while the masts snapped and the stars reeled and he roared brief orders to cut this adrift, to heave that overboard, brought the tears to her eyes, tears, she noted, of a finer flavour than any she had cried before. "I am a woman," she thought, "a real woman, at last." She thanked Bonthrop from the bottom of her heart for having given her this rare and unexpected delight. Had she not been lame in the left foot, she would have sat upon his knee.

5. This is an allusion to the fact that both Sackville-West and her husband, Harold Nicolson, were bisexual. For more on gender and bisexuality, see Brenda S. Helt in this volume (pp. 249–66).

"Shel, my darling," she began again, "tell me . . ." and so they talked two hours or more, perhaps about Cape Horn, perhaps not, and really it would profit little to write down what they said, for they knew each other so well that they could say anything, which is tantamount to saying nothing, or saying such stupid, prosy things as how to cook an omelette, or where to buy the best boots in London, things which have no lustre taken from their setting, yet are positively of amazing beauty within it. For it has come about, by the wise economy of nature, that our modern spirit can almost dispense with language; the commonest expressions do, since no expressions do; hence the most ordinary conversation is often the most poetic, and the most poetic is precisely that which cannot be written down. For which reasons we leave a great blank here, which must be taken to indicate that the space is filled to repletion.

After some days more of this kind of talk,

"Orlando, my dearest," Shel was beginning, when there was a scuffling outside, and Basket the butler entered with the information that there was a couple of Peelers downstairs with a warrant from the Queen.

"Show 'em up," said Shelmerdine briefly, as if on his own quarterdeck, taking up, by instinct, a stand with his hands behind him in front of the fireplace. Two officers in bottle-green uniforms with truncheons at their hips then entered the room and stood at attention. Formalities being over, they gave into Orlando's own hands, as their commission was, a legal document of some very impressive sort, judging by the blobs of sealing wax, the ribbons, the oaths, and the signatures, which were all of the highest importance.

Orlando ran her eyes through it and then, using the first finger of her right hand as pointer, read out the following facts as being most germane to the matter.

"The lawsuits are settled," she read out . . . "some in my favour, as for example . . . others not. Turkish marriage annulled (I was ambassador in Constantinople, Shel," she explained). "Children pronounced illegitimate (they said I had three sons by Pepita, a Spanish dancer).[6] So they don't inherit, which is all to the good. . . . Sex? Ah! what about sex? My sex", she read out with some solemnity, "is pronounced indisputably, and beyond the shadow of a doubt (what I

6. See n. 6, p. 72.

was telling you a moment ago, Shel?), female. The estates which are now desequestrated in perpetuity descend and are tailed and entailed upon the heirs male of my body, or in default of marriage"— but here she grew impatient with this legal verbiage, and said, "but there won't be any default of marriage, nor of heirs either, so the rest can be taken as read." Whereupon she appended her own signature beneath Lord Palmerston's and entered from that moment into the undisturbed possession of her titles, her house, and her estate—which was now so much shrunk, for the cost of the lawsuits had been prodigious, that, though she was infinitely noble again, she was also excessively poor.

When the result of the lawsuit was made known (and rumour flew much quicker than the telegraph which has supplanted it), the whole town was filled with rejoicings.

[Horses were put into carriages for the sole purpose of being taken out. Empty barouches and landaus were trundled up and down the High Street incessantly. Addresses were read from the Bull. Replies were made from the Stag. The town was illuminated. Gold caskets were securely sealed in glass cases. Coins were well and duly laid under stones. Hospitals were founded. Rat and Sparrow clubs were inaugurated. Turkish women by the dozen were burnt in effigy in the market-place, together with scores of peasant boys with the label "I am a base Pretender", lolling from their mouths. The Queen's cream-coloured ponies were soon seen trotting up the avenue with a command to Orlando to dine and sleep at the Castle, that very same night. Her table, as on a previous occasion, was snowed under with invitations from the Countess of R., Lady Q., Lady Palmerston, the Marchioness of P., Mrs. W. E. Gladstone, and others, beseeching the pleasure of her company, reminding her of ancient alliances between their family and her own, etc.]—all of which is properly enclosed in square brackets, as above, for the good reason that a parenthesis it was without any importance in Orlando's life. She skipped it, to get on with the text. For when the bonfires were blazing in the market-place, she was in the dark woods with Shelmerdine alone. So fine was the weather that the trees stretched their branches motionless above them, and if a leaf fell, it fell, spotted red and gold, so slowly that one could watch it for half an hour fluttering and falling till it came to rest at last, on Orlando's foot.

"Tell me, Mar,"[7] she would say (and here it must be explained, that when she called him by the first syllable of his first name, she was in a dreamy, amorous, acquiescent mood, domestic, languid a little, as if spiced logs were burning, and it was evening, yet not time

---

7. A childhood nickname of Sackville-West, which both she and her husband used later as terms of endearment.

to dress, and a thought wet perhaps outside, enough to make the leaves glisten, but a nightingale might be singing even so among the azaleas, two or three dogs barking at distant farms, a cock crowing—all of which the reader should imagine in her voice)—"Tell me, Mar," she would say, "about Cape Horn." Then Shelmerdine would make a little model on the ground of the Cape with twigs and dead leaves and an empty snail shell or two.

"Here's the north," he would say. "There's the south. The wind's coming from hereabouts. Now the brig is sailing due west; we've just lowered the top-boom mizzen; and so you see—here, where this bit of grass is, she enters the current which you'll find marked—where's my map and compasses, Bo'sun?—Ah! thanks, that'll do, where the snail shell is. The current catches her on the starboard side, so we must rig the jib-boom or we shall be carried to the larboard, which is where that beech leaf is,—for you must understand my dear—" and so he would go on, and she would listen to every word; interpreting them rightly, so as to see, that is to say, without his having to tell her, the phosphorescence on the waves; the icicles clanking in the shrouds; how he went to the top of the mast in a gale; there reflected on the destiny of man; came down again; had a whisky and soda; went on shore; was trapped by a black woman;[8] repented; reasoned it out; read Pascal; determined to write philosophy; bought a monkey; debated the true end of life; decided in favour of Cape Horn, and so on. All this and a thousand other things she understood him to say, and so when she replied, Yes, negresses are seductive, aren't they? he having told her that the supply of biscuits now gave out, he was surprised and delighted to find how well she had taken his meaning.

"Are you positive you aren't a man?" he would ask anxiously, and she would echo,

"Can it be possible you're not a woman?" and then they must put it to the proof without more ado. For each was so surprised at the quickness of the other's sympathy, and it was to each such a revelation that a woman could be as tolerant and free-spoken as a man, and a man as strange and subtle as a woman, that they had to put the matter to the proof at once.

And so they would go on talking or rather, understanding, which has become the main art of speech in an age when words are growing daily so scanty in comparison with ideas that "the biscuits ran out" has to stand for kissing a negress in the dark when one has just read Bishop Berkeley's philosophy for the tenth time. (And from this it follows that only the most profound masters of style can tell the truth, and when one meets a simple one-syllabled writer, one may conclude, without any doubt at all, that the poor man is lying.)

8. An allusion to Joseph Conrad's *Heart of Darkness* (1899).

So they would talk; and then, when her feet were fairly covered with spotted autumn leaves, Orlando would rise and stroll away into the heart of the woods in solitude, leaving Bonthrop sitting there among the snail shells, making models of Cape Horn. "Bonthrop," she would say, "I'm off," and when she called him by his second name, "Bonthrop", it should signify to the reader that she was in a solitary mood, felt them both as specks on a desert, was desirous only of meeting death by herself, for people die daily, die at dinner tables, or like this, out of doors in the autumn woods; and with the bonfires blazing and Lady Palmerston or Lady Derby asking her out every night to dinner, the desire for death would overcome her, and so saying "Bonthrop", she said in effect, "I'm dead", and pushed her way as a spirit might through the spectre-pale beech trees, and so oared herself deep into solitude as if the little flicker of noise and movement were over and she were free now to take her way—all of which the reader should hear in her voice when she said "Bonthrop"; and should also add, the better to illumine the word, that for him too the same word signified, mystically, separation and isolation and the disembodied pacing the deck of his brig in unfathomable seas.

After some hours of death, suddenly a jay shrieked "Shelmerdine", and stooping, she picked one of those autumn crocuses which to some people signify that very word, and put it with the jay's feather that came tumbling blue through the beech woods, in her breast. Then she called "Shelmerdine" and the word went shooting this way and that way through the woods and struck him where he sat, making models out of snail shells in the grass. He saw her, and heard her coming to him with the crocus and the jay's feather in her breast, and cried "Orlando", which meant (and it must be remembered that when bright colours like blue and yellow mix themselves in our eyes, some of it rubs off on our thoughts) first the bowing and swaying of bracken as if something were breaking through; which proved to be a ship in full sail, heaving and tossing a little dreamily, rather as if she had a whole year of summer days to make her voyage in; and so the ship bears down, heaving this way, heaving that way, nobly, indolently, and rides over the crest of this wave and sinks into the hollow of that one, and so, suddenly stands over you (who are in a little cockle shell of a boat, looking up at her) with all her sails quivering, and then, behold, they drop all of a heap on deck—as Orlando dropped now into the grass beside him.

Eight or nine days had been spent thus, but on the tenth, which was the 26th of October, Orlando was lying in the bracken, while Shelmerdine recited Shelley[9] (whose entire works he had by heart),

9. Percy Bysshe Shelley (1792–1822), a well-known British Romantic poet.

when a leaf which had started to fall slowly enough from a treetop whipped briskly across Orlando's foot. A second leaf followed and then a third. Orlando shivered and turned pale. It was the wind. Shelmerdine—but it would be more proper now to call him Bonthrop—leapt to his feet.

"The wind!" he cried.

Together they ran through the woods, the wind plastering them with leaves as they ran, to the great court and through it and the little courts, frightened servants leaving their brooms and their saucepans to follow after till they reached the Chapel, and there a scattering of lights was lit as fast as could be, one knocking over this bench, another snuffing out that taper. Bells were rung. People were summoned. At length there was Mr. Dupper catching at the ends of his white tie and asking where was the prayer book. And they thrust Queen Mary's prayer book in his hands and he searched hastily fluttering the pages, and said, "Marmaduke Bonthrop Shelmerdine, and Lady Orlando, kneel down"; and they knelt down, and now they were bright and now they were dark as the light and shadow came flying helter-skelter through the painted windows; and among the banging of innumerable doors and a sound like brass pots beating, the organ sounded, its growl coming loud and faint alternately, and Mr. Dupper, who was grown a very old man, tried now to raise his voice above the uproar and could not be heard and then all was quiet for a moment, and one word—it might be "the jaws of death"—rang out clear, while all the estate servants kept pressing in with rakes and whips still in their hands to listen, and some sang aloud and others prayed, and now a bird was dashed against the pane, and now there was a clap of thunder, so that no one heard the word Obey[1] spoken or saw, except as a golden flash, the ring pass from hand to hand. All was movement and confusion. And up they rose with the organ booming and the lightning playing and the rain pouring, and the Lady Orlando, with her ring on her finger, went out into the court in her thin dress and held the swinging stirrup, for the horse was bitted and bridled and the foam was still on his flank, for her husband to mount, which he did with one bound, and the horse leapt forward and Orlando, standing there, cried out Marmaduke Bonthrop Shelmerdine! and he answered her Orlando! and the words went dashing and circling like wild hawks together among the belfries and higher and higher, further and further, faster and faster they circled, till they crashed and fell in a shower of fragments to the ground; and she went in.

---

1. The drowning out of the word "obey" in the marriage service is likely an allusion to Sackville-West and Nicolson's open marriage.

CHAPTER VI

ORLANDO went indoors. It was completely still. It was very silent.
There was the ink pot: there was the pen; there was the manuscript
of her poem, broken off in the middle of a tribute to eternity. She
had been about to say, when Basket and Bartholomew interrupted
with the tea things, nothing changes. And then, in the space of three
seconds and a half, everything had changed—she had broken her
ankle fallen in love, married Shelmerdine.

There was the wedding ring on her finger to prove it. It was true
that she had put it there herself before she met Shelmerdine, but
that had proved worse than useless. She now turned the ring round
and round, with superstitious reverence, taking care lest it should
slip past the joint of her finger.

"The wedding ring has to be put on the third finger of the left
hand", she said, like a child cautiously repeating its lesson, "for it to
be of any use at all."

She spoke thus, aloud and rather more pompously than was her
wont, as if she wished someone whose good opinion she desired to
overhear her. Indeed, she had in mind, now that she was at last able
to collect her thoughts, the effect that her behaviour would have had
upon the spirit of the age. She was extremely anxious to be informed
whether the steps she had taken in the matter of getting engaged to
Shelmerdine and marrying him met with its approval. She was certainly feeling more herself. Her finger had not tingled once, or nothing to count, since that night on the moor. Yet, she could not deny
that she had her doubts. She was married, true; but if one's husband
was always sailing round Cape Horn, was it marriage? If one liked
him, was it marriage? If one liked other people, was it marriage? And
finally, if one still wished, more than anything in the whole world, to
write poetry, was it marriage? She had her doubts.

But she would put it to the test. She looked at the ring. She looked
at the ink pot. Did she dare? No, she did not. But she must. No, she
could not. What should she do then? Faint, if possible. But she had
never felt better in her life.

"Hang it all!" she cried, with a touch of her old spirit, "Here goes!"

And she plunged her pen neck deep in the ink. To her enormous
surprise, there was no explosion. She drew the nib out. It was wet,
but not dripping. She wrote. The words were a little long in coming,
but come they did. Ah! but did they make sense? she wondered, a
panic coming over her lest the pen might have been at some of its
involuntary pranks again. She read,

> And then I came to a field where the springing grass
> Was dulled by the hanging cups of fritillaries,

Sullen and foreign-looking, the snaky flower,
Scarfed in dull purple, like Egyptian girls—[1]

As she wrote she felt some power (remember we are dealing with the most obscure manifestations of the human spirit) reading over her shoulder, and when she had written "Egyptian girls", the power told her to stop. Grass, the power seemed to say, going back with a ruler such as governesses use to the beginning, is all right; the hanging cups of fritillaries—admirable; the snaky flower—a thought, strong from a lady's pen, perhaps, but Wordsworth, no doubt, sanctions it; but—girls? Are girls necessary? You have a husband at the Cape, you say? Ah, well, that'll do.

And so the spirit passed on.

Orlando now performed in spirit (for all this took place in spirit) a deep obeisance to the spirit of her age, such as—to compare great things with small—a traveller, conscious that he has a bundle of cigars in the corner of his suit case, makes to the customs officer who has obligingly made a scribble of white chalk on the lid. For she was extremely doubtful whether, if the spirit had examined the contents of her mind carefully, it would not have found something highly contraband for which she would have had to pay the full fine. She had only escaped by the skin of her teeth. She had just managed, by some dexterous deference to the spirit of the age, by putting on a ring and finding a man on a moor, by loving nature and being no satirist, cynic, or psychologist—any one of which goods would have been discovered at once—to pass its examination successfully.[2] And she heaved a deep sigh of relief, as, indeed, well she might, for the transaction between a writer and the spirit of the age is one of infinite delicacy, and upon a nice arrangement between the two the whole fortune of his works depends. Orlando had so ordered it that she was in an extremely happy position; she need neither fight her age, nor submit to it; she was of it, yet remained herself. Now, therefore, she could write, and write she did. She wrote. She wrote. She wrote.

It was now November. After November, comes December. Then January, February, March, and April. After April comes May. June, July, August follow. Next is September. Then October, and so, behold, here we are back at November again, with a whole year accomplished.[3]

This method of writing biography, though it has its merits, is a little bare, perhaps, and the reader, if we go on with it, may complain

---

1. These are lines from Sackville-West's poem *The Land*. See also n. 9, p. 78 in this volume.
2. Sackville-West was known to be a Sapphist (a woman who had sexual and romantic relationships with women), but her marriage to Nicolson protected her from, among other things, the kind of social censure that her peer Radclyffe Hall faced in 1928 for the attempted publication of *The Well of Loneliness*. See also pp. 204–08 in this volume.
3. Woolf is parodying traditional biography here for its strict adherence to chronology and reliance for its narrative structure on actions, conflict, and historical events.

Figure 7. Marmaduke Bonthrop Shelmerdine, Esquire. British Library, London, UK. From the British Library archive / Bridgeman Images.

that he could recite the calendar for himself and so save his pocket whatever sum the Hogarth Press may think proper to charge for this book. But what can the biographer do when his subject has put him in the predicament into which Orlando has now put us? Life, it has been agreed by everyone whose opinion is worth consulting, is the only fit subject for novelist or biographer; life, the same authorities have decided, has nothing whatever to do with sitting still in a chair and thinking. Thought and life are as the poles asunder. Therefore—since sitting in a chair and thinking is precisely what Orlando is doing now—there is nothing for it but to recite the calendar, tell one's beads, blow one's nose, stir the fire, look out of the window, until she has done. Orlando sat so still that you could have heard a pin drop. Would, indeed, that a pin had dropped! That would have been life of a kind. Or if a butterfly had fluttered through the window and settled on her chair, one could write about that. Or suppose she had got up and killed a wasp. Then, at once, we could out with our pens and write. For there would be blood shed, if only the blood of a wasp. Where there is blood there is life. And if killing a wasp is the merest trifle compared with killing a man, still it is a fitter subject for novelist or biographer than this mere wool-gathering; this thinking; this sitting in a chair day in, day out, with a cigarette and a sheet of paper and a pen and an ink pot. If only subjects, we might complain (for our patience is wearing thin), had more consideration for their biographers! What is more irritating than to see one's subject, on whom one has lavished so much time and trouble, slipping out of one's grasp altogether and indulging—witness her sighs and gasps, her flushing, her palings, her eyes now bright as lamps, now haggard as dawns—what is more humiliating than to see all this dumb show of emotion and excitement gone through before our eyes when we know that what causes it—thought and imagination—are of no importance whatsoever?

But Orlando was a woman—Lord Palmerston had just proved it. And when we are writing the life of a woman, we may, it is agreed, waive our demand for action, and substitute love instead. Love, the poet has said, is woman's whole existence. And if we look for a moment at Orlando writing at her table, we must admit that never was there a woman more fitted for that calling. Surely, since she is a woman, and a beautiful woman, and a woman in the prime of life, she will soon give over this pretence of writing and thinking and begin at least to think of a gamekeeper (and as long as she thinks of a man, nobody objects to a woman thinking). And then she will write him a little note (and as long as she writes little notes nobody objects to a woman writing either) and make an assignation for Sunday dusk and Sunday dusk will come; and the gamekeeper will whistle under the window—all of which is, of course, the very stuff of life and the only possible subject for fiction. Surely Orlando must have done one of these things? Alas,—a thousand times, alas, Orlando did none of them. Must it then be admitted that Orlando was one of those monsters of iniquity who do not love? She was kind to dogs, faithful to friends, generosity itself to a dozen starving poets, had a passion for poetry. But love—as the male novelists define it—and who, after all, speak with greater authority?—has nothing whatever to do with kindness, fidelity, generosity, or poetry. Love is slipping off one's petticoat and— But we all know what love is. Did Orlando do that? Truth compels us to say no, she did not. If then, the subject of one's biography will neither love nor kill, but will only think and imagine, we may conclude that he or she is no better than a corpse and so leave her.

The only resource now left us is to look out of the window. There were sparrows; there were starlings; there were a number of doves, and one or two rooks, all occupied after their fashion. One finds a worm, another a snail. One flutters to a branch, another takes a little run on the turf. Then a servant crosses the courtyard, wearing a green baize apron. Presumably he is engaged on some intrigue with one of the maids in the pantry, but as no visible proof is offered us, in the courtyard, we, can but hope for the best and leave it. Clouds pass, thin or thick, with some disturbance of the colour of the grass beneath. The sun-dial registers the hour in its usual cryptic way. One's mind begins tossing up a question or two, idly, vainly, about this same life. Life, it sings, or croons rather, like a kettle on a hob, Life, life, what art thou? Light or darkness, the baize apron of the under footman or the shadow of the starling on the grass?[4]

Let us go, then, exploring, this summer morning, when all are adoring the plum blossom and the bee. And humming and hawing, let us ask of the starling (who is a more sociable bird than the lark) what he may think on the brink of the dust-bin, whence he picks among the sticks combings of scullion's hair. What's life, we ask, leaning on the farmyard gate; Life, Life, Life! cries the bird, as if he had heard, and knew precisely, what we meant by this bothering prying habit of ours of asking questions indoors and out and peeping

---

4. In "Modern Fiction," Woolf notes that life does not unfold in an orderly procession of events and actions:

Examine for a moment an ordinary mind on an ordinary day. The mind receives a myriad impressions—trivial, fantastic, evanescent, or engraved with the sharpness of steel. From all sides they come, an incessant shower of innumerable atoms; and as they fall, as they shape themselves into the life of Monday or Tuesday, the accent falls differently from of old; the moment of importance came not here but there; so that, if a writer were a free man and not a slave, if he could write what he chose, not what he must, if he could base his work upon his own feeling and not upon convention, there would be no plot, no comedy, no tragedy, no love interest or catastrophe in the accepted style.

See *The Common Reader: First Series*, pp. 151–52.

and picking at daisies as the way is of writers when they don't know what to say next. Then they come here, says the bird, and ask me what life is; Life, Life, Life!

We trudge on then by the moor path, to the high brow of the wine-blue purple-dark hill, and fling ourselves down there, and dream there and see there a grasshopper, carting back to his home in the hollow, a straw. And he says (if sawings like his can be given a name so sacred and tender) Life's labour, or so we interpret the whirr of his dust-choked gullet. And the ant agrees and the bees, but if we lie here long enough to ask the moths, when they come at evening, stealing among the paler heather bells, they will breathe in our ears such wild nonsense as one hears from telegraph wires in snow storms; tee hee, haw haw. Laughter, Laughter! the moths say.

Having asked then of man and of bird and the insects, for fish, men tell us, who have lived in green caves, solitary for years to hear them speak, never, never say, and so perhaps know what life is—having asked them all and grown no wiser, but only older and colder (for did we not pray once in a way to wrap up in a book something so hard, so rare, one could swear it was life's meaning?) back we must go and say straight out to the reader who waits a-tiptoe to hear what life is—alas, we don't know.

At this moment, but only just in time to save the book from extinction, Orlando pushed away her chair, stretched her arms, dropped her pen, came to the window, and exclaimed, "Done!"

She was almost felled to the ground by the extraordinary sight which now met her eyes. There was the garden and some birds. The world was going on as usual. All the time she was writing the world had continued.

"And if I were dead, it would be just the same!" she exclaimed.

Such was the intensity of her feelings that she could even imagine that she had suffered dissolution, and perhaps some faintness actually attacked her. For a moment she stood looking at the fair, indifferent spectacle with staring eyes. At length she was revived in a singular way. The manuscript which reposed above her heart began shuffling and beating as if it were a living thing, and, what was still odder, and showed how fine a sympathy was between them, Orlando, by inclining her head, could make out what it was that it was saying. It wanted to be read. It must be read. It would die in her bosom if it were not read. For the first time in her life she turned with violence against nature. Elk-hounds and rose bushes were about her in profusion. But elk-hounds and rose bushes can none of them read. It is a lamentable oversight on the part of Providence which had never struck her before. Human beings alone are thus gifted. Human beings had become necessary. She rang the bell. She ordered the carriage to take her to London at once.

"There's just time to catch the eleven forty-five, M'Lady," said Basket. Orlando had not yet realised the invention of the steam engine,
but such was her absorption in the sufferings of a being, who, though
not herself, yet entirely depended on her, that she saw a railway train
for the first time, took her seat in a railway carriage, and had the
rug arranged about her knees without giving a thought to "that stu-
pendous invention, which had (the historians say) completely
changed the face of Europe in the past twenty years" (as, indeed,
happens much more frequently than historians suppose). She
noticed only that it was extremely smutty; rattled horribly; and the
windows stuck. Lost in thought, she was whirled up to London in
something less than an hour and stood on the platform at Charing
Cross, not knowing where to go.

The old house at Blackfriars, where she had spent so many pleasant days in the eighteenth century, was now sold, part to the Salva-
tion Army, part to an umbrella factory. She had bought another in
Mayfair which was sanitary, convenient, and in the heart of the fashionable world, but was it in Mayfair that her poem would be relieved
of its desire? Pray God, she thought, remembering the brightness of
their ladyships' eyes and the symmetry of their lordships' legs, they
haven't taken to reading there. For that would be a thousand pities.
Then there was Lady R.'s. The same sort of talk would be going on
there still, she had no doubt. The gout might have shifted from the
General's left leg to his right, perhaps. Mr. L. might have stayed ten
days with R. instead of T. Then Mr. Pope would come in. Oh! but
Mr. Pope was dead. Who were the wits now, she wondered—but that
was not a question one could put to a porter, and so she moved on.
Her ears were now distracted by the jingling of innumerable bells
on the heads of innumerable horses. Fleets of the strangest little
boxes on wheels were drawn up by the pavement. She walked out
into the Strand. There the uproar was even worse. Vehicles of all
sizes, drawn by blood horses and by dray horses, conveying one solitary dowager or crowded to the top by whiskered men in silk hats,
were inextricably mixed. Carriages, carts, and omnibuses seemed to
her eyes, so long used to the look of a plain sheet of foolscap, alarmingly at loggerheads; and to her ears, attuned to a pen scratching,
the uproar of the street sounded violently and hideously cacopho-
nous. Every inch of the pavement was crowded. Streams of people,
threading in and out between their own bodies and the lurching and
lumbering traffic with incredible agility, poured incessantly east and
west. Along the edge of the pavement stood men; holding out trays
of toys, and bawled. At corners, women sat beside great baskets of
spring flowers and bawled. Boys running in and out of the horses'
noses, holding printed sheets to their bodies, bawled too, Disaster!
Disaster! At first Orlando supposed that she had arrived at some

moment of national crisis; but whether it was happy or tragic, she could not tell. She looked anxiously at people's faces. But that confused her still more. Here would come by a man sunk in despair, muttering to himself as if he knew some terrible sorrow. Past him would nudge a fat, jolly-faced fellow, shouldering his way along as if it were a festival for all the world. Indeed, she came to the conclusion that there was neither rhyme nor reason in any of it. Each man and each woman was bent on his own affairs. And where was she to go?

She walked on without thinking, up one street and down another, by vast windows piled with handbags, and mirrors, and dressing gowns, and flowers, and fishing rods, and luncheon baskets; while stuff of every hue and pattern, thickness or thinness, was looped and festooned and ballooned across and across. Sometimes she passed down avenues of sedate mansions, soberly numbered 'one', 'two', 'three', and so on right up to two or three hundred, each the copy of the other, with two pillars and six steps and a pair of curtains neatly drawn and family luncheons laid on tables, and a parrot looking out of one window and a man servant out of another, until her mind was dizzied with the monotony. Then she came to great open squares with black, shiny, tightly buttoned statues of fat men in the middle, and war horses prancing, and columns rising and fountains falling and pigeons fluttering. So she walked and walked along pavements between houses until she felt very hungry, and something fluttering above her heart rebuked her with having forgotten all about it. It was her manuscript, "The Oak Tree".

She was confounded at her own neglect. She stopped dead where she stood. No coach was in sight. The street, which was wide and handsome, was singularly empty. Only one elderly gentleman was approaching. There was something vaguely familiar to her in his walk. As he came nearer, she felt certain that she had met him at some time or other. But where? Could it be that this gentleman, so neat, so portly, so prosperous, with a cane in his hand and a flower in his button-hole, with a pink, plump face, and combed white moustaches, could it be, Yes, by jove, it was!—her old, her very old friend, Nick Greene!

At the same time he looked at her; remembered her; recognised her. "The Lady Orlando!" he cried, sweeping his silk hat almost in the dust.

"Sir Nicholas!" she exclaimed. For she was made aware intuitively by something in his bearing that the scurrilous penny-a-liner, who had lampooned her and many another in the time of Queen Elizabeth, was now risen in the world and become certainly a Knight and doubtless a dozen other fine things into the bargain.

With another bow, he acknowledged that her conclusion was correct; he was a Knight; he was a Litt.D.;[5] he was a Professor. He was

5. Doctorate of Literature degree.

the author of a score of volumes. He was, in short, the most influential critic of the Victorian age.

A violent tumult of emotion besieged her at meeting the man who
had caused her, years ago, so much pain. Could this be the plaguy,
restless fellow who had burnt holes in her carpets, and toasted
cheese in the Italian fireplace and told such merry stories of Marlowe and the rest that they had seen the sun rise nine nights out of
ten? He was now sprucely dressed in a grey morning suit, had a pink
flower in his button-hole, and grey suede gloves to match. But even
as she marvelled, he made another profound bow, and asked her
whether she would honour him by lunching with him? The bow was
a thought overdone perhaps, but the imitation of fine breeding was
creditable. She followed him, wondering, into a superb restaurant,
all red plush, white table-cloths, and silver cruets, as unlike as could
be the old tavern or coffee house with its sanded floor, its wooden
benches, its bowls of punch and chocolate, and its broadsheets and
spittoons. He laid his gloves neatly on the table beside him. Still she
could hardly believe that he was the same man. His nails were clean;
where they used to be an inch long. His chin was shaved; where a
black beard used to sprout. He wore gold sleeve links; where his
ragged linen used to dip in the broth. It was not, indeed, until he
had ordered the wine, which he did with a care that reminded her
of his taste in Malmsey long ago, that she was convinced he was the
same man. "Ah!" he said, heaving a little sigh, which was yet comfortable enough, "ah! my dear lady, the great days of literature are
over. Marlowe, Shakespeare, Ben Jonson—those were the giants.
Dryden, Pope, Addison—those were the heroes. All, all are dead
now. And whom have they left us? Tennyson, Browning, Carlyle!"[6]—
he threw an immense amount of scorn into his voice. "The truth of
it is," he said, pouring himself a glass of wine, "that all our young
writers are in the pay of booksellers. They turn out any trash that
serves to pay their tailor's bills. It is an age", he said, helping himself to hors-d'oeuvres, "marked by precious conceits and wild
experiments—none of which the Elizabethans would have tolerated for an instant."

"No, my dear lady," he continued, passing with approval the tur-
bot au gratin, which the waiter exhibited for his sanction, "the great
days are over. We live in degenerate times. We must cherish the past;
honour those writers—there are still a few left of 'em—who take
antiquity for their model and write, not for pay but——" Here

6. Alfred, Lord Tennyson (1809–1892), Victorian poet who was British Poet Laureate
   from 1850 until his death. "Browning" likely refers to Robert Browning (1812–1889),
   although Elizabeth Barrett Browning (1806–1861) was the more well regarded of this
   married couple of Victorian poets during their lifetimes. Thomas Carlyle (1795–1881),
   Scottish prose writer known for his histories and essays.

Orlando almost shouted "Glawr!" Indeed she could have sworn that she had heard him say the very same things three hundred years ago. The names were different, of course, but the spirit was the same. Nick Greene had not changed, for all his knighthood. And yet, some change there was. For while he ran on about taking Addison as one's model (it had been Cicero once, she thought) and lying in bed of a morning (which she was proud to think her pension paid quarterly enabled him to do) rolling the best works of the best authors round and round on one's tongue for an hour, at least, before setting pen to paper, so that the vulgarity of the present time and the deplorable condition of our native tongue (he had lived long in America, she believed) might be purified—while he ran on in much the same way that Greene had run on three hundred years ago, she had time to ask herself, how was it then that he had changed? He had grown plump; but he was a man verging on seventy. He had grown sleek: literature had been a prosperous pursuit evidently; but somehow the old restless, uneasy vivacity had gone. His stories, brilliant as they were, were no longer quite so free and easy. He mentioned, it is true, "my dear friend Pope" or "my illustrious friend Addison" every other second, but he had an air of respectability about him which was depressing, and he preferred, it seemed, to enlighten her about the doings and sayings of her own blood relations rather than tell her, as he used to do, scandal about the poets.

Orlando was unaccountably disappointed. She had thought of literature all these years (her seclusion, her rank, her sex must be her excuse) as something wild as the wind, hot as fire, swift as lightning; something errant, incalculable, abrupt, and behold, literature was an elderly gentleman in a grey suit talking about duchesses. The violence of her disillusionment was such that some hook or button fastening the upper part of her dress burst open, and out upon the table fell "The Oak Tree", a poem.

"A manuscript!" said Sir Nicholas, putting on his gold pince-nez. "How interesting, how excessively interesting! Permit me to look at it." And once more, after an interval of some three hundred years, Nicholas Greene took Orlando's poem and, laying it down among the coffee cups and the liqueur glasses, began to read it. But now his verdict was very different from what it had been then. It reminded him, he said as he turned over the pages, of Addison's *Cato*. It compared favourably with Thomson's *Seasons*. There was no trace in it, he was thankful to say, of the modern spirit.[7] It was composed with a regard to truth, to nature, to the dictates of the human heart,

---

7. This is a backhanded dig at Sackville-West's writing style, as Woolf would have been a representative of what Greene calls the "modern spirit."

which was rare indeed, in these days of unscrupulous eccentricity.
It must, of course, be published instantly.

Really Orlando did not know what he meant. She had always carried her manuscripts about with her in the bosom of her dress. The
idea tickled Sir Nicholas considerably.

"But what about royalties?" he asked.

Orlando's mind flew to Buckingham Palace and some dusky poten-
tates who happened to be staying there.

Sir Nicholas was highly diverted. He explained that he was alluding to the fact that Messrs. —— (here he mentioned a well-known
firm of publishers) would be delighted, if he wrote them a line, to
put the book on their list. He could probably arrange for a royalty of
ten per cent on all copies up to two thousand; after that it would be
fifteen. As for the reviewers, he would himself write a line to Mr. ——,
who was the most influential; then a compliment—say a little puff
of her own poems—addressed to the wife of the editor of the ——
never did any harm. He would call ——. So he ran on. Orlando
understood nothing of all this, and from old experience did not altogether trust his good nature, but there was nothing for it but to
submit to what was evidently his wish and the fervent desire of
the poem itself. So Sir Nicholas made the blood-stained packet into
a neat parcel; flattened it into his breast pocket, lest it should disturb the set of his coat; and with many compliments on both sides,
they parted.

Orlando walked up the street. Now that the poem was gone,—
and she felt a bare place in her breast where she had been used
to carry it—she had nothing to do but reflect upon whatever she
liked—the extraordinary chances it might be of the human lot.
Here she was in St. James's Street; a married woman; with a ring
on her finger; where there had been a coffee house once there
was now a restaurant; it was about half past three in the afternoon; the sun was shining; there were three pigeons; a mongrel
terrier dog; two hansom cabs and a barouche landau. What then,
was Life?

The thought popped into her head violently, irrelevantly (unless
old Greene were somehow the cause of it). And it may be taken as a
comment, adverse or favourable, as the reader chooses to consider it
upon her relations with her husband (who was at the Horn), that
whenever anything popped violently into her head, she went straight
to the nearest telegraph office and wired to him. There was one, as
it happened, close at hand. "My God Shel", she wired; "life literature
Greene toady—" here she dropped into a cypher language which
they had invented between them so that a whole spiritual state of the
utmost complexity might be conveyed in a word or two without the
telegraph clerk being any the wiser, and added the words "Rattigan

Glumphoboo",[8] which summed it up precisely. For not only had the events of the morning made a deep impression on her, but it cannot have escaped the reader's attention that Orlando was growing up—which is not necessarily growing better—and "Rattigan Glumphoboo" described a very complicated spiritual state—which if the reader puts all his intelligence at our service he may discover for himself.

There could be no answer to her telegram for some hours; indeed, it was probable, she thought, glancing at the sky, where the upper clouds raced swiftly past, that there was a gale at Cape Horn, so that her husband would be at the mast-head, as likely as not, or cutting away some tattered spar, or even alone in a boat with a biscuit. And so, leaving the post office, she turned to beguile herself into the next shop, which was a shop so common in our day that it needs no description, yet, to her eyes, strange in the extreme; a shop where they sold books. All her life long Orlando had known manuscripts; she had held in her hands the rough brown sheets on which Spenser[9] had written in his little crabbed hand; she had seen Shakespeare's script and Milton's.[1] She owned, indeed, a fair number of quartos and folios, often with a sonnet in her praise in them and sometimes a lock of hair. But these innumerable little volumes, bright, identical, ephemeral, for they seemed bound in cardboard and printed on tissue paper, surprised her infinitely. The whole works of Shakespeare cost half a crown and could be put in your pocket. One could hardly read them, indeed, the print was so small, but it was a marvel, none the less. 'Works'—the works of every writer she had known or heard of and many more stretched from end to end of the long shelves. On tables and chairs, more 'works' were piled and tumbled, and these she saw, turning a page or two, were often works about other works by Sir Nicholas and a score of others whom, in her ignorance, she supposed, since they were bound and printed, to be very great writers too. So she gave an astounding order to the bookseller to send her everything of any importance in the shop and left.

She turned into Hyde Park, which she had known of old (beneath that cleft tree, she remembered, the Duke of Hamilton fell run through the body by Lord Mohun), and her lips, which are often to blame in the matter, began framing the words of her telegram into a senseless singsong; life literature Greene toady Rattigan Glumphoboo; so that several park keepers looked at her with suspicion and

8. Sackville-West and Nicolson used pet names for each other as well as some coded words in their correspondence with each other, but this phrasing is likely an invention of Woolf's.

9. Edmund Spenser (1552–1599), British poet best known for his epic poem *The Faerie Queen* (1590–96).

1. John Milton (1608–1674), British poet and pamphleteer, best known for his epic poem *Paradise Lost* (1667–74).

were only brought to a favourable opinion of her sanity by noticing
the pearl necklace which she wore. She had carried off a sheaf of
papers and critical journals from the book shop, and at length, flinging herself on her elbow beneath a tree, she spread these pages
round her and did her best to fathom the noble art of prose composition as these masters practised it. For still the old credulity was
alive in her; even the blurred type of a weekly newspaper had some
sanctity in her eyes. So she read, lying on her elbow, an article by
Sir Nicholas on the collected works of a man she had once known—
John Donne.[2] But she had pitched herself, without knowing it, not
far from the Serpentine. The barking of a thousand dogs sounded
in her ears. Carriage wheels rushed ceaselessly in a circle. Leaves
sighed overhead. Now and again a braided skirt and a pair of tight
scarlet trousers crossed the grass within a few steps of her. Once a
gigantic rubber ball bounced on the newspaper. Violets, oranges,
reds, and blues broke through the interstices of the leaves and spar-
kled in the emerald on her finger. She read a sentence and looked
up at the sky; she looked up at the sky and looked down at the newspaper. Life? Literature? One to be made into the other? But how
monstrously difficult! For—here came by a pair of tight scarlet
trousers—how would Addison have put that? Here came two dogs
dancing on their hind legs. How would Lamb[3] have described that?
For reading Sir Nicholas and his friends (as she did in the intervals
of looking about her), she somehow got the impression—here she
rose and walked—they made one feel—it was an extremely uncom-
fortable feeling—one must never, never say what one thought. (She
stood on the banks of the Serpentine. It was a bronze colour; spider-
thin boats were skimming from side to side.) They made one feel,
she continued, that one must always, always write like somebody
else. (The tears formed themselves in her eyes.) For really, she
thought, pushing a little boat off with her toe, I don't think I could
(here the whole of Sir Nicholas' article came before her as articles
do, ten minutes after they are read, with the look of his room, his
head, his cat, his writing-table, and the time of the day thrown in),
I don't think I could, she continued, considering the article from this
point of view, sit in a study, no, it's not a study, it's a mouldy kind of
drawing-room, all day long, and talk to pretty young men, and tell
them little anecdotes, which they mustn't repeat, about what Tupper
said about Smiles; and then, she continued, weeping bitterly, they're
all so manly; and then, I do detest Duchesses; and I don't like cake;
and though I'm spiteful enough, I could never learn to be as

---

2. John Donne (1572–1631), British poet known for his extended metaphors, called
"metaphysical conceits."
3. Charles Lamb (1775–1834), British Romantic poet and essayist.

spiteful as all that, so how can I be a critic and write the best English prose of my time?[4] Damn it all! she exclaimed, launching a penny steamer so vigorously that the poor little boat almost sank in the bronze-coloured waves.

Now, the truth is that when one has been in a state of mind (as nurses call it)—and the tears still stood in Orlando's eyes—the thing one is looking at becomes, not itself, but another thing, which is bigger and much more important and yet remains the same thing. If one looks at the Serpentine in this state of mind, the waves soon become just as big as the waves on the Atlantic; the toy boats become indistinguishable from ocean liners. So Orlando mistook the toy boat for her husband's brig; and the wave she had made with her toe for a mountain of water off Cape Horn; and as she watched the toy boat climb the ripple, she thought she saw Bonthrop's ship climb up and up a glassy wall; up and up it went, and a white crest with a thousand deaths in it arched over it; and through the thousand deaths it went and disappeared—'It's sunk!' she cried out in an agony—and then, behold, there it was again sailing along safe and sound among the ducks on the other side of the Atlantic.

"Ecstasy!" she cried. "Ecstasy! Where's the post office?" she wondered. "For I must wire at once to Shel and tell him. . . ." And repeating "A toy boat on the Serpentine", and "Ecstasy", alternately, for the thoughts were interchangeable and meant exactly the same thing, she hurried towards Park Lane.

"A toy boat, a toy boat, a toy boat", she repeated, thus enforcing upon herself the fact that it is not articles by Nick Greene on John Donne nor eight-hour bills nor covenants nor factory acts that matter; it's something useless, sudden, violent; something that costs a life; red, blue, purple; a shirt; a slash; like those hyacinths (she was passing a fine bed of them); free from taint, dependence, soilure of humanity or care for one's kind; something rash, ridiculous, like my hyacinth, husband I mean, Bonthrop: that's what it is—a toy boat on the Serpentine, ecstasy—it's ecstasy that matters. Thus she spoke aloud, waiting for the carriages to pass at Stanhope Gate, for the consequence of not living with one's husband, except when the wind is sunk, is that one talks nonsense aloud in Park Lane. It would no doubt have been different had she lived all the year round with him as Queen Victoria recommended. As it was the thought of him would come upon her in a flash. She found it absolutely necessary

4. Although Woolf wrote many reviews in the *Times Literary Supplement*, she was not a fan of academic literary criticism. In her 1932 essay "How Should One Read a Book?" she writes, "To admit authorities, however heavily furred and gowned, into our libraries and let them tell us how to read, what to read, what value to place on what we read, is to destroy the spirit of freedom which is the breath of those sanctuaries." See *The Common Reader: Second Series*, p. 258.

to speak to him instantly. She did not care in the least what nonsense it might make, or what dislocation it might inflict on the narrative. Nick Greene's article had plunged her in the depths of despair; the toy boat had raised her to the heights of joy. So she repeated: "Ecstasy, ecstasy", as she stood waiting to cross.

But the traffic was heavy that spring afternoon, and kept her standing there, repeating, ecstasy, ecstasy, or a toy boat on the Serpentine, while the wealth and power of England sat, as if sculptured, in hat and cloak, in four-in-hand, victoria and barouche landau. It was as if a golden river had coagulated and massed itself in golden blocks across Park Lane. The ladies held card-cases between their fingers; the gentlemen balanced gold-mounted canes between their knees. She stood there gazing, admiring, awestruck. One thought only disturbed her, a thought familiar to all who behold great elephants, or whales of an incredible magnitude, and that is how do these leviathans to whom obviously stress, change, and activity are repugnant, propagate their kind? Perhaps, Orlando thought, looking at the stately, still faces, their time of propagation is over; this is the fruit; this is the consummation. What she now beheld was the triumph of an age. Portly and splendid there they sat. But now, the policeman let fall his hand; the stream became liquid; the massive conglomeration of splendid objects moved, dispersed, and disappeared into Piccadilly.

So she crossed Park Lane and went to her house in Curzon Street where, when the meadow-sweet blew there, she could remember curlew calling and one very old man with a gun.

She could remember, she thought, stepping across the threshold of her house, how Lord Chesterfield had said—but her memory was checked. Her discreet eighteenth-century hall, where she could see Lord Chesterfield putting his hat down here and his coat down there with an elegance of deportment which it was a pleasure to watch, was now completely littered with parcels. While she had been sitting in Hyde Park the bookseller had delivered her order, and the house was crammed—there were parcels slipping down the staircase— with the whole of Victorian literature done up in grey paper and neatly tied with string. She carried as many of these packets as she could to her room, ordered footmen to bring the others, and, rapidly cutting innumerable strings, was soon surrounded by innumerable volumes.

Accustomed to the little literatures of the sixteenth, seventeenth, and eighteenth centuries, Orlando was appalled by the consequences of her order. For, of course, to the Victorians themselves Victorian literature meant not merely four great names separate and distinct but four great names sunk and embedded in a mass of Alexander Smiths, Dixons, Blacks, Milmans, Buckles, Taines, Paynes, Tuppers,

Jamesons—all vocal, clamorous, prominent, and requiring as much attention as anybody else. Orlando's reverence for print had a tough job set before it, but drawing her chair to the window to get the benefit of what light might filter between the high houses of Mayfair, she tried to come to a conclusion.

And now it is clear that there are only two ways of coming to a conclusion upon Victorian literature—one is to write it out in sixty volumes octavo, the other is to squeeze it into six lines of the length of this one. Of the two courses, economy, since time runs short, leads us to choose the second; and so we proceed. Orlando then came to the conclusion (opening half-a-dozen books) that it was very odd that there was not a single dedication to a nobleman among them; next (turning over a vast pile of memoirs) that several of these writers had family trees half as high as her own; next, that it would be impolitic in the extreme to wrap a ten-pound note round the sugar tongs when Miss Christina Rossetti[5] came to tea; next (here were half-a-dozen invitations to celebrate centenaries by dining) that literature since it ate all these dinners must be growing very corpulent; next (she was invited to a score of lectures on the Influence of this upon that; the Classical revival; the Romantic survival, and other titles of the same engaging kind) that literature since it listened to all these lectures must be growing very dry; next (here she attended a reception given by a peeress) that literature since it wore all those fur tippets[6] must be growing very respectable; next (here she visited Carlyle's sound-proof room at Chelsea) that genius since it needed all this coddling must be growing very delicate; and so at last she reached her final conclusion, which was of the highest importance but which, as we have already much overpassed our limit of six lines, we must omit.

Orlando, having come to this conclusion, stood looking out of the window for a considerable space of time. For, when anybody comes to a conclusion it is as if they had tossed the ball over the net and must wait for the unseen antagonist to return it to them. What would be sent her next from the colourless sky above Chesterfield House, she wondered? And with her hands clasped, she stood for a considerable space of time wondering. Suddenly she stated—and here we could only wish that, as on a former occasion, Purity, Chastity, and Modesty would push the door ajar and provide, at least, a breathing space in which we could think how to wrap up what now has to be told delicately, as a biographer should. But no! Having thrown their white garment at the naked Orlando and seen it fall short by several inches, these ladies had given up all intercourse with her these many

---

5. Christina Rossetti (1830–1894), British Victorian poet.
6. Scarves worn like a collar around the neck and top of the shoulders.

years; and were now otherwise engaged. Is nothing then, going to
happen this pale March morning to mitigate, to veil, to cover, to conceal, to shroud this undeniable event whatever it may be? For after
giving that sudden, violent start, Orlando—but Heaven be praised,
at this very moment there struck up outside one of these frail, reedy,
fluty, jerky, old-fashioned barrel-organs which are still sometimes
played by Italian organ-grinders in back streets. Let us accept the
intervention, humble though it is, as if it were the music of the
spheres, and allow it, with all its gasps and groans, to fill this page
with sound until the moment comes which it is impossible to deny
is coming; which the footman has seen coming and the maid-servant;
and the reader will have to see too; for Orlando herself is clearly
unable to ignore it any longer—let the barrel-organ sound and transport us on thought, which is no more than a little boat, when music
sounds, tossing on the waves; on thought, which is, of all carriers,
the most clumsy, the most erratic, over the roof tops and the back
gardens where washing is hanging to—what is this place? Do you
recognise the Green and in the middle the steeple, and the gates
with a lion couchant on either side? Oh yes, it is Kew! Well, Kew
will do. So here then we are at Kew, and I will show you to-day (the
second of March) under the plum tree, a grape hyacinth, and a crocus, and a bud, too, on the almond tree; so that to walk there is to
be thinking of bulbs, hairy and red, thrust into the earth in October; flowering now; and to be dreaming of more than can rightly be
said, and to be taking from its case a cigarette or cigar even, and to
be flinging a cloak under (as the rhyme requires) an oak, and there
to sit, waiting the kingfisher, which, it is said, was seen once to cross
in the evening from bank to bank.

Wait! Wait! The kingfisher comes; the kingfisher comes not.

Behold, meanwhile, the factory chimneys, and their smoke; behold
the city clerks flashing by in their outrigger. Behold the old lady taking her dog for a walk and the servant girl wearing her new hat for
the first time not at the right angle. Behold them all. Though Heaven
has mercifully decreed that the secrets of all hearts are hidden so
that we are lured on for ever to suspect something, perhaps, that
does not exist; still through our cigarette smoke, we see blaze up and
salute the splendid fulfilment of natural desires for a hat, for a boat,
for a rat in a ditch; as once one saw blazing—such silly hops and
skips the mind takes when it slops like this all over the saucer and
the barrel-organ plays—saw blazing a fire in a field against mina-
rets near Constantinople.

Hail! natural desire! Hail! happiness! divine happiness! and
pleasure of all sorts, flowers and wine, though one fades and the
other intoxicates; and half-crown tickets out of London on Sundays,
and singing in a dark chapel hymns about death, and anything,

anything that interrupts and confounds the tapping of typewriters and filing of letters and forging of links and chains, binding the Empire together. Hail even the crude, red bows on shop girls' lips (as if Cupid, very clumsily, dipped his thumb in red ink and scrawled a token in passing). Hail, happiness! kingfisher flashing from bank to bank, and all fulfilment of natural desire, whether it is what the male novelist says it is; or prayer; or denial; hail! in whatever form it comes, and may there be more forms, and stranger. For dark flows the stream—would it were true, as the rhyme hints "like a dream"—but duller and worser than that is our usual lot; without dreams, but alive, smug, fluent, habitual, under trees whose shade of an olive green drowns the blue of the wing of the vanishing bird when he darts of a sudden from bank to bank.

Hail, happiness, then, and after happiness, hail not those dreams which bloat the sharp image as spotted mirrors do the face in a country-inn parlour; dreams which splinter the whole and tear us asunder and wound us and split us apart in the night when we would sleep; but sleep, sleep, so deep that all shapes are ground to dust of infinite softness, water of dimness inscrutable, and there, folded, shrouded, like a mummy, like a moth, prone let us lie on the sand at the bottom of sleep.

But wait! but wait! we are not going, this time, visiting the blind land. Blue, like a match struck right in the ball of the innermost eye, he flys, burns, bursts the seal of sleep; the kingfisher; so that now floods back refluent like a tide, the red, thick stream of life again; bubbling, dripping; and we rise, and our eyes (for how handy a rhyme is to pass us safe over the awkward transition from death to life) fall on—(here the barrel-organ stops playing abruptly).

"It's a very fine boy, M'Lady," said Mrs. Banting, the midwife, putting her first-born child into Orlando's arms. In other words Orlando was safely delivered of a son on Thursday, March the 20th, at three o'clock in the morning.

Once more Orlando stood at the window, but let the reader take courage; nothing of the same sort is going to happen to-day, which is not, by any means, the same day. No—for if we look out of the window, as Orlando was doing at the moment, we shall see that Park Lane itself has considerably changed. Indeed one might stand there ten minutes or more, as Orlando stood now, without seeing a single barouche landau. "Look at that!" she exclaimed, some days later when an absurd truncated carriage without any horses began to glide about of its own accord. A carriage without any horses indeed! She was called away just as she said that, but came back again after a time and had another look out of the window. It was odd sort of weather nowadays. The sky itself, she could not help thinking, had changed. It was no longer so thick, so watery, so prismatic now that King Edward—see, there he was, stepping out of his neat brougham[7] to go and visit a certain lady opposite—had succeeded Queen Victoria. The clouds had shrunk to a thin gauze; the sky seemed made of metal, which in hot weather tarnished verdigris, copper colour or orange as metal does in a fog. It was a little alarming—this shrinkage. Everything seemed to have shrunk. Driving past Buckingham Palace last night, there was not a trace of that vast erection which she had thought everlasting; top hats, widows' weeds, trumpets, telescopes, wreaths, all had vanished and left not a stain, not a puddle even, on the pavement. But it was now—after another interval she had come back again to her favourite station in the window—now, in the evening, that the change was most remarkable. Look at the lights in the houses! At a touch, a whole room was lit; hundreds of rooms were lit; and one was precisely the same as the other. One could see everything in the little square-shaped boxes; there was no privacy; none of those lingering shadows and odd corners that there used to be; none of those women in aprons carrying wobbly lamps which they put down carefully on this table and on that. At a touch, the whole room was bright. And the sky was bright all night long; and the pavements were bright; everything was bright. She came back again at mid-day. How narrow women had grown lately! They looked like stalks of corn, straight, shining, identical. And men's faces were as bare as the palm of one's hand. The dryness of the atmosphere brought out the colour in everything and seemed to stiffen the muscles of the cheeks. It was harder to cry now. Water was hot in two seconds. Ivy had perished or been scraped off houses. Vegetables were less fertile; families were much smaller. Curtains and covers had been frizzled up and the walls were bare so that new brilliantly coloured pictures of real things like streets, umbrellas, apples, were hung in frames, or painted upon the wood. There was something definite and distinct about the age, which reminded her of the eighteenth century, except that there was a distraction, a desperation—as she was thinking this, the immensely long tunnel in which she seemed to have been travelling for hundreds of years widened; the light poured in; her thoughts became mysteriously tightened and strung up as if a piano tuner had put his key in her back and stretched the nerves very taut; at the same time her hearing quickened; she could hear every whisper and crackle in the room so that the clock ticking on the mantelpiece beat like a hammer. And so for some seconds the light went on becoming brighter and brighter, and she saw everything more and more clearly and the clock ticked

7. A closed one-horse carriage designed in the mid-1800s by Lord Henry Peter Brougham (1778–1868).

louder and louder until there was a terrific explosion right in her ear. Orlando leapt as if she had been violently struck on the head. Ten times she was struck. In fact it was ten o'clock in the morning. It was the eleventh of October. It was 1928. It was the present moment.

No one need wonder that Orlando started, pressed her hand to her heart, and turned pale. For what more terrifying revelation can there be than that it is the present moment? That we survive the shock at all is only possible because the past shelters us on one side and the future on another. But we have no time now for reflections; Orlando was terribly late already. She ran downstairs, she jumped into her motor-car, she pressed the self-starter and was off. Vast blue blocks of building rose into the air; the red cowls of chimneys were spotted irregularly across the sky; the road shone like silver-headed nails; omnibuses bore down upon her with sculptured white-faced drivers; she noticed sponges, bird-cages, boxes of green American cloth. But she did not allow these sights to sink into her mind even the fraction of an inch as she crossed the narrow plank of the present, lest she should fall into the raging torrent beneath. "Why don't you look where you're going to? . . . Put your hand out, can't you?"— that was all she said sharply, as if the words were jerked out of her. For the streets were immensely crowded; people crossed without looking where they were going. People buzzed and hummed round the plate-glass windows within which one could see a glow of red, a blaze of yellow, as if they were bees, Orlando thought—but her thought that they were bees was violently snipped off and she saw, regaining perspective with one flick of her eye, that they were bodies. "Why don't you look where you're going?" she snapped out.

At last, however, she drew up at Marshall & Snelgrove's and went into the shop. Shade and scent enveloped her. The present fell from her like drops of scalding water. Light swayed up and down like thin stuffs puffed out by a summer breeze. She took a list from her bag and began reading in a curious stiff voice at first as if she were holding the words—boy's boots, bath salts, sardines—under a tap of many-coloured water. She watched them change as the light fell on them. Bath and boots became blunt, obtuse; sardines serrated itself like a saw. So she stood in the ground-floor department of Messrs. Marshall & Snelgrove; looked this way and that; snuffed this smell and that and thus wasted some seconds. Then she got into the lift, for the good reason that the door stood open; and was shot smoothly upwards. The very fabric of life now, she thought as she rose, is magic. In the eighteenth century, we knew how everything was done; but here I rise through the air; I listen to voices in America; I see men flying—but how it's done, I can't even begin to wonder. So my belief in magic returns. Now the lift gave a little jerk as it stopped at the first floor; and she had a vision of innumerable coloured stuffs

flaunting in a breeze from which came distinct, strange smells; and
each time the lift stopped and flung its doors open, there was another
slice of the world displayed with all the smells of that world clinging
to it. She was reminded of the river off Wapping in the time of Elizabeth, where the treasure ships and the merchant ships used to anchor.
How richly and curiously they had smelt! How well she remembered
the feel of rough rubies running through her fingers when she dab-
bled them in a treasure sack! And then lying with Sukey—or
whatever her name was—and having Cumberland's lantern flashed
on them! The Cumberlands had a house in Portland Place now and
she had lunched with them the other day and ventured a little joke
with the old man about almshouses in the Sheen Road. He had
winked. But here as the lift could go no higher, she must get out—
Heaven knows into what 'department' as they called it. She stood
still to consult her shopping list, but was blessed if she could see, as
the list bade her, bath salts, or boy's boots anywhere about. And
indeed, she was about to descend again, without buying anything,
but was saved from that outrage by saying aloud automatically the
last item on her list; which happened to be "sheets for a double bed".

"Sheets for a double bed," she said to a man at a counter and, by
a dispensation of Providence, it was sheets that the man at that particular counter happened to sell. For Grimsditch, no, Grimsditch
was dead; Bartholomew, no, Bartholomew was dead; Louise then—
Louise had come to her in a great taking the other day, for she had
found a hole in the bottom of the sheet in the royal bed. Many kings
and queens had slept there—Elizabeth; James; Charles; George; Victoria; Edward; no wonder the sheet had a hole in it. But Louise was
positive she knew who had done it. It was the Prince Consort.

"Sale bosch!"[8] she said (for there had been another war; this time
against the Germans).

"Sheets for a double bed," Orlando repeated dreamily, for a double bed with a silver counterpane in a room fitted in a taste which
she now thought perhaps a little vulgar—all in silver; but she had
furnished it when she had a passion for that metal. While the man
went to get sheets for a double bed, she took out a little looking-glass
and a powder puff. Women were not nearly as roundabout in their
ways, she thought, powdering herself with the greatest unconcern,
as they had been when she herself first turned woman and lay on
the deck of the *Enamoured Lady*. She gave her nose the right tint
deliberately. She never touched her cheeks. Honestly, though she
was now thirty-six, she scarcely looked a day older. She looked just

---

8. Dirty German. "Bosch" was a derogatory slang word for German during the First
World War. The Prince Consort, Queen Victoria's husband, was Prince Albert of Saxe-
Coburg and Gotha, part of what is now Germany.

as pouting, as sulky, as handsome, as rosy (like a million-candled Christmas tree, Sasha had said) as she had done that day on the ice, when the Thames was frozen and they had gone skating——

"The best Irish linen, Ma'am," said the shopman spreading the sheets on the counter,—and they had met an old woman picking up sticks. Here, as she was fingering the linen abstractedly, one of the swing doors between the departments opened and let through, perhaps from the fancy-goods department, a whiff of scent, waxen, tinted as if from pink candles, and the scent curved like a shell round a figure—was it a boy's or was it a girl's?—young, slender, seductive—a girl, by God! furred, pearled, in Russian trousers; but faithless, faithless!

"Faithless!" cried Orlando (the man had gone) and all the shop seemed to pitch and toss with yellow water and far off she saw the masts of the Russian ship standing out to sea, and then, miraculously (perhaps the door opened again) the conch which the scent had made became a platform, a dais, off which stepped a fat, furred woman, marvellously well preserved, seductive, diademed, a Grand Duke's mistress; she who, leaning over the banks of the Volga, eating sandwiches, had watched men drown; and began walking down the shop towards her.

"Oh Sasha!" Orlando cried. Really, she was shocked that she should have come to this; she had grown so fat; so lethargic; and she bowed her head over the linen so that this apparition of a grey woman in fur, and a girl in Russian trousers, with all these smells of wax candles, white flowers, and old ships that it brought with it might pass behind her back unseen.

"Any napkins, towels, dusters to-day, Ma'am?" the shopman persisted. And it is enormously to the credit of the shopping list, which Orlando now consulted, that she was able to reply with every appearance of composure, that there was only one thing in the world she wanted and that was bath salts; which was in another department.

But descending in the lift again—so insidious is the repetition of any scene—she was again sunk far beneath the present moment; and thought when the lift bumped on the ground, that she heard a pot broken against a river bank. As for finding the right department, whatever it might be, she stood engrossed among the handbags, deaf to the suggestions of all the polite, black, combed, sprightly shop assistants, who descending as they did equally and some of them, perhaps, as proudly, even from such depths of the past as she did, chose to let down the impervious screen of the present so that to-day they appeared shop assistants in Marshall & Snelgrove's merely. Orlando stood there hesitating. Through the great glass doors she could see the traffic in Oxford Street. Omnibus seemed to pile itself upon omnibus and then to jerk itself apart. So the ice blocks had

pitched and tossed that day on the Thames. An old nobleman in
furred slippers had sat astride one of them. There he went—she
could see him now—calling down maledictions upon the Irish rebels.
He had sunk there, where her car stood.

"Time has passed over me," she thought, trying to collect herself;
"this is the oncome of middle age. How strange it is! Nothing is any
longer one thing. I take up a handbag and I think of an old bumboat
woman frozen in the ice. Someone lights a pink candle and I see a
girl in Russian trousers. When I step out of doors—as I do now," here
she stepped on to the pavement of Oxford Street, "what is it that I
taste? Little herbs. I hear goat bells. I see mountains. Turkey? India?
Persia?" Her eyes filled with tears.

That Orlando had gone a little too far from the present moment
will, perhaps, strike the reader who sees her now preparing to get
into her motor-car with her eyes full of tears and visions of Persian
mountains. And indeed, it cannot be denied that the most successful practitioners of the art of life, often unknown people by the way,
somehow contrive to synchronise the sixty or seventy different times
which beat simultaneously in every normal human system so that
when eleven strikes, all the rest chime in unison, and the present is
neither a violent disruption nor completely forgotten in the past. Of
them we can justly say that they live precisely the sixty-eight or
seventy-two years allotted them on the tombstone. Of the rest some
we know to be dead though they walk among us; some are not yet
born though they go through the forms of life; others are hundreds
of years old though they call themselves thirty-six. The true length
of a person's life, whatever the *Dictionary of National Biography*[9]
may say, is always a matter of dispute. For it is a difficult business—
this time-keeping; nothing more quickly disorders it than contact
with any of the arts; and it may have been her love of poetry that
was to blame for making Orlando lose her shopping list and start
home without the sardines, the bath salts, or the boots. Now as she
stood with her hand on the door of her motor-car, the present again
struck her on the head. Eleven times she was violently assaulted.

"Confound it all!" she cried, for it is a great shock to the nervous
system, hearing a clock strike—so much so that for some time now
there is nothing to be said of her save that she frowned slightly,
changed her gears admirably, and cried out, as before, "Look where
you're going!" "Don't you know your own mind?" "Why didn't you
say so then?" while the motor-car shot, swung, squeezed, and slid,
for she was an expert driver, down Regent Street, down Haymarket,

9. Woolf's father, Sir Leslie Stephen, edited the original 21-volume edition of the *Dictionary of National Biography* (London: Smith Elder and Co., 1885).

down Northumberland Avenue, over Westminster Bridge, to the left, straight on, to the right, straight on again. . . .

The old Kent Road was very crowded on Thursday, the eleventh of October 1928.[1] People spilt off the pavement. There were women with shopping bags. Children ran out. There were sales at drapers' shops. Streets widened and narrowed. Long vistas steadily shrunk together. Here was a market. Here a funeral. Here a procession with banners upon which was written "Ra—Un", but what else? Meat was very red. Butchers stood at the door. Women almost had their heels sliced off. Amor Vin—that was over a porch.[2] A woman looked out of a bedroom window, profoundly contemplative, and very still. Applejohn and Applebed, Undert—. Nothing could be seen whole or read from start to finish. What was seen begun—like two friends starting to meet each other across the street—was never seen ended. After twenty minutes the body and mind were like scraps of torn paper tumbling from a sack and, indeed, the process of motoring fast out of London so much resembles the chopping up small of identity which precedes unconsciousness and perhaps death itself that it is an open question in what sense Orlando can be said to have existed at the present moment. Indeed we should have given her over for a person entirely disassembled were it not that here, at last, one green screen was held out on the right, against which the little bits of paper fell more slowly; and then another was held out on the left so that one could see the separate scraps now turning over by themselves in the air; and then green screens were held continuously on either side, so that her mind regained the illusion of holding things within itself and she saw a cottage, a farmyard and four cows, all precisely life-size.

When this happened, Orlando heaved a sigh of relief, lit a cigarette, and puffed for a minute or two in silence. Then she called hesitatingly, as if the person she wanted might not be there, "Orlando?" For if there are (at a venture) seventy-six different times all ticking in the mind at once, how many different people are there not— Heaven help us—all having lodgment at one time or another in the human spirit? Some say two thousand and fifty-two. So that it is the most usual thing in the world for a person to call, directly they are alone, Orlando? (if that is one's name) meaning by that, Come, come! I'm sick to death of this particular self. I want another. Hence, the astonishing changes we see in our friends. But it is not altogether plain sailing, either, for though one may say, as Orlando said (being out in the country and needing another self presumably) Orlando? still the Orlando she needs may not come; these selves of which we are built up, one on top of another, as plates are piled on a waiter's

---

1. The first British edition of *Orlando* was published by Hogarth Press on October 11, 1928.
2. Likely a truncated version of *amor vincit omnia*, love conquers all (Latin).

hand, have attachments elsewhere, sympathies, little constitutions
and rights of their own, call them what you will (and for many of
these things there is no name) so that one will only come if it is rain-
ing, another in a room with green curtains, another when Mrs. Jones
is not there, another if you can promise it a glass of wine—and so on;
for everybody can multiply from his own experience the different
terms which his different selves have made with him—and some are
too wildly ridiculous to be mentioned in print at all.

So Orlando, at the turn by the barn, called "Orlando?" with a note
of interrogation in her voice and waited. Orlando did not come.

"All right then," Orlando said with the good humour people prac-
tise on these occasions; and tried another. For she had a great variety of selves to call upon, far more than we have been able to find
room for, since a biography is considered complete if it merely
accounts for six or seven selves, whereas a person may well have as
many thousand. Choosing then, only those selves we have found
room for, Orlando may now have called on the boy who cut the nigger's[3] head down; the boy who strung it up again; the boy who sat on
the hill; the boy who saw the poet; the boy who handed the Queen
the bowl of rose water; or she may have called upon the young man
who fell in love with Sasha; or upon the Courtier; or upon the
Ambassador; or upon the Soldier; or upon the Traveller; or she may
have wanted the woman to come to her; the Gipsy; the Fine Lady;
the Hermit; the girl in love with life; the Patroness of Letters; the
woman who called Mar (meaning hot baths and evening fires) or
Shelmerdine (meaning crocuses and autumn woods) or Bonthrop
(meaning the death we die daily) or all three together—which meant
more things than we have space to write out—all were different and
she may have called upon any one of them.

Perhaps; but what appeared certain (for we are now in the region
of 'perhaps' and 'appears') was that the one she needed most kept
aloof, for she was, to hear her talk, changing her selves as quickly
as she drove—there was a new one at every corner—as happens
when, for some unaccountable reason, the conscious self, which is
the uppermost, and has the power to desire, wishes to be nothing
but one self. This is what some people call the true self, and it is,
they say, compact of all selves we have it in us to be; commanded
and locked up by the Captain self, the Key self, which amalgamates
and controls them all. Orlando was certainly seeking this self as the
reader can judge from overhearing her talk as she drove (and if it is
rambling talk, disconnected, trivial, dull, and sometimes unintelligible it is the reader's fault for listening to a lady talking to herself;

3. See n. 4, p. 40.

we only copy her words as she spoke them, adding in brackets which self in our opinion is speaking, but in this we may well be wrong).

"What then? Who then?" she said. "Thirty-six;[4] in a motor car; a woman. Yes, but a million other things as well. A snob am I?[5] The garter in the hall? The leopards? My ancestors? Proud of them? Yes! Greedy, luxurious, vicious? Am I? (here a new self came in). Don't care a damn if I am. Truthful? I think so. Generous? Oh, but that don't count (here a new self came in). Lying in bed of a morning listening to the pigeons on fine linen; silver dishes; wine; maids; footmen. Spoilt? Perhaps. Too many things for nothing. Hence my books (here she mentioned fifty classical titles; which represented, so we think, the early romantic works that she tore up). Facile, glib, romantic. But (here another self came in) a duffer, a fumbler. More clumsy I couldn't be. And—and—(here she hesitated for a word and if we suggest 'Love' we may be wrong but certainly she laughed and blushed and then cried out—) A toad set in emeralds! Harry the Archduke! Blue-bottles on the ceiling! (here another self came in). But Nell, Kit, Sasha? (she was sunk in gloom: tears actually shaped themselves and she had long given over crying). Trees, she said. (Here another self came in.) I love trees (she was passing a clump) growing there a thousand years. And barns (she passed a tumbledown barn at the edge of the road). And sheep dogs (here one came trotting across the road. She carefully avoided it). And the night. But people (here another self came in). People? (She repeated it as a question.) I don't know. Chattering, spiteful, always telling lies. (Here she turned into the High Street of her native town, which was crowded, for it was market day, with farmers, and shepherds, and old women with hens in baskets.) I like peasants. I understand crops. But (here another self came skipping over the top of her mind like the beam from a lighthouse). Fame! (She laughed.) Fame! Seven editions. A prize.[6] Photographs in the evening papers (here she alluded to the 'Oak Tree' and 'The Burdett Coutts' Memorial Prize which she had won; and we must snatch space to remark how discomposing it is for her biographer that this culmination to which the whole book moved, this peroration with which the book was to end, should be dashed from us on a laugh casually like this; but the truth is that when we write of a woman, everything is out of place—culminations and perorations; the accent never falls where it does with a man). Fame! she repeated. A poet—a charlatan; both every morning as regularly

4. These quotation marks do not have partner end quotation marks. Since this punctuation was not corrected in subsequent Hogarth Press reprints of the text, I have chosen not to correct the punctuation, as Woolf may have intended to leave this long stream-of-consciousness interlude dangling.
5. Woolf read a reflective essay called "Am I a Snob?" to the Bloomsbury Group Memoir Club on December 1, 1936. See *Moments of Being*, pp. 204–20.
6. A reference to the Hawthornden Prize that Sackville-West won.

as the post comes in. To dine, to meet; to meet, to dine; fame—
fame! (She had here to slow down to pass through the crowd of
market people. But no one noticed her. A porpoise in a fishmonger's
shop attracted far more attention than a lady who had won a prize
and might, had she chosen, have worn three coronets one on top of
another on her brow.) Driving very slowly she now hummed as if it
were part of an old song, "With my guineas I'll buy flowering trees,
flowering trees, flowering trees and walk among my flowering trees
and tell my sons what fame is".[7] So she hummed, and now all her
words began to sag here and there like a barbaric necklace of heavy
beads. "And walk among my flowering trees", she sang, accenting the
words strongly, "and see the moon rise slow, the waggons go. . . . ,"
Here she stopped short, and looked ahead of her intently at the
bonnet of the car in profound meditation.

"He sat at Twitchett's table", she mused, "with a dirty ruff on. . . .
Was it old Mr. Baker come to measure the timber? Or was it Sh—p—
re? (for when we speak names we deeply reverence to ourselves we
never speak them whole). She gazed for ten minutes ahead of her,
letting the car come almost to a standstill.

"Haunted!" she cried, suddenly pressing the accelerator. "Haunted!
ever since I was a child. There flies the wild goose. It flies past the
window out to sea. Up I jumped (she gripped the steering-wheel
tighter) and stretched after it. But the goose flies too fast. I've seen it,
here—there—there—England, Persia, Italy. Always it flies fast out
to sea and always I fling after it words like nets (here she flung her
hand out) which shrivel as I've seen nets shrivel drawn on deck with
only sea-weed in them; and sometimes there's an inch of silver—six
words—in the bottom of the net. But never the great fish who lives in
the coral groves." Here she bent her head, pondering deeply.

And it was at this moment, when she had ceased to call "Orlando"
and was deep in thoughts of something else, that the Orlando whom
she had called came of its own accord; as was proved by the change
that now came over her (she had passed through the lodge gates and
was entering the park).

The whole of her darkened and settled, as when some foil whose
addition makes the round and solidity of a surface is added to it, and
the shallow becomes deep and the near distant; and all is contained
as water is contained by the sides of a well. So she was now darkened, stilled, and become, with the addition of this Orlando, what
is called, rightly or wrongly, a single self, a real self. And she fell
silent. For it is probable that when people talk aloud, the selves (of

---

7. Sackville-West, an accomplished gardener, later wrote newspaper columns about gar-
dening, which were collected in the four-volume *In Your Garden* (London: Michael
Joseph, 1951–58).

which there may be more than two thousand) are conscious of disseverment, and are trying to communicate, but when communication is established they fall silent.

Masterfully, swiftly, she drove up the curving drive between the elms and oaks through the falling turf of the park whose fall was so gentle that had it been water it would have spread the beach with a smooth green tide. Planted here and in solemn groups were beech trees and oak trees. The deer stepped among them, one white as snow, another with its head on one side, for some wire netting had caught in its horns. All this; the trees, deer, and turf, she observed with the greatest satisfaction as if her mind had become a fluid that flowed round things and enclosed them completely. Next minute she drew up in the courtyard where, for so many hundred years she had come, on horseback or in coach and six, with men riding before or coming after; where plumes had tossed, torches flashed, and the same flowering trees that let their leaves drop now had shaken their blossoms. Now she was alone. The autumn leaves were falling. The porter opened the great gates. "Morning, James," she said, "there're some things in the car. Will you bring 'em in?" words of no beauty, interest, or significance themselves, it will be conceded, but now so plumped out with meaning that they fell like ripe nuts from a tree, and proved that when the shrivelled skin of the ordinary is stuffed out with meaning it satisfies the senses amazingly. This was true indeed of every movement and action now, usual though they were; so that to see Orlando change her skirt for a pair of whipcord breeches and leather jacket, which she did in less than three minutes, was to be ravished with the beauty of movement as if Madame Lopokova[8] were using her highest art. Then she strode into the dining-room where her old friends, Dryden, Pope, Swift, Addison regarded her demurely at first as who should say Here's the prize winner! but when they reflected that two hundred guineas was in question, they nodded their heads approvingly. Two hundred guineas, they seemed to say; two hundred guineas are not to be sniffed at. She cut herself a slice of bread and ham, clapped the two together and began to eat, striding up and down the room, thus shedding her company habits in a second, without thinking. After five or six such turns, she tossed off a glass of red Spanish wine, and, filling another which she carried in her hand, strode down the long corridor and through a dozen drawing-rooms and so began a perambulation of the house, attended by such elk-hounds and spaniels as chose to follow her.

This, too, was all in the day's routine. As soon would she come home and leave her own grandmother without a kiss as come back

8. Lydia Lopokova (1891–1981), a Russian ballet dancer who was married to one of Woolf's friends, the economist John Maynard Keynes.

and leave the house unvisited. She fancied that the rooms brightened as she came in; stirred, opened their eyes as if they had been
dozing in her absence. She fancied, too, that, hundreds and thousands of times as she had seen them, they never looked the same
twice, as if so long a life as theirs had stored in them a myriad of
moods which changed with winter and summer, bright weather and
dark, and her own fortunes and the people's characters who visited
them. Polite, they always were to strangers, but a little weary; with
her, they were entirely open and at their ease. Why not indeed? They
had known each other for close on four centuries now. They had
nothing to conceal. She knew their sorrows and joys. She knew what
age each part of them was and its little secrets—a hidden drawer, a
concealed cupboard, or some deficiency perhaps, such as part made
up, or added later. They, too, knew her in all her moods and changes.
She had hidden nothing from them; had come to them as boy and
woman, crying and dancing, brooding and gay. In this window-seat,
she had written her first verses; in that chapel, she had been married. And she would be buried here, she reflected, kneeling on the
window-sill in the long gallery and sipping Spanish wine. Though
she could hardly fancy it, the body of the heraldic leopard would be
making yellow pools on the floor the day they lowered her to lie
among her ancestors. She, who believed in no immortality, could not
help feeling that her soul would come and go forever with the reds
on the panels and the greens on the sofa. For the room—she had
strolled into the Ambassador's bedroom—shone like a shell that has
lain at the bottom of the sea for centuries and has been crusted over
and painted a million tints by the water; it was rose and yellow, green
and sand-coloured. It was frail as a shell, as iridescent and as empty.
No Ambassador would ever sleep there again. Ah, but she knew
where the heart of the house still beat. Gently opening a door, she
stood on the threshold so that (as she fancied) the room could not
see her and watched the tapestry rising and falling on the eternal
faint breeze which never failed to move it. Still the hunter rode; still
Daphne flew. The heart still beat, she thought, however faintly, however far withdrawn; the frail indomitable heart of the immense
building.

Now, calling her troop of dogs to her she passed down the gallery
whose floor was laid with whole oak trees sawn across. Rows of
chairs with all their velvets faded stood ranged against the wall holding their arms out for Elizabeth, for James, for Shakespeare it might
be, for Cecil, who never came. The sight made her gloomy. She
unhooked the rope that fenced them off. She sat on the Queen's
chair; she opened a manuscript book lying on Lady Betty's table; she
stirred her fingers in the aged rose leaves; she brushed her short hair
with King James' silver brushes; she bounced up and down upon his

bed (but no King would ever sleep there again, for all Louise's new sheets) and pressed her cheek against the worn silver counterpane that lay upon it. But everywhere were little lavender bags to keep the moth out and printed notices, "Please do not touch", which, though she had put them there herself, seemed to rebuke her. The house was no longer hers entirely, she sighed. It belonged to time now; to history; was past the touch and control of the living.[9] Never would beer be spilt here any more, she thought (she was in the bedroom that had been old Nick Greene's), or holes burnt in the carpet. Never two hundred servants come running and brawling down the corridors with warming pans and great branches for the great fireplaces. Never would ale be brewed and candles made and saddles fashioned and stone shaped in the workshops outside the house. Hammers and mallets were silent now. Chairs and beds were empty; tankards of silver and gold were locked in glass cases. The great wings of silence beat up and down the empty house.

So she sat at the end of the gallery with her dogs couched round her, in Queen Elizabeth's hard armchair. The gallery stretched far away to a point where the light almost failed. It was as a tunnel bored deep into the past. As her eyes peered down it, she could see people laughing and talking; the great men she had known; Dryden, Swift, and Pope; and statesmen in colloquy; and lovers dallying in the window-seats; and people eating and drinking at the long tables; and the wood smoke curling round their heads and making them sneeze and cough. Still further down, she saw sets of splendid dancers formed for the quadrille. A fluty, frail, but nevertheless stately music began to play. An organ boomed. A coffin was borne into the chapel. A marriage procession came out of it. Armed men with helmets left for the wars. They brought banners back from Flodden and Poitiers and stuck them on the wall. The long gallery filled itself thus, and still peering further, she thought she could make out at the very end, beyond the Elizabethans and the Tudors, some one older, further, darker, a cowled figure, monastic, severe, a monk,[1] who went with his hands clasped, and a book in them, murmuring——

Like thunder, the stable clock struck four. Never did any earthquake so demolish a whole town. The gallery and all its occupants fell to powder. Her own face, that had been dark and sombre as she gazed, was lit as by an explosion of gunpowder. In this same light everything near her showed with extreme distinctness. She saw two

---

9. Parts of Knole would have been open to visitors, hence the rope and "do not touch" signs. Knole was given to the National Trust in 1946 by Charles Sackville-West, 4th Lord Sackville. The Sackville-West family still lives in private apartments at Knole by virtue of a 200-year lease.

1. Knole was originally the home of an archbishop before Henry VIII took the land for himself in 1538, around the time of the dissolution of Catholic monasteries in England.

flies circling round and noticed the blue sheen on their bodies; she
saw a knot in the wood where her foot was, and her dog's ear twitching. At the same time, she heard a bough creaking in the garden, a
sheep coughing in the park, a swift screaming past the window. Her
own body quivered and tingled as if suddenly stood naked in a hard
frost. Yet, she kept, as she had not done when the clock struck ten
in London, complete composure (for she was now one and entire,
and presented, it may be, a larger surface to the shock of time). She
rose, but without precipitation, called her dogs, and went firmly but
with great alertness of movement down the staircase and out into
the garden. Here the shadows of the plants were miraculously distinct. She noticed the separate grains of earth in the flower beds as
if she had a microscope stuck to her eye. She saw the intricacy of the
twigs of every tree. Each blade of grass was distinct and the marking of veins and petals. She saw Stubbs, the gardener, coming along
the path, and every button on his gaiters was visible; she saw Betty
and Prince, the cart horses, and never had she marked so clearly
the white star on Betty's forehead, and the three long hairs that fell
down below the rest on Prince's tail. Out in the quadrangle the old
grey walls of the house looked like a scraped new photograph; she
heard the loud speaker condensing on the terrace a dance tune that
people were listening to in the red velvet opera house at Vienna.
Braced and strung up by the present moment she was also strangely
afraid, as if whenever the gulf of time gaped and let a second through
some unknown danger might come with it. The tension was too
relentless and too rigorous to be endured long without discomfort.
She walked more briskly than she liked, as if her legs were moved
for her, through the garden and out into the park. Here she forced
herself, by a great effort, to stop by the carpenter's shop, and to stand
stock-still watching Joe Stubbs fashion a cart wheel. She was standing with her eye fixed on his hand when the quarter struck. It hur-
tled through her like a meteor, so hot that no fingers can hold it.
She saw with disgusting vividness that the thumb on Joe's right hand
was without a finger nail and there was a raised saucer of pink flesh
where the nail should have been. The sight was so repulsive that she
felt faint for a moment, but in that moment's darkness, when her
eyelids flickered, she was relieved of the pressure of the present.
There was something strange in the shadow that the flicker of her
eyes cast, something which (as anyone can test for himself by looking
now at the sky) is always absent from the present—whence its terror,
its nondescript character—something one trembles to pin through
the body with a name and call beauty, for it has no body, is as a
shadow without substance or quality of its own, yet has the power
to change whatever it adds itself to. This shadow now, while she
flickered her eye in her faintness in the carpenter's shop, stole out,

Figure 8. Orlando at the present time. © The University of Sussex and the Society of Authors as the Literary Representative of the Estate of Leonard Woolf. British Library, London, UK. From the British Library archive / Bridgeman Images.

and attaching itself to the innumerable sights she had been receiving, composed them into something tolerable, comprehensible. Her
mind began to toss like the sea. Yes, she thought, heaving a deep sigh
of relief, as she turned from the carpenter's shop to climb the hill, I
can begin to live again. I am by the Serpentine, she thought, the
little boat is climbing through the white arch of a thousand deaths.
I am about to understand. . . .

Those were her words, spoken quite distinctly, but we cannot conceal the fact that she was now a very indifferent witness to the
truth of what was before her and might easily have mistaken a sheep
for a cow, or an old man called Smith for one who was called Jones
and was no relation of his whatever. For the shadow of faintness
which the thumb without a nail had cast had deepened now, at the
back of her brain (which is the part furthest from sight), into a pool
where things dwell in darkness so deep that what they are we scarcely
know. She now looked down into this pool or sea in which everything is reflected—and, indeed, some say that all our most violent
passions, and art and religion, are the reflections which we see in
the dark hollow at the back of the head when the visible world is
obscured for the time. She looked there now, long, deeply, profoundly, and immediately the ferny path up the hill along which she
was walking became not entirely a path, but partly the Serpentine;
the hawthorn bushes were partly ladies and gentlemen sitting with
card-cases and gold-mounted canes; the sheep were partly tall Mayfair houses; everything was partly something else, as if her mind
had become a forest with glades branching here and there; things
came nearer, and further, and mingled and separated and made the
strangest alliances and combinations in an incessant chequer of light
and shade. Except when Canute, the elk-hound, chased a rabbit and
so reminded her that it must be about half past four—it was indeed
twenty-three minutes to six—she forgot the time.

The ferny path led, with many turns and windings, higher and
higher to the oak tree, which stood on the top. The tree had grown
bigger, sturdier, and more knotted since she had known it, somewhere
about the year 1588, but it was still in the prime of life. The little
sharply frilled leaves were still fluttering thickly on its branches.
Flinging herself on the ground, she felt the bones of the tree running
out like ribs from a spine this way and that beneath her. She liked
to think that she was riding the back of the world. She liked to attach
herself to something hard. As she flung herself down a little square
book bound in red cloth fell from the breast of her leather jacket—
her poem The Oak Tree. "I should have brought a trowel," she
reflected. The earth was so shallow over the roots that it seemed
doubtful if she could do as she meant and bury the book here.
Besides, the dogs would dig it up. No luck ever attended these

symbolical celebrations, she thought. Perhaps it would be as well then to do without them. She had a little speech on the tip of her tongue which she meant to speak over the book as she buried it. (It was a copy of the first edition, signed by the author and artist.) "I bury this as a tribute," she was going to have said, "a return to the land of what the land has given me," but Lord! once one began mouthing words aloud, how silly they sounded! She was reminded of old Greene getting upon a platform the other day comparing her with Milton (save for his blindness) and handing her a cheque for two hundred guineas. She had thought then, of the oak tree here on its hill, and what has that got to do with this, she had wondered? What has praise and fame to do with poetry? What has seven editions (the book had already gone into no less) got to do with the value of it?[2] Was not writing poetry a secret transaction, a voice answering a voice? So that all this chatter and praise and blame and meeting people who admired one and meeting people who did not admire one was as ill suited as could be to the thing itself—a voice answering a voice. What could have been more secret, she thought, more slow, and like the intercourse of lovers, than the stammering answer she had made all these years to the old crooning song of the woods, and the farms and the brown horses standing at the gate, neck to neck, and the smithy and the kitchen and the fields, so laboriously bearing wheat, turnips, grass, and the garden blowing irises and fritillaries?

So she let her book lie unburied and dishevelled on the ground, and watched the vast view, varied like an ocean floor this evening with the sun lightening it and the shadows darkening it. There was a village with a church tower among elm trees; a grey domed manor house in a park; a spark of light burning on some glass-house; a farmyard with yellow corn stacks. The fields were marked with black tree clumps, and beyond the fields stretched long woodlands, and there was the gleam of a river, and then hills again. In the far distance Snowdon's crags broke white among the clouds; she saw the far Scottish hills and the wild tides that swirl about the Hebrides. She listened for the sound of gun-firing out at sea. No—only the wind blew. There was no war to-day. Drake had gone; Nelson had gone. "And there", she thought, letting her eyes, which had been looking at these far distances, drop once more to the land beneath her, "was my land once: that Castle between the downs was mine; and all that moor running almost to the sea was mine." Here the landscape (it must have been some trick of the fading light) shook itself, heaped itself, let all this encumbrance of houses, castles, and woods slide off its tent-shaped sides. The bare mountains of Turkey

---

2. *The Land* had already gone through multiple printings by October 1928.

were before her. It was blazing noon. She looked straight at the baked hill-side. Goats cropped the sandy tufts at her feet. An eagle soared above her. The raucous voice of old Rustum, the gipsy, croaked in her ears, "What is your antiquity and your race, and your possessions compared with this? What do you need with four hundred bedrooms and silver lids on all your dishes, and housemaids dusting?"

At this moment some church clock chimed in the valley. The tent-like landscape collapsed and fell. The present showered down upon her head once more but now that the light was fading, gentler than before, calling into view nothing detailed, nothing small, but only misty fields, cottages with lamps in them, the slumbering bulk of a wood, and a fan-shaped light pushing the darkness before it along some lane. Whether it had struck nine, ten, or eleven, she could not say. Night had come—night that she loved of all times, night in which the reflections in the dark pool of the mind shine more clearly than by day. It was not necessary to faint now in order to look deep into the darkness where things shape themselves and to see in the pool of the mind now Shakespeare, now a girl in Russian trousers, now a toy boat on the Serpentine, and then the Atlantic itself, where it storms in great waves past Cape Horn. She looked into the darkness. There was her husband's brig, rising to the top of the wave! Up, it went, and up and up. The white arch of a thousand deaths rose before it. Oh rash, oh ridiculous man, always sailing, so uselessly, round Cape Horn in the teeth of a gale! But the brig was through the arch and out on the other side; it was safe at last!

"Ecstasy!" she cried, "ecstasy!" And then the wind sank, the waters grew calm; and she saw the waves rippling peacefully in the moonlight.

"Marmaduke Bonthrop Shelmerdine!" she cried, standing by the oak tree.

The beautiful, glittering name fell out of the sky like a steel-blue feather. She watched it fall, turning and twisting like a slow-falling arrow that cleaves the deep air beautifully. He was coming, as he always came, in moments of dead calm; when the wave rippled and the spotted leaves fell slowly over her foot in the autumn woods; when the leopard was still; the moon was on the waters, and nothing moved between sky and sea. Then he came.

All was still now. It was near midnight. The moon rose slowly over the weald.[3] Its light raised a phantom castle upon earth. There stood the great house with all its windows robed in silver. Of wall or substance there was none. All was phantom. All was still. All was lit as for the coming of a dead Queen. Gazing below her, Orlando

---

3. Woodland.

saw dark plumes tossing in the courtyard, and torches flickering and shadows kneeling. A Queen once more stepped from her chariot.

"The house is at your service, Ma'am," she cried, curtseying deeply. "Nothing has been changed. The dead Lord, my father, shall lead you in."

As she spoke, the first stroke of midnight sounded. The cold breeze of the present brushed her face with its little breath of fear. She looked anxiously into the sky. It was dark with clouds now. The wind roared in her ears. But in the roar of the wind she heard the roar of an aeroplane coming nearer and nearer.

"Here! Shel, here!" she cried, baring her breast to the moon (which now showed bright) so that her pearls glowed like the eggs of some vast moon-spider. The aeroplane rushed out of the clouds and stood over her head. It hovered above her. Her pearls burnt like a phosphorescent flare in the darkness.

And as Shelmerdine, now grown a fine sea captain, hale, fresh-coloured, and alert, leapt to the ground, there sprang up over his head a single wild bird.

"It is the goose!" Orlando cried. "The wild goose. . . ."

And the twelfth stroke of midnight sounded; the twelfth stroke of midnight, Thursday, the eleventh of October, Nineteen hundred and Twenty Eight.

INDEX[1]

A., Lord, 104
Abbey, Westminster, 31
Addison, Joseph, 91, 106, 113
Alexandra, Queen, 43
Archduchess Harriet of Finster-Aarhorn (*see* Archduke
    Harry), 61, 96, 97
Archduke, Harry, the, 130
Arlington House, 105

Bartholomew, Widow, 124, 126, 127
Bartolus, Captain Nicholas Benedict, 83, 88, 106
Basket, Butler, 126
Boswell, James, 119
Brigge, John Fenner, 69, 73
Browne, Sir Thomas, 40, 42, 48
Browning, Robert, 148

C., Marquis of, 104, 130
Canute, the elk-hound, 130
Carlyle, Thomas, 148
Carpenter, Nurse, 38
Charles the Second, King, 64
Chesterfield, Lady, 103
Chesterfield, Lord, 114, 154
Chubb, Eusebius, 122
Cicero, 55
Clorinda, 18
Consort, the Prince, 160
Cumberland, Earl of, 17, 160

Deffand, Madame du, 107
Donne, John, 48, 152
Drake, 173
Dryden, John, 91, 106, 169
Dupper, Mr., 38, 41, 45, 92, 139

Elizabeth, Queen, 12, 13, 14, 15, 16, 54
Euphrosyne, 18

---

1. Woolf's index is a spoof on the traditional index one might find in a biography. Of note is its equal treatment of nobles, famous authors, servants and other working people, and Canute the elk-hound and Pippin the spaniel. The page numbers listed here correspond to the (often idiosyncratic) page numbers included in the first Hogarth edition.

THE END

BACKGROUND AND CONTEXTS

J. C. SQUIRE

Prose-de-Société[†]

This book is easier to read than to describe. It is, indeed, very easy to read and very difficult to describe. Mrs. Woolf, who has not previously inclined to fairy tale and phantasy, has suddenly produced a book which has something in common with "Serena Blandish," "The Venetian Glass Lady," and the tales of Mr. David Garnett,[1] but which is written on a larger scale, and is of so odd and original a conception that a summary of its theme is almost impossible, and no two summaries would greatly resemble each other.

The old chroniclers, when describing the sack of cities, commonly said that the brutal victors "respected neither age nor sex." In this sole respect the author of "Orlando" resembles the pikemen of Alva and the musketeers of Tilly. The reader never knows when he is going to be whisked forward for a century, and in the middle of the story the hero calmly changes from a man into a woman. "Memory," observes Mrs. Woolf in another connection,

> is the seamstress, and a capricious one at that. Memory runs her needle in and out, up and down, hither and thither. We know not what comes next, or what follows after. Thus, the most ordinary movement in the world, such as sitting down at a table and pulling the inkstand towards one, may agitate a thousand odd, disconnected fragments, now bright, now dim, hanging and bobbing and dipping and flaunting, like the under-linen of a family of fourteen on a line in a gale of wind. (43)

The spectacle of Orlando's progress is not quite so inconsequent as the sequence of verbal, visual, and conceptual associations which flow by when the mind surrenders itself completely; for anything like that one must go to the intolerable gibberings of Miss Gertrude Stein. Mrs. Woolf is even on the hither side of [Laurence] Sterne, who said that his method was to set down one sentence and (being a clergyman) to trust to God for the next, but whose most jerky inconsequences have often a great deliberation about them.

---

† From the *Observer* (21 October 1928): 6. Copyright © Guardian News and Media Ltd. 2023. Also reprinted in *Virginia Woolf: The Critical Heritage*, ed. Robin Majumdar and Allen McLaurin (New York: Routledge, 2009), pp. 227–29. Page numbers are to this Norton Critical Edition.

1. Perhaps a reference to *Lady into Fox* (1922), by David Garnett, a member of the Blooms-bury Group and lover of Duncan Grant, who was in turn the lover of Vanessa Bell, Woolf's sister. *"Serena Blandish"*: Serena Blandish or the Difficulty of Getting Married, 1925 novel by Enid Bagnold. *"The Venetian Glass Lady"*: Perhaps a reference to Elinor Wylie's 1926 novel, *The Venetian Glass Nephew*.

Mrs. Woolf's general outline is planned and controlled; within that outline she seems to allow her narrative, which has the tenour of a day-dream, to go where it will.

Orlando, though he never goes so far as to be more than one person at one time, is a successive selection from the ancestors of a lady of our own day, for whose portrait Miss V. Sackville-West, to whom the book is dedicated, has posed. He begins as an Elizabethan nobleman-poet, a type whose features are sketched in a very characteristic page of Mrs. Woolf's prose:—

> The taste for books was an early one. As a child he was sometimes found at midnight by a page still reading. They took his taper away, and he bred glow-worms to serve his purpose. They took the glow-worms away, and he almost burnt the house down with a tinder. To put it in a nutshell, leaving the novelist to smooth out the crumbled silk and all its implications, he was a noble man afflicted with a love of literature. Many people of his time, still more of his rank, escaped the infection and were thus free to run or ride or make love at their own sweet will. But some were early infected by a germ said to be bred of the pollen of the asphodel and to be blown out of Greece and Italy; which was of so deadly a nature that it would shake the hand as it was raised to strike, cloud the eye as it sought its prey, and make the tongue stammer as it declared its love. It was the fatal nature of this disease to substitute a phantom for reality, so that Orlando, to whom fortune had given every gift—plate, linen, houses, men-servants, carpets, beds in profusion—had only to open a book for the whole vast accumulation to turn to mist. The nine acres of stone which were his house vanished; one hundred and fifty indoor servants disappeared; his eighty riding horses became invisible; it would take too long to count the carpets, sofas, trappings, china, plates, cruets, chafing dishes and other movables often of beaten gold, which evaporated like so much sea mist under the miasma. So it was, and Orlando would sit by himself, reading, a naked man. (41)

This passage may serve as an illustration of the charming manner which Mrs. Woolf has ironically fabricated for the occasion, a manner with touches of all the styles, here a paragraph in the narrative mode of the eighteenth century, here a series of little clauses with the imagery and the cadence of Euphuism.

Orlando has adventures with Love and with the Muses. Disappointments with both are the more easily overcome owing to a sudden lapse of years and his appointment by Charles II as Ambassador to the Sublime Porte. Trouble with the Turks is followed by a convenient change of success and escape into the England of Queen Anne, Pope and Addison. In Lord Palmerston's day she fell in love with a sailor and in October, 1928, the sailor, after long absence, flew to her arms (so to speak) in an aeroplane. No human novelist could quite sustain a character through such vicissitudes, that it must be admitted that Orlando is never a person. Mrs. Woolf says of her:

> She had been a gloomy boy, in love with death, as boys are; and then she had been amorous and florid; and then she had been sprightly and satirical; and sometimes she had tried prose and sometimes she had tried drama. Yet through all these changes she had remained, she reflected, fundamentally the same. She had the same brooding meditative temper, the same love of animals and nature, the same passion for the country and the seasons. (125–26)

That much is true of individuals and of families: Mrs. Woolf seems also to have the story of English literature and the English people in mind. The book, however, will no more be read for any allegorical significance it may have than for its study of a character which does not exist.

Its attractions are twofold. In the first place, Mrs. Woolf's scheme allows her, at will, to give us sidelights on manners and pictures of bygone social scenes—the Thames frozen in Jacobean days, Constantinople in Caroline days, the drawing-rooms and countrysides of several generations. When Orlando is a poet we are presented with a very amusing satirical picture of literary life; when he is an ambassador we have a glimpse of St James's and Nell Gwynn. Orlando is a thread on which many bright beads are strung—beads both bright and well turned. Secondly, Mrs. Woolf's English is always elegant, and her selection of significant details is usually sure. On occasion she is not merely interesting but amusing:

> But the doctors were hardly wiser then than they are now, and after prescribing rest and exercise, starvation and nourishment, society and solitude, that he should lie in bed all day and ride forty miles between lunch and dinner, together with the usual sedatives and irritants, diversified, as the fancy took them, with possets of newt's slobber on rising, and draughts of peacock's gall on going to bed, they left him to himself, and gave it as their opinion that he had been asleep for a week. (37)

Unfortunately the amusing passages are not very frequent; there is a wan, pervasive smile, and no more; humour can hardly be drawn out of the persons, for they change too often. I mentioned Sterne just now: to Sterne we often return, and he frequently makes us laugh aloud. To Mrs. Woolf's book, I, at least, shall not return: having discovered the outline I should enjoy it less and less at each perusal: it did not make me laugh aloud at the first. Neither did it (though there are a few beautiful phrases) give me any shock of aesthetic delight, though it never for a moment bored me. There is a sort of fatigued grace, an exquisite nebulosity, about the book. It gives the impression that the author had no gusto in the writing of it, hardly a moment of ecstasy, of devotion, of self-forgetfulness of any kind, even of mere high spirits. Did we know no more about her than this book, we might suppose that her dominant feeling was a tepid amusement at the petty futility of life—"disillusionment" is hardly the word, as we have no sense that any illusions have been lost. I have no desire to break a butterfly upon a wheel, or even to impale it upon a pin: this book is a very pleasant trifle, and will entertain the drawing-rooms for an hour: a suitable companion for the jade carving and the painted snuff-boxes. But I think that even of its kind it is not in the first order. Even a trifle, to be excellent, must have enthusiasm behind it. This book, one feels, was conceived frivolously and chancily, and carried through with too painstaking a spontaneity and too little affection or respect for the reader, the intelligence in it being immeasurably in excess of the mirth, the response to beauty, the emotional interest in history, morals, character or anything else. Possibly it is the work of a mind which, at bottom, is purely critical.

ARNOLD BENNETT

A Woman's High-Brow Lark[†]

You cannot keep your end up at a London dinner-party in these weeks unless you have read Mrs Virginia Woolf's *Orlando*. For about a fortnight I succeeded in not reading it—partly from obstinacy and partly from a natural desire for altercation at table about what ought and ought not to be read. Then I saw that Hugh Walpole had described it as 'another masterpiece', and that Desmond MacCarthy had given it very high praise.

I have a great opinion of the literary opinions of these two critics. So I bought the book and read it. I now know exactly what I think of it, and I can predict the most formidable rumpuses at future parties.

It is a very odd volume. It has a preface, in which Mrs Woolf names the names of 53 people who have helped her with it. It has,

† From the *Evening Standard* (8 November 1928): 7. Reprinted in *Virginia Woolf: The Critical Heritage*, ed. Robin Majumdar and Allen McLaurin (New York: Routledge, 2009), pp. 232–33.

too, an index. I admit some justification for the preface, but none for the index.

Further, the novel, which is a play of fancy, a wild fantasia, a romance, a high-brow lark,[1] is illustrated with ordinary realistic photographs, including several of Vita Sackville-West (a Hawthornden prize-winner), to whom the book is dedicated. The portraits of Miss Sackville-West are labelled 'Orlando'.

This is the oddest of all the book's oddities. . . .

Orlando at the end of the book has achieved an age of some four centuries. Which reminds one of the Wandering Jew and the Flying Dutchman. Half-way through the story he changes into a woman—and 'stays put'. Which reminds one of *Seraphita*, the dullest book that Balzac ever wrote.

I surmise that Orlando is intended to be the incarnation of something or other—say, the mustang spirit of the joy of life, but this is not quite clear to me.

The first chapter is goodish. It contains vivacious descriptions of spectacular matters—such as a big frost, royal courts, and the love-making of Orlando and a Muscovite girl in furs and in the open air amid the fiercest frost since the ice-age. Mrs Woolf almost convinces us of the possibility of this surely very difficult dalliance.

The second chapter shows a startling decline and fall-off. Fanciful embroidery, wordy, and naught else!

The succeeding chapters are still more tedious in their romp of fancy. Mrs Woolf does not seem to have understood that fancy must have something to play *on*. She has left out the basic substance. For example, Orlando, both as man and as woman, is said to have had many lovers, but details are given of only one love.

I shall no doubt be told that I have missed the magic of the work. The magic is precisely what I indeed have missed.

The writing is good at the beginning, but it goes to pieces; it even skids into bad grammar (e.g. on p. 262).[2] Mrs Woolf has accomplished some of the most beautiful writing of the modern age, including paragraphs that Nathaniel Hawthorne himself might have signed. *Orlando*, however, has nothing anywhere near as good as her best.

The theme is a great one. But it is a theme for a Victor Hugo, not for Mrs Woolf, who, while sometimes excelling in fancy and in delicate realistic observation, has never yet shown the mighty imaginative

1. Highbrow literature would have been seen by critics of both Woolf and her modernist peers as pretentious or overly intellectual. Woolf discusses what it means to be high-brow, middlebrow, or lowbrow in her essay "Middlebrow: A Letter Written but Not Sent," the *Atlantic* (July 1942): 43–47.
2. Bennett is likely referring to Woolf's semicolon-filled parody of Victorian prose on p. 155.

power which the theme clearly demands. Her best novel, *To the Lighthouse* raised my hopes of her. *Orlando* has dashed them and they lie in iridescent fragments at my feet.

Mrs Woolf's publishing firm, the Hogarth Press, has just issued a critical work, *The Structure of the Novel*, by Edwin Muir. In dealing with the later developments of English fiction, Mr Muir names James Joyce, Mrs Woolf and (to a less extent) Aldous Huxley as the only important innovating novelists.

I would concede him the first and the last, but I have horrid doubts about the middle term. In particular I have failed to perceive any genuine originality in the method of *Mrs Dalloway*. If originality there is, it fails in its object of presenting character.

CLEVELAND B. CHASE

Mrs. Woolf Explores the "Time" Element in Human Relations[†]

Those who open "Orlando" expecting another novel in the vein of "Mrs. Dalloway" and "To the Lighthouse" will discover, to their joy or sorrow, that once more Mrs. Woolf has broken with tradition and convention and has set out to explore still another fourth dimension of writing. Not that she has abandoned the "stream of consciousness" method which she used with such conspicuous success in her previous novels, but with it she has combined what, for lack of a better term, we might describe as an application to writing of the Einstein theory of relativity. In this new work she is largely preoccupied with the "time" element in character and human relationships, and with a statement of the exact complexion of that intangible moment, a combination of past and future of objective reality and subjective consciousness, which we refer to as the present.

> An hour [she explained], once it lodges in the queer element of the human spirit, may be stretched to fifty or one hundred times its clock length; on the other hand, an hour may be accurately represented on the timepiece of the mind by one second. * * * The most successful of practitioners of the art of life, often unknown people by the way, somehow contrive to synchronize the sixty or seventy different times which beat simultaneously in every normal human system so that when eleven strikes, all the rest chime in unison, and the present is neither a violent

† From the *New York Times* (21 October 1928): 7. Reprinted in *Virginia Woolf: The Critical Heritage*, ed. Robin Majumdar and Allen McLaurin (New York: Routledge, 2009), pp. 230–31. Page numbers are to this Norton Critical Edition.

disruption nor completely forgotten in the past. Of them we can justly say that they live precisely the sixty-eight or seventy-two years allotted them on the tombstone. Of the rest, some we know to be dead, though they walk among us; others are hundreds of years old, though they call themselves thirty-six. (53, 162)

Mrs. Woolf's hero-heroine is hundreds of years old. At the beginning of the book Orlando is a boy of 16, melancholy, indolent, loving solitude and given to writing poetry; the age is the Elizabethan; the book ends on the 11th of October, 1928, and Orlando is a thoroughly modern matron of 36, who has published a successful book of poems and has evolved a hard-earned philosophy of life. Thus, to express her very modern fourth-dimensional concepts, Mrs. Woolf has fallen back upon one of the most ancient of literary forms, the allegory. In doing so she has left the book perhaps more confused than was strictly necessary.

* * *

The rest of the novel may be divided into two parts; the first deals somewhat whimsically with Orlando's attempts to adjust herself to the conventions of nineteenth-century England. The second, and by far the most stimulating section of the book, describes Orlando at the present moment, and traces with breath-taking delicacy the influence of her past upon her present. It is in these last thirty-odd pages that the book springs startlingly to life. Up to this point it had seemed a pleasant narrative made notable by a number of passages of great beauty and by occasional bits of vivid description, but marred by a rather self-conscious facetiousness on the part of the author, an addiction to parenthetical whimsicalities that are not particularly effective.

In the closing pages of the novel Mrs. Woolf welds into a compact whole what had seemed to be a series of loosely connected episodes. In them she seems to reach down through the whole superstructure of life and to lay bare a new, or at least a hitherto unperceived, arrangement of those ephemeral flashes of memory of perception that go to make up consciousness. Throughout the ages people have remarked that time, under certain circumstances, seems much longer than under certain other circumstances. Mrs. Woolf presents concrete proof that this is not merely an impression, but a fact, by showing of what time, not as a mechanical but as a human element, consists. She has carried the "stream of consciousness" technique a step further; she has not been satisfied to present a succession of thoughts and sensations passing through the mind; she shows what is behind those thoughts and sensations, whence they spring, and how great their relative value.

In attempting to describe such subtle and illusive qualities—or should they be called quantities?—Mrs. Woolf has faced squarely one of the most puzzling technical and esthetic problems that confront contemporary novelists. The mere fact that she has stated the problem as succinctly as she does in the course of this book is immensely stimulating, whether or not one feels that she has achieved a final solution of it. It is something of a question whether the tendency of contemporary novelists to become more and more introspective can profitably be carried much further. If it is to continue, however, Mrs. Woolf has pointed out the direction in which it must develop.

CONRAD AIKEN

From the Dial[†]

That Mrs Woolf is a highly ingenious writer has been made glitteringly obvious for us in Mrs Dalloway and To the Lighthouse: which is not in the least to minimize the fact that those two novels also contained a great deal of beauty. That she is, and has perhaps always been, in danger of carrying ingenuity too far, is suggested, among other things, by her new novel, or "biography," Orlando. Whatever else one thinks about this book, one is bound to admit that it is exceedingly, not to say disconcertingly, clever. In England as well as in America it has set the critics by the ears. They have not known quite how to take it—whether to regard it as a biography, or a satire on biography; as a history, or a satire on history; as a novel, or as an allegory. And it is at once clear, when one reads Orlando, why this confusion should have arisen; for the tone of the book, from the very first pages, is a tone of mockery. Mrs Woolf has expanded a *jeu d'esprit* to the length of a novel. One might almost say, in fact—when one notes in the index that there are precisely seven references to "The Oak" (a poem which plays an important part in the story—and which in a sense is almost its ghostly protagonist) and when one recalls that Knole, a famous English house, is at Sevenoaks, (clearly the house described in the novel) that Orlando is a kind of colossal pun. More exactly, one might compare it with Alice in Wonderland; for if the latter is an inspired dream, organized with a logic almost insanely unswerving, so the former is a kind of inspired joke, a joke charged with meanings, in which the logic, if not quite so meticulous, is at any rate pressing.

† From the *Dial* (February 1929): 147–49.

There is thus an important element of "spoof" in Orlando: Mrs Woolf apparently wants us to know that she does not herself take the thing with the last [*sic*] seriousness—that she is pulling legs, keeping her tongue in her cheek, and winking, now and then, a quite shameless and enormous wink. With all this, which she accomplishes with a skill positively equestrian, she is obliged, perforce, to fall into a style which one cannot help feeling is a little unfortunate. It is a style which makes fun of style: it is glibly rhetorical, glibly sententious, glibly poetic, glibly analytical, glibly austere, by turns—deliberately so; and while this might be, and is, extraordinarily diverting for a chapter or two, or for something like the length of a short story, one finds it a little fatiguing in a full-length book. Of course, Mrs Woolf's theme, with its smug annihilation of time, may be said to have demanded, if the whole question of credibility was to be begged, a tone quite frankly and elaborately artificial. Just the same, it is perhaps questionable whether she has not been *too* icily and wreathedly elaborate in this, and taken her Orlando in consequence a shade too far towards an arid and ingenious convention. Granted that what she wanted to tell us was a fable, or allegory: that she wanted to trace the aesthetic evolution of a family (and by implication that of a country) over a period of three hundred years: and that she had hit upon the really first-rate idea of embodying this racial evolution in one undying person: need she quite so much have presumed on our incredulity? One suspects that in such a situation an ounce of ingenuousness might be worth ten times its weight in ingenuity; and that a little more of the direct and deep sincerity of the last few pages, which are really beautiful and really moving, might have made Orlando a minor masterpiece.

As it is, it is an extremely amusing and brilliant *tour de force*. It is as packed with reference, almost, as The Waste Land. Some of the references, it is true, are too esoteric—for one not in the enchanted circle—to be universally valid; and this may or may not be thought a mistake. One's private jokes and innuendoes are pretty apt to become meaningless, with the passage of time and the disappearance of the *milieu* which gave them point. This, again, is of a piece with Mrs Woolf's general air of high spirits; of having a lark; of going, as it were, on an intellectual spree; and that there is far too little of this spirit in contemporary literature we can cheerfully admit. But here too one feels inclined to enter a protest. For the idea, as has been said, is first-rate, an idea from which a poet might have evoked a profusion of beauty as easily as the djinn[1] was released from his bottle. Mrs Woolf does indeed give us a profusion of beauty and wisdom: but it is beauty and wisdom of a very special sort. Her roses

---

1. A spirit in Arabic folklore, often referred to in English as a genie.

are cloth roses, her scenes are scenes from a tapestry, her "wisdom" (that is, her shrewd and very feminine comments on men and things) has about it an air of florid and cynical frigidity, a weariness wrought into form; as if—to change the image—she were stringing for her own entertainment a necklace of beautifully polished platitudes. If only—one thinks—she could have brought an Elizabethan freshness to this admirable theme—if she could have worked her mine a little deeper, a little more honestly, a little less for diversion's sake, and a little more for poetry's; and if, finally, she were not quite so civilized, in the Kensington Gardens sense of the word, or so burdened with sophistication, or could admit now and then, if for only a moment, a glimpse into the sheer horror of things, the chaos that yawns under Bloomsbury—but then this book would not have been the charming *jeu d'esprit* that it is; it would have been something else.

HELEN MACAFEE

From the Yale Review[†]

It is the right and the nature of the artist to renew the forms of expression inherited from great predecessors by impressing upon them his own intense being. Mrs. Woolf, who has chosen fiction as her chief literary medium, has from the first shown herself impatient of the old categories, and now in her latest novel she declares her independence openly in the subtitle, "a biography". This extraordinary work, bearing as it does the clear stamp of her mind in its maturity, might in a sense have been called an autobiography. Readers who are interested in such matters may find in it a whole philosophy of creative literature, a subtle speculation upon personality and recorded time.

"Orlando" is a boldly conceived and finely executed dramatization of the civilized current of three centuries, imagined as flowing through the veins of a person who existed in the flesh as a man—a very young Englishman—during the spacious days of Elizabeth, was mysteriously transformed into a woman about the time of Queen Anne, and is under George V (and will always remain) in the prime of the years that consummate youth. In each of her novels Mrs. Woolf has done with a sure hand the thing she set out to do—most often it has been to refine with the utmost resourcefulness upon a theme not in bare outline of great magnitude. "Orlando" may be taken as

† From the *Yale Review* 18.2 (Winter 1929): xvi. Reprinted in *Virginia Woolf: The Critical Heritage*, ed. Robin Majumdar and Allen McLaurin (New York: Routledge, 2009), p. 237.

an answer to those who have questioned whether she could handle with equal success a larger scheme and implications of greater scope. It is a book rich in humanity, a spirited prose epic of intellectual adventure.

ELIZABETH BOWEN

Orlando by Virginia Woolf[†]

Virginia Woolf's *Orlando* was first published in London in October of 1928. I remember the book was regarded with some mistrust by one generation—my own, at that time "the younger." We in our twenties during the '20s, were not only the author's most zealous readers, but, in the matter of reputation, most jealous guardians. Her aesthetic became a faith; we were believers. We more than admired, we felt involved in each of her experimental, dazzling advances. Few of us (then) knew the still-conservative novels of her first period; a minority had informed itself of *The Mark on the Wall* and *Kew Gardens*, hand-printed and issued in 1919 by the original Hogarth Press. She broke full upon us, it would be correct to say, with *Jacob's Room*, 1922, on which followed *Mrs Dalloway*, 1925; then, while we were still breathless, *To the Lighthouse*, 1927. What now, what next? Next came *Orlando*. It was *Orlando*'s fate to come hard on the heels of the third of those masterpieces, of which each had stimulated a further hope. We regarded this book as a setback. Now, thirty-two years later, I wonder why this should have been so.

One trouble was, I imagine, our peculiar attitude to this writer's art. Defending it as we did against all comers—"stupids," dissidents, or the unseeing critic—we were ready, should so desperate a need arise to defend it against the artist herself. Never had we foreseen that we might be required to! The virtue of the art was, for us, its paradox: sublimating personality into poetry, it had—as art—the chastity of the impersonal. Before we had read *Orlando*, indeed for some time before it was "out," we scented the book as a transgression. Unofficial advance publicity was unfortunate, the more so because it was unofficial. This *Orlando*—we did not care for the sound of it! The book was, we gathered, in the nature of a prank, or a private joke; worse still, its genesis was personal. Inspired by a

---

[†] From "Afterword" in *Orlando*, Signet Classics edition (New York: New American Library, 1960), pp. 216–22. Reproduced with permission of Curtis Brown Group Ltd, London, on behalf of the Literary Executors of the Estate of Elizabeth Bowen. Reprinted in *The Mulberry Tree*, ed. Hermione Lee (New York: Harcourt, Brace, Jovanovich, 1986), pp. 131–36. In the few instances where the Signet edition differs from the later reprint in *The Mulberry Tree*, the version in *The Mulberry Tree* has been used.

romantic friendship, written for the delectation of the romantic
friend, it was likely to be fraught with playful allusion. Nor was that
all—a distinguished sympathetic and "special" coterie had contributed to the invention known as *Orlando*. That Virginia Woolf should
have intimates was a shock.

Most of us had not met Virginia Woolf; nor did we (which may
seem strange) aspire to do so. She did not wish to be met. Her
remoteness completed our picture of her, in so far as we formed a
picture at all. Exist she must (or writing could not proceed from her),
but we were incurious as to how she did. What she looked like, we
had not a remote idea; authors' photographs did not, then, ornament
book jackets. Our contentment with not knowing Virginia Woolf
today would appear extraordinary, could it even be possible? We visu-
alized her less as a woman at work than as a light widening as it
brightened. When I say, "She was a name, to us," remember (or if
you cannot remember, try to imagine) what a name can be, surrounded by nothing but the air of heaven. Seldom can a living artist
have been so—literally—idealized.

Malevolent autumn of '28—it taunted us with the picture of the
lady given to friends, to the point of fondness, and jokes, to within
danger of whimsicality. Ourselves, we were singularly uncoordi-
nated, I see now, as generations go. When I hear it said, as sometimes I do today, that Virginia Woolf's reputation was built up by a
sophisticated coterie, I ask myself, "Whom can they possibly mean?"
We, the ardent many, were rank-and-file provincials, outlanders,
freelances, students (to me, in 1922, reading *Jacob's Room*, Bloomsbury meant University College, London). We ran, if into anything,
into floating groups, loose in formation, governed by vague affini-
ties. Then scorning fringes of coteries, we have remained, I notice,
unwilling to form their nucleus in our later days—not, I hope,
hostile, but non-attachable. Nevertheless, what we heard of *Orlando*
galled us. We were young enough to feel out of it.

What we loathed was literary frivolity. So this was what Virginia
Woolf could be given over to, if for an instant we took our eye off
her—which, to do us justice, we seldom did? Cloak-and-dagger stuff.
The finishing touch was the success the book enjoyed with our
elders—*Orlando* charmed its way into the forts of middle-aged folly.
"Your Mrs Woolf has so often puzzled us. But *this* book of hers is
delightful! We see what you mean!" Betrayed . . .

We, naturally, read *Orlando*. We knew neither how to take it nor
what to make of it; it outwitted us. Up to this year, I had never read
it again.

The position as to *Orlando* has now changed. Or, better, the book
itself has a position it lacked before—it belongs to what is central
and main in the writer's work, instead of appearing, as it once did,

to hover on the questionable periphery. There has been time, since Virginia Woolf's death to stand back and view her work as a whole—still more, to see the whole as a thing of structure (in so far as an artist's whole art is like a building) or of inevitable growth (in so far as a whole art is like a tree). Though what does one mean by "a whole art"? Seldom does a writer lay down his pen or a painter his brush with calculated finality, saying "This is for ever; I have done!"

Death, other than in very old age, is an arbitrary interruption, the snipping of a cord at what seems often a fortuitous point. Rather, in Virginia Woolf's case, say her achievement within her fifty-nine years of life seems more, rather than less, significant now that we judge it steadily, as a whole. Up to 1941, that is, while she was living and at work, judgement was bound to be piecemeal, book by book. Temporary mists, misprisions, prejudices, sometimes intervened. From those mists' evaporation nothing she did gains more than *Orlando*. That *Orlando* was beautiful nobody doubted: what we now see is that it is important—and why.

It was important to the writer. She was the better, one feels certain, for writing it; in particular, for doing so when she did. More irresponsible than the rest of her work in fiction, it has the advantage of being less considered and more unwary. This book corresponds with a wildness in her, which might have remained unknown of—unless one knew her. This was a rebellion on the part of Virginia Woolf against the solemnity threatening to hem her in. *Orlando* is, among other things, rumbustious; it is one of the most high-spirited books I know.

Personal memories of Virginia Woolf cast, for me, their own light upon *Orlando*, though I certainly never spoke to her of the book, heard her speak of it, or attempted to find my way back to it while I knew her. Friendship with her—chiefly laughter and pleasure, and an entering, in her company, into the rapture caused her by the unexpected, the spectacular, the inordinate, the improbable, and the preposterous—filled out nine years of the lengthy interval between my first and second readings of *Orlando*. From her I learned that one can be worse than young and foolish; for she was the epitome of the young and foolish; it is among the glories of *Orlando* that it is in some ways a foolish book. It is not disorganized—on the contrary, is a miracle of "build"—but it is rhapsodical. Half-way through her creative life, she desired a plaything—also a mouthpiece. Shyness is absent from *Orlando*; in what sometimes are rhetorical exclamations, sometimes lyrical flashes like summer lightning, she voices herself on the subject of art, time, society, love, history, man, woman. The book is a novelist's holiday, not a novel.

By definition, *Orlando* is a fantasy. What is that? A story that posits "impossible" circumstances and makes play with them. Fantasy may juggle with time and space, and ignore, for instance, the law of gravity. Infinitely less fortunate is the novel, a work of imagination fettered to earthly fact and subject to dire penalty if it break the chain—one slip on the part of the novelist as to "reality" and his entire edifice of illusion totters and threatens to tumble down. At the same time, the licence accorded the fantastic is not boundless— the probable must enter his story *somewhere*. Should it fail to do so, interest is lost. Against extraordinary events, he must balance (in some sense) ordinary, or at least credible, characters. Where would *Wonderland* and *Through the Looking Glass* be without the prim, dogmatic lucidity of the temperamentally *un*adventurous Alice? Virginia Woolf, whom the "musts" of the novel bored, fell in without complaint with the laws of fantasy. Her Orlando—that is, her central character—though redeemed by grace, genius, and breeding from being "ordinary," is *as a character* absolutely convincing. To the change of sex, to the mysterious flight of time—centuries slipping by like months in the country—he-she reacts in a manner one cannot challenge—psychologically, all is extremely sound. And the more transitory, lesser cast are touched in, manipulated, with great adroitness. Nothing in *Orlando*, other than the outright impossible, seems improbable. Ironically, fantasy made Virginia Woolf a more thoroughgoing "straight," one might say assiduous, novelist than she was wont to be. The entire thing was a pleasure—she did not "have to;" she was out of school.

What a performance *Orlando* is, simultaneously working on amazement and suspending disbelief! At the start, a sixteen-year-old aristocrat, male, proffering a bowl of rose water to the ancient Queen Elizabeth I; at the close, a woman of thirty-six, still Orlando, under an oak tree in the moonlight, in the reign of Britain's King George V—the month October, the year 1928, the exact day probably that of the publication of *Orlando*. The change of sex took place in Constantinople, where Orlando was being ambassador, towards the end of the seventeenth century. The longing to be a poet which consumed the youth has been realized by the woman, who has combined this with giving birth to a son. Exquisite social comedy has enjoyed a run of, roughly, three-and-a-half centuries, partly in London, partly in the great Kentish country house. The Victorian age has been survived. Love has seared its way into a young breast, never to be forgotten, always to be associated with a Jacobean Thames ice carnival lasting a winter. Among the series of grand effronteries with which Orlando handles English history, there appear to be a few inadvertent errors—surely St. Paul's acquires a dome sooner than it did? The enormous sense of release that runs through the book is partly an affair of effortless speed, mobility, action—carriages dashing, whips cracking, mobs swaying, ice islands twirling doomfully down the river. By contrast, I remember Virginia Woolf—back to being a novelist, writing *Between the Acts*—coming down the garden path from her studio, saying, "I've spent the whole of the morning trying to move people from the dining-room into the hall!"

I have a theory—unsupported by anything she said to me, or, so far as I know, to anyone—that Virginia Woolf's writing of *Orlando* was a prelude to, and in some way rendered possible, her subsequent writing of *The Waves*, 1931. Outwardly, no two works of fiction could be more different; yet, did the fantasy serve to shatter some rigid, deadening, claustrophobic mould of so-called "actuality" which had been surrounding her? In *To the Lighthouse* (coming before *Orlando*), she had reached one kind of perfection. This she could not surpass; therefore, past it she could not proceed. In *Orlando*, delicacy gives place to bravura, to rhetoric. It was a breaking-point and a breathing-space at the same time, this fantasy. She returned to the novel, to *The Waves*, with—at least temporarily—a more defiant attitude to the novel's "musts."

Captive in the heart of the book *Orlando*, in the midst of the splendid changing and shifting scenes, are accounts of the sheer sensation of writing, more direct than this writer has ever given us. For instance:

> At this moment . . . Orlando pushed away her chair, stretched her arms, dropped her pen, came to the window, and exclaimed, 'Done!'
>
> She was almost felled to the ground by the extraordinary sight which now met her eyes. There was the garden and some birds. The world was going on as usual. All the time she was writing the world had continued.
>
> 'And if I were dead, it would be just the same!' she exclaimed.

There is a touch of hallucination about "reality;" creative Orlando was right, so was his-her creator. Virginia Woolf's vision conferred strangeness, momentarily, on all it fell on; it was, I believe, her effort to see things as they were apparent to *other* people that wore her down. The bus, the lamp-post, the teacup—how formidable she found them, everyday things. Nothing of an ordeal to her, however, were melodrama or panorama—she was at home with, or within, either.

Orlando, about which we who were young then were so stupid in 1928, is, I perceive, a book for those who are young. How does it strike those who are young now?

Title page of Thomas Dekker's *The Great Frost* (London: Henry Gosson, 1608).

VIRGINIA WOOLF

From A *Room of One's Own*†

Chapter Six

Next day the light of the October morning was falling in dusty shafts through the uncurtained windows, and the hum of traffic rose from the street. London then was winding itself up again; the factory was astir; the machines were beginning. It was tempting, after all this reading, to look out of the window and see what London was doing on the morning of the 26th of October 1928. * * *

* * * Now it was bringing from one side of the street to the other diagonally a girl in patent leather boots, and then a young man in a maroon overcoat; it was also bringing a taxi-cab; and it brought all three together at a point directly beneath my window; where the taxi stopped; and the girl and the young man stopped; and they got into the taxi; and then the cab glided off as if it were swept on by the current elsewhere.

The sight was ordinary enough; what was strange was the rhythmical order with which my imagination had invested it; and the fact that the ordinary sight of two people getting into a cab had the power to communicate something of their own seeming satisfaction. The sight of two people coming down the street and meeting at the corner seems to ease the mind of some strain, I thought, watching the taxi turn and make off. Perhaps to think, as I had been thinking these two days, of one sex as distinct from the other is an effort. It interferes with the unity of the mind. Now that effort had ceased and that unity had been restored by seeing two people come together and get into a taxi-cab. The mind is certainly a very mysterious organ, I reflected, drawing my head in from the window, about which nothing whatever is known, though we depend upon it so completely. Why do I feel that there are severances and oppositions in the mind, as there are strains from obvious causes on the body? What does one mean by "the unity of the mind," I pondered, for clearly the mind has so great a power of concentrating at any point at any moment that it seems to have no single state of being. It can separate itself from the people in the street, for example, and think of itself as apart from them, at an upper window looking down on them. Or it can think with other people spontaneously, as, for instance, in a crowd waiting to hear some piece of news read out. It can think back through its fathers or through its

† From A *Room of One's Own* (New York: Harcourt Brace and Company, 1929), pp. 95–104.

mothers, as I have said that a woman writing thinks back through
her mothers. Again if one is a woman one is often surprised by a
sudden splitting off of consciousness, say in walking down Whitehall, when from being the natural inheritor of that civilization, she
becomes, on the contrary, outside of it, alien and critical. Clearly
the mind is always altering its focus, and bringing the world into
different perspectives. But some of these states of mind seem, even
if adopted spontaneously, to be less comfortable than others. In order
to keep oneself continuing in them one is unconsciously holding
something back, and gradually the repression becomes an effort. But
there may be some state of mind in which one could continue without effort because nothing is required to be held back. And this
perhaps, I thought, coming in from the window, is one of them. For
certainly when I saw the couple get into the taxi-cab the mind felt
as if, after being divided, it had come together again in a natural
fusion. The obvious reason would be that it is natural for the sexes
to co-operate. One has a profound, if irrational, instinct in favour
of the theory that the union of man and woman makes for the
greatest satisfaction, the most complete happiness. But the sight of
the two people getting into the taxi and the satisfaction it gave me
made me also ask whether there are two sexes in the mind corresponding to the two sexes in the body, and whether they also require
to be united in order to get complete satisfaction and happiness? And
I went on amateurishly to sketch a plan of the soul so that in each
of us two powers preside, one male, one female; and in the man's
brain the man predominates over the woman, and in the woman's
brain the woman predominates over the man. The normal and comfortable state of being is that when the two live in harmony together,
spiritually co-operating. If one is a man, still the woman part of his
brain must have effect; and a woman also must have intercourse
with the man in her. Coleridge perhaps meant this when he said
that a great mind is androgynous. It is when this fusion takes place
that the mind is fully fertilized and uses all its faculties. Perhaps a
mind that is purely masculine cannot create, any more than a mind
that is purely feminine, I thought. But it would be well to test what
one meant by man-womanly, and conversely by woman-manly, by
pausing and looking at a book or two.

   Coleridge certainly did not mean, when he said that a great mind
is androgynous, that it is a mind that has any special sympathy with
women; a mind that takes up their cause or devotes itself to their
interpretation. Perhaps the androgynous mind is less apt to make
these distinctions than the single-sexed mind. He meant, perhaps,
that the androgynous mind is resonant and porous; that it trans-
mits emotion without impediment; that it is naturally creative,

incandescent and undivided. In fact one goes back to Shakespeare's mind as the type of the androgynous, of the man-womanly mind, though it would be impossible to say what Shakespeare thought of women. And if it be true that it is one of the tokens of the fully developed mind that it does not think specially or separately of sex, how much harder it is to attain that condition now than ever before. Here I came to the books by living writers, and there paused and wondered if this fact were not at the root of something that had long puzzled me. No age can ever have been as stridently sex-conscious as our own; those innumerable books by men about women in the British Museum are a proof of it. The Suffrage campaign was no doubt to blame. It must have roused in men an extraordinary desire for self-assertion; it must have made them lay an emphasis upon their own sex and its characteristics which they would not have troubled to think about had they not been challenged. And when one is challenged, even by a few women in black bonnets, one retaliates, if one has never been challenged before, rather excessively. That perhaps accounts for some of the characteristics that I remember to have found here, I thought, taking down a new novel by Mr A, who is in the prime of life and very well thought of, apparently, by the reviewers. I opened it. Indeed, it was delightful to read a man's writing again. It was so direct, so straightforward after the writing of women. It indicated such freedom of mind, such liberty of person, such confidence in himself. One had a sense of physical well-being in the presence of this well-nourished, well-educated, free mind, which had never been thwarted or opposed, but had had full liberty from birth to stretch itself in whatever way it liked. All this was admirable. But after reading a chapter or two a shadow seemed to lie across the page. It was a straight dark bar, a shadow shaped something like the letter "I". One began dodging this way and that to catch a glimpse of the landscape behind it. Whether that was indeed a tree or a woman walking I was not quite sure. Back one was always hailed to the letter "I". One began to be tired of "I". Not but what this "I" was a most respectable "I"; honest and logical; as hard as a nut, and polished for centuries by good teaching and good feeding. I respect and admire that "I" from the bottom of my heart. But—here I turned a page or two, looking for something or other—the worst of it is that in the shadow of the letter "I" all is shapeless as mist. Is that a tree? No, it is a woman. But . . . she has not a bone in her body, I thought, watching Phoebe, for that was her name, coming across the beach. * * *

What, then, it amounts to, if this theory of the two sides of the mind holds good, is that virility has now become self-conscious—men, that is to say, are now writing only with the male side of their brains. It is a mistake for a woman to read them, for she will inevitably look for something that she will not find. It is the power of suggestion that one most misses, I thought, taking Mr B the critic in my hand and reading, very carefully and very dutifully, his remarks upon the art of poetry. Very able they were, acute and full of learning; but the trouble was that his feelings no longer communicated; his mind seemed separated into different chambers; not a sound carried from one to the other. Thus, when one takes a sentence of Mr B into the mind it falls plump to the ground—dead; but when one takes a sentence of Coleridge into the mind, it explodes and gives birth to all kinds of other ideas, and that is the only sort of writing of which one can say that it has the secret of perpetual life.

But whatever the reason may be, it is a fact that one must deplore. For it means—here I had come to rows of books by Mr Galsworthy and Mr Kipling—that some of the finest works of our greatest living writers fall upon deaf ears. Do what she will a woman cannot find in them that fountain of perpetual life which the critics assure her is there. It is not only that they celebrate male virtues, enforce male values and describe the world of men; it is that the emotion with which these books are permeated is to a woman incomprehensible. It is coming, it is gathering, it is about to burst on one's head, one begins saying long before the end. That picture will fall on old Jolyon's head; he will die of the shock; the old clerk will speak over him two or three obituary words; and all the swans on the Thames will simultaneously burst out singing. But one will rush away before that happens and hide in the gooseberry bushes, for the emotion which is so deep, so subtle, so symbolical to a man moves a woman to wonder. So with Mr Kipling's officers who turn their Backs; and his Sowers who sow the Seed; and his Men who are alone with their Work; and the Flag—one blushes at all these capital letters as if one had been caught eavesdropping at some purely masculine orgy. The fact is that neither Mr Galsworthy nor Mr Kipling has a spark of the woman in him. Thus all their qualities seem to a woman, if one may generalize, crude and immature. They lack suggestive power. And when a book lacks suggestive power, however hard it hits the surface of the mind it cannot penetrate within.

And in that restless mood in which one takes books out and puts them back again without looking at them I began to envisage an age to come of pure, of self-assertive virility, such as the letters of professors (take Sir Walter Raleigh's letters, for instance) seem to forebode, and the rulers of Italy have already brought into being. For one can hardly fail to be impressed in Rome by the sense of unmitigated masculinity; and whatever the value of unmitigated masculinity upon the state, one may question the effect of it upon the art of poetry.[1] At any rate, according to the newspapers, there is a certain anxiety about fiction in Italy. There has been a meeting of academicians whose object it is "to develop the Italian novel". "Men famous by birth, or in finance, industry or the Fascist corporations" came together the other day and discussed the matter, and a telegram was sent to the Duce expressing the hope "that the Fascist era would soon give birth to a poet worthy of it". We may all join in that pious hope, but it is doubtful whether poetry can come of an incubator. Poetry ought to have a mother as well as a father. The Fascist poem, one may fear, will be a horrid little abortion such as one sees in a glass jar in the museum of some county town. Such monsters never live long, it is said; one has never seen a prodigy of that sort cropping grass in a field. Two heads on one body do not make for length of life.

However, the blame for all this, if one is anxious to lay blame, rests no more upon one sex than upon the other. All seducers and reformers are responsible: Lady Bessborough when she lied to Lord Granville; Miss Davies when she told the truth to Mr Greg.[2] All who have brought about a state of sex-consciousness are to blame, and it is they who drive me, when I want to stretch my faculties on a book, to seek it in that happy age, before Miss Davies and Miss Clough were born, when the writer used both sides of his mind equally. One must turn back to Shakespeare then, for Shakespeare was androgynous; and so were Keats and Sterne and Cowper and Lamb and Coleridge. Shelley perhaps was sexless. Milton and Ben Jonson had a dash too much of the male in them. So had Wordsworth and Tolstoi. In our time Proust was wholly androgynous, if not perhaps a little too much of a woman. But that failing is too rare for one to complain of it, since without some mixture of the kind the intellect seems to predominate and the other faculties of the mind harden and become barren. However, I consoled myself with the reflection that this is perhaps a passing phase; much of what I have said in obedience to my promise to give you the course of my thoughts will seem out of date; much of what flames in my eyes will seem dubious to you who have not yet come of age.

---

1. Woolf is referring here to the rise of futurism, an aesthetic movement that originated in Italy and was expounded by poet Filippo Tommaso Marinetti (1876–1944) in his "Manifesto of Futurism," published in Le Figaro, February 20, 1909. Futurism became associated with Fascism in the 1920s.
2. Henrietta Ponsoby (née Spencer), Countess of Bessborough (1761–1821), who had an affair with Granville Leveson-Gower, first Earl Granville (1773–1846). Emily Davies (1830–1921), British feminist and one of the founders of Girton College. William Rathbone Greg (1809–1881) published a pamphlet titled "Why are Women Redundant?" (London: N. Trübner and Co., 1869), which argued that one way to reduce the population of unmarried women in Britain would be to expatriate them by the thousands to former British colonies.

Even so, the very first sentence that I would write here, I said, crossing over to the writing-table and taking up the page headed Women and Fiction, is that it is fatal for anyone who writes to think of their sex. It is fatal to be a man or woman pure and simple; one must be woman-manly or man-womanly. It is fatal for a woman to lay the least stress on any grievance; to plead even with justice any cause; in any way to speak consciously as a woman. And fatal is no figure of speech; for anything written with that conscious bias is doomed to death. It ceases to be fertilized. Brilliant and effective, powerful and masterly, as it may appear for a day or two, it must wither at nightfall; it cannot grow in the minds of others. Some collaboration has to take place in the mind between the woman and the man before the art of creation can be accomplished. Some marriage of opposites has to be consummated. The whole of the mind must lie wide open if we are to get the sense that the writer is communicating his experience with perfect fullness. * * *

THE WELL OF LONELINESS
CENSORSHIP TRIAL

The Well of Loneliness, a novel by Radclyffe Hall published in July 1928 by Jonathan Cape publishers, was the subject of a campaign initiated by James Douglas, editor of the *Sunday Express* newspaper, to suppress the novel due to its depiction of sapphic lives and loves. Loosely autobiographical, the novel is a bildungsroman (a novel of development) featuring the protagonist Stephen Gordon, who identifies as an "invert" (what we today might call a trans masculine person who is attracted to feminine women). Douglas was successful in his campaign to censor the novel in England, where it was declared obscene and ordered to be destroyed on November 16, 1928. Virginia Woolf and Vita Sackville-West corresponded about the suppression campaign, and Woolf and her literary friends prepared to testify in court in support of the novel. None of the authors who prepared to testify were called to the stand during the proceedings, nor was Hall allowed to testify, although she asked to speak on behalf of her novel. In *A Room of One's Own*, Woolf alludes to the trial before mentioning the possibilities of same-sex desire between women to her audience: "I am sorry to break off so abruptly. Are there no men present? Do you promise me that behind that red curtain over there the figure of Sire Chartres Biron is not concealed? We are all women, you assure me? Then I may tell you that the very next words I read were these—'Chloe liked Olivia.' Do not start. Do not blush. Let us admit in the privacy of our own society that these things sometimes happen. Sometimes women do like women."[1]

1. Virginia Woolf, *A Room of One's Own* (New York: Harcourt Brace and Co., 1981 [1929]), 82.

Many scholars of *Orlando* comment on the timing of the publication of Woolf's novel in October 1928, in between the campaign against *The Well of Loneliness* (beginning in August 1928) and the trial verdict (November 16, 1928). Both Woolf and Sackville-West, despite being lovers, were also married to men, which Woolf suggests via *Orlando* may have helped both women escape the censorship that Hall endured. When Orlando resumes writing seriously after the writer's block induced by her lack of a proper wedding ring, the "spirit of the age" gives her a pass: "As she wrote she felt some power (remember we are dealing with the most obscure manifestations of the human spirit) reading over her shoulder, and when she had written 'Egyptian girls', the power told her to stop. . . . Are girls necessary? You have a husband at the Cape, you say? Ah, well, that'll do" (141). Regardless of how or why Woolf's novel escaped direct censorship in the UK, which is a matter for critical interpretation, *Orlando* engages with the debate over censorship of Hall's novel and the representation of gender and sexual diversity in early 20th-century English literature.

From Edinburgh Evening News[†]

"I emphatically claim that my book is eminently Christian," declared Miss Radclyffe Hall in a statement last night regarding the request by the Home Secretary to her publishers to discontinue issuing her new book, "The Wells of Loneliness." The action of the Home Office, she said, meant that two years of incessant work, following upon many years of deep study, had suffered at the hands of wilful ignorance and of prejudice which amounted to persecution. "In 'The Wells of Loneliness' I have given the public an accurate psychological study of one of the most pressing problems of the day in all its complicated and heartrending aspects. I have dared to call attention to facts which I, for one, consider should be recognised, for I am one of those who believe in the truth, who believe that suppressing the truth we incur a grave public danger. I also believe that the intelligent and thoughtful public wants the truth, and the reception, almost universal, accorded to my book has confirmed me in this belief.

"I also claim that, far from encouraging depravity, my book is calculated to encourage mutual understanding between normal persons and the inverted, which can only be beneficial to both and to society at large. I am proud and happy to have taken up my pen in defence of the persecuted. As a pioneer, I have been attacked, but then pioneers must always expect that fate, and the attacks in

† From *Edinburgh Evening News* (24 August, 1928).

my case, whatever their material consequences to my book, have not come from those whose approval would have conferred any honour."

[Transcript from *The Well of Loneliness* Trial][†]

Before:

Sir Chartres Biron

(Chief Magistrate).

The Director of Public Prosecutions.

—v—

Jonathan Cape and Leopold Hill.

Transcript of the Shorthand Notes of Barnett, Lenton & Co., 40 Chancery Lane, London, W.C.2.

COUNSEL FOR THE PROSECUTION: MR. EUSTACE FULTON, instructed by The Director of Public Prosecutions.

COUNSEL FOR THE DEFENDANT CAPE: MR. NORMAN BIRKETT, K.C., and MR. HERBERT METCALF, instructed by Messrs. Rubinstein, Nash, & Co.

COUNSEL FOR THE DEFENDANT HILL: MR. J.S. MELVILLE, K.C. and MR. WALTER FRAMPTON, instructed by Messrs. Rubenstein, Nash, & Co.

Judgment

The Magistrate: Before delivering my judgment in this case I thought it right to consider this book which is the subject of these proceedings in the light of the statements made by the learned Counsel for the Defence, for whose assistance in the matter I should like to say at once I am very much indebted.

First of all, one thing is clear which does not seem to have been clearly appreciated, that no question of censorship arises here at all. The only question here for me to decide is whether this book is an obscene libel according to the common law of this country because, although the proceedings under which this book has been raised are in the execution of a Statute, I have to be satisfied before I can order this book to be seized and to be destroyed (if I come to that conclusion) that at common law it is an obscene libel.

---

† From the National Archives, CUST 49/1057. Original transcript dated Friday, November 16, 1928. Transcribed by the editor of this Norton Critical Edition.

In the course of this case the issue has been very considerably simplified. It was contended at first by the Defence that this book nowhere in any way related to physical misconduct between these women; that was put forward and strongly urged by the Defence in this case on behalf of the publisher, Mr. Jonathan Cape; it was put forward in cross-examination, and subsequently, Mr. Norman Birkett in his very interesting speech drew a subtle distinction between what he called "inverts" and what he called "perverts." As I understood his speech, "invert" is a term used to describe women who, born with certain masculine tendencies are therefore or thereby born with an inclination in certain directions which make them averse to relationship with and intellectual sympathy with the male sex; that in consequence of that, which is an accident of birth for which they are not responsible, they are forced into intercourse (I use the word in its[1] [benign sense?) with] their own sex and companionship with their own sex, which might very easily be misunderstood by a censorious world; that, therefore, they should be deserving of sympathy, liable as they are to be misunderstood; and it is said that appeal to that sympathy is the purpose of this book. I confess, having read it, that I was amazed at that contention being put forward, and I was not surprised when, after the adjournment, Mr. Norman Birkett announced that he was not in a position to contend any further that this book did not relate to unnatural offences between women in every sense of those words. But he urged, and Mr. Melville also urged in a forcible speech, that there was nothing in this book which in any way outraged decency, that the subject was dealt with, I think he used the term somewhere in the course of his speech, with restraint, and I think he used the term "reverence"— that there was nothing in the book of any kind which would induce people to indulge in these horrible practices, that there was nothing in the book which could be said in any way to defend these unnatural practices or (he used the term) which was to their glorification. That of course very much simplifies the issue which I have to try.

Before I say more, I should like to say that there seems to have been a considerable misunderstanding about the meaning of the word "obscene". People very often do use words without any definite idea of what their meaning is, and it is suggested that this book cannot be described fairly as an obscene book because there are no gross words or filthy words in it; and that because it is, as it is said, well written therefore it is to be regarded as a work of literature, and, therefore, not properly a subject of these proceedings. First of all, in consulting a standard dictionary to find out what the real meaning of "obscene" is, I find it is defined as:

1. The typed transcript is missing a line here.

"Offensive to chastity, delicacy or decency, or presenting to the mind something that decency, delicacy and purity forbids to be exposed; offensive to the moral sense because of a tendency to excite lustful passions." That is of peculiar interest, because when I look at what must guide me in arriving at a decision in this case, that is the test of an obscene book as laid down by that great Judge Chief Justice Cockburn in the leading case of The Queen v. Hicklin, Law Reports, 3 Queen's Bench Cases, page 360, he there says:

"I think the test of obscenity is this, whether the tendency of the matter charged as obscenity is to deprave and corrupt those whose minds are open to such immoral influences, and into whose hands a publication of this sort may fall". It is interesting to find how the dictionary definition of "obscenity" so nearly is within the meaning of the exact words used in the legal test of what is or is not an obscene publication.

* * * I might say this at once: with regard to the point that this book is well written, and, therefore, should not be the subject of these proceedings, that is an entirely untenable proposition. I agree that this book has some literary merit, defamed, as I think everybody who has read it will admit, with certain deplorable lapses of taste; but the mere fact that the book is well written can be no answer to these proceedings, because otherwise we should be in their preposterous position, that because it is well written the most obscene book would be free from such proceedings. It is quite obvious to anybody of intelligence that the better an obscene book is written the greater the public to whom the book is likely to appeal. The more palatable the poison the more insidious.

To deal with what really now is the substantial question before me, which is Mr. Melville's contention, does this book as a whole defend unnatural practices between women, and, as he puts it, does it glorify them? * * *

[Examines examples from The Well.]

This being the tenor of this book, I have no hesitation whatever in saying that it is an obscene libel, that it would tend to corrupt those into whose hands it should fall, and that the publication of this book is an offence against public decency, an obscene libel, and I shall order it to be destroyed.

* * *

CRITICISM

Culture and History

JANE DE GAY

Virginia Woolf's Feminist Historiography in *Orlando*†

Virginia Woolf made a seminal contribution to feminist literary history and provided the discipline with some of its most memorable quotations. In *A Room of One's Own,* she urged her audience of female students at Cambridge University to 'rewrite history' by seeking out figures neglected by conventional (patriarchal) histories in order to trace a female tradition, a concept she described as 'thinking back through our mothers'.[1] She sketched how such a tradition might look, tracing a line from Lady Winchilsea and Aphra Behn, Fanny Burney and Jane Austen through to George Eliot and the Brontës, considering how the conditions of these writers' lives affected their work, and also looking at how gender might influence their use of language and choice of genre. Behind Woolf's historical sketch lies an imaginative attempt to reclaim lost origins: Woolf notes that there was no female Shakespeare because conditions in the Renaissance would have made it impossible for a woman to write for the theatre. She creates an imaginary starting-point for her history by sketching a fictional biography of Shakespeare's sister, Judith, whose life could only have ended in failure and suicide. Woolf concludes by urging her audience to imaginatively reclaim these lost origins in their own writings:

> Now my belief is that this poet who never wrote a word and was buried at the cross-roads still lives. She lives in you and in me . . . for great poets do not die; they are continuing presences; they need only the opportunity to walk among us in the flesh. This opportunity, as I think, it is now coming within your power to give her. (108)

† From *Critical Survey* 19.1 (2007): 62–72. Reprinted with permission. Page numbers to this Norton Critical Edition appear in brackets.
1. Virginia Woolf, *A Room of One's Own* (London: Grafton, 1977 [1929]), 72.

Woolf never developed this female literary history in a sustained, systematic, non-fictional form, although she put her ideas into practice by writing essays about obscure female writers and, in the last years of her life, she began to make notes for an alternative literary history and drafted two essays, 'Anon' and 'The Reader'. However, Woolf did try out such a history in *fictional* form in her fantasy novel *Orlando: A Biography*, which she was writing as she began preparing *A Room of One's Own*. Within her fantastic narrative and through her protagonist, a writer who lives for 350 years and changes sexes part-way through, Woolf traces the changing conditions for writers, and reflects upon the effect of gender on their experiences. Furthermore, by incorporating parodies of literary and social history and biography into *Orlando* Woolf also critiques scholarly apparati for viewing the past, thus developing her ideas about the writing and rewriting of history. This article will demonstrate that Woolf alludes and responds to specific debates about the form literary history should take; the significance of the past to the present; and the importance of the imagination in engaging with the past.[2]

Orlando reflects Woolf's profound ambivalence about prevalent models of history. This is most evident in her treatment of periodisation which, as Sally Greene has noted, had been a key organising feature of Victorian historical discourse.[3] On the surface, *Orlando* is organised along the lines of clearly demarcated literary periods—the Renaissance, the Restoration, the Enlightenment, the Romantic era, the Victorian period and the present—but these categories become unstable for they are frequently treated ironically. Woolf's narrator attempts at several points to characterise the literature of a particular period, but the method is rendered ridiculous by the sheer excess of the connections made. This may be seen in Woolf's hyperbolic account of Orlando's writing style during the Restoration period:

> For it is for the historian of letters to remark that he had changed his style amazingly. His floridity was chastened; his abundance curbed; the age of prose was congealing those warm fountains. The very landscape outside was less struck about with garlands and the briars themselves were less thorned and intricate. Perhaps the senses were a little duller and honey and cream less seductive to the palate. Also that the streets were better drained

---

2. A discussion of Woolf's engagement with debates about biography in *Orlando* lies outside the scope of this piece. For an account of this, see Suzanne Raitt, *Vita and Virginia: The Work and Friendship of V. Sackville-West and Virginia Woolf* (Oxford: Oxford University Press, 1993), chapter 1.
3. Sally Greene, 'Introduction', in *Virginia Woolf: Reading the Renaissance*, ed. Sally Greene (Athens: Ohio University Press, 1999), 19. Subsequent page references are given within the article.

and the houses better lit had its effect upon the style, it cannot be doubted.[4]

This passage may be read more narrowly as Woolf's critique of the sociological approach to literary history developed by her father, Sir Leslie Stephen. His method is seen at its most schematic in *English Literature and Society in the Eighteenth Century*, in which he proposes a model whereby literary history develops in a series of reactive changes led by key writers responding to their audiences and reflecting the main concerns of their time. For example, he sees Swift and Pope as expressing prevalent upper-class disaffection with the Walpole government, and Defoe as writing for the emerging middle class. Stephen's conclusion expresses the holistic approach at its most extreme through the notion of each generation advocating a 'Return to Nature' so that 'literature must be produced by the class which embodies the really vital and powerful currents of thought which are moulding society'.[5] Woolf's suggestion that Orlando's changing style bears the direct impress of the changing countryside and changing gastronomic tastes may be read as a *reductio ad absurdam* of this argument.

Although Woolf's own method was essentially sociological—*A Room of One's Own*, after all, seeks to demonstrate the effect of the conditions of production on the quality of writing—her satire of Stephen's views arises from a perception that his emphasis on the influential classes was deeply ideological. Questions of gender are central here for, while Stephen had neglected gender entirely, Woolf shows that it is a significant factor determining how people write and whether they can be arbiters of taste. So, where Stephen was interested in male writers who both expressed and helped to influence the ideas of their time, Woolf sought out individuals (chiefly women) who tried to retain artistic integrity in opposition to contemporary trends. Stephen's history focuses on mainstream and influential writers, dividing the century into a series of 'schools' gathered under key, male figures including Pope (whom he claims as a 'leading figure', p. 109), Defoe, Johnson and Boswell. *Orlando*, by contrast, depicts an aspiring writer (female from the seventeenth century onwards), who does not achieve any recognition until the twentieth century, when her poem *The Oak Tree* is published and wins a prize. Canonical authors are viewed through Orlando's eyes, and this perspective is often used to cut them down to size: quite

---

4. Virginia Woolf, *Orlando: A Biography*, ed. R. Bowlby (Oxford: Oxford University Press, 1992), 108–109 [60]. Subsequent page references are given within the article.
5. Sir Leslie Stephen, *English Literature and Society in the Eighteenth Century* (London: Duckworth, 1904), 218. Subsequent page numbers are given in the article.

literally so, in the case of Pope, who (perhaps in a direct riposte to
Stephen) is described as a 'little gentleman', and rendered silent:

> Then the little gentleman said,
> He said next,
> He said finally,*
>> *These sayings are too well known to require repetition,
>> and besides, they are all to be found in his published works.
>> (193) [108]

The novel demonstrates some of the constraints Orlando experiences after becoming a woman: she hides her manuscript when
people come in (169) [100] (an anecdote from the life of Jane Austen which Woolf cited in *A Room of One's Own*) and becomes aware
of a taboo against describing 'sullen and foreign-looking' girls,
although this had been perfectly acceptable when she had been
male (252–3) [141].

Woolf's quarrel with Stephen's approach is at its most cutting in
her treatment of the concept of 'the spirit of the age' which rever-
berates throughout his work, but is satirised by being repeated *ad
nauseum* in *Orlando*. Stephen opens his work on eighteenth century
literature with the statement that literature is valuable as 'one manifestation of what is called "the spirit of the age"' (2) and it quickly
emerges that this statement applies specifically to the work of the
great male writers. Stephen's gender bias may be seen in *Hours in a
Library*, where he praises Sir Walter Scott for expressing the spirit
of his age, but criticises Charlotte Brontë for being out of tune with
hers, arguing that if she had read Hegel or Sir William Hamilton,
'her characters would have embodied more fully the dominating
ideas of the time'.[6] Brontë is criticised both for neglecting the works
of two male writers and for apparently ignoring the status quo by
not giving in to the 'dominating' ideas of her time.

In *Orlando*, Woolf satirises the idea of 'the spirit of the age' as a
regulatory ideological force. Significantly, this is at its strongest in
the nineteenth-century section where 'the spirit of the age' persis-
tently affects Orlando's behaviour, making her embarrassed at the
idea of pregnancy, censoring her writing and compelling her to marry
(225, 252–3, 232) [125, 140–41, 129]. Since marriage has never
appealed to Orlando, this development may be seen as the result of
violent coercion.

Woolf's satire of 'the spirit of the age' is double-edged, for although
she mocks Stephen's method of characterising literary periods, she
also uses periodisation to dismiss Victorian ideas as outmoded prod-
ucts of their time. She alludes to Stephen's contemporary John

6. Sir Leslie Stephen, *Hours in a Library,* 3 vols (London: Smith, Elder, 1874–79), vol. 3, 332.

Ruskin in a very similar way when she uses *The Storm Cloud of the Nineteenth Century* to characterise that period. Ruskin had claimed that a 'storm-cloud' or 'plague-cloud' was 'peculiar to our own times',[7] and Woolf parodies this by describing the arrival of the nineteenth century as the descent of a fog influencing every aspect of life: 'A turbulent welter of cloud covered the city. All was darkness; all was doubt; all was confusion. The Eighteenth century was over; the Nineteenth century had begun' (216) [120]. She mocks Ruskin's model of sweeping change again when she distinguishes the Edwardian from the Victorian era, by linking the change in monarch improbably with changes in the weather, as a celebration of the lifting of the Ruskinian storm-cloud: 'The sky itself . . . had changed. It was no longer so thick, so watery, so prismatic now that King Edward . . . had succeeded Queen Victoria. The clouds had shrunk to a thin gauze' (282–3) [157–58]. This frivolous and comic indication of a change in era is underwritten by a sense that the quality of life *had* changed for the better by the twentieth century, for modernity is welcomed in the form of the motor car and electric lighting, and celebrated for breaking through the gloom of Victoriana. Thus whilst mocking Ruskin, Woolf uses his process of periodisation to separate her own age from the nineteenth century.

Woolf's attitude towards Victorian periodisation may thus be seen as profoundly ambivalent. Although she used it as a method of distancing herself from the Victorians, she also distrusted the way in which their formulations of history threatened to make the past inaccessible to later generations. The latter impulse may be seen in the closing section of the novel, where moments from the past flash back into the present day. Here Woolf attacks history as a discourse that kills off the past: we are told that Orlando's house, now a tourist attraction, 'belonged . . . to history; was past the touch and control of the living', but that Orlando's vivid memories counteract this by conjuring up an active past from the empty space: 'The gallery . . . was as a tunnel bored deep into the past. As her eyes peered down it, she could see people laughing and talking . . . Dryden, Swift and Pope' (304) [169]. Here the past is represented spatially rather than temporally, so that it still exists to be viewed from the present. Literary history is especially accessible in this way, for books remain to be rediscovered by future generations: this idea is epitomised in *Orlando* by the cameo appearances by Shakespeare, from the Elizabethan era to the twentieth century, when Orlando envisages Shakespeare and cries 'Haunted! ever since I was a child' (21, 157, 299) [13, 89, 166].

7. John Ruskin, *The Storm Cloud of the Nineteenth Century* (Orpington: George Allen, 1884), 1.

Woolf's suspicions about moralistic and schematic approaches to literary and cultural history are seen at their strongest in her treatment of the Renaissance. This movement forms the emotional backbone for *Orlando*: firstly because the narrative begins in the late sixteenth century, and this starting-point becomes a frequent point of reference for what comes afterwards; and secondly because proportionately more space is allocated to the Elizabethan and Jacobean eras, with more than half the book covering the period from the late sixteenth century to the Restoration era. Yet Woolf had to grapple with Victorian ideas and conceptions here, too, for Victorian scholars were influential in shaping the idea of the Renaissance, as Sally Greene (19) points out. A close reading of Woolf's treatment of the Renaissance in *Orlando* reveals that she engaged with Victorian debates over the nature of the period in submerged allusions to the views of Ruskin, Pater, John Addington Symonds and Vernon Lee (Violet Paget) in particular. (Significantly, Leslie Stephen had not contributed to this debate, for he wrote little on Elizabethan literature and so, by entering this discussion, Woolf was able to move on to literary territory that her father had not already claimed.)

John Ruskin, who made one of the first attempts to demarcate the Renaissance period in *The Stones of Venice*, attacked it on moral and aesthetic grounds which were closely linked to questions of gender. The arrival of the Renaissance saw the 'first corruptions introduced into the Gothic schools', which manifested themselves as 'over-luxuriance and over-refinement' or, more tellingly from a gender point of view, as a 'decline, into luxury and effeminacy as the strength of the school expires'.[8] Ruskin criticised the height of the Renaissance for demonstrating a lack of religious faith by giving classical mythology and Christian symbolism equal prominence in art, and he saw the seeds of the fall of Venice being sown in this period, diagnosing the symptoms in Biblical terms as vainglory and the sin of pride in science, state and system (III, 35). Ruskin's third and final phase was the 'corruption of the renaissance itself', which he characterised by a 'grotesque' spirit of 'idiotic mockery' (III, 121). Having established that architecture was corrupted by the Renaissance, Ruskin concludes by urging a return to the Gothic forms of the more pious Middle Ages.

As Sally Greene (23) has suggested, Woolf's account of the Great Frost in the seventeenth-century section of *Orlando* may be read as a satire of Ruskin's view of the Renaissance as a frost that swept away the values of the Middle Ages: 'the Renaissance frosts came, and all perished' (I, 225). Although Woolf partly agrees with Ruskin

---

8. John Ruskin, *The Stones of Venice*, 3 vols (London: Smith, Elder, 1851), vol. 3, 2–4, 7. Subsequent volume and page references are given within the article.

by criticising the decadence of the courtiers who celebrate wildly as country-folk lose their livelihoods, she nonetheless detects an inner spark which Ruskin had categorically denied was there. She notes that the 'moon and stars blazed with the hard fixity of diamonds' and describes a bumboat woman who appears full of life although frozen beneath the Thames (35) [21]. Orlando, in the first throes of his love for a Russian princess, Sasha, comes to life inside: 'the ice turned to wine in his veins; he heard the waters flowing and the birds singing' (39) [23]. Ruskin's devastating Renaissance frosts are thus rewritten as the start of revival and reawakening, so that his linear historical model of decline is replaced with a cyclical one of natural renewal.

Woolf's depiction of the Renaissance as a fire beneath the ice echoes the view of Walter Pater, a Victorian critic of a different school from Ruskin: 'Filled as our culture is with the classical spirit, we can hardly imagine how deeply the human mind was moved, when, at the Renaissance, in the midst of a frozen world, the buried fire of ancient art rose up from under the soil'.[9] As Perry Meisel has pointed out, Woolf knew Pater's work and frequently adopted his metaphors in her own criticism but hid her indebtedness to him by rarely referring to him directly in her essays.[1] The dynamic in *Orlando* is slightly different, for Woolf ironically acknowledges herself and all writers to be 'perpetually in the debt' of Pater in a mock 'Preface' to the novel (5) [5], lifting the weight of Pater's legacy whilst also signalling that his ideas play a part in the book's argument.

Pater, together with J. A. Symonds and Vernon Lee, countered Ruskin's moralistic attack on the Renaissance by arguing that it initiated the advancement of personal and political freedoms. Pater celebrated the movement for the very reasons that Ruskin rejected it, seeing it as an era of intellectual and sensual enjoyment which saw a healthy liberalisation of thought and broadening of perspectives. He detected the earliest signs of the Renaissance in the Middle Ages, evidenced in a 'spirit of rebellion and revolt against the moral and religious ideas of the time. In their search after the pleasures of the senses and the imagination, in their care for beauty, in their worship of the body, people were impelled beyond the bounds of the Christian ideal' (26). Orlando's discovery of sexuality with Sasha is a moment of joyful liberation of the sort that Pater associated with the Renaissance.

---

9. Walter Pater, *The Renaissance: Studies in Art and Poetry* (London: Macmillan, 1888 [1873]), 193. Subsequent page references are given within the article.
1. Perry Meisel, *The Absent Father: Virginia Woolf and Walter Pater* (New Haven and London: Yale University Press, 1980), xiii. Subsequent page references are given within the article.

Pater, Symonds and Lee also offered Woolf (like her contemporary Lytton Strachey) an antidote to conventional models of history. As Hilary Fraser has noted, all three were criticised in their time for being 'unhistorical' and for writing history as literature, and all three have been largely ignored by historiographers.[2] They offered Woolf a more helpful approach to periodisation than either Stephen or Ruskin. Pater and Symonds saw the Renaissance as originating in the Middle Ages and continuing to their own time: Symonds argued that 'we still participate' in 'the onward progress of the Renaissance';[3] Pater saw the Renaissance continuing in the work of William Blake, Victor Hugo and the eighteenth-century German art critic Johann Joachim Wincklemann. Woolf's sense of the past as alive and active, seen in Orlando's long memory and her visions of the past, reflects this spirit. Woolf may have used Pater to support her belief that one can resist the spirit of the age. Pater described Wincklemann as 'a relic of classical antiquity, laid open by accident to our alien, modern atmosphere' (232). Woolf's description of Orlando's inability to accommodate herself to the nineteenth century follows very similar lines: 'it is probable that the human spirit has its place in time assigned to it; some are born of this age, some of that; and now that Orlando was grown a woman . . . the lines of her character were fixed, and to bend them the wrong way was intolerable' (233) [129].

These critics proved helpful to Woolf by suggesting not only that the Renaissance spirit was alive in the present but that it played a vital role in modernity. Pater, for example, defined the Renaissance quite literally as a rebirth, where classical learning went alongside 'the coming of what is called the "modern spirit"' (113). Meisel argues that Woolf's 'greatest anxiety about Pater is that she had inherited modernism rather than created it herself' (52), but it may be more accurate to say that Woolf found Pater congenial because he expressed her view that one must tap into the past in order to discover the modern. As Juliet Dusinberre has argued, the idea of the Renaissance had two different resonances for Woolf: 'her affinity on many different levels with the early modern period, and her own sense of being reborn through the creation of an alternative tradition of reading and writing whose roots go back to the Elizabethans and beyond'.[4] This second dimension inclines towards Pater, for, as Sally Greene notes, he helped Woolf see the Renaissance as a process of discovery that could happen at any time, a 'founding yet also

---

2. Hilary Fraser, *The Victorians and Renaissance Italy* (Oxford: Blackwell, 1992), 213–15 (230).
3. J. A. Symonds, *A Short History of the Renaissance in Italy*, ed. A. Pearson (London: Smith, Elder, 1893), 3.
4. Juliet Dusinberre, *Virginia Woolf's Renaissance: Woman Reader or Common Reader?* (Basingstoke: Macmillan, 1997), 5.

renewable movement'; and through this she used 'its liberating spirit' to support her feminist politics and modernist aesthetic (24).

Lee and Pater set a precedent for Woolf and Strachey by using fiction as a mode for exploring historical developments. For example, Lee had used a fictional life of a painter to trace the lost origins of the Renaissance.[5] Pater and Lee shared an impressionistic approach to the past, privileging subjective responses to art and literature over objective, scholarly attempts to analyse the period. Lee distinguished her work from that of a historian: 'I have seen . . . what I might call the concrete realities of thought and feeling left behind by the Renaissance, and then tried to obtain from books some notion of the original shape and manner of wearing these relics, rags and tatters of a past civilization'.[6] Having spent most of her life in Italy, Lee formed her conception of the Renaissance from the art and architecture she saw around her, using book learning to bolster these ideas.

Woolf's conception of the past—and of the Renaissance in particular—was similarly subjective and, in the case of *Orlando*, rooted in a sense of place. She conceived the central, historical idea for the novel whilst visiting her lover Vita Sackville-West at her ancestral home of Knole in Kent. In her diary, Woolf recalls seeing a cart bringing wood to be chopped and Sackville-West saying that 'she saw it as something that had gone on for hundreds of years'. Woolf goes on to fantasise about Knole's history: 'All the centuries seemed lit up, the past expressive, articulate; not dumb & forgotten; but a crowd of people stood behind, not dead at all; not remarkable; fair faced, long limbed; affable; & so we reach the days of Elizabeth quite easily'.[7] Here, Woolf gives history a voice and revives long-dead people in her imagination to create an intimate link between herself and the Elizabethan age. Woolf expressed this sense of intimacy with the past by basing the character of Orlando on Sackville-West, drawing details of his/her life from Sackville ancestors and basing Orlando's estate on Knole. This link between past and present had resonances for Sackville-West, who had lost Knole when her father died and the estate passed to a male cousin. As Nigel Nicolson has noted, Woolf in *Orlando* had 'identified [Vita] with Knole for ever': 'Virginia by her genius had provided Vita with a unique consolation for having been born a girl, for her exclusion from her inheritance, for her father's death earlier that year'.[8]

5. Vernon Lee, 'A Seeker of Pagan Perfection, being the Life of Domenico Neroni, Pictor Sacrilegus', in *Renaissance Fancies and Studies* (London: Smith, Elder, 1895), 163–231.
6. Vernon Lee, *Euphorion: being Studies of the Antique and the Medieval in the Renaissance*, 2 vols (London: T. Fisher Unwin, 1884), vol. I, 16.
7. Virginia Woolf, *Diary*, 5 vols, ed. A. O. Bell and A. McNeillie (Harmondsworth: Penguin, 1979–85), vol. III, 125.
8. Nigel Nicolson, *Portrait of a Marriage* (London: Weidenfeld and Nicolson, 1990), 190.

Orlando demonstrates that imagination and empathy provide more powerful ways of staking a claim to the past than either patrilineal inheritance laws or conventional models of history.

Orlando, therefore, enacts the imaginative search to rediscover lost origins which Woolf had advocated in *A Room of One's Own,* by using Orlando's long life to trace a heritage for a twentieth-century woman writer back to the Renaissance. In satirising the methods of Stephen and Ruskin, she rejected Victorian patriarchal metanarratives, which had left out the history of women writers and had attempted to package the past in ways which reinforced patriarchal ideologies. Instead she inclines to a school of critics who sought to tap into the past and release its energies, and who used the strategies of fiction to bring history alive and make it live in the present. By placing Woolf's feminist historiography in the tradition of Pater and Lee, we can see why Woolf made her fullest and most sustained attempt to rewrite history in *Orlando* rather than in a nonfictional work: for Woolf, the imagination provided the only satisfactory medium for embracing the lost past.

ABBY BARDI

"In Company of a Gipsy": The "Gypsy" as Trope in Woolf[†]

[T]hus, attended by a lean dog, riding a donkey, in company of a gipsy, the Ambassador of Great Britain at the Court of the Sultan left Constantinople.

Virginia Woolf, *Orlando*[1]

Halfway through Virginia Woolf's *Orlando* (1928), the title character, who lives for over three hundred years, wakes up and discovers that he has become a woman. Although Woolf evidently does not intend us to take this novel entirely seriously, it is clear from the contemporaneous *A Room of One's Own*[2] that she is quite serious about deconstructing the boundaries of gender; in *Orlando*, she calls its categories into question by depicting them as permeable, even arbitrary. In so doing, she flies in the face of her Victorian forebears, as was her wont, critiquing and complicating the prevailing model

---

[†] From "'In Company of a Gipsy': The 'Gypsy' as Trope in Woolf and Brontë," *Critical Survey* 19.1 (2007): 40–44, 46–47, 48–50. Reprinted with permission. Page numbers to this Norton Critical Edition appear in brackets.
1. Virginia Woolf, *Orlando: A Biography* (New York: Harcourt Brace Jovanovich, 1929 [1956]), 140 [76]. Subsequent page references will be cited parenthetically within the text.
2. The lecture that was to become *A Room of One's Own* was delivered in October, 1928.

of male/female as binary opposition.[3] Orlando's sudden, mysterious transformation from male to female initially appears to reflect this binary: 'Orlando was a man till the age of thirty; when he became a woman, and has remained so ever since' (139) [76]. However, his/her transition is complicated when Orlando enters into a somewhat indeterminate state, escaping from both Constantinople and gender by running away with a 'gipsy tribe' (140) [76].

In representing Gypsies,[4] Woolf was drawing upon a literary trope that had been well established in the previous century. Gypsies play significant roles in a variety of works, including Jane Austen's *Emma* (1815), Sir Walter Scott's *Guy Mannering* (1815), Emily Brontë's *Wuthering Heights* (1847), Matthew Arnold's 'The Scholar Gypsy' (1853), and George Eliot's *The Mill on the Floss* (1860) and *The Spanish Gypsy* (1868).[5] At mid-century, George Borrow's autobiographical novels of Gypsy life, *Lavengro* (1851) and *Romany Rye* (1857), fuelled interest in a culture that was seen as mysterious, closed to outsiders and exotic, and was often eroticised.[6] The Gypsy Lore Society, founded in 1888, formalised this growing interest and led to considerable scholarship.[7] For non-Romanis, the Romani population of Britain represented an Other that was simultaneously foreign and indigenous; despite research into their culture on the part of Borrow and the generation of 'Gypsiologists' that succeeded him, both in Britain and on the continent, Gypsies remained fundamentally inaccessible, and their identity was complicated by a lack of accurate information about them.[8] As Janet Lyon has argued, the 'fabled insularity of "Gypsy" communities was proof of a radical alterity' and she asserts that the literary 'Gypsy' is a 'multivalent' *gadže* (non-Romani) creation'.[9] It is this *gadže* creation' and not an accurate portrayal of the Romani people that is ubiquitous in nineteenth- as well as early twentieth-century literature.

Kirstie Blair has argued convincingly that in *Orlando*, Woolf draws upon a twentieth century trope of the Gypsy that 'haunts texts

3. See Thomas Laquer, *Making Sex: Body and Gender from the Greeks to Freud* (Cambridge, Mass.: Harvard University Press, 1990).
4. I am using the term 'Gypsy', rather than Rom or Roma, throughout this essay to represent literary, as opposed to historical, constructions of the Romani people. Like Gypsy identity, these terms are themselves contested, and it is difficult to ascertain which are 'correct'.
5. Interestingly, D. H. Lawrence's novella, *The Virgin and the Gipsy*, was written in 1926, two years before *Orlando*, but was not published until 1930, after Lawrence's death.
6. According to David Mayall, Borrow's work inspired 'a wide range of Gypsiologists' and 'is thought to have brought the cult of Gypsyism into widespread popularity'; *Gypsy Identities 1500–2000: From Egipcyans and Moon-men to the Ethnic Romany* (London: Routledge, 2004), 156.
7. See Angus Fraser, 'A Rum Lot', in *100 Years of Gypsy Studies*, ed. Matt Salo (Cheverly, Maryland: The Gypsy Lore Society, 1990).
8. See Mayall, *Gypsy Identities*, for a discussion of contestations and multiple constructions of Gypsy identity by non-Romani groups.
9. Janet Lyon, 'Gadže Modernism', *Modernism/Modernity* 11.3 (2004), 517–38 (518).

about desire between women in this period',[1] as well as idiosyncratic references to Gypsies by Woolf's lover, Vita Sackville-West, of whom *Orlando* is an affectionately parodic biography. In Sackville-West's correspondence with her other lovers, particularly the novelist Violet Trefusis, Blair reads their numerous mentions of Gypsies as representations of lesbian desire and finds evidence that Woolf adopted Vita's trope of 'gypsiness' in their relationship.[2] Throughout *Orlando*, Woolf is playfully alluding to the family history of the Sackville-Wests: Vita's mother, Victoria, was the illegitimate daughter of Lord Sackville and a Spanish Gypsy known as 'Pepita'.[3] When Orlando marries the dancer Rosina Pepita, reputedly a Gypsy, this revises Lord Sackville's association with the real Pepita; and Orlando's vexed relationship with property—which the Gypsies are said to abjure—echoes Vita's relationship with the Sackville estate, Knole. The complex and seemingly androgynous relationship between Orlando and her husband Shelmerdine mirrors that of Vita and her husband, Harold Nicolson, and Vita's and Virginia's own playful relationship to gender.

In the trope of the Gypsy, I argue, Woolf finds resonance with the protean quality with which she represents gender; like gender in *Orlando*, Gypsies constitute a floating signifier whose signified, scholarship notwithstanding, managed to elude the grasp of their *gadže* observers. Their contested identity is apparent from their first appearance in the British isles in the early sixteenth century,[4] and it is perhaps because of the semantic vacuum they presented that an identity was constructed for them by writers, lawmakers, Gypsiologists and others. That Gypsies represented escape, freedom, and 'aberrant femininity' has been noted by literary critics;[5] as Deborah Nord has argued, 'gypsydom function[ed] imaginatively as an "escape" from English conventionality at the borders of English society itself'.[6] The historian David Mayall states that 'foreign origin was the basis around which images were drawn of [the Gypsies as]

---

1. Kirstie Blair, 'Gypsies and Lesbian Desire: Vita Sackville-West, Violet Trefusis, and Virginia Woolf', *Twentieth-Century Literature* 50.2 (Summer 2004), 141–66 (142).
2. See Blair, 'Gypsies and Lesbian Desire', 156–57. According to Blair, Sackville-West and Trefusis went so far as to learn Romany so as to have a 'secret (or semisecret, given widespread interest in Romany) vocabulary to express desire and love' (151).
3. See Victoria Glendinning, *Vita: The Life of Vita Sackville-West* (Hardmondsworth: Penguin, 1984), 2.
4. These debates continue to the present day: see Mayall, *Gypsy Identities* (54–63 and 188, *passim*).
5. See George K. Behlmer, 'The Gypsy Problem in Victorian England', *Victorian Studies* 28 (Winter 1985), 231–53; and Katie Trumpener, 'The Time of the Gypsies', *Critical Inquiry* 18 (Summer 1992), 843–84; Deborah Nord, '"Marks of Race": Gypsy Figures and Eccentric Femininity in Nineteenth-century Women's Writing', *Victorian Studies* 41 (Winter 1998), 189–210; and Michelle Mancini, 'The Pursuit of Gypsyness in Nineteenth-century Britain', unpublished dissertation (University of California, Berkeley, 2000).
6. Nord, '"Marks of Race"', 190.

a romantic people, living an idle, natural, *al fresco* life'; they were thought to be 'dark, supple, agile and handsome, possessing a temperament that was wild, fierce, and defiant',[7] and possessing 'a sexual appetite matched only by their wanderlust'.[8] Judith Okely, in her anthropological study *The Traveller-Gypsies,* examines the prevalent stereotype of the Gypsy woman as 'sensual, sexually provocative, and enticing' and 'thought to be sexually available and promiscuous in her affections'.[9] Representations of Gypsies as objects of desire are complicated by equally powerful negative stereotypes. Throughout the nineteenth and early twentieth centuries, legislation was continually enacted that characterised Gypsies as 'vagrants, rogues, beggars, and vagabonds';[1] the nineteenth century 'reformer' George Smith 'of Coalville' described them as 'a people who "live like pigs and die like dogs"'.[2] Mayall states that while romantic conceptions of Gypsies are common, they are often accompanied by images of 'criminality, parasitism and deceit, with the nomadic Gypsy strangers appearing as a threat and danger to health, property, and person'.[3] The history of Gypsy identity in Britain was complicated by this strange confluence of negative and positive stereotypes that informed on the one hand, the phenomenon of 'Gypsiology' and on the other, centuries of anti-Gypsy legislation and oppression.[4]

In *Orlando,* it is from this pastiche of stereotypes that Woolf appears to draw in representing the Gypsies as exotics whose existence on the perimeters of European culture offers Orlando a respite from the confines of both aristocratic society and gender. This article will argue that similar disruptions of gender binaries are legible in references to Gypsies in Charlotte Brontë's *Villette* (1853), in which Gypsies are associated with challenges to social, sexual and gender norms. I do not claim that Woolf was consciously basing her representation of Gypsies on Brontë's, though it is worth noting that Woolf said of Brontë, 'we are steeped through and through with her genius'.[5] But I would suggest that Brontë and Woolf were both

7. David Mayall, *Gypsy-travellers in Nineteenth-century Society* (Cambridge: Cambridge University Press, 1988), 71.
8. Ibid., 76.
9. Judith Okely, *The Traveller-Gypsies* (Cambridge: Cambridge University Press, 1983; rpt. 1998), 201–202.
1. David Mayall, *English Gypsies and State Policies* (Hertfordshire: University of Hertfordshire Press, 1995), 31.
2. Quoted in Mayall, *English Gypsies,* 35. See also Okely, who quotes an eighteenth-century farmer who described local Gypsies as 'miscreants' and their 'loose women' as 'a parcel of Rogues and Trollops', *The Traveller-Gypsies,* 201.
3. Mayall, *Gypsy Identities,* 1.
4. It must be noted that the sorts of negative stereotypes found in references to Gypsies in British legislation resembled those that informed the Nazi persecution of Gypsies during World War II.
5. Virginia Woolf, '*Jane Eyre* and *Wuthering Heights*' in *The Common Reader: First Series* (New York: Harcourt Brace, 1925; rpt. 1953), 160.

'steeped' in the same prevailing stereotypes about Gypsies—their association with sexuality, with freedom and openness, and with challenges to the increasingly rigid categories of social and sexual roles. By examining Brontë's use of the Gypsy trope in *Villette* through the lens of *Orlando*, this article hopes to shed some light on the function of the Gypsy trope and its effects on gender in both novels.

* * * [T]he Gypsy trope signals that gender has been destabilised. This is explicit in *Orlando*: during her interlude with the 'gipsy tribe', Orlando temporarily inhabits the space between gender binaries in an ambiguous state between her previous life as a man and her new female identity. The ambiguity is reflected in her apparel: she 'dresse[s] herself in those Turkish coats and trousers which can be worn indifferently by either sex' (139) [76]. When she leaves the Gypsies, however, her clothes manifest a definite transition; now 'in the dress of a young Englishwoman of rank', she reflects that up to this point, 'she had scarcely given her sex a thought' and opines that 'perhaps the Turkish trousers, which she had hitherto worn had done something to distract her thoughts' (153) [82]. Here, Gypsyness calls attention to the extent to which for Orlando, and for Woolf, gender is to a large degree, perhaps entirely, performative. Orlando characterises the gender of the Gypsies themselves in ambiguous terms, stating that 'the Gypsy women, except in one or two very important particulars, differ very little from Gypsy men' (153) [82]. The implication is that while there are anatomical differences between Gypsy men and women, and these differences are 'very important', the cultural gap between men and women that is so cavernous in European society is not significant among the Gypsies because their costume is so similar; their difference in terms of biological sex may be 'important', but the difference in terms of socially constructed categories of gender is minimal.

When Orlando moves back into European society, however, gender there is foregrounded. As Orlando leaves the Gypsies and assumes the dress of an Englishwoman, she (for she is clearly female now) realises the significant role her clothing plays in her change of gender: 'it was not until she felt the coil of skirts about her legs and the Captain offered, with the greatest politeness, to have an awning spread for her on deck that she realised, with a start the penalties and privileges of her position' (153) [82–83]. She lists the disadvantages of being a woman: these primarily have to do with the maintenance of her appearance, which is conflated with the maintenance of chastity: 'there's the hairdressing. . . . That alone will take an hour of my morning. . . . there's staying and lacing; there's washing and powdering; there's changing from silk to lace and from lace to paduasoy; and there's being chaste year in year out' (157) [84]. Whereas the culture of the Gypsies has provided Orlando with a respite from the strictures of sex roles, European society insists upon conformity to a demanding female role whose costume enforces the limitations placed on female sexuality.

Certainly, *Orlando* deconstructs gender as a way of playfully masking homoeroticism, or what Karen Lawrence terms 'the poly-morphous possibilities of bisexuality'.[6] In depicting the Gypsies' androgyny as lacking in erotic power, Woolf is not making an argument that a heterosexual, binary model of gender is a neces-sary component of desire; rather, I would argue, she suggests that for Orlando, sexuality resides in an acknowledgement of the tremen-dous complexity of gender. Not only is Orlando herself both man and woman, but her husband, Shelmerdine, with whom she has a child, appears to be so as well: 'An awful suspicion rushed into both their minds simultaneously: "You're a woman, Shel!" she cried. "You're a man, Orlando!" he cried' (252) [134]. This complication of gender has an immediate erotic effect on them: 'For each was sur-prised at the quickness of the other's sympathy, and it was to each such a revelation that a woman could be as tolerant and free-spoken as a man, and a man as strange and subtle as a woman, that they had to put the matter to proof at once' (258) [137]. For Orlando, it would appear that it is not the absence of gender that constructs sexual desire, but gender's multiplicity.

*   *   *

Whereas Brontë's depiction of the effects of costume—or the lack thereof—on the performance of gender is implicit, Woolf's narrator in *Orlando* addresses this issue quite directly:

> The difference between the sexes is, happily, one of great pro-fundity. Clothes are but a symbol of something hid deep beneath. . . . Different though the sexes are, they intermix. In every human being a vacillation from one sex to the other takes place, and often it is only the clothes that keep the male or female likeness, while underneath the sex is the very opposite of what it is above. (189) [101–02]

The narrator goes on to list some of the ways in which Orlando her-self is a combination of allegedly male and female traits, stating that 'it was this mixture in her of man and woman, one being upper-most and then the other, that often gave her conduct an unexpected turn' (189) [102] and adding, '[w]hether, then, Orlando was most man or woman, it is difficult to say, and cannot now be decided'

6. Karen R. Lawrence, 'Orlando's Voyage Out', *Modern Fiction Studies* 38 (Spring 1992), 253–77 (255).

(190) [102]. This philosophy of gender has much more in common with the indeterminacy of the Gypsies' gender during Orlando's interlude with them than with the binary approach to gender later demonstrated when she returns to London. Like Brontë, Woolf has represented Gypsyness in a key moment as a sign of the breakdown, at least temporarily, of accepted gender binaries.

However, while Woolf's depiction of the Gypsies' destabilising effects on gender is similar in some ways to Brontë's, it differs greatly in terms of their association with sexuality: whereas the power of the 'gipsy-giantess' in *Villette* resides in her palpable eroticism, in *Orlando*, there is nothing remotely sexual about Orlando's associations with the Gypsies. Although she is a woman alone, the only threat they appear to pose to her is to her life, not to her 'chastity',[7] and while she considers marrying and settling among them, she is forced to abandon this idea because of her philosophical differences with them, so there is never any possibility of sexual relations between them. Indeed, Orlando's stay with the Gypsies appears to offer her a respite not just from gender, but from sexuality. While Orlando's life as a man has been filled with women who were said to be 'dying for love' of him, as well as with 'passionate embraces' from mysterious women, and her life as a woman is replete with flirtatious sailors and persistent suitors, her time with the Gypsies presents her with no opportunities for similar liaisons. Here Woolf, unlike Brontë, works against the traditional stereotype of Gypsies as 'free-living and free-loving'; in fact, they seem to be asexual, as if the lack of significant gender difference that Orlando notes is an impediment to their sexuality. While gender for Woolf is a performance, it is one that is essential to eroticism.

* * *

I would argue that for both Woolf and Brontë, the Gypsy trope represents a ready-made challenge to the nineteenth century project of disciplining gender and sexuality with which Woolf, in reacting against her Victorian predecessors, grapples; for Woolf and Brontë, Gypsy figures, in their multiple challenges to the status quo, disrupt this project. In making the case for Brontë as Woolf's antecedent here, I am not suggesting that the Gypsies in *Orlando* appear because of a direct connection to Brontë's novels. Rather, I would argue that both writers are drawing from the multiple possibilities opened up by the indeterminacy of Gypsy identity and its analogies to gender, and that it is Gypsies' inherent semantic ambiguity that helps enable the dislocation of social mores and the

---

7. This is a ludicrous concept for someone who has been having sexual dalliances for several hundred years.

deconstruction of accepted notions of gender and sexuality, and ultimately, of race, class and empire, when they enter a text.

JULIE VANDIVERE

The Bastard's Contention: Race, Property, and Sexuality in Virginia Woolf's *Orlando*†

How is it that we've never seen all the bastards in *Orlando*?[1] Most of us have read the novel as a rich text that, even though it has an excoriation of sexual definition at its base, also manages to engage with a wide range of other issues, including time, history, death, writing, and nature.[2] But we have not, to this point, considered the bastard, and we should. After all, in the pivotal lawsuit that follows Orlando for three hundred years, bastardy is a crucial factor; the suit claims that Orlando "was an English Duke who had married one Rosina Pepita, a dancer; and had had by her three sons, which sons now declaring that their father was deceased, claimed that all his property descended to them."[3] Orlando can only keep the estate because the "children [are] pronounced illegitimate" (Woolf, *Orlando*, 254–55) [135]. This direct allusion to misbegotten heirs and the way the threat of the lawsuit threads its ways through the second half of the novel should alert us to pay attention to the bastards; Woolf uses them to show that primogeniture, race, and nationality—foundations on which English wealth and citizenship were built at the beginning of the twentieth century—were, in fact, flimsy constructs whose boundaries were constantly transgressed. Through the figure of the bastard, *Orlando* reveals the ways that a supposedly racially pure and monogamously produced English system of authority and control was undermined by those it rejected: bastards, and non-white, non-English progenitors.

---

† From *Modernism/modernity* 28.1 (January 2021): 91–105, 110–16. © 2021 Johns Hopkins University Press. Reprinted with permission of Johns Hopkins University Press. Page numbers to this Norton Critical Edition appear in brackets. Most images have been omitted from this excerpt.

1. This argument forms part of my nearly completed monograph, *Fetal Wars: Birth Registration, Bastardy, and the Rise of Modernism*.

2. The criticism on *Orlando* is both broad and deep, demonstrating the potential of Woolf's novel to provoke a diversity of thinking. Notable recent criticism that deals with gender transgressions or metamorphosis include Jessica Berman, "Is the Trans in Transnational the Trans in Transgender?," *Modernism/modernity* 24, no. 2 (2017): 217–44; Georgia Johnson, "Queer Lives: Wilde, Sackville-West, and Woolf," in *A History of English Autobiography*, ed. Adam Smyth (Cambridge: Cambridge University Press, 2016), 269–83; and Pamela Caughie, "The Temporality of Modernist Life Writing in the Era of Transsexualism: Virginia Woolf's *Orlando* and Einar Wegener's *Man Into Woman*," *Modern Fiction Studies* 59, no. 3 (2013): 501–25.

3. Virginia Woolf, *Orlando: A Biography* (New York: Harcourt, Brace, 1928), 168 [91].

To contemporary ears, the word "bastardy" sounds more offensive than "illegitimacy." Nevertheless, "bastard" and "bastardy" were legal terms in England until the middle of the twentieth century, and, historically, these words did not carry the stigma they do today. More importantly, as Jenny Bourne Taylor delineates in her study of bastardy in the nineteenth century, the term "bastardy" has a much richer meaning than the term "illegitimacy"; bastardy's definition also includes that which is adulterated, imitative, and spurious. Taylor argues that legitimacy is based on a binary between legitimate and illegitimate, while bastardy points to the twisted historical basis of the term that is not rooted in a binary. Taylor argues that the bastard is "an identity constructed as an aporia."[4] In this light, illegitimacy is to legitimacy similar to what homosexual is to heterosexual, while the word "bastard" operates conceptually more like the word "queer"; that is, it opens up possibilities of meanings that would be foreclosed by a simple binary. Of course, the relationship between sexual preference and conditions of birth is in other ways not at all analogous. Terms that denote conditions of birth and sexual orientation carry both social and legal heft, but "illegitimate" and "bastard" are legal categories that have been used historically to define privilege, ownership, and citizenship. In social realms, they have less weight. As histories of bastardy show, the appellation often carried no social stigma at all.[5] In contrast, categories of sexual preference bear tremendous social force; individuals are often excluded from social groups based on their sexual orientation.

Creating a category that outlines what is or is not bastardy is vital to the legal structure of a country because it is a nation's framing of what is native and alien. "Legitimate" birth invariably strives to create a body of citizens who are defined by two factors: whether their birth is in line with the state's ambitions and whether their birth reinforces existing hierarchies. In other words, the purpose of legitimacy laws has been both to corral the population and to create a pecking order within it. France, England, Spain, and Germany have had very different political structures and so possessed very different legitimacy laws at the beginning of the twentieth century.[6] Even

4. Jenny Bourne Taylor, "Representing Illegitimacy in Victorian Culture," in *Victorian Identities: Social and Cultural Formations in Nineteenth-Century Literature*, ed. Ruth Robbins and Julian Wolfreys (New York: St. Martin's Press, 1996), 119–42, 121.

5. For histories of bastardy, Jenny Bourne Taylor's helpful summaries of bastardy laws are found in "Nobody's Secret: Illegitimate Inheritance and the Uncertainties of Memory," *Nineteenth-Century Contexts* 21, no. 4 (2000): 565–92. A more complete history is Ivy Pinchbeck and Margaret Hewitt's *Children in English Society*, 2 vols. (London: Routledge and Kegan Paul, 1969–73). Also informative are Jenny Teichman, *Illegitimacy: A Philosophical Examination* (Oxford: Blackwell, 1982); and the collection of essays, *Illegitimacy in Britain, 1700–1920*, ed. Alysa Levene, Thomas Nutt, and Samantha Williams (New York: Palgrave Macmillan, 2005).

6. Editors Peter Laslett, Karla Oosterveen, and Richard M. Smith's *Bastardy and its Comparative History: Studies in the History of Illegitimacy and Marital Nonconformism in*

within English laws, legitimacy laws for centuries have diverged dramatically since they were rooted in two entirely different systems—the Common and the Ecclesiastical.[7] Ecclesiastical law strove to ensure that unsupported mothers and children would not tax the parishes. Historically, the Christian Church created legitimacy laws that, although they could be capricious, created a liberal definition of illegitimacy: a child was presumed legitimate unless there was irrefutable evidence to the contrary, and any child could be named as legitimate whose parents married each other at any point. Common law, however, strove to assure the integrity of property and royal inheritance and asserted a much stricter definition of legitimacy on the disposition of titles, wealth, and privilege.[8]

By the dawn of the twentieth century, however, the contradictions caused by the 1857 Matrimonial Causes Act and the 1858 Legitimacy Declaration Act set the two parallel systems at odds with each other. The first act was meant to preclude economic breakdown, while the second was meant to secure consistent and predictable patterns of wealth. Both acts sought to modernize the bifurcated system by moving matrimonial and legitimacy issues to the Common law courts, but the effect was, rather, to join two incompatible definitions of legitimacy. By the early twentieth century, legitimacy had become what Taylor calls a "Gordian knot of tangled and conflicting laws within the nation, within the empire, and within the Western world" ("Representing Illegitimacy," 185). As Taylor points out, while English jurists attempted to create these distinctions between legitimate and not, "they knew that the bastard was a slippery creature, an elusive figure that highlighted the mutable meanings of the family—as based on legal fiction, blood relations or ties of social affection and obligation—itself" (174).

Britain, France, Germany, Sweden, North America, Jamaica, and Japan (London: Edward Arnold, 1980) provides the most through side-by-side comparison of bastardy laws. See also Lewellyn Hendrix, Illegitimacy and Social Structures: Cross-Cultural Perspectives on Nonmarital Birth (Westport, CT: Bergin and Garvey, 1996).

7. See Alan Macfarlane, "Illegitimacy and Illegitimates in English History," in Bastardy and its Comparative History, 71–85, 73.

8. William Blackstone explains that under civil law in England, bastards are "filius nullius," "the sons of nobody." "Being thus the sons of nobody, they have no blood in them, at least no heritable blood" (The Commentaries of Sir William Blackstone, Knight, on the Laws and Constitution of England, ed. William Curry [London: Oxford, 1796], 65, 148). The illegitimate child was seen as issue of no one, having no parents or kin. He was prohibited from inheriting property or joining guilds, a condition which would have kept him out of most professions. These strict prohibitions, designed to maintain the power of the crown, largely accomplished just that. After the Statute of Merton, England had few illegitimate challengers to the throne, despite the legions of illegitimate children that the kings and queens of England produced. Although the illegitimate children were not able to inherit directly from their wealthy parents, they were often given wealth as a gift and/or married to the royalty of other countries (Teichman, Illegitimacy, 56).

The Underpinnings of Bastardy in Orlando

The novel's most pointed reference to bastardy appears in the account of the lawsuit that follows Orlando for three hundred years. The sequence and substance of the trial, as scholars have noted, closely mirrors the real-world legitimacy trial that in 1910 pitted Vita Sackville-West's uncle, Henry, against Vita's parents, Victoria (Henry's sister) and Lionel Edward.[9] Henry claimed that his parents, Pepita and Lionel Sackville-West, had been married at the time of his birth, and, therefore, he should be recognized as their legitimate and legal heir. Lionel Edward (Victoria's husband) contended the opposite. Lionel Edward argued that Victoria and Henry's parents had never married; as such, the estate should pass to him since he was the couple's nephew. Indeed, what made the case so alluring were the complicated relationships within this aristocratic family: Victoria was simultaneously the sister to the plaintiff (Henry) and wife, as well as first cousin, to the defendant (Lionel Edward). As a woman, Victoria had no legal claim to the money. But if her husband inherited the estate (by virtue of also being her cousin), Victoria and her daughter, Vita, would benefit in a way that would have been impossible if the estate was granted to her brother Henry. Therefore, in 1910, Vita's parents found themselves in the awkward position of arguing that Henry, and by extension, Victoria, should be declared bastards.[1]

The parallels between the Sackville-West lawsuit and the fictional lawsuit in *Orlando* are obvious. The first, and most obvious, is the fact that both mothers have the name Pepita. The second is that both cases revolve around the question of whether or not the mother had been legally married at the time of her child's birth. The third is that both the real and the fictional son argue that they are legitimate heirs to their family fortune, and their claims threaten to bankrupt a well-known and aristocratic English family. The fourth and final parallel is that both cases end happily for the English aristocracy: in both, the union of Lord and Gypsy is deemed unlawful, the children are proclaimed bastards and sent packing, and the aristocratic families retain their estates and titles. This

---

9. See Abby Bardi, "'In Company of a Gipsy': The 'Gypsy' as Trope in Woolf and Brontë," *Critical Survey* 19, no. 1 (2007): 40–50, 41.

1. The basic contours of the 1910 Sackville-West legitimacy trial were well known and were covered in newspapers around the world. Vita Sackville-West also recounted the trial in detail in her 1937 biography of her mother and grandmother entitled *Pepita* (London: Hogarth Press, 1937), 210–29. Vita Sackville-West's biographers, the Sackville-West family, and others have relied on this account. In particular, see Robert Sackville-West, *Inheritance: The Story of Knole and the Sackvilles* (London: Bloomsbury, 2010), 206; Victoria Glendinning, *Vita: A Biography of Vita Sackville-West* (New York: Quill, 1983), 35; and Robert Sackville-West, *The Disinherited: A Story of Family, Love, and Betrayal* (London: Bloomsbury, 2014), 210–25.

clear biographical nesting in the 1910 trial sets up the context whereby the novel reaches out to the historical events and conditions to examine the ways that race, land rights, and perceptions of women's sexuality were changing in the early twentieth century.

Bastardy and Race in Orlando

First, let us turn to the question of race. Woolf's view of race in *Orlando* has been understood as naïve, if not bigoted. Woolf conflates Turks and Gypsies, gives a Spanish name to a Turkish Gypsy, identifies a Negress only as an object of sexual desire, and, most egregiously, begins the novel with a racist scene of conquest. The tendency among readers has been to argue that Woolf uses a stable and shallow view of race in order to contrast the instability of gender or to tease out the meaning of individual categories of race.[2] Certainly, part of Woolf's muddling about race comes simply from an early twentieth-century xenophobia that bound the idea of a racialized body as one associated with geographical distance. As historians such as Edward Beasley, Jeffrey Green, and Paul Rich have shown, until the 1930s, race was "generally synonymous with 'nation' in British liberal discourse," and racialized subjects were often seen as foreigners.[3] Woolf's interchangeable use of Gypsy, Moor, Turk, Blackamoor, and Negress would, therefore, have been typical of the cultural perspective of the time—a perspective that blurred the distinction between racial and ethnic identity.

---

2. Jaime Hovey reads race in *Orlando* as a reaction to post–World War I concerns about "Englishwoman's dubious racial . . . loyalty" ("'Kissing a Negress in the Dark': Englishness as a Masquerade in Woolf's *Orlando*," *PMLA* 112, no. 3 [1997]: 393–404, 394). Erzsebet Zelinka, Celia R. Caputi Daileader, Ching-fang Tseng, Erica L. Johnson, and Deborah Cohler all draw from Hovey's reading and see the stability of race in *Orlando* as foil to the instability of gender. See Erzsebet Zelinka, "Virginia Woolf's Oriental Discourse in *Orlando*," *Gender Studies* 1, no. 7 (2008): 51–69, 55; Celia R. Caputi Daileader, "Othello's Sister: Racial Hermaphroditism and Appropriation in Virginia Woolf's *Orlando*," *Studies in the Novel* 45, no. 1 (2013): 56–79, 58; Ching-fang Tseng, "'Jour de Ma Vie': Englishness, the Exotic Other, and the Sublime in Virginia Woolf's *Orlando*," *NTU Studies in Language and Literature* 34 (2015): 57–90, 62; Erica L. Johnson, "Giving up the Ghost: National and Literary Haunting in *Orlando*," *Modern Fiction Studies* 50, no. 1 (2004): 110–28, 114; Deborah Cohler, *Citizen, Invert, Queer: Lesbianism and War in Early Twentieth-Century Britain* (Minneapolis: University of Minnesota Press, 2010), 174–81. Karen Kaivola acknowledges her debt to Hovey but argues that race is also destabilized. See "Revisiting Woolf's Representations of Androgyny: Gender, Race, Sexuality, and Nation," *Tulsa Studies in Women's Literature* 18, no. 2 (1999): 235–61, 253.

3. Paul B. Rich, *Race and Empire in British Politics* (Cambridge: Cambridge University Press, 1986), 3. In particular, Jeffrey Green provides a close reading of how racial minorities were read at the turn of the century. He carefully chronicles the ways that racialized individuals either blended into English identity by marrying Anglo-British women or were seen as foreigners and celebrated as performers, spectacles, or exotic diplomats. See Jeffrey Green, *Black Edwardians: Black People in Britain from 1910 to 1914* (New York: Frank Cass Publishers, 1998), 1–14. See also Rich, *Race and Empire*, 18.

However, by looking more closely at the issue of bastardy and the scholarship on miscegenation in British history, we can see that *Orlando* offers insights into the ways that racialization was folded into a population whose systems of control presumed whiteness. Orlando, on his/her traipse through the history of England, picks up and carries along with him/her the bits and pieces of different English concepts of race as they presented over the course of three hundred years. Woolf alludes to race in both story and pictures, challenging the reader to see that, because of bastardy, assumptions of whiteness in a presumably English line are false and revealing the English "race" as hybrid in the most basic sense. The English body alone—no matter how white, native, royal, or wealthy—cannot establish the differentiation between racial categories that would award racial supremacy to any one group. More importantly, Woolf uses bastardy to expose the English "race" as hybrid in a more complex way. Woolf's bastard sits as a metaphor for what Homi Bhabha calls "third space," an articulation of something that "challenges our sense of the historical identity of culture as a homogenizing, unifying force."[4] Thus, race in *Orlando* stresses two points. First, the English body cannot assert the differentiation between two racial categories that would establish supremacy. Second, *Orlando* does more than simply establish that there is not differentiation between dark and light, Black and white, foreign and native; *Orlando* also establishes bastardy as the culprit that secretly mingles and melds racial categories.

The most explicit evidence of *Orlando*'s engagement with the racially hybrid body lies in the allegorical creature on the cover of the first edition. It is, as J. H. Stape has noted, a reproduction of a sixteenth-century painting that was thought to depict Thomas Sackville-West, advisor to Queen Elizabeth and Vita's ancestor who secured the Knole estate (fig.1).[5] Although there were many paintings of Thomas readily available at the time Vita and Virginia were choosing which portrait to include in the novel, the two ignored them all and instead chose a painting that offers an image unlike all the others.[6] What distinguishes the chosen portrait is that while the face and attire resemble a sixteenth-century Anglo-English nobleman, the body does not. Beneath the figure's neck lies the unmistakable markers of a Black body. The painting, destroyed

4. Homi K. Bhabha, *The Location of Culture* (London: Routledge, 1994), 375.
5. J. H. Stape, "'The Man at Worthing' and the Author of 'The Most Insipid Verse She Had Ever Read': Two Allusions in *Orlando*," *Virginia Woolf Miscellany* 50 (1997): 5–6.
6. Virginia reminded Vita in a letter to bring "the photograph of the man at Worthing" (Virginia Woolf to V. Sackville-West, April 17, 1928, in *The Letters of Virginia Woolf*, ed. Nigel Nicolson and Joanne Trautmann, vol. 3, *1923–1928* [Boston, MA: Houghton Mifflin, 1980], 484). In June of the same year, Leonard wrote to the Museum of Worthing to ask for permission to use the photograph (Stape, "'The Man at Worthing,'" 6).

Fig. 1. Hogarth Press first edition dustcover of *Orlando* depicting Thomas Sackville, 1928, painted by an unknown artist during the late sixteenth century and held until 1944 by the Worthing Museum Art Gallery, UK.

during the bombing of London in World War II, was described by L. F. Salzman in a way that underscores the figure's composite identity as both Black and white:

> It shows a three-quarter length figure of a negro, or Moor—for his skin is dark brown and not black. He is naked except for a metal gorget or neckpiece and a waistline [*sic*] . . . The right arm, adorned with a bracelet and, higher up, a bangle of pearls, holds a jeweled hilt of a sword, which passes behind the figure. This head, almost full face, emerges from a ruff and is that of a Northern European, a man of about 40 with dark hair and

close-trimmed beard. The shield . . . shows a landscape in which two satyrs side by side, one almost hidden by the other, each carrying a banner, are driving before them three deer towards a tree.[7]

To understand the implication of this composite figure, we need to turn to the extensive work done on race by early modern historians like Lynda Boose, Andrew Curran, and Roxann Wheeler who have determined that, during the Renaissance, dark skin carried very different significance than it did in the twentieth century but that these "protoracial ideologies" would have persisted.[8] These older conceptions, as multiple historical scholars show, indicate that during this period "the black man [was] representable" (Boose, "'The Getting of a Lawful Race,'" 47). As Isabel Wilkerson notes in her recent work on caste in America, Caucasian is a relatively recent term that emerged only in 1795.[9] Notions of difference in the sixteenth and seventeenth centuries were based not on skin color but on religion and wealth. Clothing signified whether an individual was Pagan or Christian and wealthy or poor, categories of difference that persisted through much of the eighteenth century (Wheeler, Complexion of Race, 14)![1]

While today it might seem that the differentiation between Christian and Pagan would make the Moor an outsider, in Thomas Sackville's time, to be Christian meant to be not Catholic. Thomas Sackville, in fact, was involved in elevating the standing of the Moor in England. As Queen Elizabeth fended off attacks from Rome and Spain, who were together seeking to make England Catholic once again, she reached for support to the Sultan Zuldan Murad of the far more powerful Ottoman Empire. During this period, as Vita chronicles in Knole and the Sackvilles, Thomas Sackville was the Queen's Lord Treasurer and "absent from none of the councils of the nation."[2] He was even imprisoned in Rome in 1568 on suspicion

---

7. L. F. Salzman, "A Sixteenth-Century Portrait," Sussex Notes and Queries 8, no. 8 (1941): 205–7, 205.
8. Roxann Wheeler, The Complexion of Race: Categories of Difference in Eighteenth-Century British Culture (Philadelphia: University of Pennsylvania Press, 2000), 9. See Lynda E. Boose, "'The Getting of a Lawful Race': Racial Discourse in Early Modern England and the Unrepresentable Black Woman" in Women, "Race" and Writing in the Early Modern Period, ed. Margo Hendricks and Patricia Parker (Abingdon, VA: Routledge, 1994), 35–54, 47. Andrew Curran identifies the creation of blackness with the mid-eighteenth century, noting that the development of race reveals far more about Europeans than it does about Africans (The Anatomy of Blackness; Science and Slavery in an Age of Enlightenment [Baltimore, MD: Johns Hopkins University Press, 2011], 3). Wheeler narrows the window, ascribing the creation of race to the last quarter of the eighteenth century (The Complexion of Race, 9).
9. Isabel Wilkerson, Caste: The Origins of Our Discontents (New York: Random House, 2020), 65.
1. See also Edward Beasley, The Victorian Reinvention of Race: New Racisms and the Problem of Grouping in the Human Sciences (London: Routledge, 2010), 11.
2. Vita Sackville-West, Knole and the Sackvilles (Kent: Ernest Benn Limited, 1984), 47.

of being a spy for Elizabeth (Sackville-West, *Knole*, 47). As Jerry Brotton has shown, the British and Ottoman Empires created a philosophical sympathy that cast them as allied against the sacrilege of the Catholic Church. Elizabeth presented herself to the Moorish Sultan as the "most mighty defender of the Christian faith against all kind of idolatries, of all that live among the Christians, and falsely profess the name of Christ."[3] The Sultan's admiration was also colored with language that sought to align their beliefs as a way to find common ground against the power of the pope, addressing her as "most wise governor of the causes and affairs of the people and family of Nazareth."[4] The intensity of the powerful Moor's admiration was evident when he spoke of the Queen to others. One of the Queen's agents reported to her that the Shah had said, "I make more account of you coming from the queen of England than of any from Spain," because Philip II "cannot govern his own country but is governed by the Pope" (Brotton, *Sultan and the Queen*, 70). In fact, as Brotton writes, the agent went so far as to claim that the Moor thought of himself to "be a very earnest Protestant of good religion and living" (70). Distancing themselves from the common enemy of the Pope, the pair, the Moor and the Anglican, stretched their philosophies to see themselves as united combatants against the Catholic outsider.

While Woolf hints at this history and the racialization of the Anglo-English line in her chosen portrait for *Orlando*'s dustcover illustration, the image makes no connection between race and bastardy. Elsewhere in the novel, however, this linkage becomes explicit. For example, midway through the narrative, Orlando, considering his own racial composition, points out "a certain darkness in his complexion" and "wondered if, in the season of the Crusades, one of his ancestors had taken up with a Circassian peasant woman" (Woolf, *Orlando*, 121) [66]. In a later scene, the gypsies are described as having "looked upon her [Orlando] as one of themselves . . . her dark hair and dark complexion bore out the belief that she was, by birth, one of them and had been snatched by an English Duke from a nut tree when she was a baby" (141–42) [77].

One can also see the mix of racial signifiers produced by bastardy in another image inserted into the novel. In the photograph identified in the text as "Orlando about the year 1840," the figure sports what multiple critics have observed to be a hodgepodge of racial

3. Cited in Jerry Brotton, *The Sultan and the Queen: The Untold Story of Elizabeth and Islam* (New York: Penguin Press, 2016), 2–3.
4. Quoted in Jerry Brotton, *This Oriental Isle: Elizabethan England and the Islamic World* (London: Penguin Press, 2016), 94.

allusions [page 132 in this volume].[5] Christine Fouirnaies identifies the clash and clutter of patterns and accessories in Sackville-West's attire and argues that Woolf here dissociates Sackville-West from her noble guise, distancing her from the Sackvilles and preventing Vita from becoming conflated with her aristocratic identity.[6] Similarly, Jane Garrity comments on the "mishmash of sartorial signifiers"—a plaid kilt-like skirt, a soft, velvet Renaissance cap, and incongruously, a flowered gypsy blouse or shawl—and argues that they are all meant to convey Vita Sackville-West's mixed identity as both English and Gypsy.[7] The photograph's hodgepodge of racial allusions echoes the myriad racial allusions in *Orlando*. In the novel, the origin of the English white and non-white lineage varies from scene to scene: in Constantinople, the Gypsies see Orlando as the product of a cross-racial coupling, while his alignment with Othello, as Daileader has remarked, shifts its focuses, muddling the impression of whether Sasha or Orlando might be dark skinned.[8]

In creating a variety of racial identities for Orlando that morph from scene to scene, Woolf exposes the ways in which the racial hybridity I mentioned earlier is endemic to the English population. And it is her use of bastardy that identifies the more complex and

5. In this photograph, Woolf carefully planned a masquerade, asking Vita, "Should I hire a wig for you? or can you make up?" (Virginia Woolf to V. Sackville-West, October 30, 1927, in Nicolson and Trautmann, *Letters*, 3:434).
6. Christine Fouirnaies, "Was Virginia Woolf a Snob? The Case of Aristocratic Portraits in *Orlando*," *Woolf Studies Annual* 22 (2016): 21–40, 33.
7. Jane Garrity, "Fashioning Photographic Syntax in *Orlando*" (paper, Annual Conference of the Modernist Studies Association, Pittsburgh, PA, November 7, 2014).
8. Orlando and Sasha come upon the Punch and Judy production of *Othello*, just before they are to flee. Orlando finds himself unusually moved and reflects passionately that "the frenzy of the Moor seemed to him his own frenzy, and when the Moor suffocated the woman in her bed it was Sasha he killed with his own hands" (Woolf, *Orlando*, 57 [32]). Cohler marks the integration of the Moor's racial identity into Orlando's self-composition, while Daileader reads the scene as a complicated superpositioning of biracial couples, noting that the scene not only contains the Moor and the white woman from *Othello*, but, that the narrator's description of the interlude repeats the lines from the duet in *The Merchant of Venice* as the Jew's daughter and the Christian prepare for their escape (Cohler, *Citizen, Invert, Queer*, 178). Daileader observes: "Thus, in this densely allusive conclusion to Orlando's first chapter, two Shakespearean, fugitive, interracial couples get superimposed upon Orlando and the Russian princess on the eve of their planned flight. Like Desdemona, Sasha is suspected of having betrayed the hero: like Jessica, she will come disguised 'in her cloak and trousers, booted like a man'" ("Othello's Sister," 62; Woolf, *Orlando*, 59 [33]). In that same passage, Daileader highlights the similarities between these lines in *Orlando*—"The night was dark; it was pitch dark; but it was such a night as this that they had waited for; it was on such a night as this that they had planned to fly"—and these lines from *The Merchant of Venice*:

> The moon shines bright. In such a night as this,
> When the sweet wind did gently kiss the trees
> And they did make no noise—in such a night.

(*Orlando*, 57 [32]; William Shakespeare, *The Merchant of Venice*, in *William Shakespeare: The Complete Works*, ed. Gary Taylor and Stanley Wells [Oxford: Oxford University Press, 1988], 5.1.1–3).

radical racial hybridity, the way bastardy exists as a "third space." The bastard child represents the interstices in the collision of concepts of race and concepts of the law, giving "rise to something different, something new and unrecognizable, a new area of negotiation of meaning and representation."[9] To that point, historian Emily Bartels argues that, given the history of darker-skinned people in England (one that goes back almost a thousand years), racial hybridity is simply part of the English composition, and terms like "the Moor" or "Gypsy" serve "as a site where competing, always provisional axes of identity come dynamically into play, disrupting our ability" to compartmentalize race.[1] In this equation, the Moor and Gypsy are signs of racial diversity that are components of *all* English heritage.

The more crucial and compelling element of this British hybridity is the English tendency to create sexual relations between individuals of different races rather than within their own national and ethnic group: one outcome of which is children. Sydney Collins notes that such alliances are not common in other societies but "in Britain, however, miscegenation between white women and non-white men is a general pattern."[2] The inclination to pursue interracial relationships and produce racially diverse children persisted into the twentieth century and has been noted by more contemporary critics such as David Olusoga who asserts that anti-black riots erupted in 1919 because non-English white men from the colonies objected to the interracial relationships they witnessed in England.[3] Moreover, children of mixed races were so common throughout England's history, argues Peter Fryer, that although records of their lives are so obscure and scattered that they have for the most part been forgotten by their descendants, there must nevertheless, "be many thousands of British families who, if they traced their roots back to the eighteenth or early nineteenth century, would find among their ancestors an African or person of African descent."[4]

9. Homi K. Bhabha and Jonathan Rutherford, "The Third Space: Interview with Homi Bhabha," in *Identity: Community, Culture, Difference*, ed. Jonathon Rutherford (London: Lawrence and Wishart, 1990), 207–21, 211.
1. Emily Bartels, *Speaking of the Moor: From "Alcazar" to "Othello"* (Philadelphia: University of Pennsylvania Press, 2009), 7.
2. Sydney Collins, *Coloured Minorities in Britain: Studies in British Race Relations Based on African, West Indian, and Asiatic Immigrants* (London: Lutterworth Press, 1957), 23.
3. David Olusoga quotes a 1919 *Times* that reports "In the post war situation many [blacks] married Liverpool women and while it is admitted that some of them made good husbands the intermarriage of black men and women, not to mention other relationships, has excited much feeling" (*Black and British: A Forgotten History* [London: MacMillan Press, 2017], 459).
4. Peter Fryer, *Staying Power: The History of Black People in Britain* (London: Pluto Press, 2010), 235.

The question then becomes, how were these hybrid children presented and incorporated within English culture, particularly in the
first decades of the twentieth century, and especially during the
years Woolf was writing her novel about the gender-switching,
racially complex nobleman? Deborah Cohen argues that one of the
essential structuring principles for class and wealth in late nine-
teenth- and early twentieth-century Britain was the organization of
secrets around who was illegitimate and who was a racially hybrid
child.[5] As many historians of Asia recount, only those who were
deemed sufficiently white to pass among English peers of the upper
and middle classes were shipped home by British agents.[6] Maintaining the secret of bastardy and the racialization of the family line
became one of the most important elements of class structures:
"Keeping a secret, like keeping a servant," contends Cohen, "was one
way . . . to define the middle class" (*Family Secrets*, 8). Cohen argues
that, as ideas about race became calcified through the course of the
nineteenth century, the existence of darker-skinned offspring was
driven underground (45). Maintaining the secret held class and
family structures in place. Families were "transparent within . . . and
opaque from without" (4). The path of the secret defined the intricacies of class structures themselves. "Family secrets were shared
secrets, whether by a pair of relatives or a populous clan, and therefore required the constant management of information, both inside
and outside the family. Who should be told what, who could and
could not be trusted" (6). Seen in this context, Woolf's *Orlando* can
be understood as having divulged secrets about racialization within
a supposedly white, Anglo-Saxon line, and in so doing, violated the
practice of maintaining class identity.

5. Deborah Cohen, *Family Secrets: Shame and Privacy in Modern Britain* (Oxford: Oxford
   University Press, 2018).
6. In the early nineteenth century, a company agent, John Palmer, made this distinction
   clear as he considered what to do with his young charges: "The two eldest [who] are
   almost as fair as European children . . . should be sent to Europe. I could have made
   no distinction between the children if the youngest was of a complexion that could
   possibly escape detection; but as I daily see the injurious consequences resulting from
   bringing up certain [darker-skinned] native children at Home, it is become a question
   in my own mind how far I should confer a service in recommending the third child"
   (William Dalrymple, *White Mughals: Love and Betrayal in Eighteenth-Century India*
   [New York: Viking, 2003], 40). As William Dalrymple summarizes, "It was decided in
   the end that the 'dark' child should stay in India and try to make his way as a clerk,
   while the others were shipped to Britain to try their luck there" (40). Maria Graham,
   writing in 1813, makes the color distinction explicit, declaring "it a cruelty to send
   children of colour to Europe, where their complexion must subject them to perpetual
   mortification" (*The Journal of a Residence in India* [Edinburgh: George Ramsay, 1813],
   128). The British poor, however, did not seem to worry about degrees of darkness as
   strongly. Historians, including Peter Fryer, note the presence of multi-racial children
   of all shades from the Renaissance on and remark that the children, "the fruit of . . .
   mutual love" between Black men and white women, no longer saw "themselves as con-
   stituting a distinct black community. They were part of the British poor" (*Staying
   Power*, 235).

Such racial subterfuge would have been familiar to Vita Sackville-West and Virginia Woolf from their own families and friends. And they would have known how to integrate racially distinct lineages into the homes and hearths of Englishness. Vita's own "mixed" pedigree was flashed in newspaper headlines around the world as the 1910 legitimacy trial pitted the "Gypsy" line against the "English" line, exposing the spurious motivation behind designations of race. The irony, of course, is that both parties in the lawsuit were the children of the "Gypsy" Pepita de Oliva and thus were equally racialized.

Woolf was equally well-equipped to handle racial complexity. The family structure of Woolf's close friend Lytton Strachey illustrates the phenomenon of integrated "dark" blood that Cohen discusses as a central part of Imperial England. Strachey's grandmother Julia had two Indian half-siblings, Cecilia and Robert, and both were raised as white and English. The same pattern of racial co-mingling occurred in the following generation when Strachey's mother was asked by her favorite brother to help raise his four Indian-born children. In keeping with English practice at the time, she took them in and raised them alongside her other children until they went to boarding school.[7]

Woolf's own family tree indicates a similar incorporation of racial diversity. Woolf's father's first wife, Minny Thackeray, had an Indian aunt and Indian cousins (her father, William Makepeace Thackeray had an Indian half-sister and a "black niece" who came and stayed with the Thackerays when Minny was eleven). In addition, Woolf's great-aunt, Julia Cameron, had two Indian stepchildren (her husband, Charles Hay Cameron, had fathered them before he met Julia). Julia never indicated she was bothered by the miscegenation, for after all, she and Woolf's grandmother Maria were two of the five beautiful Pattle sisters who were deeply embedded within Indian culture. They spoke Hindustani among themselves, appeared in Indian adornment and were teased for their dusky Indian beauty and "Pondicherry eyes."[8] Their Indian heritage came through the maternal line; one of Woolf's ancestors was a Hindu Bengali woman

---

7. Barbara Caine, *Bombay to Bloomsbury: A Biography of the Strachey Family* (Oxford: Oxford University Press, 2006), 45–46.
8. In his biography of the family, Malcolm Allbrook writes that, "The arrival from Calcutta of four of Sara's sisters, Julia Margaret (Cameron), Maria (Jackson), Virginia (Somers) and Sophia (Dalrymple), over the next few years brought the formation of a network that was unashamedly and assertively Anglo-Indian, and willing to exhibit their Indianness in a way that appealed to London society" (*Henry Prinsep's Empire: Framing a Distant Colony* [Acton: Australian National University Press, 2014], 83). The sisters "exhibited the exotic and idealised aspects of Anglo-Indian culture, dressing in oriental costumes, speaking Hindustani amongst themselves, serving Indian cuisine" (85).

who, upon marriage to a French soldier, took the name Maria Monica.[9]

I recount the history of the period and the genealogy of Vita Sackville-West and Virginia Woolf because it reveals the profound way that bastardy incorporated racialization into a supposedly pure Anglo-English line. The bastard's existence, especially when he breaks the codes of racist culture, apart from any philosophy he or she might espouse (like Vita's ham-handed elitism and xenophobia), represents the absolute embodiment of liminal space from which new possibilities can emerge. As Boose explains, the interpolation of race in a child through a mother, "threatens nothing less than the wholesale negation of white patriarchal authority" ("The Getting of a Lawful Race," 46). While a "racially mixed" "bastard" male (such as Henry Sackville) may challenge the structures that exclude him, the existence of "racially mixed" "bastard" women creates seepage throughout the philosophy of white supremacy and its belief in the essential and unitary nature of race. She, therefore, "destroys the system, essentially swallowing it up within the signification of her body" (47). The daughter may pass as white, but she is not, nor will her heirs be, "white," and there is no rule that white patriarchy can impose that will subvert a woman's ability to corrupt the presumptions of white, male control. Bastardy in *Orlando* brings this principle to light: in the novel, we witness the whole cloth of an imagined single racial identity dissolve, much in the way that Orlando's gender bending undermines a single gender identity.

Bastardy and Property

Since its publication, readers often interpret *Orlando* as Woolf's metaphorical gift of Knole to Sackville-West. Vita, barred by her gender from inheriting her home, would somehow be consoled by fictional ownership.[1] Though perhaps it's nice to think of the novel as a sort of romantic memento, such a reading obscures the significant ways in which the novel responds to early twentieth-century notions

---

9. Dalrymple traces his own genealogy (which is also Virginia Woolf's) and concludes that a maternal ancestor, Maria Monique, had been Indian ("White Mischief," *The Guardian*, December 8, 2002, * * *). In addition, amateur genealogists have traced the line from Virginia to the Indian maternal ancestor. See "Therese Josephe (Blin de Grincourt) de l'Etang (1768–1866)," *WikiTree*, accessed October 28, 2020 * * *.

1. Among others, see Sophie Blanch, "Contested Wills: Reclaiming the Daughter's Inheritance in Vita Sackville-West's *The Edwardians*," *Critical Survey* 19, no. 1 (2007): 73–83, 73; Victoria L. Smith, "'Ransacking the Language': Finding the Missing Goods in Virginia Woolf's *Orlando*," *Journal of Modern Literature* 29, no. 4 (2006): 57–75, 64; and Sarah Edwards, "'Permanent preservation for the benefit of the nation': The Country House, Preservation, and Nostalgia in Vita Sackville-West's *The Edwardians* and Virginia Woolf's *Orlando*," in *Modernism and Nostalgia: Bodies, Locations, Aesthetics*, ed. Tammy Clewell (London: Palgrave Macmillan, 2013), 93–110, 93.

of primogeniture inheritance and participates in subverting the existent system by flaunting primogeniture's vain and bootless insistence on legitimate birth.

At first glance it seems that *Orlando* reinforces established views of primogeniture: Orlando is able to keep his estate only because his sons with Rosina Pepita are declared illegitimate. Nevertheless, the complications of bastardy seep through the narrative, ridiculing the mandates of primogeniture as the condition of inheritance. Woolf's first undermining of land rights appears in the preface when she thanks C. P. Sanger, without whose knowledge of "real property the book would not have been written" (*Orlando*, vii) [5]. Some scholars, Helen Southworth and Caroline Webb among others, see the comment as humorous, while others, like Frank Baldanza and Jamie McDaniel, see it as serious.[2] McDaniel, for example, surmises that Woolf includes Sanger because his work illustrates the ways in which the patrilineal system-based inheritance on lineal heirs of a particular class, and that "sex defines that class" ("The Power of Renewable Resources," 719).

Nevertheless, what has remained unaddressed is the fact that Woolf's focus on Sanger's "knowledge of the law of real property" directs attention to inheritance and bastardy. In the essay to which Woolf refers, Sanger describes the "remarkable . . . symmetry" of pedigree that involves illegitimate birth, the marriage of cousins, and the co-mingling of Gypsy and English heredity.[3] This "symmetry" is precisely the very issue at the heart of the 1910 trial of the Sackville-Wests. Sanger's essay pointedly asks how Heathcliff—whom Emily Brontë describes as a "dark skinned gypsy"—"sets out with success to acquire all the property of two families" through the marriage of cousins.[4] Not only is Heathcliff the fictional stand-in for the aspiring Henry Sackville-West's familial claims and Gypsy blood but, as Q. D. Leavis bluntly states, "clearly Heathcliff was originally the illegitimate son."[5] He thereby mirrors Henry Sackville-West's bastardy.

2. See Helen Southworth, "Virginia Woolf's *Orlando* Preface, the Modernist Writer, and Networks of Cultural, Financial, and Social Capital," *Woolf Studies Annual* 18 (2012): 75–107; Caroline Webb, "Listing to the Right: Authority and Inheritance in *Orlando* and *Ulysses*," *Twentieth Century Literature* 40, no. 2 (1994): 190–204; Frank Baldanza, "*Orlando* and the Sackvilles," *PMLA* 70, no. 1 (1955): 274–79; and Jamie L. McDaniel, "The Power of Renewable Resources: *Orlando*'s Tactical Engagement with the Law of Intestacy," *Gender and History* 24, no. 3 (2012): 718–34.
3. C. P. Sanger, "The Structure of Wuthering Heights," *The Reader's Guide to "Wuthering Heights*," accessed December 10, 2018 * * *.
4. Emily Brontë, *Wuthering Heights* (London: Penguin, 2003), 4.
5. Queenie Dorothy Leavis, "A Fresh Approach to *Wuthering Heights*," in *Collected Essays*, vol. 1, *The Englishness of the English Novel*, ed. Ghan Singh (Cambridge: Cambridge University Press, 1984), 228–64, 231. Eric Solomon first noted the possibility in "The Incest Theme in *Wuthering Heights*," *Nineteenth-Century Fiction* 14, no. 1 (1959):

Though Woolf's reference to Sanger is the first of the book's references to bastardy, the most important involves Orlando herself when she is presented with the results of the lawsuit. Orlando's control of her ancestral lands depends on both marriage and the production of an heir. A few critics have noted this clause, including Jane Maher, Nancy Cervetti, and Robert Preissle, and have outlined the significance of pregnancy and birth in *Orlando*.[6] Cervetti and Preissle even observe that Orlando was pregnant before she met and married Shel (Cervetti, "In the Breeches," 170; Preissle, "Society's Child," 15). However, what none of these readers consider is why the timing of the birth might weigh as importantly in inheritance issues as the question of whether the child is male or female.

While canonical, continental, and Scottish law allowed heirs to be rendered legitimate and able to inherit by a subsequent wedding, English Common Law forbade such an allowance, insisting that a legal wedding precede not only birth but conception. Orlando's pregnancy clearly doesn't meet this standard, because it began at some undetermined point before Orlando's fateful fall on the bog and her subsequent romantic rescue by the man who would become her husband. Indeed, Orlando's first awareness of her pregnancy takes place significantly earlier in the chapter when she reflects that she "would have to buy a crinoline, and then (here she blushed) a bassinette" (Woolf, *Orlando*, 236) [125]. The bassinette requires no explanation, but the crinoline, a structured petticoat, was required to conceal "the deplorable fact; which every modest woman did her best to deny until denial was impossible; the fact that she was about to bear a child" (234–35) [124]. The following lines clarify that the reflection is not a general observation on the nature of womanhood but on Orlando's present condition as an unmarried, pregnant woman: "And if the spirit of the age blew a little unequally, the crinoline being blushed for before the husband, her ambiguous position must excuse her (even her sex was still in dispute) and the irregular life she had lived before" (236) [125]. Although nuptials with Shel will follow, and the birth will take place within a legal union, the pregnancy clearly preceded the espousal. Therefore, Shel is not the child's legal father; Orlando's son, the heir, is a bastard of an

80–83. Many other readers, including Leavis, concur (see "A Fresh Approach," 206). Bardi, in her discussion of the gypsy trope, picks up on the similarities between the two novels in their treatment of birth illegitimacy and Gypsy identity and compares the two ("In Company of a Gipsy," 40–44). She does not, however, ascribe the similarities to anything other than coincidence or similar cultural perspectives.

6. Jane Maree Maher, "Prone to Pregnancy: *Orlando*, Virginia Woolf and Sally Potter Represent the Gestating Body," *Journal of Medical Humanities* 28, no. 1 (2007): 19–30; Nancy Cervetti, "In the Breeches, Petticoats, and Pleasures of *Orlando*," *Journal of Modern Literature* 20, no. 2 (1996): 165–75; Robert Preissle, "Society's Child: Orlando's Son," *Virginia Woolf Miscellany* 66 (2004): 15, 20–21.

unknown father.[7] Woolf carries this critique of marriage as the condition for land rights even further as she sketches the procedure whereby Orlando is saddled with the lawsuit that will threaten his estates.

During the central scene of the novel, as Orlando reposes unconscious in his long and transformative slumber that will transform him into a woman, his secretaries come across a certificate:

> A deed of marriage, drawn up, signed and witnessed between his Lordship, Orlando, Knight of the Garter, etc., etc., etc., and Rosina Pepita, a dancer, father unknown, but reputed a gipsy, mother also unknown but reputed a seller of old iron in the market-place over against the Galata Bridge. (132) [72–73]

Upon reading the document, the secretaries understandably look "at each other in dismay": this single document—if authentic—means that any child produced with the clearly racialized Rosina Pepita will inherit titles and lands, thereby complicating England's silent insistence on white racial purity (133) [73].

Woolf's emphasis on a marriage certificate to determine the course of inheritance directs attention back to the Sackville-West trial because the fictional marriage certificate tropes the very controversial piece of paper that won the Sackville-Wests their fortune in the 1910 trial. As in *Orlando*, the conclusion of the 1910 trial rested on the existence of a marriage certificate. While the fictional marriage certificate proves the union of Orlando and Rosina Pepita, the actual marriage certificate supposedly proved that Pepita had been wedded to someone else in Spain before meeting Lionel Sackville-West and would thereby be unable to produce any legitimate heirs, including Henry. The 1853 Spanish marriage certificate was of such importance because all of the other evidence provided to the 1910 court had been compromised. The judge, basing his ruling on this sole document, denied the claims of the aspiring "bastard" Henry and awarded the estate to Vita's parents. The ruling read:

> Pepita in her lifetime produced to Mr. Sackville-West a certificate of her marriage extracted from the church register on the 11th November, 1853 and this certificate was found among her papers at her death. It contains none of the alterations now appearing in the Register itself. . . . I therefore dismiss the Petition with costs.[8]

---

7. Preissle argues that the father of Orlando's child is, thus, "society," a paternity that seems viable although legally useless ("Society's Child," 15) * * *.
8. West, or Sackville-West v. Attorney-General, 1897–1910, Petition of Ernest Henri Jean Baptiste Sackville West, TS 18/247, The National Archives, Kew, UK.

With the case decided, the Sackville-Wests took possession of the estate and fortune and the defeated Henry returned to France where he, penniless and bereft, soon put a gun to his head and took his life. Ironically the 1853 Spanish marriage certificate that won the fortune for Vita's family had been the focus of another trial that took place in Spain in 1909, a year before the trial in England, but has never been discussed in any public or scholarly forum. The transcript of that trial resides in the 1910 court documents in the British National Archives.[9] Like the English trial, the Spanish trial worked to establish the course of Pepita's matrimony and, ultimately, turned to the same 1853 Spanish marriage certificate that the Sackville-Wests used the following year to secure their triumph.[1]

In Spain, the lawsuit turned out differently. After an extensive examination, Spanish handwriting experts declared the Sackville-Wests' 1853 marriage certificate a sloppy fake. The court ruled that the marriage certificate contained legal inconsistencies that never would have been present in an official Spanish document, including bogus seals, inaccurate signatures, and unnecessary flourishes. In addition, Spanish experts determined that each of the apparently different signatures was, in fact, written by a single person. The greatest evidence of the document's fraudulence was the fact that it had been written entirely with a steel pen, a device that in 1853 "was not in use at that time in the sacristies" (West v. Attorney-General). The Spanish court concluded that the evidence was overwhelming that the Sackville-West certificate was nothing but a crude fake and so ruled against the English aristocracy.[2]

However, while it would certainly be titillating to propose that the Sackville-Wests stole the property outright, the truth, although initially less exciting, has much wider cultural implications. The Sackville-Wests won the case on the basis of a document they knew to be forged, but the court documents also make clear that Henry Sackville also manipulated documents in an effort to win the case.

---

9. The transcript of the Spanish trial sits among the papers for the 1910 trial at the National British National Archives in Kew, London, England (TS 18/247). Because many of names are the same and it has been translated into English, it's easy to overlook. However, it resides in the same box.

1. The 1909 Spanish trial sought to discover who had altered the records that detailed the alleged marriage between Juan de Oliva and Pepita. The court was not interested in inheritance but in vandalism.

2. The existence of the transcript from the 1909 Spanish trial not only undermines the findings from the 1910 English trial but also destabilizes the story perpetuated by Vita Sackville-West in Pepita and Nigel Nicolson in Portrait of a Marriage. Nicolson sums up the relationship in a nicely dismissive, easily understood stereotype: "A family which belonged to the highest Edwardian society were quarrelling publicly about inheritance—the inheritance of one of the most historic houses and titles in England, and a large sum of money—all because a young diplomat had fallen in love with a Spanish ballerina sixty years before and made her his mistress" (Portrait of a Marriage: Vita Sackville-West and Harold Nicolson [London: Weidenfeld and Nicolson, 1990], 65).

Both parties battled to prove an impossible proposition, that legitimate birth is a fixed concept and is a sufficiently sound base from which to build a system of wealth and political influence. The 1910 Sackville-West trial illustrated the ways that the twentieth-century developments in international communication and travel disclosed the contradictory nature of these laws and indeed on the structures of property that they were constructed to protect. When the two very different definitions of bastardy collided in the courts—one English and one Spanish—the very laws on which inheritance and the perpetuation of authority had been based crumbled. England structured its bastardy laws to create a clear and ordered ascendancy to govern that was based on a single racial type within a small group of families. Spain, in contrast, was from the eighth century to the fifteenth century the contested ground between Europeans and Moors, Catholicism and Islam. The strong influence of the polygamous Moors introduced the possibility of multiple partners who would produce children of different racial definitions. Further, in the ongoing conflict between Moors and Christians, the Christians were motivated by the "prime necessity" of "an increase of the Christian population to defend against the Moors."[3] This imperative led to a definition of legitimacy with flexible categories and no insistence on racial purity which had, even in the twentieth century, little correspondence to English bastardy laws. One British legal scholar marveled in disbelief at the system in the eighteenth century, declaring with surprise that "bastards were on equal footing with legitimate children."[4] *Orlando* captures a moment at the beginning of the twentieth century when a system of control whose foundation relied on a fixed definition of race and legitimacy failed.

3. Ralph Burke Ulick, *A History of Spain: From the Earliest Times to the Death of Ferdinand the Catholic* (London: Londmans, Green, 1900), 1:404.
4. Matthew Bacon, *A New Abridgement of the Law* (London: A. Strahan and M. Woodfall, 1778), 1:77. The delineation of legitimates in the nineteenth century in Spain was not straightforward. The Spanish system creates an almost endless variation of designations of legitimate and illegitimate that allows movements within and between the categories. While English law allowed only two categories of bastards (special and regular), the 1805 Spanish Civil Code had two broad categories, legitimate and "natural," and multiple designations within the category of "natural": bastards (*fornecinos*), or the illegitimate children (*nothos*) who are born from adulterous intercourse; the children of prostitutes (*manceres*), the suprious (*espurios*), that is, children born of a concubine, and those begotten on a relation, or on a religious woman (*religiosa*), who are called incestuous. See D. Ignatius Jordan de Asso y del Rio and D. Miguel de Manuel y Rodriguez, *Institutes of the Civil Law of Spain*, trans. Lewis F. C. Johnston (London: Butterworth and Son, 1825), 72–73. Almost all these categories could find a path to legitimacy, including the marriage of the parents, a decree from the king or pope, a male entering the military service, or a female marrying a distinguished person. Failing all these options, a child could be legitimated by a simple "public deed" or "letter of writing" (*Institutes of the Civil Law of Spain*, 73). In the absence of all of these options, the Spanish Civil Code allowed more possibilities, for a father could adopt any adult male in order to make him his heir and pass on all inheritances to him (75).

Woolf's wry attack on property rights can also be seen in her use of Constantinople as the site of the novel's climactic scene. By choosing Constantinople for Orlando's transformation, Woolf imagines a system that would be free of fixed definitions of race and land rights based on national definition. Constantinople was a city very much on both Leonard Woolf's and Virginia's radar in the years preceding the publication of *Orlando*, precisely because it required the sort of thinking about race and property that is at the heart of *Orlando*. In 1917, Leonard published *The Future of Constantinople*, a tract that identifies the city as the historical hub of five different "European subject races," "races" which he identifies as German, Russian, Austrian, French, and British.[5] Apart from these "races," Leonard identifies Constantinople as the historical epicenter of religious groups, including "Moslems" and "Christians" (*The Future of Constantinople*, 19). Leonard's solution to the co-existence of competing national and religious definitions of nationhood is to allow Constantinople to exist without constraints of national definition that would allow a sole nation to define the terms of property. This internationalism, he explains, "sprang from the wonderful discovery that national interests are often promoted better by international co-operation than by international competition" (16). Leonard argues that abolishing nationhood and, by extension, state-sanctioned land rights at the most racially and nationally diverse juncture in Europe is the only solution that will produce peace.

Nagihan Haliloğlu perceptively argues that Leonard Woolf's view of Constantinople as free of state-sanctioned land rights did not go far enough, and that Virginia Woolf's early observations on Constantinople offer a more radical view.[6] Haliloğlu's reading is in line with the work done by scholars including Anna Snaith, Michèle Barrett, and Laura Doan who have shown that Virginia Woolf's knowledge and commitment to radical geopolitics and anti-imperialism surpassed Leonard's.[7] Haliloğlu believes Virginia's perspective takes in individual subjectivities in a way that Leonard's does not. Of particular interest to the young Virginia was the commingling of Christianity, Islam, and secularity in her 1906 travel writings. She writes in those early essays that in the mosques, "crosses have become safe patterns without meaning," and that the mosques

---

5. Leonard Woolf, *The Future of Constantinople* (London: George Allen and Unwin, 1917), 14.
6. Nagihan Haliloğlu, "Constantinopolitan Modernities: Leonard Woolf, Virginia Woolf and Halide Edib" (paper, International Virginia Woolf Conference, University of Kent, Canterbury, UK, June 23, 2018).
7. Michéle Barrett, "Virginia Woolf's Research for *Empire and Commerce in Africa* (Leonard Woolf, 1920)," *Woolf Studies Annual* 19 (2013): 83–122; Anna Snaith, "Leonard and Virginia Woolf: Writing against Empire," *The Journal of Commonwealth Literature* 50, no. 1 (2015): 19–32.

themselves are "not a temple of religion as we understand the word, it is surely a temple of something."[8] Just as the mosques exemplify to Virginia an easy mélange, so do the people. Wandering through the streets, she sees "a real town of flesh and blood" where the inhabitants "will offer you fragments of many different languages in order that you may choose your own" (Woolf, *Passionate Apprentice*, 353, 352). The English tourist was just part of the diverse array, for "no one stopped to look at us, and the eccentricities of all our dresses seemed but part of the ordinary composition" (353).

Therefore, by 1927, when she began writing *Orlando*, Woolf had both a personal understanding of Constantinople as a national and racial crossroads and a sophisticated and critical philosophy about the failures of land rights based on traditional national models. Constantinople is presented in the novel as a medley, both a symbolic and real city that would defy national and racial definitions. It is a place where it's possible for a man to become a woman, where an English nobleman can contemplate his own racialization and bastardy, and where that same nobleman can impregnate a Gypsy woman, thereby setting in motion another strain of racialization in English identity through bastardy. Constantinople displays the viability of what Woolf articulates in Rustum's beliefs, a free, untamed and unchallenged land. Simply "the whole earth is ours," a vision that haunts Orlando even when she returns to England and hears the "raucous voice of old Rustum, the gipsy," who demands, "what is your antiquity and your race, and your possessions compared with this?" (*Orlando*, 148, 326) [80, 174]. This deep and cutting critique of property, race, and inheritances shows the sophistication that Barrett notes when she asserts that Virginia Woolf brought into her marriage a "familiarity with liberal critiques of the evils of imperialism" ("Virginia Woolf's Research," 114). Woolf honed critical skills with the factual research she did on imperialism with Leonard, and then used fiction to flesh out the interstitial space where racialization and private property are compromised by the reality of illegitimate birth.

* * *

Conclusion

In 1928, eighteen years after Victoria Sackville-West won the Sackville-West estate with a forged marriage certificate that legally established her bastardy, the dowress received an early copy of

---

8. Virginia Woolf, *A Passionate Apprentice: The Early Journals, 1897–1909*, ed. Mitchell A. Leaska (London: Pimlico, 2004), 350.

Woolf's *Orlando*. The novel filled Victoria with volcanic rage; she scrawled angry graffiti across the book's pages, urged family members to condemn the novel, and begged her contacts not to review it. She even visited bookstores, hiding copies of *Orlando* under other books to discourage sales.[9] Finding no satisfaction in the public realm, she glued a photograph of Virginia in her own copy of *Orlando* and captioned it, "the awful face of a mad woman whose successful mad desire is to separate people from each other."[1] Then, in fury, she wrote directly to Woolf, exclaiming: "probably you do not realize how *cruel* you have been" (*Letters*, 3:548n2). But perhaps, after all, Woolf did know, for in *Orlando*, the very sharp feminist revealed Victoria's secrets, and in so doing, signaled how bastardy marks the fragility of extant structures of authority, an insight the young Orlando also articulates after he loses Sasha. Bereft, he spends his nights wandering his ancient house, descending, in despair, into the "ghastly sepulcher" of the basement, among the skulls and cobwebs. There he concludes that—despite the sturdiness of the walls in the house above, the sanctity of his heritage, and the line of portraits that asserted linear descent—the truth was held in the basement, among the cobwebs and careless disposal of skulls, for there he realized that "all pomp is built upon corruption" (*Orlando*, 71) [39]. In *Orlando*, Woolf asserts that beneath the English aristocratic house, at the core of its very foundation, lies a rot of bastardy, and that it will ultimately dissolve all presumption of nobility, national or racial purity, and female fidelity.

9. Hermione Lee, *Virginia Woolf* (New York: Vintage Press, 1999), 206.
1. Virginia Woolf to Edward Sackville-West, October 22, 1928, in Nicolson and Trautmann, *Letters*, 3:548n2.

Genders and Sexualities

BRENDA S. HELT

Passionate Debates on "Odious Subjects": Bisexuality and Woolf's Opposition to Theories of Androgyny and Sexual Identity†

Since 'bisexual' was rarely used to describe a sexual identity type until the 1960's, it might seem anachronistic to use the word to describe the coexistence of sexual desire and affections for both men and women in the same individual in literary work of the early twentieth century. Yet the fact that 'bisexual' was *not* an identity category indicating a type of person in this period is precisely what makes an investigation of Woolf's use of bisexuality and bisexual desire important. Bisexuality has several functions in Woolf's work. Those functions, though, are obscured if desire is conflated with sexual identity, or if Woolf's depictions of desire are understood solely in terms of autobiographical self-expression rather than authorial strategy.

In her work of the 1920's, Woolf challenged trends to construe same-sex desire as a distinguishing characteristic of a sexual type as well as the essentialist ideas about male and female character traits that underlie theories of androgyny. She instead gave voice to a much older understanding of women's same-sex desires as common to *most* women and promoted those desires as epistemologically, aesthetically, and politically more useful to women than the bifurcated sexual identities and beliefs about dual-gendered minds promoted by sexologists and some members of the avant-garde.

Woolf opposed both the reduction of desire to sexuality and the concept of dyadic (i.e., homo/hetero) sexual identity itself—a

† From *Queer Bloomsbury*, ed. Brenda S. Helt and Madelyn Detloff (Edinburgh: Edinburgh UP, 2016), pp. 114–31. © Brenda S. Helt, 2016. This essay was first published in *Twentieth-Century Literature* 56.2 (2010): 131–67, prefaced by a five-page encomium by Linda Hutcheon. It is republished here in excerpted form (approximately half its original length) with the kind permission of *TCL* and Edinburgh University Press through PLSclear. Page numbers to this Norton Critical Edition appear in brackets.

concept just gaining currency in the 1920's and 30's. Her work instead frames same-sex desire and sexuality as common, ordinary, harmonious with women's desire for and sexual relations with men, and even useful in achieving marital bliss. Thus she disentangles bisexual desire from androgyny and sexual identity. As she does so, she dispenses with the male-promoting concepts of androgyny and androgynous genius, and recoups the imaginative and creative possibilities associated with bisexual desire for women. With this in mind, I examine the function of bisexual desire in *Orlando* and *A Room of One's Own*, understanding it as a challenge to the new hetero/homo dichotomy that Woolf believed to be producing another social invention: a culturally widespread homophobia that isolated women from other women, emotionally, politically, and professionally.

Sex Talk Becomes High Modernist Philosophy

In 'Old Bloomsbury', Woolf narrates the advent of modernism among those quintessential modernists, the Bloomsbury Group. As Virginia and Vanessa sat talking one day in 1906, the drawing room door opened and Lytton Strachey emerged from the shadows, pointing a finger at a stain on Vanessa's dress.

> 'Semen?' he said. Can one really say it? I thought and we burst out laughing. With that one word all barriers of reticence and reserve went down. . . . Sex permeated our conversation. The word bugger was never far from our lips. We discussed copulation with the same excitement and openness that we had discussed the nature of good. (195)

Bloomsbury's fascination with sexuality was consistent with that of other avant-garde groups now considered modernist. In the inter-war period, women and men who aspired to be avant-garde began to distinguish themselves by openly debating the latest sexual theories in mixed company, and by producing literary and artistic works that openly engaged in these debates. By 1922, Woolf could term this new openness 'a great advance in civilization', one for which, she implied, Bloomsbury was directly responsible ('Old Bloomsbury' 196).

Bloomsbury's ideas about sexuality were heavily influenced by sexual scientists from Otto Weininger to Freud, and both bisexuality and androgyny were key points of debate in these discussions. Though its important role in the epistemological history of sexuality is no longer obvious, bisexuality was central to sexology's congenitalist theories of sexuality and sexual identity. The mid-nineteenth-century medical study of the physical hermaphrodite—sometimes termed a 'bi-sexual'—initiated hypotheses in Germany that there might be a corresponding type who was psychologically both male and female: a 'psychic hermaphrodite'. Psychic hermaphroditism was understood by some sexologists to account for 'inversion' in general, but for others it explained a type that might have sexual relationships with both men and women: a 'psychosexual hermaphrodite'.

Because late-nineteenth-century medical science had presumed that 'hermaphrodites'—the term then used to describe intersexed persons—were either male or female, sexologists such as Havelock Ellis reasoned that psychologically, too, people were either male or female, though in rare cases their psychological sex might not accord with their biological one.[1] In arguing that some rare 'types' of people are born 'sexual inverts'—that is, the sex of their mind is the 'opposite' of that of their body—Ellis eschewed 'third sex' theories popular with German scientists like Hirschfeld and French authors like Gautier to describe people who did not fit into a binary sex/gender paradigm. In so doing, he also dismissed the association of sexual bisexuality with gendered 'bi-sexuality' or 'androgyny' in favour of the hetero/homo dyad.

Freud, too, found the conflation of bisexuality with gender dimorphism as well as sexual bisexuality problematic, since it caused a slippage between gender identification and sexual desire. One of Freud's most significant departures from other sexual scientists was his belief that homosexuality was a neurosis rooted in early childhood developmental problems. Such a theory necessitated the hypothesis that all human beings are congenitally 'bisexual'—born psychologically dual-gendered—and that they acquire an identification with one sex or the other through a complex psychological mechanism by which they come to desire the parent of the opposite sex, and *only* that parent. The fact that both Ellis and Freud found gendered duality (androgyny) and sexual bisexuality incompatible with their theories of homosexuality is characteristic of the general consternation these two concepts with their single signifier were causing among scientists. In London during the interwar period, then, 'bisexuality' was a floating signifier. Primarily a scientific term, the word rarely referred to a mature adult's sexual attraction to people of both sexes, a state most early twentieth-century scientists, Freud included, believed to exist only in very young children, in people of 'primitive' cultures, or in those passing through a transitional phase between the two true sexual dispositions, heterosexuality and homosexuality.

1. On the medical profession's shift to an either/or understanding of biological sex with regards to 'hermaphrodites', see Dreger 15–45. See also Foucault vii–xvii.

By the early 1920's the appropriation of sexological theories to valorise homosexuality and bisexuality in men was well established among the well-educated in London, Cambridge, and Oxford. So common was this stance at Cambridge that young men like Leslie Runciman felt the need to apologize for their attraction to women (Tindall 47). In later life, Rosamond Lehmann explained Runciman's apologetic attitude about his sexual attraction to women as a response to a trend among young men at Cambridge to prefer sexual relationships with other men, since they were understood to be sexually, because intellectually, more stimulating: 'He thought it was an intellectual disgrace to marry' (qtd. in Hastings 68).

That this particular manifestation of homosexuality among young men at Cambridge in the late teens and twenties was considered a 'trend' or 'fashion' by first-generation Bloomsberries is clear in a 1925 letter from Woolf to Jacques Raverat:

> Mrs Joad . . . now has a room of her own, and walks out with various Cambridge young men, who are not entirely devoted to the fashionable foible of loving their own sex. . . . Have you any views on loving one's own sex? All the young men are so inclined, and I can't help finding it mildly foolish; though I have no particular reason. For one thing, all the young men tend to the pretty and ladylike, for some reason, at the moment. They paint and powder, which wasn't the style in our day at Cambridge. I think it does imply some clingingness. (*Letters* 3:155)

Here Woolf's critique of a younger generation's performance of homosexuality as style is similar to that of friends such as Lytton Strachey and E. M. Forster, who scoffed at some men's avowed preference for what Strachey facetiously termed 'the higher sodomy', a pretentious intellectualization of same-sex but nonsexual relationships that masked a preciosity and misogyny of which they disapproved. (Forster's character Clive in *Maurice* is a higher sodomite, for example.) The persona of the effeminate 'sodomite' performed by some of the Bright Young Things—Cecil Beaton, Stephen Tennant, Edward Sackville-West—also seemed to appropriate sexological theories of inversion that much of first-generation Bloomsbury had rejected in favour of the socialist, feminist, and egalitarian theories and practices of Edward Carpenter. Though fascinated and amused by the youthful gender-play of the Bright Young Things, Woolf did not endorse the logic implied by the fashions of inversion that retrospectively were interpreted as evolving sexual identities.

For some interwar women, this fashion of sexual inversion took the form of the mannish lesbian. Although that persona did not resonate as sexually 'deviant' with the larger public until after the 1928 obscenity trial of Radclyffe Hall's *The Well of Loneliness*, the mannish lesbian was recognizable to groups of the *cognoscenti* prior to the trial, as attested to by her presence in works such as Lawrence's *The Rainbow* (1915) and *The Fox* (1922), Lehmann's *Dusty Answer* (1927), and Mackenzie's *Extraordinary Women* (1928). The theory of sexual inversion could not account for same-sex attractions in feminine and bisexual women, especially those whose partners were not masculine. Some interwar women therefore appropriated a competing sexological theory popularized in the scientific community by sexologist Otto Weininger, who hypothesized that those attracted to others of their sex were born neither male nor female, but both: they were 'sexually intermediate types' (*Sex and Character* 5–10, 51). For Weininger, 'the woman who attracts and is attracted by other women is herself half male' and that 'homosexuality in a woman is the outcome of her masculinity and presupposes a higher degree of development' (66).

Unlike her lover Vita Sackville-West and some of her younger male friends, Woolf disagreed with understandings of sexual desire that were based on gender stereotypes, performed as gender dysphoria, and construed as essential sexual identities. It was specifically these understandings of identity as a problem of gender (or 'sexual') inversion that she termed 'perversion' in a 1930 letter to Ethel Smyth (*Letters* 4:200). Though Woolf could find cross-dressing and gender-play creative and fun, as *Orlando* illustrates, she did not accept conflations of gender and desire as grounds upon which to construct identity, nor did she endorse the evolving theories that rendered sexuality part of an aesthetics of identity. Ridiculing the self-presentations of Eddy Sackville-West and other 'effeminate sodomites' as 'silly', 'pretty', and 'trivial' in her letter to Smyth, Woolf portrayed such costuming as a cover for shallow thinking (*Letters* 4:200).

Women's Ordinary Bisexuality

As historians such as Carroll Smith-Rosenberg, Lillian Faderman, Martha Vicinus, and Sharon Marcus have shown, there is a long tradition in Great Britain and the US of positive understandings of women's intimate affective and often sexual relationships with other women. Together, the research of these four scholars demonstrates that the stigmatization of women's intimate relationships with other women (as indicative of deviant sexual identities) is a fairly recent development. In *Fashioning Sapphism*, Laura Doan argues that the trial of Hall's *Well* crystallized an image of 'the lesbian' as mannish for the general population in England, thereby paralleling for women the stigma the Oscar Wilde trials had generated for men (1–30). Yet even before the Hall trial Woolf foresaw the danger for women and for feminism of replacing older understandings of women's

'romantic friendships' and undefinable same-sex loves with an easily
identifiable masculine-gendered sexual type or with a Freudian
understanding of homosexuality as neurotic sexual subjectivity.

In her work of the twenties, Woolf depicts the eroticism of those
long-standing positive portrayals of women's intimate friendships
(intimacies that are neither gendered masculine nor exclusive of
similar relationships with men) and promotes them as more desirable than exclusively homo- or heterosexual relationships. For example, a major theme of *A Room of One's Own* is the complexity of
women's lives and minds, their experiences of desire, their relationships with each other, and, importantly, men's inability to understand and depict these. She criticizes male scientific presumptions
about the desires and minds of women. 'Where shall I find that elaborate study of the psychology of women by a woman?' Woolf asks
her audience of educated young women, exhorting them to write
such studies (*Room* 81).

Woolf's fictional novelist, Mary Carmichael, begins the work of
portraying women's relationships with other women in their full
complexity. Woolf considers Carmichael's depiction of two professional women who not only share a laboratory but even *like* each
other as entirely new in literature. Chloe and Olivia like each other.
But that fact does not preclude their liking men as well, a point
Woolf makes explicit. Olivia has two children and a husband, and
leaves Chloe at the lab to go home to be with them (87–8). The mention of Olivia's children and husband specifically contradicts the
increasingly popular association of lesbianism with feminists and
professional women, an association given wide publicity by the
Radclyffe Hall trial. Far from hinting that Chloe and Olivia are lesbians, Woolf thus refutes the association of feminism with lesbianism. Woolf does *not* mean to deny that women who work together
might also experience erotic feelings for each other, however. Woolf
instead reinforces an understanding that she implies has long been
held among women, though rarely documented in print: women's
love for other women is a highly desirable and empowering emotive
force common to *most* women, and not an identifying characteristic
of a rare sexual type.

That so-called 'perversion' and friendship merge into each other,
rather than marking women as distinct types, is an important point
in most of Woolf's work and is intimated in her letter to Smyth:

> Where people mistake, as I think, is in perpetually narrowing
> and naming these immensely composite and wide flung
> passions—driving stakes through them, herding them between
> screens. But how do you define 'Perversity'? What is the line
> between friendship and perversion?' (*Letters* 4:200)

For her, 'perversion' is consistent with friendship—these are intimate relationships, which Woolf values, not sexual types. Woolf's criticism in the letter is aimed at the appropriation of scientific concepts of perversion, not at sexual and affective relationships.

Nobody's Androgyny

Both the androgyne and the genius have a heritage privileging men and maleness more generally. Thus Woolf's challenges to sexological theories of gender inversion and dyadic sexual identities necessarily included theories of androgyny popular with modernists and other elite circles. In the companion pieces *Orlando* and *A Room*, Woolf shows that the androgynous mind is presently an impossibility precisely because of the social realities accompanying embodiment. In both works Woolf takes up but ultimately rejects the prevalent notion that the gifted artist must have an androgynous mind. Woolf shows that what it means to be man or woman depends upon social conditions, and these conditions differ based on the biological sex of the body. One cannot know what it is to be 'womanly' unless one has walked down Whitehall in a woman's body, for example, or tried to engage in intellectual conversation with Milton or Pope while wearing voluminous skirts and decorously pouring out tea. And learned men and men of genius do not, in fact, somehow manage to escape their sex and 'remov[e] themselves above the strife of tongue and the confusion of body' to 'issu[e] the result of their reasoning and research in books which are to be found in the British Museum' (*Room* 25). Woolf's emphasis in *A Room* on the subconscious misogyny of every man writing on 'sex—woman, that is to say' from the honourable Professor von X to 'men who have no apparent qualification save that they are not women' is one she has previously broached in *Orlando* (*Room* 27). Alexander Pope, the genius figure in that novel, becomes enraged when Orlando inadvertently offends him and therefore 'avenge[s]' himself by 'present[ing]' her instantly with the rough draught of a certain famous line in the 'Characters of Women'' (214) [115].

Although *Orlando* is certainly in part a 'love letter' to Vita Sackville-West, it also furthers a theoretical argument between the two women concerning gender and desire, especially in relation to first-wave feminism.[2] Sexological thinking authorizes Sackville-West's essentialism. She herself claimed that she exemplified 'the perfectly accepted theory that cases of dual personality do exist, in which the feminine and the masculine elements alternately

---

2. Nigel Nicolson calls *Orlando* 'the longest and most charming love letter in literature' in his depiction of his mother's various loves in *Portrait of a Marriage* (202).

preponderate' (qtd. in Nicolson 106). Sackville-West's conflation of
sex, gender, and sexual desire caused her to believe she was actually a 'different person'—a male person—when she was amorous or
sexual with women, and she would often dress according to the sex
she felt she was embodying at the moment (qtd. in Nicolson 105).
Her purported ability to shift between the two sexes allowed her to
claim to be that most rare of types among 'civilized' societies: a 'bisexual' or 'psychosexual hermaphrodite' in 1920s sexological par-
lance, or a *female* androgyne or even androgynous genius.

Orlando disputes this notion that gender has a biological essence.
A main contention of the novel is that nobody can know what it is
to be either a man or a woman without having lived in the body of
one. Putting on trousers and making love to women does not make
one a man. *Orlando* should be read, then, as part one of Woolf's two-
part contradiction of theories of the writer or artist as androgynous
genius, or as member of the intermediate sex or of the third sex, all
of which share the same basic premise: men are essentially active
and intellectual, women are essentially passive and sensual, and so
the ideal gifted type is a biological male born with a touch of womanly sensibilities.

Woolf's theories of gender, sexuality, and desire take into account
the social reality of living as a woman in society and the ways that
reality is formative of one's mind or psyche, and, therefore, of one's
opportunities and talents. *Orlando* shows that only by living corpo-
really as both a man and a woman and being understood by both
one's society and one's intimates as one and then the other can a
person hope to obtain an androgynous mind. Even then, the necessity of always being treated as one or the other would cause a person to think predominantly as one or the other. Because a body will
always be interpellated as either male or female, even the sex-
changing Orlando can partake only fleetingly of an androgynous
mind. For a few days after her sex change, Orlando 'seemed to vacillate' between the two sexes, 'she was man; she was woman; she
knew the secrets, shared the weaknesses of each' (158) [85]. But for
Woolf this momentarily androgynous state is not to be recommended. It is 'a most bewildering and whirligig state of mind to be
in', and, immediately after her first experience of being courted by
a man, Orlando begins to adopt a woman's perspective and to perform her gender as a woman—a woman the sight of whose legs might
even cause a sailor a nasty fall from the mast (158–9) [84–85].

Woolf shows that the experience of being treated as a woman—and
she implies that Orlando's first experience includes the sexual—is
responsible for Orlando's move from the temporary and confusing
state of androgyny towards a woman's perspective: 'it is plain that
something had happened during the night to give her a push towards

the female sex, for she was speaking more as a woman speaks than as a man, yet with a sort of content after all' (159) [87]. And when Orlando returns as a woman to her family estate in England, her servants and suitors quickly begin to treat her as one. She, in response, develops an interest in decorating the many rooms of the mansion and a care for her dress and person. The social realities accompanying the possession of a woman's body quickly begin to occlude the insights she had garnered living in the body of the 'opposite' sex.

Woolf differed strongly with Sackville-West's ideas regarding what we today might call her 'bisexuality'. Though Orlando changes sex during the novel, just as Sackville-West claimed she felt she did based upon the sex of the person she was in love with at the moment, Orlando's sex is often not the 'opposite' of that of her beloved. Orlando actually changes sex only once; her subsequent changes are changes of clothing only, and seem primarily nods to convention, though her cross-dressing provides opportunities for sexual play. Orlando's desires, though, are consistently free-flowing and completely irrespective of sex and gender. When Orlando is a young man, he is powerfully attracted to Sasha before he is able to discern her sex. Prior to discovering her to be a woman, he notes the 'extraordinary seductiveness which issued from the whole person', a person who looks remarkably like a boy (*Orlando* 37–8) [21]. When he believes her to be a boy, he wants to 'tear his hair with vexation' at the thought that he cannot embrace the object of his desire (38) [21]. Later, after Orlando becomes a woman, she continues to love Sasha, for

> if the consciousness of being of the same sex had any effect at all, it was to quicken and deepen those feelings which she had had as a man. For now a thousand hints and mysteries became plain to her that were then dark. . . . and if there is anything in what the poet says about truth and beauty, this affection gained in beauty what it lost in falsity. (161) [88]

Knowing the truth about women through the experience of being a woman makes women more desirable, suggesting that women are ordinarily better judges of women than are men, an idea consistent with Woolf's normalizing of same-sex desire in *Mrs. Dalloway*, *To the Lighthouse*, and *A Room*.

After being courted by men and learning of the limitations that British society places on its women, Orlando takes to changing her sex, figuratively, with her clothing, by which 'device' she 'reap[s] a twofold harvest . . . and enjoy[s] the love of both sexes equally' (221) [118]. And if her mention of the names of Nell and Kit along with Sasha when musing on love late in the novel is any indication, we can assume Orlando's enjoyment of 'the love of both sexes' included

same-sex sexual relations (311) [118]. After her marriage to Shelmerdine, a man with whom she is 'passionately in love' (251) [134], and
whom she even likes (264) [140], Orlando begins writing exotic, sensual poetry in which girls appear, a fact that can be overlooked by
the 'spirit of the age' only because she has 'a husband at the Cape'
(265) [141].

The difference I am noting here between Sackville-West's and
Woolf's theories of bisexuality is similar to and evocative of two significant differences between sexological theories and Freudian
ones, though Woolf goes further than Freud, whose work she did
not actually read until 1939.[3] Whereas most of the sexologists conceived of anatomical sex and sexual desire as inextricable, homosexual desire being explained as occasioned by a disparity between
the anatomical and the 'true' or psychical sex (or the sex of the
'soul'), Freud's separation of sexual instinct from sexual object
and both from sexual aim in his *Three Essays on the Theory of
Sexuality* effectively disentangled sex from sexuality. In Woolf's
work, unlike Freud's, bisexual desire seems to be the most common experience of *adults*. Furthermore, Woolf's theories of sexuality foreground the ways social realities such as class systems,
financial means, physical bodies, epistemologies of sexuality and
gender, and hegemonic power structures determine the possibilities for a given individual of bringing desires to consciousness and
pursuing them.

Unlike both the sexologists and some of her friends, Woolf was
not striving to develop a modernist category or definition of a sexual type. Woolf's approaches to issues of sexuality were instead integrated in a literary focus on what she called 'an ordinary mind on
an ordinary day' ('Modern Fiction' 149). Most of Woolf's characters
are ordinary; they are not rare types with unusual thoughts and
desires. In *Mrs. Dalloway*, the importance that the mature Clarissa
Dalloway gives to being once kissed by Sally Seton as a young woman
epitomizes Woolf's focus on the ordinary. Even Orlando, who sometimes seems to imagine himself/herself to be extraordinary, is actually quite ordinary. Orlando is unusual only in her/his fantasy
elements: physical sex change, multi-centuried longevity, extreme
wealth and privilege as a member of the aristocracy. In *Orlando*,
Woolf simultaneously plays with and challenges Sackville-West's
contention that she is a rare type because she is able psychically to
change sexes, an ability Woolf calls 'something that happens to most
people without being thus plainly expressed':

3. For Woolf's unwillingness to read Freud until 1939, see Lee 68.

Different though the sexes are, they intermix. In *every human being* a vacillation from one sex to the other takes place, and often it is only the clothes that keep the male or female likeness, while underneath the sex is the very opposite of what it is above. Of the complications and confusions which thus result *every one* has had experience; but here we leave the general question and note only the odd effect it had in the particular case of Orlando herself. (*Orlando* 189; my emphasis) [102]

Finding oneself intermittently thinking 'like a man' and 'like a woman' is not, for Woolf, an identifying feature of a rare type of person. Everyone does it. Effectively stating that all adults are androgynous, Woolf disrupts both the notion that gender has an essence and the belief that only rare types have the experience of thinking or feeling like both a man and a woman. If everyone is androgynous, then androgyny is nobody's distinguishing characteristic, nobody's rare trait.

If Woolf believes that everyone 'vacillates' between the two sexes, then, does she also believe that everyone also experiences Orlando's 'love of both sexes equally'? The answer, I think, is not to be found in *Orlando*, but in Woolf's earlier novels, in which bisexual desire is experienced by extremely ordinary characters that, in other hands, would be mere stereotypes: Rachel Vinrace of *The Voyage Out*; Jacob Flanders and Dick Graves of *Jacob's Room*; Clarissa Dalloway of *Mrs. Dalloway*; Mr. Bankes, Mr. Ramsay, and Charles Tansley of *To the Lighthouse*. What people do with their bodies in respect to fulfilling (or not) their desires depends on socially constituted realities differing by geographical locale, historical moment, economic resources, social standing, and biological constraints, including the psychic constraints that the individual develops as a result of being interpellated as a gendered subject. Woolf carefully removes all but the latter of these constraints for Orlando, so that Orlando's story demonstrates that gender is socially constructed, even performative, and that desire is naturally and commonly polymorphous or bisexual when released from social strictures.

A Room of One's Own, too, demonstrates that the daily experience of living in a given sexed body is exactly what makes a mind 'womanly' or 'manly'; nobody can escape the effect of this experience on the psyche. As is typical of her essays, Woolf begins her disquisition by positing a question or placing in question a popular maxim. In the case of the androgyny thesis in *A Room*, the maxim is Coleridge's statement that 'a great mind must be androgynous'. Woolf begins the interrogation of this maxim by maintaining that Coleridge's hypothesis was invoked for her by the sight of a man and woman getting into a taxi, a common enough occurrence, but one which, she pretends, made her speculate as to whether there might be 'two sexes in the mind corresponding to the two sexes in the body', which might

> also require to be united in order to get complete satisfaction and happiness. . . . It is when this fusion takes place that the mind is fully fertilised and uses all its faculties. Perhaps a mind that is purely masculine cannot create, any more than a mind that is purely feminine. (102)

To most scholars, this passage has seemed to offer clear evidence that Woolf agreed with those who believed in the superiority of the androgynous mind. But Woolf's variations on this theme only begin with the taxi. Less often quoted is a passage just previous:

> For certainly when I saw the couple get into the taxi-cab the mind felt as if, after being divided, it had come together again in a natural fusion. The obvious reason would be that it is natural for the sexes to co-operate. One has a profound, if irrational, instinct in favour of the theory that the union of man and woman makes for the greatest satisfaction, the most complete happiness. (101–02)

In a statement theorizing the aesthetic superiority of an androgynous mind, Woolf interposes the figure of the male-female couple and refers to marriage. One explanation for this might be that Woolf enjoyed being married, an idea she facetiously implies to be radically retrogressive not only in her reference to the 'irrational instinct', but also in a 1925 letter to Sackville-West: 'But then, in all London, you and I alone like being married' (*Letters* 3:221). Her inclusion of male-female love in her consideration of the theory of androgynous superiority therefore could be read as a corrective to this homosocial/homoerotic paradigm that had elicited so much misogynistic speculation among some young men at Cambridge.

While Woolf may agree with those arguing that it is impossible to find an androgynous mind 'like Shakespeare's' in a woman, her reasons are different from those bandied about among young men at Cambridge.[4] These reasons form the basic arguments of *A Room*, and are the same as those she gives for the dearth of great women writers: the lack of women's financial and material independence, the want of reasonably reputable educational institutions for women,

4. The taunt 'Where's the woman Shakespeare?' was a prime nonsequitur being used in the late 1920s by male undergraduates in the heated debate over granting women full access and equal degrees at Cambridge. For an in-depth discussion of the controversy over women's attempts to be granted full titular degrees at Cambridge in the 1920s, see McWilliams-Tullberg 142–208. For a discussion of the ways in which *A Room* specifically engages in this debate, as well as the ramifications of that engagement for contemporary feminist theory, see Cucullu.

the fact that women are not admitted into the libraries of the great universities, the burden of raising children and caring for men—in short, a history of patriarchal subjection. Woolf writes,

> Coleridge certainly did not mean, when he said that a great mind is androgynous, that it is a mind that has any special sympathy with women; a mind that takes up their cause or devotes itself to their interpretation. Perhaps the androgynous mind is less apt to make these distinctions than the single-sexed mind. (102)

A Room as a whole is engaged in encouraging women to write history, psychology, even science from a woman's perspective, not an androgynous one. The mind's ability to 'make these distinctions' is extremely important to Woolf. They make a woman with her 'single-sexed mind' psychologically a woman.

Many of the problems women writers have faced historically are caused by marriage, however, and others are exacerbated by it, as Woolf implies throughout A Room. So what are we to make of this apparent privileging of the heterosexual couple in Woolf's riff on androgynous creativity? The answer is inherent in the metaphor itself, which Woolf does not originate, but only exposes as inherently debilitating for women. She elaborates upon it further a few pages later: 'Some collaboration has to take place in the mind between the woman and the man before the act of creation can be accomplished. Some marriage of opposites has to be consummated' (108). The natural result of such a coupling for a man, who here is 'the writer', is that 'once his experience is over', he 'must lie back and let his mind celebrate its nuptials in darkness. He must not look or question what is being done' (108). But the natural result of that coupling for a woman is radically different: the carrying, birthing, and raising of the child that is the 'artistic creation' in the extended metaphor. Woolf, who hated lectures and didacticism, simply gives her readers the conceptual tools to deconstruct the metaphor of the androgynous mind for themselves.[5] The logic, however, is simple: the metaphorical consummation of the androgynous mind's 'marriage of opposites' invokes a social and biological reality that is different for men and women. The highly limiting material conditions of a woman's life in a patriarchal society—the exposure of which is a main purpose of A Room—makes the free and equal union of the male and female a material impossibility.

In A Room, then, we can understand Woolf to question the possibility of androgyny for anyone, male or female, since here, as in

---

5. Woolf's dislike of lecturing and didacticism is perhaps most ardently set forth in her essay 'Why?' in which she blames these customs for 'incit[ing] the most debased of human passions—vanity, ostentation, self-assertion, and the desire to convert' (231).

Orlando, material conditions are shown to suffuse the experience of being 'womanly' or 'manly'. 'Intellectual freedom', Woolf writes, 'depends upon material things' (112). And material things are socio-culturally prescribed and proscribed: the way one is required to dress, for instance, which is exposed as a seriously restrictive physical factor in *Orlando*; or the fact that one is denied entrance to libraries or parliamentary buildings, a limitation with which *A Room* is much concerned; or the social mandate to marry and to bear and raise children, an underlying issue in much of Woolf's fiction. Such limitations cause Woolf to set forth what we might term, after W. E. B. Du Bois, a theory of women's 'double consciousness':

> Again if one is a woman one is often surprised by a sudden splitting off of consciousness, say in walking down Whitehall, when from being the natural inheritor of that civilisation, she becomes, on the contrary, outside of it, alien and critical. (*Room* 101)

Since the androgynous mind is the 'undivided' mind (102), and the thinking woman notices the inequities that surround her far too much for her mind to remain undivided, the state of androgyny is currently impossible for women.

Polymorphous Desire and the Flight of the Imagination

In Woolf's work, the female artist is not constructed according to the cultural mythos of genius. Rather, the notion of genius tends to be exposed as a cultural device for maintaining a reverence or mythical fiction about writing, painting, and the arts in general that keeps women from attempting to achieve recognition in those arts. But what then are the ramifications of dismissing both 'androgyny' and 'genius' for Woolf's particular theorizations of the woman artist? More to the point, what does bisexuality or bisexual desire have to do with it? To answer this, I want to turn from *A Room* back again to *Orlando*. One might think that the most interesting passage in *Orlando* for a person interested in Woolf's use of bisexuality would be her explicit reference to Orlando's ability to 'enjoy[ ] the love of both sexes equally' (221) [118]. But I want to call attention to what is to me a more illuminating passage of the novel, one that underscores Woolf's *aesthetic* use of that polymorphous desire we now term 'bisexuality': her belief in what it does for the artist.

For Woolf, it is not the ability to think both 'like a woman' and 'like a man' that enables artistic creativity and production. In Woolf's work, conscious indulgence of the ability of one's mind to range freely and contemplate openly *all* desires, even those that are socially proscribed, is necessary for full intellectual and artistic freedom.

Thinking through desire, not sex or sexuality, is central to Woolf's concept of the artist. Some of the most important lines in Woolf's work for understanding her use of desire—including the desire that causes Orlando to indulge her 'love of both sexes equally'—are those towards the end of the novel, in which the narrator contemplates the way unhampered polymorphous desire enables artistic inspiration:

> So here then we are at Kew, and I will show you to-day . . . under the plum tree, a grape hyacinth, and a crocus, and a bud, too, on the almond tree; so that to walk there is to be thinking of bulbs, hairy and red, thrust into the earth in October; flowering now; and to be dreaming of more than can rightly be said and to be taking from its case a cigarette or cigar even, and to be flinging a cloak under (as the rhyme requires) an oak, and there to sit, waiting the kingfisher, which, it is said, was seen once to cross in the evening from bank to bank.
>   Wait! Wait! The kingfisher comes; the kingfisher comes not. (293) [156]

Creativity, imagination, and inspiration are here symbolized by the kingfisher, a bird whose ability to dive into flowing water and emerge with a fish has made it a symbol of sudden artistic inspiration mysteriously pulled from the depths of the unconscious. Somewhat more complex is the imagery of budding floral life in the passage. The phallic image of the 'bulbs, hairy and red, thrust into the earth' and productive of flowers together with the nipple-like buds of the almond is fairly obviously evocative of the heterosexual reproductive sex act. And yet the image is queered by the fact that the hyacinth has a long tradition of associations with male homosexuality, as well as by the crocus, traditional symbol of a virginally pure and specifically female bliss, a symbol Woolf has already used in *Mrs. Dalloway* to represent Sally and Clarissa's youthful same-sex love.[6] The lush confusion and proliferation of floral sexual imagery here connects both reproductive and non-reproductive sexuality with the creative process of reflection. All these symbols of sex and desire figure into the 'more than can rightly be said' of what the once-male-now-female poet Orlando is contemplating as she performs the modern woman's gender-bending activity of smoking, possibly even a cigar, in a public park while sitting on the ground absorbed in thought, awaiting inspiration. Implicitly, this unfettered

6. Woolf's use of the crocus is esoteric, sometimes symbolizing female same-sex desire, as in *Orlando*, sometimes symbolizing the essence of meaning, such as that a writer attempts to convey in her/his work, as in her essay 'The Patron and the Crocus', sometimes symbolizing both together, as in *Mrs. Dalloway*: 'a match burning in a crocus; an inner meaning almost expressed' (47). For a discussion of the symbolism in the latter, see Sparks.

contemplation of a polymorphous diversity of desires and dreamed of pleasures invokes the intellectual depths from which that fish, that inspiration, will come.

Where women's sexual desire is concerned, it is not limited to the heterosexual keeping of 'an assignation for Sunday dusk' with the gamekeeper and 'slipping off one's petticoat', which Woolf has earlier figured as 'love—as the male novelists define it' (*Orlando* 269) [144]. 'Love' includes that, surely, and Orlando has a baby boy on the very next page as if to prove it, but it also includes 'the love of both sexes equally' in which Orlando has been engaging throughout the novel. What is more, it includes the seemingly nonsexual 'splendid fulfilment of natural desires for a hat, for a boat, for a rat in a ditch' (294) [156]. To return to the language Woolf uses in her letter to Smyth, the 'narrowing and naming' of 'these immensely composite and wide flung passions' does not serve the modern female artist, who depends on her ability to render in her artwork the beauty of desire in its multiple and uncharacterisable forms.

Woolf's juxtaposition of the beauty of uncategorisable desires against the 'dullness' of sexual identities constructed according to what she calls 'physical feeling' is perhaps made clearer in another passage in the letter to Smyth, in which she remarks on the 'illusion' that presses her to create her fiction. After revealing her previous tendency to 'wheel round and gallop the other way' in response to her own merely physical attraction to two or three 'obtuse, gallant, foxhunting and dull' men earlier in her life, she tells Ethel:

> Perhaps this shows why Clive . . . always called me a fish. Vita also calls me fish. And I reply (I think often while holding their hands, and getting exquisite pleasure from contact with either male or female body) 'But what I want of you is illusion—to make the world dance'. More than that, I cannot get my sense of unity and coherency and all that makes me wish to write the Lighthouse etc. unless I am perpetually stimulated. Its [*sic*] no good sitting in a garden with a book; or collecting facts. There must be this fanning and drumming—of course I get it tremendously from Leonard—but differently—Lord Lord how many things I want—how many different flowers I visit . . . (*Letters* 4:200)

For Woolf, what is 'silly', 'dull', and 'trivial' about certain early-twentieth-century evolving sexual identities, then, is the over-emphasis on the merely physical aspects of desire, an emphasis she understands to be shared by the sexual scientists, the 'effeminate sodomites', and the 'mannish lesbians' alike. On the whole, Woolf's work is far more interested in desire than it is in sex, sexuality, and sexual identity. What her biography-writing narrator facetiously states in *Orlando* might be understood as Woolf's personal authorial mantra nonetheless: 'But let other pens treat of sex and sexuality; we quit such odious subjects as soon as we can' (139) [76]. Desire is so multiple, so varied, that the search to satisfy it must not be bounded by constructed limitations such as gender and sexuality. And it is that search itself, and not the physical satisfaction of every desire, that engenders the inspiration that makes possible, makes necessary, Woolf's art.

WORKS CITED

Cucullu, Lois. 'Exceptional Women, Expert Culture, and the Academy'. *Signs* 29.1 (2003): 27–54.

Doan, Laura. *Fashioning Sapphism: The Origins of a Modern English Lesbian Culture.* New York: Columbia UP, 2001.

Dreger, Alice Domurat. 'Doubtful Sex'. *Hermaphrodites and the Medical Invention of Sex.* Cambridge: Harvard UP, 1998. 15–45.

Ellis, Havelock. *Sexual Inversion.* Vol. 2. of *Studies in the Psychology of Sex.* 3rd ed. Rev. and enlrgd. Philadelphia: Davis, 1915.

Faderman, Lillian. *Surpassing the Love of Men: Romantic Friendship and Love Between Women from the Renaissance to the Present.* New York: Morrow, 1981.

Foucault, Michel. Introduction. Herculine Barbin. *Being the Recently Discovered Memoirs of a Nineteenth-Century French Hermaphrodite.* Transl. Richard McDougall. New York: Random House, 1980. vii–xvii.

Freud, Sigmund. *Three Essays on the Theory of Sexuality.* 1905. *Standard Edition of the Complete Psychological Works,* 24 vols. Vol. 7. Ed. and trans. James Strachey. London: Hogarth, 1953. 133–245.

Hastings, Selina. *Rosamond Lehmann.* 2002. London: Vintage, 2003.

Lee, Hermione. *Virginia Woolf.* New York: Random, 1996.

Marcus, Sharon. *Between Women: Friendship, Desire, and Marriage in Victorian England.* Princeton, NJ: Princeton UP, 2007.

McWilliams-Tullberg, Rita. *Women at Cambridge: A Men's University—Though of a Mixed Type.* London: Gollancz, 1975.

Nicolson, Nigel. *Portrait of a Marriage: Vita Sackville West and Harold Nicolson.* Chicago: U of Chicago P, 1973.

Smith-Rosenberg, Carroll. 'The Female World of Love and Ritual: Relations between Women in Nineteenth-Century America'. *Signs* 1.1 (1975): 1–29.

Sparks, Elisa Kay. '"A Match Burning in a Crocus": Modernism, Feminism, and Feminine Experience in Virginia Woolf and Georgia O'Keeffe.' *Virginia Woolf: Emerging Perspectives. Selected Papers from the Third Annual Conference on Virginia Woolf.* New York: Pace UP, 1994. 296–302.

Tindall, Gillian. *Rosamond Lehmann: An Appreciation.* London: Chatto & Windus / Hogarth, 1985.

Vicinus, Martha. *Intimate Friends: Women Who Loved Women, 1778–1928*. Chicago: U of Chicago P, 2004.

Weininger, Otto. *Sex and Character*. London: Heinemann, 1907.

Woolf, Virginia. *The Letters of Virginia Woolf*. Ed. Nigel Nicolson and Joanne Trautmann. 6 vols. New York: Harcourt, 1975–1980.

———. 'Modern Fiction'. *The Common Reader: First Series*. Ed. Andrew McNeillie. San Diego: Harcourt, 1984. 146–54.

———. *Mrs. Dalloway*. 1925. New York: Harcourt, 1953.

———. 'Old Bloomsbury'. *Moments of Being*. Ed. Jeanne Schulkind. 2nd ed. San Diego: Harcourt, 1985. 179–201.

———. *Orlando: A Biography*. 1928. San Diego: Harcourt, 1956.

———. *A Room of One's Own*. 1929. San Diego: Harcourt, 1957.

———. 'Why?' *The Death of the Moth and Other Essays*. San Diego: Harcourt, 1942. 227–34.

MARGARET HOMANS

On Rereading Woolf's *Orlando* as Transgender Text[†]

This chapter reads recent reinterpretations of Virginia Woolf's *Orlando* and offers a new rereading of the novel itself in order to address the problem of how transgender histories can be located (found, or placed) in representational works from historical epochs that precede our own time's fast-changing formations of gender and sexuality. Starting with critical debates about how transgender readings can and cannot be done, I show how recent efforts to enlist *Orlando* as a transgender fiction do not do justice either to the novel or to the needs of transgender reading subjects. I then reread the novel with a focus not on the alluring central character but on the novel's narrative form—specifically, the narrative's voices. Compared to prior transgender readings of *Orlando*, this reading method offers a potentially more satisfying way to read for transgender presences in a literary work of the past. My rereading is thus both a new reading of one novel and a contribution to methods of transgender reading; it is also a polemic in favor of the vital work of rereading. With two exceptions (a play and a film) the rereadings that I discuss and perform are not recyclings, since they do not take apart and recombine the material they read; instead, turning to the past to

---

† From *Contemporary Revolutions: Turning Back to the Future in 21st-Century Literature and Art*, ed. Susan Stanford Friedman (London: Bloomsbury Academic, 2018), pp. 212, 221–28, 232–36. © Margaret Homans and Susan Stanford Friedman, 2018, Bloomsbury Academic, an imprint of Bloomsbury Publishing Plc. Page numbers to this Norton Critical Edition appear in brackets.

move into the future, they treat the literary text as an infinitely renewable resource.

* * *

Rereading Orlando: *Narrative Form as Transgender Text*

What case, then, can be made for rereading *Orlando* "unhistorically" as a lively object for transgender studies, without either universalizing Orlando's vacillation ("we are all transsexuals") or minoritizing the novel as an account of a model character? (By rereading I mean reading with awareness of prior readings, reading the text while also responding to the history of its readings.) Can *Orlando* be useful to readers as a transgender text because of, rather than despite, the novel's figurative power and representational complexity? Is there a way to read so as to locate—not only to place, but also to find—a transgender "latent presence" in the novel, seen not as a failed work of realism, but as the marvelous and fantastical "representation" that it is?

* * * [Alexander] Eastwood affirms an unhistorical theory of transgender reading that relies on listening for [Wai Chee] Dimock's "resonances" and shared affect rather than on finding documentable historical connections or plausible transgender characters. This approach has proved productive for recent rereadings of *Orlando*. [Chris] Coffman listens for *Orlando*'s "resonances with contemporary transgender narratives" and "cross-historical reverberations" not by trying to align Orlando the character with contemporary transgender identities but by finding common ground between Orlando's "anti-identitarian" politics and contemporary feminist politics (paragraphs 24, 35).[1] Similarly, Lucas Crawford finds *Orlando* to be not about the rightly or wrongly gendered body but about gender as transitory affect. Instead of focusing on the sex-change scene and the narrator's musings about gender and clothes (cited in virtually all readings of transgender Orlando including Coffman's), Crawford highlights Orlando's "wandering poetic feeling" (171) in the modern scenes.[2] Both of these rereadings sidestep the opposition between "reality" and "representation" (or between minoritizing and

---

1. Because it focuses on politics rather than character, this reading resembles without exactly duplicating the 1990s postmodern alliance between queer and feminist readings of Orlando's vacillation.
2. Crawford cites as an example the moment when Orlando steps outside the department store and experiences feelings from all across her long history: "'Nothing is any longer one thing. . . . Someone lights a pink candle and I see a girl in Russian trousers. When I step out of doors . . . I see mountains. Turkey? India? Persia?' Her eyes filled with tears" (223, quoted in Crawford 173) [162]. Crawford also finds transgender affect in Orlando's feeling like "scraps of torn paper tumbling from a sack" (225, Crawford 174) [163]. There is nothing intrinsically trans about the feelings these passages present, but a reader seeking transgender resonances could find them there.

universalizing readings) by expanding what counts as the reality of transgender life—politics for Coffman, affect for Crawford—so that Woolf's novel can be seen to contain that reality as a "latent presence."

Rereading for resonances, Coffman also locates a transgender presence in *Orlando* by reading for form. For Coffman, the extension of the narrative of gender change over time "thwart[s] readers assumptions about the coherence of life narratives" and so constitutes a formally transgender narrative structure (paragraph 21).[3] Building on Coffman, Pamela Caughie likewise reads *Orlando* as formally transgender, enjoying the pun that translates "transgender" into French as "transgenre" and shifting the emphasis away from character: "The transsexual in *Orlando* is the narrative's organizing principle, not its subject," she writes; "*Orlando* provides not the transsexual's life but a different way to narrate that life" ("Temporality" 507, 518) [excerpted with its original title in this volume, pp. 276–94]. Like Coffman's, her formal reading focuses on the novel's nonstandard temporality: its folding and compressing of times and its stretching of the hero's story across centuries.[4] For Caughie, the novel's queer temporality and its mixing of genres are sufficient to mark its form as transgender. But, I argue, other features of the narrative are more explicitly gendered than either the resonances heard by Crawford and Coffman or the nonnormative temporality emphasized by Coffman and Caughie, and I will show how these features—perhaps more persuasively—make *Orlando* legible as a latently transgender text.

Although literary forms are not intrinsically gendered, they can become saturated with gendered meanings at particular historical moments.[5] *Orlando's* narrative abounds in (mostly) satirical replicas of just such historically contingent gendered forms. These forms

---

3. This aspect of the novel also aligns it with the anti-linear temporality of contemporary gender transitions that are not one-way, as discussed by Nael Bhanji and Aren Aizura.
4. Caughie builds on Coffman's reading of the narrative's refusal of "coherence," contrasting what she sees as the queer temporality of Orlando's life to Lili Elbe's one-way "bridge" (517), but she also disagrees with Coffman, claiming here and in an earlier essay that Orlando's gender identity becomes "unbounded." Caughie also places a premium on historicizing; comparing Orlando to Hirschfeld and Lili Elbe, she sees the novel's queer temporality and instability as historical, not just artifacts of contemporary reading. [Magnus Hirschfeld (1838–1965), sexologist and founder of the German Institute for Sexual Science (1919–33). Lili Elbe (later Lili Ilse Elvenes) (1882–1931), Danish painter and subject of the co-authored memoir *Man Into Woman* (1933). See Caughie (p. 277) and Rose (p. 294) in this volume—*Editor.*]
5. Rachel Blau DuPlessis shows that forms can carry gendered meanings at particular historical junctures; for example, romance novel plots of the eighteenth and nineteenth centuries are "scripts of heterosexual romance" (2) that normalize and naturalize social conventions. Following DuPlessis, Susan Stanford Friedman shows that Woolf genders narrative masculine and deploys "lyric strategies" linked to the female domain of feeling to "subvert" narrative's grip on women's lives (162). But in different cultural locations, the genders of these forms may be reversed.

were gendered for Woolf, and they remain gendered for twenty-first-century readers, although what their resonant presence in the novel can mean for readers has not remained static. The highly conspicuous plot of Orlando's gender change is counterpointed—not in any neat way paralleled—by a less visible and more complex sequence of gender changes and contradictions in the narration. As Suzanne Young observes, "The work tries on a breathtaking array of period styles, from the rhetorical ornament of Euphuism and the digressiveness of Sterne to the bizarre collages of surrealist prose" (170).[6] These styles carry gendered meanings, and, recycled by being taken out of context and juxtaposed in unexpected ways, they make the narration—the voice of the biographer and the other voices the narration summons—an important location of transgender resonance.[7]

Woolf initially dreamed up the book in a distinctively feminine mode: a "Defoe narrative," a "fantasy to be called 'the Jessamy Brides'" about two women, based on real-life couples, with "Sapphism . . . to be suggested." In a diary entry in March 1927, she anticipates the book will be "an escapade . . . great fun to write" (131). But when she wrote it the next year, the first few chapters conjoin a lighthearted and ironic romantic fantasy, coded feminine,[8] to the conventionally masculine genre of great-man biography, the model for which was her father Leslie Stephen's *Dictionary of National Biography*, which profiles only men, with the exception of George Eliot. The balance of these gendered voices is shifting and unstable, with the fantasy elements constantly disrupting but never entirely silencing the biographer's dogged pursuit of the truth. For example, Chapter 3, in which Orlando changes sex, begins with the lumbering voice of the seventeenth-century biographer:

> It is, indeed, highly unfortunate, and much to be regretted that at this stage of Orlando's career, when he played a most important part in the public life of his country, we have least information to go upon. (88) [64]

The biographer goes on to list Orlando's ambassadorial accomplishments and then describes the fire that destroyed his papers. Here the mocking tone of the fantasist starts to break through, making fun of the document-obsessed biographer:

6. Young does not see these styles as gendered, finding only that their artifice is like what she calls the "artifice" of transsexuality. That Young can call transsexuality a form of "artifice" shows how much trans discourse has changed in the twenty years since her essay appeared. She aligns the send-up of literary conventions with the refusal to give the protagonist a fixed identity, finding there is no nature in the novel's presentations of either art or gender.

7. I thank Scarlet Luk, whose dissertation-in-progress on transgender and nonbinary narrators (though not on Woolf) opened up for me the possibility of this way of reading.

8. Drawing on the work of Diana Wallace, Elizabeth English sees *Orlando* building on the distinctly feminized genre of historical romance, for example, by Sir Walter Scott (114).

> Often the paper was scorched a deep brown in the middle of
> the most important sentence. Just when we thought to eluci-
> date a secret that has puzzled historians for a hundred years,
> there was a hole in the manuscript big enough to put your fin-
> ger through. [65]

This intrusively anatomical image requires the reader to stop and
imagine the dignified biographer incongruously poking his finger
through the precious manuscript; more likely, the disembodied finger is that of the fantasist, hijacking the narrative to poke holes in
the biographer's high-minded but deluded belief in truth. The paragraph concludes:

> We have done our best to piece out a meagre summary from
> the charred fragments that remain; but often it has been nec-
> essary to speculate, to surmise, and even to make use of the
> imagination. [65]

With this remark the biographer yields the narrative to the fantasist, who takes over the story for the sex-change scene that follows,
even though the biographer also struggles hysterically to preserve
control. This shift in the narrative voice, from coded-masculine to
coded-feminine, tracks with the story of Orlando's sex change itself.
   But because the narrative voice or voices never stay the same,
running through a pastiche of period styles as the centuries advance,
the early chapters' gendered duel between stodgy biographer and
fantasy writer gives way to other, differently gendered contests for
control of the narrative. Another such struggle occurs near the start
of Chapter 5, which opens with a pastiche elaboration of Ruskin's
"storm-cloud of the nineteenth century" describing the rain and
damp that permeate England, leading to "unparalleled profusion"
in home decoration, clothing, verbiage, and human fertility, and
thence to the British Empire and to rigid gender difference (Beer
144–46). When Orlando takes out the manuscript of her poem "The
Oak Tree," she finds her hand cannot control her pen, which at first
produces a spreading blot and then "the most insipid verse she had
ever read in her life" (actual verses by Letitia Elizabeth Landon),
including:

> She was so changed, the soft carnation cloud
> Once mantling o'er her cheek like that which eve
> Hangs o'er the sky, glowing with roseate hue,
> Had faded into paleness . . . (174) [127]

Unlike the intrusive finger at the beginning of Chapter 3, whose fantastic, feminized subversion of the stodgy male biographer is a welcome interruption, this disembodied and distinctly feminine pen

pouring out Victorian clichés has interrupted not only Orlando's pride in authorship but also the male biographer's (at this point) less obtrusively gendered narration. The pen continues to make "one lachrymose blot after another" (177) [129] until Orlando resolves the "tingling" in her ring finger by finding a husband, who arrives at the climax of a Brontë parody, *Wuthering Heights* and *Jane Eyre* sent up as floridly sentimental gothic romances (180–83) [129]. The pen that took over Orlando's hand with its "mellifluous fluencies" (177) [129] has now taken over the narrative itself.

The narration of the novel's final chapter involves further contentious gendered conversations between the biographer's tradition-bound style and other voices that question, intrude, and finally take charge. The biographer finds nothing to say as Orlando completes "The Oak Tree" in the late Victorian period: he needs action in order to narrate, and would settle for love in this case, since (in his androcentric view) "love . . . is woman's whole existence"; but he looks for love "as the male novelists define it," and Orlando is merely kind, faithful, and generous (198) [144]. Besides, she is busy writing: her writing disables his. As a woman writer, Orlando invents modern poetry ("'A toy boat on the Serpentine,' and 'Ecstasy,'" she repeats to herself, while discovering that what "matters" is "something useless, sudden, violent; something that costs a life; red, blue, purple; a spirit; a splash," 211 [153]) and, with modernist compression, she summarizes all of Victorian literature in six lines. The fusty biographer, resisting Orlando's feminist modernity and preferring the "sixty volumes octavo" approach to literary criticism, finds no room in his prolix narrative for the last of Orlando's "six lines" (214) [155].

This gendered sparring echoes earlier struggles for control of the narrative, and in the next episode the biographer recalls his long-ago conjuring of a Baroque masque to delay the revelation of Orlando's sex change. Seeking now to avoid a similarly naked revelation (Orlando is about to give birth), the biographer wishes in vain "that, as on a former occasion, Purity, Chastity, and Modesty would push the door ajar and provide, at least, a breathing space" (214) [155]. Admitting he no longer controls "these ladies," the biographer looks for distraction elsewhere, and in place of the masque's comforting affirmation of gender hierarchy, the biographer describes a scene in Kew Gardens that is far from orderly and that, surprisingly, reproduces Orlando's own modernist style:

> I will show you to-day (the second of March) under the plum tree, a grape hyacinth, and a crocus, and a bud, too, on the almond tree; so that to walk there is to be thinking of bulbs, hairy and red, thrust into the earth in October; flowering now; and to be dreaming of more than can rightly be said, and to be

> taking from its case a cigarette or cigar even, and to be flinging
> a cloak under (as the rhyme requires) an oak, and there to sit,
> waiting the kingfisher, which, it is said, was once seen to cross
> in the evening from bank to bank. (215) [156]

Brenda Helt, reading *Orlando* as a bisexual text, argues that this passage shows "how polymorphous desire enables artistic inspiration" (154). The passage can surely be described as bisexual or polymorphous in terms of desire, or as trans or nonbinary in terms of gender. More striking, in the context of the chapter, is that the biographer speaks these lines only moments after yearning for his old heteronormative allies, Purity and her friends. The biographer's voice and narrative project seem to have merged with or capitulated to the feminized lyricism—now given a positive, modernist spin—that it has been his long endeavor to denigrate and defeat.

Following this passage, the biographer casts doubt on masculine authority, wondering whether "natural desire . . . is what the male novelist says it is" (216) [157] and critiquing the *Dictionary of National Biography* itself, which has subtended the biographer's project of creating a linear, rational narrative of Orlando's life. Such an approach to life-writing, the biographer now admits, fails to capture the subjectivity of time and can capture only "six or seven" of a person's thousands of selves (226) [164]. Still, he cannot adjust to the alternative style required to convey how little Orlando cares about having won a prize:

> we must here snatch time to remark how discomposing it is for
> her biographer that this culmination and peroration should be
> dashed from us on a laugh casually like this; but the truth is
> that when we write of a woman, everything is out of place . . .
> the accent never falls where it does with a man. (228) [165]

Again linking modernist style with women's writing (and echoing Woolf's 1919 manifesto "Modern Novels," where "the accent falls a little differently," 35), the biographer concedes the limitations of male-defined biography. From here on, the voice of the biographer gives way to a voice that more compatibly records Orlando's thoughts in free indirect discourse, "ecstasy" being the repeated keynote, as if Orlando, the modernist woman artist standing outside herself, were performing her own narration.

Anyone who has read *Orlando* will recognize the changeable voice of the narration, sometimes coextensive with the narrow-minded biographer, sometimes outside or beyond him and channeling the variably gendered voices that I have discussed. In the examples I have detailed, the narration does not so much combine masculine and feminine styles, as we might expect from Woolf's celebration of androgyny a year later in *A Room of One's Own*, as lurch from one to another in crosscutting interruptions, even as what counts as masculine and feminine changes from era to era. As the narration crosses back and forth over the gender line, a reader could locate a "latent" transgender "presence" in the narration itself. This array of voices represents a more complex figure of transgender presence (and one that takes into account more of the text) than the relatively simple one-way transition that comes into view when the minoritizing reader focuses on the protagonist as a person. Nor can the transgender presence in the narration be mistaken for the universalizing, appropriative mode of "representation" to which [Susan] Stryker objects, for it never congeals into an allegorical figure.

If *Orlando*'s form might be said to offer transgender resonances to the attuned rereader, it could also be said to approximate Sandy Stone's claim that "transsexuals [constitute not a third gender but] a *genre*—a set of embodied texts whose potential for *productive* disruption of structured sexualities . . . has yet to be explored" (231).[9] For Stone to call transsexuals a genre or "a set of embodied texts" instead of a gender goes a step beyond the commonsense claim for language's powers of social construction that she also makes when she shows that, in order to obtain surgical intervention, early transsexuals had to conform to surgeons' binary gender narratives. Stryker too notes language's constructive power in "My Words to Victor Frankenstein," which concludes that transsexual "monstrosity" is an effect of mislabeling: "phallogocentric language . . . is the scalpel that defines our flesh" (250). But how can a transsexual, or any person, "be" a text? Stryker may be glossing Stone's claim about genre when she announces a "transgender aesthetic" that her essay embodies or "replicate[s]." The essay flamboyantly mixes genres by juxtaposing literary criticism, personal reflection, a poem, and a section titled "theory." Stryker explains:

> I wanted the formal structure of the work to express a transgender aesthetic by replicating our abrupt, often jarring transitions between genders—challenging generic classification with the forms of my words just as my transsexuality challenges the conventions of legitimate gender. (245)

In this account, Stryker's text itself becomes a transgender body. In contrast to Stryker's more recent insistence that "reality" is distinct from and more valuable than "representation" ("[De] Subjugated" 2), the older essay's creative literary experimentation with a "transgender aesthetic" of "jarring transitions," together with its narrator's identification with the fictional monster, suggests that the Stryker

---

9. Caughie alludes to this claim, too, when she calls the novel a "transgenre" narrative.

of 1994 could join Stone in imagining transgender as a literary genre, and transsexuals as embodied texts.[1] Read in such a context, which collapses the distinction between "representation" and "reality," *Orlando* could not be dismissed * * * as *mere* representation, since the novel's multiply gendered narration could be seen, somewhat like the "transgender aesthetic" of Stryker's essay, if not exactly to "replicate" the "jarring transitions" of transgender embodiment, at least to offer transgender resonances for today's readers to hear.

Thus a transgender body may be locatable in Woolf's text, but it isn't, or isn't only, to be found in the person of Orlando; rather, if we follow the lead of Stryker's 1994 essay instead of her later views, Orlando's character is a signpost or decoy alerting the reader to listen for the transgender resonances that can be heard in the narration itself.

✳ ✳ ✳

Works Cited

Aizura, Aren Z. "The Persistence of Transgender Travel Narratives." In *Transgender Migrations: The Bodies, Borders, and Politics of Transition.* Ed. Trystan T. Cotten. New York: Routledge, 2012, 139–56.

Beer, Gillian. *Arguing with the Past: Essays in Narrative from Woolf to Sidney.* London: Routledge, 1989.

Bhanji, Nael. "Transcriptions: Homing Desires, (Trans)sexual Citizenship, and Racialized Bodies." In *The Transgender Studies Reader 2.* Eds. Susan Stryker and Aren Z. Aizura. New York: Routledge, 2013, 512–26.

Caughie, Pamela. "The Temporality of Modernist Life Writing in the Era of Transsexualism: Virginia Woolf's *Orlando* and Einar Wegener's *Man Into Woman.*" *Modern Fiction Studies* 59.3 (2013), 501–25.

Coffman, Chris. "Woolf's *Orlando* and the Resonances of Trans Studies." *Genders* 51 (2010), n.p.; paragraphs 1–35. Web. * * *

Crawford, Lucas. "Woolf's Einfülung: An Alternative Theory of Transgender." *Mosaic* 48.1 (2015), 165–81.

---

1. To say that transsexuals are a genre is not to say that they are merely fictional, but rather to say that we live in, as, and by our representations. To be fair, Stryker's statement about "a transgender aesthetic" could be read with a different emphasis: if literary form (merely) "replicates" or serves as an analogy for ("just as") transsexuality, then the two remain ontologically distinct and the statement could be seen to anticipate—not contradict—Stryker's later insistence that "reality" is distinct from and more important than "representation." But the tone of the 1994 passage differs from that of the later statement, indicating a wish to unite representation and reality, not divide them.

Dimock, Wai Chee. "A Theory of Resonance." *PMLA* 112.5 (1997), 1060–71.

DuPlessis, Rachel Blau. *Writing beyond the Ending: Narrative Strategies of Twentieth-Century Women Writers*. Bloomington: Indiana University Press, 1985.

Eastwood, Alexander. "How, Then, Might the Transsexual Read? Notes toward a Trans Literary History." *Transgender Studies Quarterly* 1.4 (2014), 590–604.

English, Elizabeth. *Lesbian Modernism: Censorship Sexuality, and Genre Fiction*. Edinburgh: Edinburgh University Press, 2015.

Friedman, Susan Stanford. "Lyric Subversion of Narrative in Women's Writing: Virginia Woolf and the Tyranny of Plot." In *Reading Narrative: Form, Ethics, Ideology*. Ed. James Phelan. Columbus: Ohio State University Press, 1989, 162–85.

Helt, Brenda S. "Passionate Debates on 'Odious Subjects': Bisexuality and Woolf's Opposition to Theories of Androgyny and Sexual Identity." *Twentieth Century Literature* 56.2 (2010), 131–67.

Stone, Sandy. "The Empire Strikes Back: A Posttranssexual Manifesto." 1991. Rpt. *The Transgender Studies Reader*. Eds. Susan Stryker and Stephen Whittle. New York: Routledge, 2006, 221–35.

Stryker, Susan. "(De)Subjugated Knowledges: An Introduction to Transgender Studies." In *The Transgender Studies Reader*. Eds. Susan Stryker and Stephen Whittle. New York: Routledge, 2006, 1–17.

Stryker, Susan. "My Words to Victor Frankenstein above the Village of Chamounix: Performing Transgender Rage." *GLQ* 1.2 (1994), 237–54.

Wallace, Diana. *The Woman's Historical Novel: British Women Writers, 1900–2000*. Basingstoke: Palgrave Macmillan, 2005.

Woolf, Virginia. *The Diary of Virginia Woolf*. Ed. Anne Olivier Bell assisted by Andrew McNeillie. Vol. III. New York: Harcourt Brace, 1980.

———. "Modern Novels." 1919. In *The Essays of Virginia Woolf*. Ed. Andrew McNeillie. Vol. III: 1919–1924. San Diego: Harcourt Brace, 1988.

———. *Orlando: A Biography*. 1928. Orlando, FL: Harcourt, 2006.

Young, Suzanne. "The Unnatural Object of Modernist Aesthetics: Artifice in Woolf's *Orlando*." In *Unmanning Modernism: Gendered Re-Readings*. Eds. Elizabeth Jane Harrison and Shirley Peterson. Knoxville: University of Tennessee Press, 1997, 168–87.

PAMELA L. CAUGHIE

[Time's Queer Force: Modernist Life Writing in the Era of Transsexualism][†]

> Consider what immense forces society brings to play upon each of us, how that society changes from decade to decade . . . ; well, if we cannot analyse these invisible presences, we know very little of the subject of the memoir; and again how futile life writing becomes.
> —Virginia Woolf, "A Sketch of the Past"

In a conversation with Bruno Latour, historian and philosopher of science Michel Serres provides a metaphor that captures modernist life writing's temporality. Our experience of time, says Serres, resembles a crumpled handkerchief rather than a flat plane, where the past folds in on the present, pressing on it at difference places, and the present folds in on the past, pressing on it from behind in that the present redacts our understanding of what the past has become (60).[1] Virginia Woolf shares this understanding of the proximity of the present and the past in her classic life writing narrative, *Orlando*, as in her memoir, "A Sketch of the Past," begun in 1939, where she dates each reminiscence to include the present moment in which she writes as "a platform to stand upon" (75). In writing a life, and in reading life writing, one unavoidably encounters the past from some present vantage point, some immediate stimulus that revisions that past, and thus the present as the past's future, gathering up moments in time that resonate with the present moment. In this sense, Orlando's composition of "The Oak Tree" over three centuries is not fantastic, a temporal aberration, but emblematic of how writing and reading work. "The present when backed by the past," writes Woolf, "is a thousand times deeper than the present when it presses so close you can feel nothing else" ("Sketch" 98). Likewise, the past when backed by the present is far deeper, more yielding than when visited as a discrete period, as if only a moment in time.

In this essay, I read Woolf's 1928 mock biography, *Orlando*, whose eponymous protagonist changes from a man into a woman midway

---

† From "The Temporality of Modernist Life Writing in the Era of Transsexualism: Virginia Woolf's *Orlando* and Einar Wegener's *Man Into Woman*," *Modern Fiction Studies* 59.3 (Fall 2013): 501–07, 512–25. © 2013 Johns Hopkins University Press. Reprinted with permission of Johns Hopkins University Press. Title updated at request of the author. Page numbers to this Norton Critical Edition appear in brackets.

1. Concerning Serres's notion of time in relation to presentism, see Gajowski. Walter Benjamin's historical materialism similarly conceives history as folded into different moments in time. Benjamin's concept of history as a "constellation" of past and present, not a fixed moment in time to be mined as a source of meaning for an event or artwork, captures the concept of temporality that informs Woolf's life writings.

through her life, in relation to the discourse of transsexualism in the modernist era. In particular, I compare *Orlando* with the contemporaneous *Man into Woman: An Authentic Record of a Change of Sex*, the biography-memoir of Danish artist Einar Wegener, who, as Lili Elbe, can lay claim to the title of the first transsexual. Although transsexualism as we study it today emerged out of early-twentieth-century scientific discoveries and technologies, such as synthetic hormones and advances in plastic surgery, it was also engendered by modernist aesthetics, formal innovations responding to and shaping a changing social discourse of sexuality and subjectivity. By focusing on the nexus of scientific experimentation with the real and aesthetic experimentation with representation as reciprocal cultural forms, I uphold the power of literature, not just the promise of science, to reshape notions of gender and identity in the modernist era. Insofar as it offers new ways to read sexual and gender identity *as narrative*, modernist aesthetics makes textual analysis as critical as cultural history to contemporary transgender studies. Instead of taking the transsexual as the subject of Woolf's novel, as many critics do, I take this figure as its object of thought, one that led Woolf to produce a model of modernist life writing in the era of transsexualism that I call a "transgenre."[2]

Orlando serves as the prototype of the transgenre, one that reconfigures in life writing narratives not only notions of gender but also of time, identity, history, and the very nature of writing and reading. Recently the French, for whom the word "genre" (gender) refers not to sexuality but to linguistics, have begun to use "transgenre" to translate the English "transgender." "Transgenre," then, when used in French, foregrounds linguistic differences and distinctions in works about gender. I adopt the French "transgenre" in English for narratives treating transgender lives that transfigure conventions of narrative diegesis.[3] Transsexual life writing, as other scholars have noted, disrupts conventions of narrative logic by defying pronominal stability, temporal continuity, and natural progression. It thereby demands a new genre, a transnarrative. Woolf reached this insight in writing *Orlando,* remarking in her diary that she doubted she would write another novel after *Orlando,* that she would need another name for her fiction (*Diary* 3, 176). Transnarratives cross genres—for example, medical, psychological, judicial, journalistic,

2. The play on "gender" and "genre" informs other readings of *Orlando*, though the term "transgenre" appears in only one, Anne Ciecko's essay on Sally Potter's *Orlando*, to refer specifically to new filmic genres. For other essays that read *Orlando* in terms of contemporary gender and transgender theory, see Coffman, Craps, and Taylor; for readings that treat the relation between gender and genre in *Orlando*, see Boehm and Young.

3. Coined in the 1990s, "transgender" serves as an umbrella term that includes transsexualism, with or without surgical intervention, as well as cross-dressing and various practices defying conventional notions of gender.

anthropological, philosophical, autobiographical, fictional—as in the case of *Orlando* with its generic mix of biography and fantasy, philosophy and literary history, poetry and prose. They cross—or more accurately, crisscross—temporal moments as the protagonist transitions in gender and in time. Of necessity, transnarratives emphasize the artifice of gender, even while maintaining its naturalness. The term "transgenre" extends Sandy Stone's provocative suggestion in her 1991 landmark essay, "The Empire Strikes Back," that transsexuals be considered "not as a class or problematic 'third gender,' but rather as a *genre*—a set of embodied texts whose potential for *productive* disruption of structured sexualities and spectra of desire has yet to be explored" (165). That potential has been explored by Virginia Woolf in *Orlando*.

Insofar as it reconceives the very concept and form of life writing, *Orlando* radically refigures the narrative of transsexualism presented in Lili Elbe's more conventional tale. Using transsexualism as an organizing metaphor in the construction of a life, as Woolf does in *Orlando*, produces a different understanding of temporality and of those "invisible presences" that society "brings to play on each of us" and that Woolf complains have "never been analysed in any of those Lives which I so much enjoy reading" ("Sketch" 80). *Orlando* breaks down arbitrary historical divisions, renews the past in the present, immerses us in time, dramatizes how life and literature acquire a shape, and a value, within multiple pasts and always in relation to a present moment. Woolf makes the art of prose fiction, specifically temporality and narration, central to identity. When in the early stages of writing *Orlando* Woolf was fascinated by a newspaper article about a young woman who became a man (Bell v. 2, 132), that moment provided not so much the subject for her fictionalized biography as the occasion for re-conceptualizing the subject of life writing.

Transsexualism in the Modernist Era

> The modern is a period, in fact, most likely to produce a work like *Orlando*.
>
> —Suzanne Young, "The Unnatural Object
> of Modernist Aesthetics"

As gender historians and modernist scholars have noted, the modernist era witnessed tremendous change in concepts of sexual and gender identity.[4] Psychoanalysts, sexologists, and endocrinologists

---

4. Mary Evans dates this insight to feminist literary scholars of the 1970s and 1980s: "Collectively, these critics [Ann Douglas, Elaine Showalter, and Alice Jardine] argued that what occurred at the end of the nineteenth and the beginning of the twentieth centuries was a denaturalization of gender. Partly as a result of the intellectual

challenged the sacrosanct nineteenth-century belief in sexual dimorphism in positing a universal bisexuality.[5] Anthropologists wrote about the tradition of the man-woman, men dressing and living as women, in various cultures. The modern girl cut her hair, dressed in pants, smoked in public, and rode the subway, arousing anxiety about "masculine women and feminine men."[6] Newspaper and later radio accounts of women living as men, and men as women, were widespread. The journal *Urania* was founded in the 1910s explicitly to resist distinct, and binary, sexual categories.[7] When we consider the many modernist literary works that treat transsexualism and what we call today transgender,[8] Woolf's comment "No age can ever have been as stridently sex-consciousness as our own" (*A Room* 99) that I once took as a profound insight into the modernist era seems a rather banal understatement.

Less noted among modernist scholars is that the term "transsexualism" was coined in 1923 (would that it were 1922!) by Magnus Hirschfeld, founder of the Institute for Sexual Science in Berlin, where the first transsexual surgeries were performed, a fact relevant to the changes noted above. In his article "The Intersexual Constitution," Hirschfeld coined "transsexualism" to describe the adoption of the gender role opposite to birth sex by men and women who held an unswerving conviction that they were assigned the wrong sex. Yet already in *Transvestites*, where Hirschfeld created the category of transvestism to distinguish cross-dressing from homosexuality, the lack of a single term to capture the various experiences of his

---

influence of Freud and psychoanalysis, and partly because human experience began to be less immediately controlled by 'nature' and the 'natural', it began to be possible to disturb conventional assumptions about masculinity and femininity. Within this literary tradition the most important work was Virginia Woolf's *Orlando* . . ." (72–73).

5. According to Brenda Helt, bisexuality at this time referred to personality, not sexual orientation. Sigmund Freud, Otto Weininger, and Havelock Ellis are among those who promoted a theory of bisexuality. Helt argues that the various understandings of this concept made bisexuality a "floating signifier" (135), its many meanings "reflected and propagated the conflation of concepts now understood as distinct: biological sex, gender, desire, sexual preference, sexual identity, and intellectual and artistic superiority" (136). The same might be said of "transvestite" and "transsexual" as Magnus Hirschfeld defined them.

6. This phrase comes from the title of a popular American song, "Masculine Women, Feminine Men," produced by Okeh Records in 1926, with words by Edgar Leslie and music by James V. Monaco. For more on these changes, see Caughie.

7. In 1916 British feminist Thomas Baty (also known as Irene Clyde) founded *Urania,* a journal that advocated for cross-gender identification and the dissolution of sexual categories. Baty, who would be considered transgender today, also founded the Aëthnic Union in 1912. See Oram, "Feminism" and "Cross-dressing." For newspaper accounts of transgender in the 1920s and 1930s, see Oram, *Her Husband Was a Woman.*

8. The list includes Sherwood Anderson's "The Man Who Became a Woman," the Tiresias episode in T. S. Eliot's *The Waste Land,* the Circe chapter of James Joyce's *Ulysses,* Willa Cather's *One of Ours* (all works from that emblematic year 1922), all cited by Michael North in *Reading 1922,* as well as Radclyffe Hall's *The Well of Loneliness,* and writings by Gertrude Stein, Ernest Hemingway, Djuna Barnes, Bryher, and Virginia Woolf, among others. As North writes, much modernist literature was concerned in some way with the reorientation of gender and "a more general transsexuality" (191–92).

subjects led him to describe, if not yet name, transsexuals.[9] Despite such taxonomic efforts to distinguish categories of transvestite, transsexual, and homosexual, inversion, intersexuality, and bisexuality, sexual categories were in flux in the modernist era. Confusion among them reigned then as it does now, with Hirschfeld himself conflating them at times.

When gender historians and modernist scholars caution us against imposing our contemporary notions of gender and sexuality on a previous era, they themselves impose a more coherent set of definitions on early-twentieth-century scientific and popular narratives than the literature supports. Historian Alison Oram, for example, warns scholars against asserting a transhistorical identity for the transsexual, "reading the confused category of the early twentieth-century invert as evidence of a past transsexual subject" ("Cross-dressing" 279). In "Fin de Siècle, Fin de Sexe: Transsexuality and the Death of History," Rita Felski cautions that metaphoric uses of transsexuality, such as those employed by postmodern and feminist theorists, elide historical differences in concepts of, and investments in, gender (150). Such caveats can prevent naïve readings and prove useful for scholarship, as, for example, when Brenda Helt says that the fact that bisexuality was not yet a sexual identity in the 1920s, that it referred to personality not sexual orientation, makes it useful as a textual strategy in *Orlando* (131) [see p. 249 in this volume]. In point of fact, however, past usage of sexual terms was not stable. Even though many critics insist that the word queer, for example, which appears frequently in modernist literature, did not yet carry homosexual connotations, it was beginning to be sexualized in the modernist era. It is as difficult to say when the term transsexual achieved sufficient coherence and stability to be marked as distinct from present usage as it is to say precisely when a transsexual's transition from one sex to another begins and ends.

Such anxiety about imposing our present notions on past writings risks under-reading the present moment, the platform on which we stand, in reading the past. In guarding against the conflation of historical moments we may suppress their proximity. Confusion in terminology in modernists texts, whether Hirschfeld's or Woolf's, is not something to clear up in terms of our present knowledge but something to realize and negotiate in our readings of modernist-era writing and its social formations. As Gertrude Stein blandly reminds us in "How Writing is Written," "everybody is contemporary with his period" (488), a seemingly simple if not simplistic assertion that

---

9. According to Meyerowitz, as early as 1916 German sexologist Max Marcuse published an article on the "drive for sex transformation" (18), distinguishing this drive from inversion or cross-gender identification, which both Hirschfeld and Ellis referred to as transvestism. Meyerowtiz says Hirschfeld's transvestite is today's transsexual.

raises profound questions of what it means to read the past. To understand the modernist past in its contemporaneity, Stein suggests, it is not enough just to recapture that past as it was; one must also appreciate the modernist sense of time as synchronous, not linear.[1] Historicizing cannot itself be a transhistorical act, flattening out different temporalities in reading across historical time. That is not time as a crumpled handkerchief but time as a sequence of discrete eras. A modernist reading of the past reads synchronically, across the folds of the handkerchief. Further, the metaphoric use of transsexuality is precisely one means by which to negotiate such narratives and their historical differences. Metaphors enable us to read sexual identity as a historically-specific narrative.[2] Woolf's transsexual metaphorically links temporality (*trans* as movement) with sex and sexuality. Such metaphors do not elide the past but encode it in the writing of the present and future.

Reading across the folds of Hirschfeld's writings provides a deeper insight into what he means by transsexualism. In *Transvestites* Hirschfeld argues that it is a mistake to imagine male and female as two "fully separate entities," asserting that "the constantly present merging of both into one . . . is the core for the genesis and substance of personality" (18). Yet in that work, Darryl Hill argues, Hirschfeld created a sexual category premised on a theory that disavowed sexual categories. Even a cursory reading of *Transvestites*, Hill argues, reveals not only that Hirschfeld's definition of transvestite differs from our own (someone who cross-dresses for sexual excitement) but also that in interpreting his source material, Hirschfeld ignored crucial aspects of his subjects' experiences, exposing tensions and contradictions between their stories and his reading of them (316).[3] Hirschfeld's study shows, Hill concludes, what other historians of sexuality have found: namely, that his subjects resisted the definitions and interpretations imposed on them by medical science (318). Historians need to listen to, in George

---

1. Stein's concept of time in this essay, as in "Composition as Explanation," is as important as her concept of writing. Stein's use of the continual present, influenced by William James's theory of time as a continual flow of present moments, arranges historical events and ideas to indicate their coincidence or coexistence. Such synchrony is evident in Woolf's biographical novels *Jacob's Room* and *Orlando* as well. As Armstrong writes, "Modernism works . . . with notions of temporality which overlap, collide, and register their own incompletion . . . the *dynamization* of temporality is one of the defining features of modernism" (*Cultural History* 9).

2. Fredric Jameson's imperative "always historicize" might itself be read as an implicit metaphor in which the tenor, the historical past, can only be implied. In responding to calls to historicize, we would do well to keep in mind Hayden White's conception of historical narrative as an extended metaphor.

3. Hill did not have access to Hirschfeld's sources (they were destroyed when the Nazis raided Hirschfeld's institute in 1933), an important contextual difference to keep in mind when comparing his and Hirschfeld's readings of the subjects' life narratives.

Chauncey's phrase, "the elusive evidence of the ordinary" (qtd. in Hill 319), Hill argues, not just read the works of the authorities.

Where Hirschfeld sought to distinguish transvestites from homo-sexuals "to remove legal and medical obstacles to sexual and gender variance" (Meyerowitz 21), Hill seeks to privilege personal narra-tives. Hirschfeld's study, as Hill notes, relies on published letters, news reports, case studies, interviews, and popular publications about cross-dressing men and women. If we were to read it as an example of a modernist transgenre, it would necessarily offer con-tradictory evidence and produce conflicting interpretations, work-ing against any effort to establish the truth about transvestism, or transsexualism, whether that truth comes from medical science or personal narratives. The sexologist's or psychoanalyst's case study, as Michael Levenson notes, is itself a modernist experimental nar-rative form that offers a "new metaphysics of character, . . . an over-lay of past and present" (83). Giving a name, transvestism, and later transsexualism, to such "elusive evidence" traced across various genres creates a generic distinction rather than a definitive category or a new sexual identity, as Hirschfeld is presumed to do. In other words—specifically Sandy Stone's—we can read the transvestite or transsexual in Hirschfeld's writing as a genre.

Missing in Hill's reading is any awareness of the subjects' con-scious construction of their narratives to create the kinds of dis-tinctions they, or their doctors, desire. If you want to be understood as a transsexual and not as a female impersonator, as one of Hirschfeld's subjects insists, then you must assume a certain sub-ject position within narratives of desire and sexuality. Hirschfeld's notion of the "constantly present merging" of sex differences cap-tures that sense of changing *narrative* position and need not be read as a new *subject* position. The discrepancy between the posi-tion the subject assumes in the narrative and the way s/he is posi-tioned in Hirschfeld's reading and other source materials requires of us a different kind of reading, that is reading people the way many of us have learned to read characters, taking into account narrative conventions and narrative time, the temporal span of a story, and the historical and social contexts within which the narratives oper-ate. Such a practice requires reading across genres rather than hold-ing any one genre—the personal narrative, the medical treatise, the official biography—as authoritative. I am not suggesting that personal narratives should be discounted, as Stone says autobio-graphical accounts by transsexuals are often dismissed by the med-ical establishment (155); rather, personal accounts should be read as narratives.

What Hirschfeld faced in writing about sexual and gender expe-riences that defy conventional categories resembles what Orlando's biographer faces in trying to write about his elusive subject. Narrating the life of a subject who changes sex certainly taxes conventions of life writing, yet so do the minutiae of daily life that no single account can hope to capture. "The elusive evidence of the ordinary" describes perfectly the kind of details provided in so many modernist narratives. The typist scene in *The Waste Land*, Bloom's perambulations through Dublin in *Ulysses*, the detritus of everyday life that clutters *Jacob's Room* come to mind as famous examples. Orlando, like Jacob Flanders, is neither a traditional character presented through his actions in the world, the kind of biographical figure Woolf found objectionable, nor a modernist character presented through "the atoms as they fall" ("Modern Fiction" 155), the kind of impressionistic interiority that has long defined modernist fiction. The transsexual in *Orlando* is the narrative's organizing principle, not its subject. The "elusive evidence of the ordinary" in such modernist texts does not necessarily prove the authority (in this case, Hirschfeld) wrong, as Hill implies; instead, insofar as it characterizes the contemporaneity of modernist life writing, whether fiction or nonfiction, such evidence suggests a way of reading the modernist past commensurate with its terminological confusion and temporal conflations. In both his writings and in his life's work at his institute in Berlin, Hirschfeld was a modernist, constructing new narratives of embodiment and new metaphors of gender.[4]

* * *

Time's Queer Force

> On all sides writers are attempting what they cannot achieve, are forcing the form they use to contain a meaning which is strange to it.
> —Virginia Woolf, "The Narrow Bridge of Art"

Woolf's transsexual narrative makes the art and artifice of gender self-conscious. The story begins in Elizabethan England with Orlando as a young boy brandishing his sword at a Moor's head, and ends in the moment of its writing, the eleventh of October 1928, with Orlando as a thirty-something woman shopping at Marshall & Snelgrove's. In this fantastic tale, subtitled a biography (which, to Woolf's amusement, led at least one bookstore to shelve it under that genre), the eponymous protagonist lives for over three centuries, changing somewhere in the seventeenth century from a man to a woman. *Orlando* has all the trappings of a biography—an index,

---

4. In suggesting we read Hirschfeld as a modernist writer, I support recent scholarship on the Weimar Republic that seeks the continuities between literary culture and the new sciences. See, for example, Veronika Fuechtner.

photographs, and other authenticating documents, such as letters
and lists, and a preface by the author, in which she thanks, among
others, literary figures, living and dead, and the British Museum and
Record Office. Throughout the narrative, the biographer-narrator
reflects on the difficulty of writing a biography, especially for someone like Orlando who spends much of his/her time in solitude, thinking and writing. In this way the narrative keeps the focus on the
writing itself as part and parcel of the subject's life.

   Orlando shares a number of motifs and themes with other transsexual narratives, in addition to the requisite sex change. There is
the synecdoche of the leg whereby a single appendage comes to signify sexual identity, both masculinity and femininity at different
points in the narrative as in history. There are explicit references to
contemporaneous theories of sexual identity (as in the clothes philosophy passage discussed below); heightened attention to pronouns
(as in the first line of the novel: "He—for there could be no doubt of
his sex" [13] [9]); reflections on memory and the past as transfigured
by sexual difference; and elements of melancholy and the maca-
bre (though these are as much a homage to Sir Thomas Browne
and the fin-de-siècle decadents as they are signifiers of the abject
lives of sexual dissidents). But more important for understanding
Woolf's transgenre as a model for life writing in the age of transsexualism are its differences from other transsexual narratives.

   An obvious difference is the treatment of the sex change. In
Orlando as in no other transnarrative, the sex change is instanta-
neous, "unanticipated" and "undesired," as Karen Kaivola notes
(235), even though the narrative defers acknowledgment of the
change through an elaborate masque figuring the three female
virtues: Purity, Chastity, Modesty. That long digression mocks the
notion of a sex change as a momentous and temporally specific event,
as the clock striking October 11, 1928, in the last chapter mocks
the historian's measurement of time, as if either sexes or eras were
discrete units that followed one another in succession. The narrator's matter-of-fact account and the insouciance with which Orlando
responds to the change present this "incredibly fantastic" event as,
if not commonplace, at least not uncommon:[5] "Orlando looked himself up and down in a long looking-glass, without showing any signs
of discomposure, and went, presumably, to his bath" (138) [75]. The
treatment of this extraordinary event, as Kaivola notes, extends
"the particularity of Orlando to a more general human truth" (235)—
the truth that "one's life is not confined to one's body," as Woolf

---

5. In his introduction to *Man into Woman*, sexologist Haire refers to Wegener's story as
   "incredibly fantastic" (v).

writes in "A Sketch of the Past" (84), or to *one* body. Importantly, Orlando's life suggests that the transsexual's watchword might not be "I'm trapped in the wrong body" but "I'm sick to death of this particular self. I want another" (*Orlando* 308) [163].

The homecoming scenes in these two narratives illustrate the protagonists' different attitudes. When Orlando returns to her ancestral home after the sex change, there is some initial confusion as the servants greeting her, "overcome with emotion," remark "Milord! Milady! Milady! Milord!" (169) [92]. Yet no one, the narrator observes, "showed an instant's suspicion that Orlando was not the Orlando they had known" (170) [92]. Overjoyed to be home, Orlando settles back in to his (now her) old routines and picks up her writing where he had left off. * * * Orlando * * * continues writing the poem she began as a young man throughout the novel, finishing it as a modern woman, welcoming desire "in whatever form it comes," she says, "and may there be more forms, and stranger" (294) [157].

Initially Orlando, newly female, loves women, out of habit: "As all Orlando's loves had been women, now, through the culpable laggardry of the human frame to adapt itself to convention, though she herself was a woman, it was still a woman she loved" (161) [87]. Eventually the power of bodily mimesis, and the pressure of Victorian convention, compel her to love and marry a man, though one whose gender is as suspect as Orlando's. Even this acquiescence, though, is presented not just as a performance of femininity, and a subversive one at that, but as indispensable for her writing. Comparing her "obeisance to the spirit of her age" (265) [141] to a traveler smuggling a box of cigars through customs, Orlando thinks:

> She had just managed, by some dexterous deference to the spirit of the age, by putting on a ring and finding a man on a moor, by loving nature and being no satirist, cynic, or psychologist— any one of which goods would have been discovered at once— to pass its examination successfully. And she heaved a deep sigh of relief. . . . Orlando had so ordered it that she was in an extremely happy position; she need neither fight her age, nor submit to it; she was of it, yet remained herself. Now, therefore, she could write, and write she did. (266) [141]

Here Woolf articulates her own strategy in this narrative, her ability to write freely about contraband topics, such as those that resulted in the censoring of Théophile Gautier and Radclyffe Hall, without resorting to the satiric impulse that saved Compton Mackenzie and

Djuna Barnes. She does so by giving us a protagonist who is neither wrongly sexed nor tragically gendered.

Read in the context of its cultural moment, *Orlando* thematizes new concepts of sexual identity circulating in scientific discourses and popular culture. Lisa Carstens identifies the following passage from *Orlando* with Sir Henry Head's theory of the self as a reiteration of postures the body performs over time, a theory that anticipates Bourdieu's concept of the *habitus*: "The change of clothes had, some philosophers will say, much to do with it. Vain trifles as they seem . . . they change our view of the world and the world's view of us" (187) [101]. * * * The next passage, however, contradicts this view, asserting that "Clothes are but a symbol of something hid deep beneath. It was a change in Orlando herself that dictated her choice of a woman's dress and a woman's sex" (188) [101–02]. Many contemporary memoirs by transsexuals espouse this notion that sexual difference is ontological; something "deep beneath" dictates the outward change.[6] Lili Elbe eventually adopts this view.

But two sentences later, the narrator offers yet another view in the statement often quoted as Woolf's theory of androgyny: "For here again, we come to a dilemma. Different though the sexes are, they intermix. In every human being a vacillation from one sex to the other takes place, and often it is only the clothes that keep the male or female likeness, while underneath the sex is the very opposite of what is above" (189) [102]. This notion of a permanent bisexuality is the one articulated by Hirschfeld in *Transvestites*, a view that became dominant among sexologists in the 1920s. The novel is often said to uphold this androgynous concept of sexual identity.[7] Yet more important than which theory of identity Woolf may hold is her capturing the coexistence of conflicting notions of sexual identity that vary not only among sexologists and writers, but even within any one writer's works.

In its very narrative form *Orlando* disrupts the sexual dimorphism theorists of transsexualism and transsexual narratives like Lili Elbe's so often fall back on. The metaphor of the bridge, prominent in

6. Carstens argues that this passage expresses Woolf's belief in a core, if multiple, self (42). The insistence that the protagonist has no choice runs through narratives of sexual dissidents, such as in Foucault's *Herculine Barbin*, *The Well of Loneliness*, *Man into Woman*, and Boylan's *She's Not There*.

7. Woolf uses the more familiar concept of androgyny rather than the newly coined transsexualism. These concepts were in flux at the time. Kari Weil in *Androgyny and the Denial of Difference*, distinguishes between the androgyne as an "aesthetic ideal," or "cultural conceit," and the hermaphrodite as the physical condition (11). Yet Earl Lind (also known as Ralph Werther) in *Autobiography of an Androgyne* (1918) uses "androgyne" (19) for the lived identity, the actual physical and psychic condition, and sees the hermaphrodite as the aesthetic ideal (19–20).

transsexual narratives, appears in Lili's memoir when she imagines that she has "built a slender bridge across that abyss which separates man and woman" (270). For Woolf, the metaphor of the bridge applies to experiments in the writing, not on the body. The narrow bridge of art, the title of an essay Woolf published in August 1927 shortly before she began *Orlando,* signifies the passage to a new prose genre, one capable of presenting an affective equivalent of the modernist era's new reality, "an age," Woolf says, "when we are not fast anchored where we are" ("Narrow Bridge" 11). Who better to serve as an emblem of this age of the unmoored than the transsexual? Like Lili Elbe, Orlando articulates the dilemma of those who choose or are forced to change their sex. Yet she does so in terms that capture the sensate experience that characterizes the new genre Woolf envisions at this time, whether the new biography (the title of an essay she wrote the same month she began *Orlando*) or the new novel. This new genre "will differ from the novel as we know it now chiefly in that it will stand further back from life" ("Narrow Bridge" 18) dispensing with fiction's "fact-recording power," and resembling poetry in expressing "emotions toward such things as roses and nightingales, the dawn, the sunset, life, death, and fate" ("Narrow Bridge" 19).

The poetry of this new transgenre is evident in a scene from *Orlando* that appears in some form in nearly every transsexual memoir, where the protagonist must account for her or his past life as the other sex. Voyaging home from Turkey after the sex change and seeing the cliffs of England for the first time as a woman, Orlando remarks that "she would have been hard put to it to explain to Captain Bartolus . . . that she, who now trembled on his arm, had been a Duke and an Ambassador" (162) [88]. Yet a passage that begins with the fact of the sex change ends with the sensate experience of life: "How explain to him that she, who had been lapped like a lily in folds of paduasoy, had . . . lain with loose women among treasure sacks in the holds of pirate ships on summer nights when the tulips were abloom and the bees buzzing off Wapping Old Stairs?" (162) [88]. For the transsexual who conceives the narrow bridge as a passage from one sex to the other, the past becomes a burden and a conundrum. In *Orlando,* that same conundrum devolves into a series of tactile, visual, and aural sensations that life writing must capture if we are to know the subject of the memoir.[8] The problem *Orlando*

8. As Catherine Neale Parke points out, *Orlando* conveys to readers the sense of what it felt like—physically, emotionally, intellectually, spiritually—to be Orlando "at precise moments of her male and female lives" (72). "The felt sense of living more than one life" comes not from the change of sex, I would argue, but from a change in emphasis in modernist life writing.

considers is not just how to account for yourself when your present sex does not match your past, but how to capture the minutiae of everyday life left out of so much life writing.

The figure of the transsexual gives potency and urgency to life writing's ultimate dilemma: how to account for oneself? * * * Orlando * * * conceives herself in terms of the "seventy-six different times all ticking in the mind at once" and as many as "two thousand and fifty-two" selves "built up, one on top of another, as plates are piled on a waiter's hand" (308) [163–64], at once juxtaposing different temporal moments and accelerating into the future, beyond the boundaries of any single life, in a memorable instance of modernist temporality. In the final chapter, one long meditation on time, the rapid changes of bodily sensations, memories and desires that compose the self at any one moment are figured through the wonder of modern technology: "the process of motoring fast out of London so much resembles the chopping up small of body and mind, which precedes unconsciousness and perhaps death itself that it is an open question in what sense Orlando can be said to have existed at the present moment" (307) [163]. The bridge Orlando crosses is "the narrow plank of the present" (299) [159], that "raging torrent" of sights, sounds, objects and impressions that swirl around her as she motors through London. From the time the clock strikes the present moment, the narrative presents us with a "configuration" (Benjamin 262), in Benjamin's sense, of present and past: "'When I step out of doors—*as I do now*,' here she stepped on to the pavement of Oxford Street, 'What is it that I taste? Little herbs. I hear goat bells. I see mountains. Turkey? India? Persia?' Her eyes filled with tears" (305; emphasis added) [162]. * * * *Orlando* dramatizes the persistence of the past in the present, making narrative temporality crucial to identity. *Orlando* insists that writing and identity, textuality and sexuality, the grammatical and the gendered, are learned together.

The frequent changes in the narration's temporal pacing, the many pauses in the story, as when the biographer looks out of the window while Orlando writes, the numerous anachronisms in the form of both analepsis and prolepsis, the thematizing of time—all serve to accentuate time's queer force:

> Time, unfortunately, though it makes animals and vegetables bloom and fade with amazing punctuality has no such simple effect upon the mind of man. The mind of man, moreover, works with equal strangeness upon the body of time. An hour, once it lodges in the queer element of the human spirit, may be stretched to fifty or a hundred times its clock

length. . . . It would be no exaggeration to say that [Orlando] would go out after breakfast a man of thirty and come home to dinner a man of fifty-five at least. Some weeks added a century to his age, others no more than three seconds at most. (98–99) [53–54]

Why do critics remark that Orlando barely ages in nearly four centuries when the span between 16 and 36 is enormous? Like Walter Benjamin's "Theses on the Philosophy of History," Woolf's narrative suggests, in Freeman's words, "a potentially queer vision of how time wrinkles and folds as some minor feature of our own sexually impoverished present suddenly meets up with a richer past, or as the materials of a failed and forgotten project of the past find their uses now, in a future unimaginable in their time" (163). The transsexual in *Orlando* is a figure of such future embodiment. The centrality of writing in this narrative, the emphasis on metaphoric language and literary history and the explicit discussions of writing's difficulties, present life writing not as an account of a life lived, but as the deliberate shaping of a narrative of a life that might be lived, and livable. The modernist transgenre as represented by *Orlando* is not about being true to life in the factual sense but about the consequences for living of telling a different kind of story. *Orlando* reemplots (Hayden White's term) life writing by changing the value readers tend to attach to certain kinds of facts and events, such as treating a sex change as mundane and the seasonal alterations of nature as a miraculous transformation. In this way, *Orlando* provides not the transsexual's life but a different way to narrate that life, one that can be more life-sustaining than the avowedly true-to-life account of Lili Elbe.

Orlando's closing chapter gathers up specific moments in time, particular scenes, scents and objects, and folds them into the present moment. "The past," writes Elizabeth Grosz in *The Nick of Time*, "is always already contained in the present, not as its cause or its pattern but as its latency, its virtuality, its potential for being otherwise" (254–55). This sense of the past informs Woolf's novel. In the closing pages of *Orlando*, the "pressure of the present" is unrelenting—"Braced and strung up by the present moment she was also strangely afraid, as if whenever the gulf of time gaped and let a second through some unknown danger might come with it" (321) [170]—until the narrative ends with the last stroke of midnight on the day Woolf finished the novel. The next stroke will take us into the future, the day after the writing stops.

A Wrinkle in Time

> The transaction between a writer and the spirit of the age is one of infinite delicacy.
>
> —Virginia Woolf, *Orlando*

Has anyone ever asked why Woolf makes her Vita-figure a transsexual? She wants to pay homage to Vita's aristocratic heritage, to acknowledge her bi-sexuality, to make her into a fantastic larger-than-life figure, but is a sex change necessary for that? What the sex change emphasizes is not transition from one thing to another but transformation over time. Gender in *Orlando* is a historically specific cultural process, a matter of literary forms and legal institutions, psychology and medicine, fashion and social customs. Woolf's point here anticipates Foucault's in *The History of Sexuality*: namely, that gender and sexuality are constructed over time through an array of institutions and discourses. Woolf happened to be constructing a life of Vita, an exceptional person in terms of sexuality and gender, at the moment when new scientific models of gender and a new vocabulary of sex and sexuality were being formed. Setting Vita's life in a fictional version of that emerging discourse produces the modernist transgenre that invites us to read across temporal moments.

By providing an account of the past in terms of what is to come and representing the future as if it had already occurred, *Orlando* is a proleptic narrative. Beyond imagining the physical transformation of a man into a woman that is not to become a reality for several more years, *Orlando* models a reading of the past with an eye toward the future that opens the possibility of a new form of life writing, a way of encountering what has not yet been, what has not yet entered the historical record. The transsexual in this novel becomes a fantastic figure of future forms of relationality and intimacy, of desire, happiness and pleasure. Having laid her parents' ghosts to rest in *To the Lighthouse*, and with that past its familial model of intimacy, Woolf creates in *Orlando* a new model of home, marriage, and companionship, one more in keeping with Vita's life as well as the transsexual's life, but that also opens up possibilities of affiliation and affection for any individual. The family in *To the Lighthouse* gives way to heritage in *Orlando*, and the house expands beyond the nuclear family and a few close friends to embrace a society of strangers. Orlando's relation to parents, husband and child are no more significant—indeed, with the exception of Shel, much less significant—than her relation to lovers, servants, dogs, trees, and objects. That the transsexual Jan Morris cites *Orlando* in her autobiography gives new meaning to Suzanne Raitt's insight that the novel's ending opens into the future, extending "the boundaries of

who we are, and of who we might be" (qtd. in Taylor 215). The figure of the transsexual allows for a truer depiction of the genre called
life writing, which by definition is about the multitude of ways of
inhabiting time and space, than does the conventional single-sexed
subject. The transsexual's life narrative essentially changes the definition of life writing itself.

    * * * [W]e need a narrative logic that can provide a different tem-
porality of embodiment. This narrative logic, which we find in
Orlando, is more in keeping with its time in its *sense* of time than in
anything it says about sexological discourses of the day. For *Orlando's*
temporality is as queer as its eponymous protagonist. In [his] book,
In a Queer Time and Place, * * * Jack Halberstam uses "queer"
(1) to refer to modes of temporality outside the structure of reproductive and family time, of generational inheritance and capital
accumulation—the very temporality Woolf exposes in *Orlando.*
Halberstam, like Woolf, argues for changes in conceptions of narrative, not in order to get the story right, not to make the narrative
match the body or the body match the narrative (as Jay Prosser
argues transsexual narratives do)—that is, not in the name of the
real or the authentic, but in order to disrupt our notions of the real
and our investments in authenticity.[9] As a fantasy, *Orlando,* in Halberstam's words, refuses "to privilege the literal over the figurative"
(87). It is the insistence on the factually correct over the imaginatively and emotionally true that mars many transnarratives. Rather
than looking for literal transsexuals in the modernist past, then, we
might look to modernist literature as offering new narratives of
embodiment that enable new configurations of gender and sexual
identity.

    Reading in this way invites us to experience the transgenre's tem-
poral logic. From the platform of our present moment overbrimming
with trans terms, we can recognize the transsexual as a proleptic
subject, already there in the past, but not yet there in language.
Woolf foresaw this experience of ours when she wrote, in the final
pages of the manuscript, "words have yet to be coined for the selves
have never been numbered" (280). *Orlando* establishes the trajec-
tory—or transjectory—of the transgenre, where temporality is synchronous and recursive, the future is before us, and behind. It is
both of its time and ours.

---

9. In *Second Skins,* Jay Prosser argues that surgery and hormones allow the transsexual
   to create a narrative about the body that enables the transsexual to become a subject,
   albeit one that is subject to binary notions of gender. Telling a coherent story about
   one's experiences as a transsexual is the first step toward transitioning to a new body.
   In this sense, the body comes to match the narrative, the narrative the body.

WORKS CITED

Armstrong, Tim. *Modernism: A Cultural History*. Cambridge: Polity, 2005.

Bell, Anne Olivier, ed. *The Diary of Virginia Woolf*. 5 vols. New York: Harcourt, 1980.

Bell, Quentin. *Virginia Woolf: A Biography*. New York: Harcourt, 1972.

Benjamin, Walter. "Theses on the Philosophy of History." 1940. *Illuminations*. Ed. Hannah Arendt. Trans. Harry Zohn. New York: Schockent, 1969.

Boehm, Beth. "Fact, Fiction, and Metafiction: Blurred Gen(d)res in *Orlando* and *A Room of One's Own*." *Journal of Narrative Technique* 22.3 (1992): 191–204.

Bourdieu, Pierre. *Distinction: A Social Critique of the Judgement of Taste*. Trans. Richard Nice. Cambridge: Harvard UP, 1984.

Carstens, Lisa. "The Science of Sex and the Art of Self-Materializing in *Orlando*." In *Virginia Woolf Out of Bounds: Selected Papers from the Tenth Annual Conference on Virginia Woolf*. Ed. Jessica Berman and Jane Goldman. New York: Pace UP, 2001. 39–45.

Caughie, Pamela. "Passing as Modernism." *Modernism/modernity* 12.3 (2005): 385–406.

Ciecko, Anne. "Transgender, Transgenre, and the Transnational: Sally Potter's *Orlando*." *Velvet Light Trap* 41 (1998): 19–34.

Coffman, Chris. "Virginia Woolf's *Orlando* and the Resonances of Trans Studies." *Genders* 51 (2010). n. pag. Web. 20 Jan. 2012.

Conor, Liz. *The Spectacular Modern Woman: Feminine Visibility in the 1920s*. Indianapolis: Indiana UP, 2004.

Craps, Stef. "How to Do Things with Gender: Transgenderism in Virginia Woolf's *Orlando*." *Image into Identity: Constructing and Assigning Identity in a Culture of Modernity*. Ed. Michael Wintle. New York: Amsterdam, 2006. 175–90.

Evans, Mary. *Gender and Social Theory*. Philadelphia: Open UP, 2003.

Felski, Rita. "Fin de Siècle, Fin de Sexe: Transsexuality and the Death of History." *Doing Time: Feminist Theory and Postmodern Culture*. New York: New York UP, 2000. 137–53.

Freeman, Elizabeth. "Introduction." *Queer Temporalities*. Spec. issue of *GLQ: A Journal of Lesbian and Gay Studies* 13.2–3 (2007): 159–76. *Project Muse*. Web. 20 Jan. 2012.

Fuechtner, Veronika. *Berlin Psychoanalytic: Psychoanalysis and Culture in Weimar Republic Germany and Beyond*. Berkeley: U of California P, 2011.

Gajowski, Evelyn. "Beyond Historicism: Presentism, Subjectivity, Politics." *Literature Compass*, 7/8 (2010): 674–91. *Wiley Online Library*. Web. 21 Feb. 2012.

Genette, Gérard. *Narrative Discourse: An Essay on Method*. Trans. Jane E. Lewin. Ithaca: Cornell UP, 1972.

Grosz, Elizabeth. *The Nick of Time: Politics, Evolution, and the Untimely*. Durham: Duke UP, 2004.

Halberstam, Jack. *In a Queer Time and Place: Transgender Bodies, Subcultural Lives*. New York: New York UP, 2005.

Haire, Norman. Introduction. *Man into Woman: An Authentic Record of a Change of Sex*. Ed. Neils Hoyer. Trans. H. J. Stenning. New York: E. P. Dutton, 1933. v–xii.

Helt, Brenda. "Passionate Debates on 'Odious Subjects': Bisexuality and Virginia Woolf's Opposition to Theories of Androgyny and Sexual Identity." *Twentieth-Century Literature* 56.2 (2010): 131–67. *EBSCO*. Web. 21 Jan. 2012.

Hill, Darryl B. "Sexuality and Gender in Hirschfeld's *Die Transvestiten*: A Case of 'The Elusive Evidence of the Ordinary.'" *Journal of the History of Sexuality* 14.3 (2005). 316–32.

Hirschfeld, Magnus. *Transvestites: The Erotic Drive to Cross Dress*. Trans. Michael A. Lombardi-Nash. Buffalo, NY: Prometheus, 1991.

Hoyer, Niels, ed. *Man into Woman: An Authentic Record of a Change of Sex*. Trans. H. J. Stenning. New York: E. P. Dutton, 1933.

Kaivola, Karen. "Revisiting Woolf's Representations of Androgyny." *Tulsa Studies in Women's Literature* 18.2 (1999): 235–61. *JSTOR*. Web. 25 Jan. 2012.

Levenson, Michael. *Modernism*. New Haven: Yale UP, 2011.

Meyerowitz, Joanne. *How Sex Changed: A History of Transsexuality in the United States*. Cambridge: Harvard UP, 2002.

North, Michael. *Reading 1922: A Return to the Scene of the Modern*. New York: Oxford UP, 1999.

Oram, Alison. "Cross-dressing and Transgender." *Palgrave Advances in the Modern History of Sexuality*. Ed. H. G. Cocks and Matt Houlbrook. New York: Palgrave Macmillan, 2006.

———. "Feminism, Androgyny and Love Between Women in Urania, 1916–1940." *Media History* 7.1 (2001). 57–70. *Ebsco*. Web. 25 Jan. 2012.

———. *Her Husband was a Woman! Women's Gender-crossing in Modern British Popular Culture*. New York: Routledge, 2007.

Parke, Catherine Neale. *Biography: Writing Lives*. New York: Routledge, 2002.

Serres, Michel, with Bruno Latour. *Conversations on Science, Culture, and Time*. Trans. Roxanne Lapidus. Ann Arbor: U of Michigan P, 1995.

Stein, Gertrude. "How Writing is Written." *The Gender of Modernism: A Critical Anthology*. Ed. Bonnie Kime Scott. Bloomington: Indiana UP, 1990. 488–95.

Stone, Sandy. "The Empire Strikes Back: A Posttranssexual Manifesto." *Camera Obscura* 2.29 (1992): 150–76.

Taylor, Melanie. "True Stories: *Orlando*, Life-Writing and Transgender Narrative." *Modernist Sexualities*. Ed. Hugh Stevens. Manchester: Manchester UP, 2000. 202–18.

Weil, Kari. *Androgyny and the Denial of Difference*. Charlottesville: U of Virginia P, 1992.

Werther, Ralph. *Autobiography of an Androgyne*. 1918. New Brunswick: Rutgers UP, 2008.

White, Hayden. "The Historical Text as Literary Artifact." *The Norton Anthology of Theory and Criticism*. 2nd ed. Ed. Vincent B. Leitch. New York, 2010. 1536–53.

Woolf, Virginia. *The Diary of Virginia Woolf.* 5 vols. Ed. Anne Oliver Bell. New York: Harcourt, 1980.

———. "Modern Fiction." 1919. *The Common Reader: First Series.* New York: Harcourt, 1925. 150–58.

———. "The Narrow Bridge of Art." 1927. *Granite and Rainbow.* New York: Harcourt, 1958. 11–23.

———. *Orlando: A Biography.* 1928. New York: Harcourt, 1956.

———. *A Room of One's Own.* 1929. New York: Harcourt, 1981.

———. "A Sketch of the Past." *Moments of Being.* 2nd ed. Ed. Jeanne Schulkind. New York: Harvest, 1985.

Young, Suzanne. "The Unnatural Object of Modernist Aesthetics: Artifice in Virginia Woolf's *Orlando*." *Unmanning Modernism: Gendered Re-readings*. Ed. Elizabeth Jane Harrison. Knoxville: U of Tennessee P, 1997: 168–87.

GWEN ROSE

Unsolicited/Unrepresentative: The Ethics of Virginia Woolf's Portrayal of the Transgender in *Orlando*, as Compared to Lili Ilse Elvenes's *Man Into Woman*[†]

Lili Ilse Elvenes's *Man Into Woman* and Virginia Woolf's *Orlando* both chronicle the life narratives of a single protagonist who, in each case, begins their life assigned male at birth, but identifies as a woman by text's end. Though Lili is the subject of her own text, leading to an easy classification as "auto-biography," editorial and

---

[†] A version of this essay appears in *Virginia Woolf and Ethics. Selected Papers from the 31st Annual International Conference on Virginia Woolf*, ed. Amy Smith (Clemson: Clemson University Press, 2024). Reproduced by permission of Gwen Rose. Page numbers to this Norton Critical Edition appear in brackets.

co-authorial intersections in its composition—it was completed and published after her death—lead some scholars to classify *Man Into Woman* as semi-fictional.[1] This creates a generic similarity to the fictional *Orlando*, which, given Woolf's inclusion of some of the personal characteristics and family history of Vita Sackville-West, to whom this text is devoted and on whom the titular protagonist is supposedly based, also challenges the distinctions between fact and fiction.[2] Treating both Orlando and Lili strictly as literary characters—declining, notably, the urge to view Elvenes's text as a completely factual chronicle of her life—one can ask the extent to which each textual character is, or is not, representative of a genuine transgender identity.

The concept of representation is of pivotal importance for people from marginalized identity groups and central to the premise of this paper. Trans representation affirms that "trans people have always been here."[3] Romain Chareyron argues that representation "is always *for someone* . . . [it] has real effects within society—it tends to shape people's understanding of individuals and phenomena."[4] The presence of negative representations results in the proliferation of outdated stereotypes and damaging tropes about trans people.[5] Accordingly, trans people have recently called for "realistic depictions of trans people that do not sensationalize them and leave room for their voices to be heard."[6]

In examining *Man Into Woman* and *Orlando*, I ask what is at stake in interpreting Orlando as a trans character, or even adjacent to transness. Complicated and diverse though transgender identities are, a key component, perhaps the one universal truth amongst the subjective diversity of trans self-identification—which we might call "transness"—is just that: the self-originating sense of such an identity, a conscious rejection of sex as assigned at birth in favor of

1. Madelyn Detloff, "The Binary Bind: Inversion, Intersexuality and Interest in a Very Queer Künstlerroman," in *Man Into Woman: A Comparative Scholarly Edition*, edited by Pamela L. Caughie and Sabine Meyer (New York: Bloomsbury Academic, 2020), 229; and Pamela L. Caughie and Sabine Meyer, "Introduction," in *Man Into Woman: A Comparative Scholarly Edition*, edited by Pamela L. Caughie and Sabine Meyer (New York: Bloomsbury Academic, 2020), 28–44.
2. Brenda Helt, "Passionate Debates on 'Odious Subjects': Bisexuality and Woolf's Opposition to Theories of Androgyny and Sexual Identity," in *Queer Bloomsbury*, edited by Brenda Helt and Madelyn Detloff (Edinburgh: Edinburgh UP, 2016), 118, 120–3; and Maria DiBattista, "Introduction," in *Orlando: A Biography*, edited by Mark Hussey (Orlando: Harcourt, 2006), xliii–li.
3. "LGBT History Month: Trans People Have Always Been Here," *Stonewall* (accessed Apr. 2, 2023); and Jay Prosser, "Some Primitive Thing," in *Palatable Poison: Critical Perspectives on The Well of Loneliness*, edited by Laura L. Doan and Jay Prosser (New York: Columbia UP, 2001), 133–4.
4. Romain Chareyron, *Trans Identities in the French Media: Representation, Visibility, Recognition* (Lanham: Lexington Books, 2022), 7.
5. Ibid., 8–9.
6. Ibid., 11.

formulating oneself as something else. Despite the incredible diversity of transness, all trans people share their active rejections of cisgender identities: trans people take control of their own self-expression as what Jay Prosser calls "constructing subjects."[7] In reading *Orlando* alongside Elvenes's *Man Into Woman*, I highlight a pivotal difference between Orlando and other trans characters in modernism, and suggest the former, ultimately lacking this self-constructing sense, should be read as *other* than transgender.

   Orlando has at times been explicitly labeled "transsexual life writing,"[8] establishing perhaps unintentionally a basis for assuming that the titular character expresses a transgender identity. Pamela Caughie argues that Woolf uses "transsexualism as an organizing metaphor in the construction of a life,"[9] and what happens to the character of Orlando works well as a "metaphor" for exploring identities, particularly that of women within British society. However, while this metaphor relies on Orlando's bodily transformation, fantastically changing from the body of a cis man to that of a cis woman, this change precedes any articulation on Orlando's part for such a change: there is no sense that Orlando felt any previous need to change his/her gender. Without, then, any of sense of his/herself as a "constructing subject" in his/her own narrative of transness, the text actually reinforces the idea that gender stems from physical biology, rather than from any desire on Orlando's part to self-actualize a female gender identity. The "metaphor" of transness overtakes and overrides any opportunity for what Gayle Salamon calls "embodied subjectivity":[1] a trans person's sense of themselves that intersects with the body and embodiment, yet is not derived from the body. It is a necessary deviation given that the umbrella term "trans" indicates an identity inconsistent with a person's assigned sex at birth, or in Orlando's case, biological sex, since his/her body becomes entirely that of a cis woman. Orlando's transformation is one part of what separates him/her from other trans characters in literary modernism, in fact, a combination of the way that gender identity is in fact largely an afterthought in the text overall, derived from Orlando's body but without reflection on the protagonist's part. Instead, when Orlando delves into introspection at all, the focus is on gender roles and the restrictions on women in British society: Orlando's transformation is a means to this end for Woolf.

---

7. Jay Prosser, *Second Skins: The Body Narratives of Transsexuality* (New York: Columbia UP, 1998), 8.
8. Pamela L. Caughie, "The Temporality of Modernist Life Writing in the Era of Transsexualism: Virginia Woolf's *Orlando* and Einar Wegener's *Man Into Woman*," *Modern Fiction Studies*, vol. 59, no. 3 (2013), 503.
9. Caughie, "Modernist Life Writing," 503.
1. Gayle Salamon, *Assuming a Body: Transgender and Rhetorics of Materiality* (New York: Columbia UP, 2010), 2.

One reason for comparing Orlando with Lili Elbe, specifically, is because both of their narratives involve alterations to the bodies of the protagonists. In medical narratives of trans identities popular in the latter half of the twentieth century, some came to feel that bodily changes were what defined a transgender person: according to this (outdated) lens, both Orlando and Lili would be trans characters. Caughie and Sabine Meyer, editors of the recent scholarly edition of Elbe's *Man Into Woman*, have noted that Lili, who expresses some highly idiosyncratic views about her identity, should not be read as "a standard-bearer for some generalized trans experience."[2] All the same, Lili *does* possess a "transsubjectivity,"[3] which, distilled to its simplest essence—that, consciously and explicitly, she feels prior to transitioning that her male sex as assigned at birth does not accurately reflect who she feels herself to be—resonates strongly with present-day understandings of trans identity. Orlando, meanwhile, *lacks* this self-constructing directive: she becomes a woman simply because his/her body changes, not because she expresses any internal desire to do so. Moreover, after his/her transformation, his/her chief struggles concern the realm of social habits and learned behaviors: s/he never fears being misgendered, never struggles with doubt. Lili, unlike Orlando, experiences dysphoria and fears of rejection—but accompanying her much more conscious and personal process of bodily change, she also experiences euphoria and the restorative joy of a realized and affirmed transgender identity, which is a pivotal and *positive* part of trans identity—the *euphoria* that is so rarely represented in media, while dysphoria is. Caughie has cautioned against seeking out "literal trans[gender people] in the modernist past,"[4] but all the same, perhaps when we can identify them, via their fully realized transsubjectivities, characters like Lili with a fully realized sense of transsubjectivity are representative of transgender people in the modernist era in a way that Orlando is not.

Furthermore, and problematically, Orlando's gender is derived from his/her biology from the text's opening page, where the narrator declares that "there could be no doubt of his sex, though the fashion of the time did something to conceal it,"[5] implying a biologically male figure underneath somewhat feminine clothing. Likewise, his/her transformation is noted quite simply: Orlando awakens from a deep sleep and her "nakedness"[6] reveals him/her to be a

---

2. Caughie and Meyer, "Introduction," 10.
3. Salamon, *Assuming a Body*, 5.
4. Caughie, "Modernist Life Writing," 520.
5. Virginia Woolf, *Orlando: A Biography*, edited by Mark Hussey (Orlando: Harcourt, 2006), 11 [9].
6. Ibid., 102 [75].

woman. S/he "st[ands] upright" and "look[s] himself up and down" while the narrator states: "Orlando had become a woman—there is no denying it."[7] The implication is that Orlando's body has changed, that there could be "no denying it" based on her physical form and therefore her gender has changed as well. Yet Orlando doesn't reflect on this at all, has no subjective position on the matter: the narrator, who could provide some clarity, instead leaves the question to "biologists and psychologists," evades the issue entirely, espousing the view that "sex and sexuality" are "odious subjects."[8] We also learn that, other than his/her bodily change, "Orlando remained precisely as [s]he had been."[9] That his/her mind remains the same yet his/her gender has changed reinforces the conflation of sex and gender inherent in Orlando's gender identity, and Woolf effectively rejects the opportunity for Orlando to formulate a trans-subjective position at this crucial juncture. Chris Coffman argues that Woolf "uses the fantastic to foreground the slow pacing of Orlando's shifts in gender presentation and comportment,"[1] but in largely avoiding the free indirect discourse so common to her other works, Woolf fails to explain how the character herself actually understands her gender. Instead, Orlando seems to experience this change as simply something that has happened to him/her, something to which she must adjust. Coffman characterizes this as a refusal "to use narrative to create a coherent sense of the development of a singular identity."[2] Orlando need not commit to a singular, fixed, identity—but seems to experience neither euphoria *or* dysphoria, no reflection on her body *at all*, and this both leaves her gender to be defined *by* her biology—the very assignation that trans people reject—and reinforces the impression that Orlando's identity isn't defined by gender at all.

Her one significant moment of reflection on her gender happens later, just before she arrives back in England, when she seems "to vacillate" between man and woman but is also "not sure to which she belong[s]."[3] By the end of the same page, she aligns herself with women, and refers to men as "the other" sex—but there is no elaboration on how or why she has reached this conclusion. When she cries, "Praise God that I'm a woman," the narrator cautions us against the "extreme folly . . . of being proud of [one's] sex,"[4] again complicating our understanding of why, if not simply because of his/

7. Ibid., 102 [75].
8. Ibid., 103 [76].
9. Ibid., 102 [75].
1. Chris Coffman, "Woolf's *Orlando* and the Resonances of Trans Studies," *Genders*, no. 51: (2010).
2. Ibid.
3. Woolf, *Orlando*, 117 [85].
4. Ibid., 119 [87].

her altered biology, Orlando has ultimately chosen this identity.
Coffman, criticizing Jack Halberstam and Prosser and arguing that
their theories lead to "[a] proliferati[on of] different boxes for
identity,"[5] argues that Orlando's incoherence is a positive feature: that
Orlando defies categorization. Yet this argument would seem to
place Orlando outside the otherwise broad and inclusive trans
umbrella—if Orlando rejects all categories by refusing to reflect on
her own identity, then there would be no basis for assuming that she
embodies a transgender identity. It is not "incoherence" of identity
that would be non-representative; the trans umbrella is broad, and
inclusive of those who are questioning or unsure of their identity.[6]
Rather, it is Orlando's lack of articulation on his/her identity: while
he/she seems to align his/herself with womanhood on his/her passage back to England, the lack of explanation for this conclusion
seems to imply the default, once again, of his/her gender identity
simply aligning with that of his/her biological sex at that time.

Orlando's rare moments of introspection are often reserved for
other matters: his/her reflections on what it means to be a woman
are effectively utilized as a metaphorical thought experiment of what
someone with the learned behaviours, attitudes, and privileges of a
man would think if forced by circumstances to explore instead the
role of a woman. We learn that while living with the Roma people,
"she had scarcely given her sex a thought,"[7] but it is striking that
Orlando would have given his/her gender no thought whatsoever in
the time directly succeeding her transformation. After his/her later
moment of indecision, his/her reflections on board the *Enamoured
Lady* are largely concerned with gender *roles* and societal expectations as she reacclimates to English society. Madelyn Detloff highlights the role of camp in this criticism of gender roles, for example,
when Orlando bares an ankle, and later, in Orlando's dreary and
unsolicited courtship with the Archduke Harry.[8] Camp and satire
take centre stage, and Orlando's status as an ostensibly transgender
woman becomes merely a means to exploring this end. Caughie, too,
compares the "bridge" between genders that Orlando embodies as
more of an experiment in writing than an exploration of the body.[9]
Orlando does occupy a unique subjective space where s/he can
explore the conventions that restrict women with self-knowledge of
male privilege, but the opportunity here for him/her to reflect on

5. Coffman, "Woolf's *Orlando*," para 25.
6. T. Benjamin Singer, "Umbrella," *Transgender Studies Quarterly*, vol. 1, no. 1–2 (2014),
260.
7. Woolf, *Orlando*, 113 [82].
8. Madelyn Detloff, "Camp Orlando (or) *Orlando*," *Modernism/modernity*, vol. 23, no. 1
(2016), 19–20.
9. Caughie, "Modernist Life Writing," 515.

what it means to be *transgender* is missed; Orlando only reflects on what it means to be a *woman* in society.

Orlando is also based, at least loosely, on Woolf's lover, Vita Sackville-West. Vita is willing to articulate her sense of herself: Brenda Helt notes that she believed herself to be able to "shift between the two [binary genders]" according to dress, context, and sexual desire.[1] Vita is, quite possibly, expressing a sort of transsubjectivity in this articulation of becoming a different gender, a possible analogue to a modern genderfluid identity—yet Woolf offers no indication that Orlando occupies a similar subjective position. Orlando echoes Vita most when, after his/her transformation, s/he dresses as a man and seeks out female sex workers,[2] but these scenes highlight Orlando's "love of both sexes equally,"[3] that is, her bisexuality, and s/he does not formulate or express a transsubjective position in these encounters that would be comparable with Vita's.

For Lili, on the other hand, her assigned sex at birth is a source of constant concern to her, and until she transitions, she struggles to situate herself in the world. Historically, Lili Elbe was one of the first transgender people to undergo a medical transition, and *Man Into Woman* chronicles her life both before and after this moment. Caughie and Meyer point out factual inaccuracies in the text, and Lili is not a perfect antecedent to modern transgender people, to be sure. In describing her life prior to transitioning, she talks about Andreas Sparre, the deadname she uses for herself in the text, in the third person, as if Andreas were another person with whom she shared a single body, before being able to live completely as Lili after her second surgery. But the textual Lili can be thought of as a semifictional character who still provides a poignant point of comparison with Orlando, as another figure of literary modernism who undergoes a physical transition, but who consciously seeks out this change and also reflects much more meaningfully upon what it means for her.

Lili's pre-transition despair and despondency, while living a double, semi-closeted life, stem at least partially from the fact that she cannot imagine living as herself. She does not view total and final separation from the supposedly separate persona of Andreas as possible until she meets the surgeon who performs her gender-affirming surgeries and helps her attain legal status as a woman. Pivotally, though, this change is driven by Lili herself; she feels that she "was never intended to be anything but a woman."[4] The Andreas persona

---

1. Helt, "Passionate Debates," 120.
2. Woolf, *Orlando*, 158–61 [115–16].
3. Ibid., 117 [118].
4. Lile Elbe, *Man Into Woman: A Comparative Scholarly Edition*, edited by Pamela L. Caughie and Sabine Meyer (New York: Bloomsbury Academic, 2020), 148.

willingly—enthusiastically even—submits to a procedure that they both believe will eliminate this part of her and allow the Lili persona to take sole possession of their body. Lili's desire for bodily change is a conscious process, as the two personas agree that suicide was inevitable had the transition not been possible. After her second surgery, only Lili is present, Andreas seemingly gone forever—Lili has transitioned, is now fully "out" as trans. It is as if she has been newly birthed, but through her own volition, in her own words: "fully conscious through her own pangs."[5]

Lili is poignantly aware of the tenuous nature of her position within society; she knows that people look upon her as a "phenomenon" and associates this with negative feelings.[6] She also fears being misgendered when out in public,[7] and her sister's constant deadnaming and rejection of her transition is particularly painful to her, as she feels that she has "to demonstrate every day" to her sister that she is, in fact, a woman.[8] Salamon describes this challenge for trans people, the difficulty of reconciling how they are "perceived from the outside" compared with their internal sense of themselves.[9] But something we also see in Lili is the pure euphoria that life as a woman brings her after her transition. She is "happy . . . walking quite naturally like a young woman among other young women."[1] These moments provide a powerful antidote to her fears; she feels "secure and salvaged."[2] "How delightful it is to be addressed as 'madam,'" she writes:[3] the congruence of how she is perceived and how she wishes to be perceived is euphoric, and these simple joys are representative of the less-discussed, *positive* side of transgender lived experiences. For Lili, after her transition, these small moments, interspersed throughout the narrative as she navigates other challenges, cannot be undervalued; she finds in them the reconciliation of outer and inner perceptions—her gender is *affirmed*, and it is because of her deeply felt sense of transsubjectivity that she is able to articulate how and why this matters to her.

Orlando must suffer through the odious routines of decorum and convention, but his/her sense of gender *identity* is not an issue for her at any time, even after an incredible transformation. Lili, meanwhile, must actively work to come into her own, and, as a result, is able to express a deep appreciation for being seen and validated as a woman. This pivotal difference between Lili and Orlando

5. Ibid., 194.
6. Ibid., 135.
7. Ibid., 146.
8. Ibid., 176.
9. Salamon, *Assuming a Body*, 4.
1. Elbe, *Man Into Woman*, 145.
2. Ibid., 145.
3. Ibid., 159.

highlights what *Orlando*, as both a text and a character, lacks. Transgender identification cannot exist without introspection; it must be consciously actualized. Lili does that; it is Lili who feels real. Lili provides a baseline for the limits of reading Orlando—an interesting experiment and an endlessly fascinating character, to be sure—but not, perhaps, a transgender one.

MADELYN DETLOFF

Camp Orlando (or) *Orlando*†

In her "Notes on 'Camp,'" Susan Sontag asserts that "camp taste is a kind of love, love for human nature".[1] This love makes camp, despite its frequent flamboyant bitchiness, different from attempts at humor that derive from homophobia, transphobia, misogyny, or other forms of bigotry. Not all forms of drag are camp, nor are they all beneficent. But drag and camp have a special affinity that exceeds their mutual tendency toward parodic hyperbole. Camp's "love for human nature" distinguishes it from malicious cattiness, while drag's love for gendered nature is what distinguishes it from demeaning mimicry of the other. Moreover, drag and camp are both resource-rich practices, employing what Eve Kosofsky Sedgwick calls a "communal, historically dense exploration of a variety of reparative practices."[2]

In that spirit, I analyze the reparative cultural work of a camped-up version of Virginia Woolf's *Orlando*—itself arguably a masterpiece (or mistresspiece?) of camp sensibility.[3] My intent is not to show that Woolf's writing is campy—although it is, often—nor to argue that drag is campy—although it too is, often. Rather, I aim to elucidate a feature of camp's rhetorical functioning—a queer form of dramatic irony that creates an insider group which is *in the know* (and thus is in a position to appreciate the sublime, bitchy social critique leveled by camp) and an outsider group which is *not in the know* and often the target of camp's barbed wit. This sort of dramatic irony is similar to the successful joke as Ted Cohen explains it, which presumes

† From *Modernism/modernity* 23.1 (2016): 18–22. © 2016 Johns Hopkins University Press. Reprinted with permission of Johns Hopkins University Press. Page numbers to this Norton Critical Edition appear in brackets.

1. Susan Sontag, "Notes on Camp," in *Against Interpretation* (New York: Picador, 2001), 291.
2. Eve Kosofsky Sedgwick, "Paranoid Reading and Reparative Reading," in *Novel Gazing*, ed. Eve Kosofsky Sedgwick (Durham: Duke University Press, 1997), 28.
3. George Piggford, for example, calls *Orlando* an exemplar of "Bloomsbury camp biography" in "Camp Sites: Biographies of Queer Bloomsbury," *Queer Forster*, ed. Robert K. Martin and George Piggford (Chicago: University of Chicago Press, 1997), 97–101, and the novel has made the short list of Allan Pero's canon of camp modernism in "A Fugue on Camp," *Modernism/modernity* 23.1 (2016): 28–36.

and creates a sense of intimacy between the teller and the audience. Cohen describes this intimacy as

> the shared sense of those in a community. The members know that they are in this community, and they know that they are joined there by one another. When the community is focused on a joke, the intimacy has two constituents. The first constituent is a shared set of beliefs, dispositions, prejudices, preferences, et cetera—a shared outlook on the world, or at least part of an outlook. The second constituent is a shared feeling—a shared response to something.[4]

Camp similarly depends on a "shared set of beliefs, dispositions, prejudices, preferences" and fosters a "shared feeling"—what Sontag calls a "kind of love . . . for human nature." Moreover, it is my hunch, although it cannot be proved in the space of this brief piece, that the queer dramatic irony of camp as performed in and by modernist texts can nuance our understanding of modernist irony, so often associated with alienation and disillusion. For those *in the know*, camp's irony effects a communal interpellation within an alienating world, and this seems to be an important aspect of camp's taste for love.

In an act of misdirection comparable to Leonard Woolf's when he called Virginia "the least political animal since Aristotle invented the definition," Sontag herself disclaims camp's political force, calling it "disengaged, depoliticized—or at least apolitical" ("Notes on 'Camp,'" 277).[5] This pronouncement grossly underestimates the political force of "love for human nature," disavowing camp's close kinship with satire, arguably camp's straight-acting cousin. Drag, too, is a mode of misdirection that takes our eyes off the sleight of hand concealing the artifice of seemingly natural gender identities. Judith Butler most famously made this point, analyzing drag as a form of mimicry that exposes and undermines the naturalness of heteronormative gender performance, itself always already a form of masquerade. "In imitating gender," says Butler, "drag implicitly reveals the imitative structure of gender itself—as well as its contingency."[6] Butler derives her analysis of drag from, among other psychoanalytic and philosophical theories, Esther Newton's 1972 anthropological study *Mother Camp* (*Gender Trouble*, 174). Butler thus puts into words what others implicitly demonstrate through camp: that *how* one does a thing—act the man or play the

---

4. Ted Cohen, *Jokes: Philosophical Thoughts on Joking Matters* (Chicago: University of Chicago Press, 2001), 28.

5. Leonard Woolf, *Downhill All the Way: An Autobiography of the Years 1919 to 1939* (New York: Harcourt Brace Jovanovich, 1967), 27.

6. Judith Butler, *Gender Trouble: Feminism and the Subversion of Identity* (New York: Routledge, 1999), 175.

woman—may be more significant than *what*, if anything, lies beneath that performance. As Allan Pero notes * * *, "camp is the authenticity of affectation, . . . one of the triumphs of affect over sense, . . . the enemy of identity" (28–29). And camp is the sassy queer friend of love, love that is key to the successful, campy critique of gender politics in Woolf's *Orlando*.

In *Orlando*, Woolf's own hyperbolic spoofs of normative gender performance successfully leverage the risk of being too *much*. The narrator's many references to Orlando's shapely legs flirt with this form of hyperbole, moving from Queen Elizabeth's ogling of his fine legs [15], to the narrator's later aside—"he had a pair of the shapeliest legs that any Nobleman has ever stood upright upon" [62]—to Orlando's ultimate discovery that a mere glimpse of her shapely legs would be enough to startle a man into missing his footing and nearly falling to his death: "If the sight of my ankles means death to an honest fellow, who, no doubt, has a wife and family to support, I must, in all humanity, keep them covered" [84–85]. As hyperbole, the scene of a sailor almost falling off a mast because of the glimpse of a woman's ankles playfully turns the tables on gender stereotypes of women as the "weaker sex." Clearly men must be fairly weak and vulnerable if they can be killed by an accidental peek at an ankle. But for those in the know—for those who know that the character Orlando is modeled on Woolf's lover, Vita Sackville-West—the narrator's praise of Orlando's killer legs delivers the pleasure of being in on the open secret, of witnessing a seduction-by-novel in progress.

The scenes depicting the Archduke Harry's courtship of Orlando, on the other hand, are gloriously bathetic, intimating the tedium of eighteenth-century heterosexual courtship rituals through the invention of a game called "fly loo" (guessing which lump of sugar a fly will land on), which, like whist or piano playing, occupies the time while the business of courtship is conducted (181) [98]. Taken out of the context of camp sensibility that the novel so playfully builds up, this example, like other scenes of heteronormative hyperbole in the novel, would be too preposterous to function as a plausible critique of dominant gender roles. As a send-up of parlor culture, however, it is magnificent.

Adaptations of Woolf's work face the risk of being "too much" as well, which is perhaps why few undertake them. Failed adaptations of Woolf too often take themselves too seriously, straightening out her camp sensibility in order to present the text as political polemic. Such earnest adaptations prove unfaithful to Woolf's sensibility—getting the period costumes or lines from the diary right are mere attempts at verisimilitude, not fidelity. Jessica Thebus's production of Sarah Ruhl's adaptation of *Orlando* pleasantly surprised me, therefore, with its fidelity to the novel's camp sensibility, with its arch send-ups of the British nobility, of "high" literature, of "gloire," of politics, of biography. Drag, not surprisingly, played a key role in this performance, which ran from March 10 to April 10, 2011, at the Court Theatre in Chicago. The chorus (whom Ruhl employs to convey the narrator/biographer's voice) consisted of four male-appearing actors wearing corset-like bustiers and anatomically revealing leggings. (The stage direction in the script indicates that the chorus "may be cast without regard to gender.")[7] Costume designer Linda Roethke explains that she conceived of the chorus costumes after coming across a Len Prince photo of drag performer Charles Busch sporting tighty-whities (clearly showing the bulge of his genitals beneath the briefs), a bustier, and a wig cap [see front cover of this volume].[8]

Many treatments of androgyny deemphasize gender, but Roethke's design (and the performers' embodiment of it) does not; instead, it fleshes out Woolf's critique of gender ideology via gender hyperbole and materializes her lampooning of masculine sartorial vanity (a frequent motif in Woolf's work). Such peacocking is literalized in campy drag, epitomizing Allan Pero's observation * * * that "camp is not the enemy of masculinity; it merely critiques the sublimity of its earnestness."

The stage adaptation of *Orlando* (already a farcical parody biography) amplifies the novel's playful disdain for verisimilitude, making ontological referentiality a delightfully impossible game of "who's on first?" In act 1, scene 2, for example, one of the chorus members is double cast as Queen Elizabeth. Hence when the remainder of the chorus proclaims, quoting directly from Woolf's *Orlando*, that "he had been kissed by a queen without knowing it," the audience is treated to a delightful double entendre, knowing that the queen is also a queen (Ruhl, *Chekhov's "Three Sisters" and Woolf's "Orlando,"* 132). In a Butlerian sense, this pileup of citation on citation allows for a critique of essentialism without resorting to the high seriousness of Sally Potter's filmic adaptation of *Orlando*.[9] While I would gladly see that film over and over just to see Tilda Swinton in her lavish costumes (and none at all), in my estimation Potter's film is ultimately too artistically earnest to communicate the gist of Woolf's *Orlando*, which is delightful precisely because it is so bawdy, grotesque, hyperbolic . . . and loving of human nature even when it does not come packaged in the shape of Tilda Swinton. If we can adore, admire, and empathize with the bathetically grandiose and self-abasing but simultaneously self-affirming pronouncements of a

---

7. Sarah Ruhl, *Chekhov's "Three Sisters" and Woolf's "Orlando": Two Renderings for the Stage* (New York: Theatre Communications Group, 2013), 120.
8. Linda Roethke, email correspondence with the author, March 8, 2013.
9. *Orlando*, dir. Sally Potter (Adventure Pictures, 1992).

troupe of drag queens in awkwardly revealing underwear and wig caps, then perhaps we can be more accepting of our own and others' less outré transgressions of normative gender. To indulge in camp taste is, after all, to love—and self-love in the face of misogynistic, homophobic, or transphobic hate is a potent form of transformational politics.

Virginia Woolf: A Chronology

1882   January 25, Adeline Virginia Stephen born in London.
1895   May 5, death of mother Julia Prinsep Stephen.
1897   July 19, death of half-sister Stella Duckworth Hills.
1904   February 22, death of father, Leslie Stephen.
        Moves from 22 Hyde Park Gate to 46 Gordon Square in
        Bloomsbury. With her siblings, hosts Bloomsbury "Thursday
        Evenings" at 46 Gordon Square.
1905   Teaches weekly at Morley Memorial College for Working
        Men and Women in London.
1906   November 20, death of brother Thoby Stephen.
1907   February 7, sister Vanessa Stephen marries Clive Bell.
        April 12, moves with brother Adrian Stephen to 29 Fitzroy
        Square.
1909   February 17–18, Lytton Strachey proposes marriage to
        Virginia and then retracts.
1911   April, travels to Turkey.
1912   August 19, marries Leonard Woolf.
1914   Brother Adrian Stephen marries Karin Costelloe.
1915   Leases (with Leonard) Hogarth House, Richmond.
        March 26, *The Voyage Out* published by Gerald Duckworth
        and Company.
1917   July, Hogarth Press publishes its first book, *Two Stories* by
        Virginia and Leonard Woolf.
1919   July 1, purchases (with Leonard) Monk's House in Rod-
        mell, Sussex.
        October 20, *Night and Day* published by Gerald Duckworth
        and Company.
1922   October 24, *Jacob's Room* published by Hogarth Press.
        December 14, meets Vita Sackville-West.
1924   Leases (with Leonard) 52 Tavistock Square.
        January 1, Hogarth Press becomes the publisher for the
        International Psychoanalytic Library, which includes the
        English-language translations for Sigmund Freud's works.
        July 5, visits Knole and Long Barn with Vita.
        September 14–15 Vita visits Virginia at Monk's House.

1925   April 23, *The Common Reader* published by Hogarth Press.
        May 14, *Mrs Dalloway* published by Hogarth Press.
        December 17–20, stays at Long Barn with Vita; the two become lovers.

1926   January 20, Vita leaves for Teheran, Persia (Tehran, Iran).
        May 16, Vita returns to England and Virginia and Vita spend time together as lovers throughout the summer.
        October 27, Vita's long poem *The Land* is published by Heinemann.

1927   January 28, Vita leaves for Teheran.
        March 8, conceives of the idea of *Orlando*.
        May 5, *To the Lighthouse* published by Hogarth Press.
        June 16, Vita awarded the Hawthornden Prize for *The Land*.
        October 8, begins writing *Orlando*.

1928   January 28, Lionel Sackville-West, 3rd Lord Sackville, dies.
        March 17, finishes first draft of *Orlando*.
        October, lectures on women and fiction at Newnham and Girton Colleges.
        October 2, US limited edition of *Orlando* published.
        October 11, *Orlando* published by Hogarth Press.
        October 18, US edition of *Orlando* published.

1929   October 24, *A Room of One's Own* published by Hogarth Press.

1931   October 8, *The Waves* published by Hogarth Press.

1932   October 13, *The Common Reader: Second Series*, published by Hogarth Press.

1933   October 5, *Flush* published by Hogarth Press.

1937   March 15, *The Years* published by Hogarth Press.
        July 18, death of nephew, Julian Bell, in the Spanish Civil War.

1938   June 2, *Three Guineas* published by Hogarth Press.

1939   August 17, leases (with Leonard) 37 Mecklenburgh Square.
        September 1, World War II begins.
        Resides primarily at Monk's House in Sussex during WWII.

1940   July 25, *Roger Fry* published by Hogarth Press.
        September 7, German "Blitzkrieg" bombing begins in England.
        September 10, Mecklenburgh Square house bombed in air raid.
        September 23, Hogarth Press moved to Hertfordshire.
        October, former home at 52 Tavistock Square destroyed in air raid.
        October 21, publishes "Thoughts on Peace in an Air Raid" in *The New Republic*.

1941   March 28, dies by suicide (drowning) in River Ouse.
        July, *Between the Acts* published by Hogarth Press.

Selected Bibliography

WORKS BY VIRGINIA WOOLF

The Voyage Out. 1915. New York: Harcourt, Inc., 1948.

Night and Day. 1920. New York: Harcourt, Brace, Jovanovich, 1948.

Jacob's Room. 1922. New York: Harcourt, Brace, Jovanovich, 1950.

The Common Reader: First Series. 1925. New York: Harcourt, Inc., 1964.

Mrs. Dalloway. 1925. Edited by Anne Fernald, Norton Critical Edition. New York: W. W. Norton, 2021.

To the Lighthouse. 1927. Edited by Margaret Homans, Norton Critical Edition. New York: W. W. Norton, 2023.

Orlando: A Biography, The Cambridge Edition of the Works of Virginia Woolf. Edited by Suzanne Raitt and Ian Blyth. New York: Cambridge UP, 2018.

A Room of One's Own. 1929. New York: Harcourt Brace and Company, 1981.

The Waves. 1931. New York: Harcourt, Inc., 1959.

The Common Reader: Second Series. 1932. Edited by Andrew McNeillie. New York: Harcourt, Brace, Jovanovich, 1986.

Flush: A Biography. 1933. New York, Harcourt Brace and Company, 1933.

The Years. 1937. New York, Harcourt Inc., 1965.

Three Guineas. 1938. New York: Harcourt, Inc., 1966.

Roger Fry: A Biography. 1940. New York: Harcourt, Brace, Jovanovich, 1968.

Between the Acts. 1941. New York: Harcourt, Inc. 1969.

The Death of the Moth and Other Essays. Edited by Leonard Woolf. New York: Harcourt, Brace, Jovanovich, 1942.

The Moment and Other Essays. Edited by Leonard Woolf. New York: Harcourt, Brace, Jovanovich, 1948.

The Essays of Virginia Woolf, vols. 1–4. Edited by Andrew McNeillie. New York: Harcourt, Brace, Jovanovich, 1986–1994.

The Essays of Virginia Woolf, vol. 5. Edited by Stuart N. Clarke. New York: Houghton Mifflin Harcourt, 2010.

The Essays of Virginia Woolf, vol. 6. Edited by Stuart N. Clarke. New York: Chatto and Windus, 2011.

The Letters of Virginia Woolf, vols. 1–6. Edited by Nigel Nicolson and Joanne Trautmann. New York: Harcourt, Brace, and Company, 1977–1982.

Freshwater: A Comedy. Edited by Lucio P. Ruotolo. New York: Harcourt Brace Jovanovich, 1976.

The Diary of Virginia Woolf. Edited by Anne Olivier Bell and Andrew McNeillie. New York: Harcourt, Brace, Jovanovich, 1977–1984.

A Passionate Apprentice: The Early Journals. Edited by Mitchell A. Leaska. New York: Harcourt, Brace, Jovanovich, 1990.

Moments of Being, 2nd ed. Edited by Jeanne Schulkind. New York: Harcourt Brace and Company, 1985.

WORKS ABOUT VIRGINIA WOOLF

Barrett, Eileen, and Morgan Cramer, eds. *Virginia Woolf: Lesbian Readings*. New York: New York University Press, 1997.

Beer, Gillian. *Virginia Woolf: The Common Ground*. Ann Arbor: The U of Michigan P, 1996.

Bell, Quentin. *Virginia Woolf: A Biography*. New York: Harcourt, Brace, Jovanovich, 1972.

Berman, Jessica, ed. *A Companion to Virginia Woolf*. Hoboken, NJ: Wiley-Blackwell, 2016.

Cuddy-Keane, Melba. *Virginia Woolf, the Intellectual, and the Public Sphere*. New York: Cambridge UP, 2003.

Detloff, Madelyn. *The Value of Virginia Woolf*. New York: Cambridge UP, 2016.

Fernald, Anne E., ed. *The Oxford Handbook of Virginia Woolf*. New York: Oxford UP, 2021.

Froula, Christine. *Virginia Woolf and the Bloomsbury Avant-Garde*. New York: Columbia UP, 2005.

Goldman, Jane. *The Feminist Aesthetics of Virginia Woolf*. New York: Cambridge UP, 2001.

Hussey, Mark. *Virginia Woolf A–Z: The Essential Reference to Her Life and Writings*. New York: Oxford UP, 1995.

Lee, Hermione. *Virginia Woolf*. New York: Random House, 1996.

Randall, Bryony, and Jane Goldman, eds. *Virginia Woolf in Context*. New York: Cambridge UP, 2012.

Scott, Bonnie Kime. *In the Hollow of the Wave: Virginia Woolf and Modernist Uses of Nature*. Charlottesville: U of Virginia P, 2012.

Silver, R. Brenda. *Virginia Woolf Icon*. Chicago: U of Chicago P, 2000.

Simpson, Katheryn. *Virginia Woolf: A Guide for the Perplexed*. New York: Bloomsbury, 2016.

Zwerdling, Alex. *Virginia Woolf and the Real World*. Berkeley: U of California P, 1986.

WORKS BY VITA SACKVILLE-WEST

Sackville-West, V. *Knole and the Sackvilles*. London: William Heinemann, 1922.

Sackville-West, Vita. *The Land*. London: William Heinemann, 1926.

———. *Pepita*. New York: Doubleday, Doran, and Co., 1937.

WORKS ABOUT VITA SACKVILLE-WEST

Glendinning, Victoria. *Vita: A Biography of Vita Sackville-West*. New York: Quill, 1983.

Nicolson, Nigel. *Portrait of a Marriage: Vita Sackville-West and Harold Nicolson*. Chicago: The U of Chicago P, 1998.